W9-ADA-698

More Critical Acclaim for the Fiction of

JOAN JOHNSTON

"Joan Johnston does short contemporary Westerns to perfection."

—*Publishers Weekly*

"Like LaVyrle Spencer, Ms. Johnston writes of intense emotions and tender passions that seem so real that the readers will feel each one of them."

—*Rave Reviews*

"Johnston warms your heart and tickles your fancy."

—New York *Daily News*

"Joan Johnston continually gives us everything we want . . . fabulous details and atmosphere, memorable characters, a story that you wish would never end, and lots of tension and sensuality."

—*Romantic Times*

Other Bitter Creek novels by Joan Johnston

The Rivals
The Price
The Loner
The Texan
The Cowboy
Texas Woman
Comanche Woman
Frontier Woman

Also by Joan Johnston

Colter's Wife
No Longer a Stranger

JOAN
JOHNSTON

THE
NEXT
MRS.
BLACKTHORNE

East Moline Public Library
740 - 16th Avenue
East Moline, IL 61244

POCKET BOOKS
New York London Toronto Sydney

This book is a work of fiction. Names, characters, places and incidents are products of the author's imagination or are used fictitiously. Any resemblance to actual events or locales or persons, living or dead, is entirely coincidental.

An *Original* Publication of POCKET BOOKS

POCKET BOOKS, a division of Simon & Schuster, Inc.
1230 Avenue of the Americas, New York, NY 10020

Copyright © 2005 by Joan Mertens Johnston, Inc.

All rights reserved, including the right to reproduce
this book or portions thereof in any form whatsoever.
For information address Pocket Books, 1230 Avenue
of the Americas, New York, NY 10020

ISBN 0-7394-5915-5

POCKET and colophon are registered trademarks of
Simon & Schuster, Inc.

Front cover design by Lisa Litwack; cover images by Gary
Villet/GettyImages and Stockbyte/GettyImages

Manufactured in the United States of America

ACKNOWLEDGMENTS

I want to thank Elizabeth Saunders, the deputy clerk in charge of the Austin Division of the U.S. District Court for the Western District of Texas, for her invaluable assistance with details about the federal court in Austin. If there are mistakes, they are mine.

My editor Maggie Crawford has the soul of patience, the cheerfulness of a good friend when you need one, and the amazing savvy to make my work better. Thank you, Maggie.

I am in awe of the effort it takes by so many people in a publishing house to get a novel to market and ensure its success there. To everyone at Pocket Books, especially my publisher Louise Burke, you are the best!

My agent Robert Gottlieb is always there when I need him and does his work so well that I don't need him often. Just know how much I appreciate all you do.

I could never be a writer if I didn't have good

12 Dypt 2005

05105 6801

friends to get me through the tough chapters. You know who you are.

And to my mother, who passed away this year, I know you're up there watching. And that you're proud of me. And that you'll like this one even better than the last. You always do.

"I can't believe Dad's marrying that uppity, French-speaking, redheaded bit—" Kate Grayhawk cut herself off before she called her father's prospective wife the B-word. She glanced at her uncle North, who was brushing down his horse in an adjacent stall. "You've met Jocelyn, haven't you, Uncle North. What do you think of her?"

"Are you done grooming that animal?" he asked.

Kate turned back to the bay gelding she'd ridden across her uncle's Texas hill country ranch that morning, sending the brush down the animal's back in long, soothing strokes. "Miss Montrose is only twenty-five—just six years older than me," Kate continued. "Dad was married to her sister, for heaven's sake."

"If I'm not mistaken," he said, "Jocelyn's sister died two years ago, leaving your dad a widower."

Kate flushed. "He should be marrying Mom."

That was the crux of Kate's problem. She couldn't believe her forty-six-year-old father and thirty-five-year-old mother were going to throw away this last chance at finding happiness together. "If Grandpa King hadn't kept them apart, Mom and Dad would have gotten married before I was born, instead of never getting married at all."

Her uncle gave a noncommittal grunt and continued grooming his horse.

Kate lifted the bay's black mane and brushed the animal's sweaty neck. Kate's waist-length black hair was caught up in a ponytail to keep it off her neck, but the leftover curls at her nape were damp from the heat. "I wish I knew how to make Dad change his mind about that French ambassador's daughter he seems to think is so perfect for him."

"I believe her father was ambassador *to* France," her uncle corrected. "She was born in Connecticut."

Kate shot her uncle a narrow-eyed look. "Whatever. Dad shouldn't be marrying some blue-blooded Eastern tenderfoot. If that wedding happens next month, Mom's heart is going to be broken into so many pieces, it'll never mend."

Kate watched for another look of censure, but her uncle seemed totally absorbed in the glossy black stallion he was brushing. She'd learned over the years that Uncle North never sympathized, never offered advice, never offered to solve her problems. In fact, sometimes his ice blue eyes were so cold, they made her shiver. When she was a kid, she'd dubbed him North *Pole*, he'd seemed so remote and unfeeling.

She'd also noticed that whenever she poured out her troubles to her uncle, they somehow miraculously got resolved. She was sure Uncle North was paying attention, listening to every word she said. She knew he cared about her and wanted her to be happy. He just had a little trouble showing his feelings.

Which wasn't surprising, considering that King Grayhawk was his father, and he'd had two really bad stepmothers after Grandpa King had divorced North's mother. Kate knew for a fact that Grandpa King didn't listen. And he didn't care about anyone but himself.

The situation between her parents would have been resolved long ago if her two grandfathers, King Grayhawk and Jackson Blackthorne, hadn't been mortal enemies. But Blackjack had stolen away Eve DeWitt—the woman King loved—and married her. What made the theft so much more heinous was the fact that Blackjack never loved Eve. His heart had always belonged to another woman. He'd married Eve only for the fifty thousand acres of good DeWitt grassland in Texas she'd brought with her as a dowry. The two men had been on opposite sides of the fence ever since.

It was no wonder that when her father got her mother pregnant all those years ago, Grandpa King had taken advantage of the situation to exact revenge by forbidding them to marry.

But her parents were meant to be together like oatmeal and raisins. Like eggs and bacon. Like pancakes and syrup.

Kate realized she was hungry. Her horseback ride with Uncle North had started at daybreak, and the sun was well up. She had an hour's drive ahead of her, to get back to her condo near UT. She was finishing her freshman year at the University of Texas at Austin, and she'd left her homework sitting when she'd come to spend the weekend on Uncle North's ranch. Her brushstrokes came faster until her uncle lifted his head and pierced her with a look from his ice blue eyes.

"You giving that horse a good brushing?" he asked.

"Yessir." Kate slowed her hand, but her mind was still working a mile a minute. "What if I pretended to break a leg?" she said. "That would get Mom and Daddy here in a hurry."

"It also might make your mom take chances getting here," North said.

Kate bit her lower lip. When she'd called and left a message that she was in trouble a year ago, her mom had caused an accident because she was driving too fast, trying to get home to help Kate. "I see what you mean," she said. "Maybe you could tell Mom you need her help with something, and I could ask Daddy to come help me with something."

"I manage fine by myself," North said. "And Libby—your mom—knows it."

Kate's face twisted in disgust. "You could pretend—"

"No."

The curt word sounded final. Absolutely, positively firm. Kate would get no help plotting from Uncle North, that was for sure.

"You finished?" he asked.

Kate ran her hand along the bay's glossy back and said, "Yep."

North slapped his horse on the rump, left the stall, and headed out of the barn without another word.

Kate chewed on her lower lip, staring at her uncle's broad, powerful back and long legs as he strode into the sunshine. In the past, she'd been happy to rely on one of Uncle North's miracles to accomplish the impossible. But he hadn't seemed the least bit interested in helping her get her mother and father back together. And she knew for a fact Uncle North didn't like the Blackthornes—which included her father—one little bit.

Kate squinted as she stepped out of the barn into the blistering Texas sun. She waited for her eyes to adjust to the light as she stared out over the grassy hills dotted with the purple remnants of April bluebonnets. There wasn't much time before her father's wedding—to the wrong woman. Just one month. Her mother's—and father's—happiness was just too important to leave to chance.

She was just going to have to come up with a miracle of her own.

1

Jocelyn Montrose didn't mean to cavesdrop. But the arguments and shouting coming from the library at the Castle, the legendary ranch house at Bitter Creek, were hard to ignore. Her future husband, Clay Blackthorne, was being verbally attacked in that room.

Those assaulting him were his family—his twin brother Owen and sister-in-law Bay, his younger sister Summer and brother-in-law Billy Coburn, and his father Blackjack and stepmother Ren. Clay's brother Trace and his wife, Callie, were on the speakerphone from Australia, where Trace owned a cattle station.

Jocelyn pressed her cheek against the wall next to the slightly open door, peeked inside and listened.

"You see what a reliable advisor Morgan DeWitt turned out to be," Owen snarled, his hand on the SIG P226 he wore as a Texas Ranger. "That bastard was an out-and-out thief and murderer."

"Morgan's suggestion to incorporate the Bitter Creek Cattle Company and sell stock seemed sound

EAST MOLINE PUBLIC LIBRARY

to me," Clay replied. "The DeWitt ranch is incorporated, and they've never had a problem. I didn't know
until a year ago that Morgan was anything less than
the astute advisor he seemed to be."

"We incorporated Bitter Creek on your advice,"
Summer said angrily.

"A suggestion I made based on—"

"That sonofabitch's advice," Blackjack interrupted.
"This is getting us nowhere. The question is, how do
we stop that bastard—whoever he is—from buying up
a controlling interest in the Bitter Creek Cattle
Company?"

The silence was deafening.

"This is a disaster," Trace said from the speakerphone on Blackjack's desk.

"It's not my fault!" Summer shot back.

"I wasn't blaming you," Trace said.

Jocelyn saw Clay's jaw tighten. It was clear they
blamed him. She wanted to walk into that room and
put her arms around him and comfort him. But he'd
forbidden her to attend the family meeting. She
wasn't Clay's wife yet, as he'd made very clear to her
earlier this morning.

They'd arrived at Bitter Creek last night to make
final preparations for the wedding and had discovered
that all hell had broken loose. Clay's rejection of her
offer of support, her plea to be allowed to stand by his
side, still stung.

"Anybody got a useful suggestion how to get us out of this fix?" Billy said, his dark-eyed gaze moving from grim face to grimmer face around the room.

Jocelyn felt her heart sink. No one seemed to have any idea how to stop the anonymous corporate raider who was threatening to steal the Blackthornes' heritage. In a hostile takeover, the existing management was usually terminated. Summer and Billy ran the ranch, but the Blackthornes had owned Bitter Creek, a property in South Texas the size of a small northeastern state, for nearly a hundred and fifty years. The new management would have the power to do whatever they wanted—even sell the ranch to strangers.

"Maybe this raider just wants greenmail," Trace suggested.

"What's that?" Bay asked from her seat in one of the two horn-and-hide chairs in front of Blackjack's desk.

"He makes a quick profit by threatening to take control and then selling the stock back at a premium— more than it's really worth," Clay explained to his sister-in-law as he poured himself another glass of Jack Daniels from the bar.

Jocelyn watched Blackjack, who sat in a swivel chair at his desk, down a glass of whiskey in two swallows.

Clay's stepmother laid a hand on Blackjack's shoulder and said, "It would be worth any price to save Bitter Creek, wouldn't it?"

"It's blackmail, plain and simple," Blackjack said, slamming his empty glass on the old-fashioned wooden desk. "And I'll be damned before I'll pay it!"

"What else is left?" Summer said, her voice breaking. "You won't consider a poison pill or a scorched earth defense or . . ."

Jocelyn heard Summer swallow a sob as she turned into Billy's open arms, and then Billy saying, "It's all right, sweetheart. We'll think of something."

But what she heard was more deathly silence.

Apparently the Blackthornes were unwilling to use the few methods of shark repellent—ways to discourage an unfriendly takeover—still available to them. A poison pill was anything that might make the target company stock less attractive, like authorizing a new series of preferred stock that gave shareholders the right to redeem shares at a premium after the takeover.

Jocelyn shuddered when she considered the scorched earth defense. That involved the target company disposing of its crown jewels—its most desirable property—to thwart the takeover. The Blackthornes might be able to save the assets of the Bitter Creek Cattle Company from being confiscated by a corporate raider—if they sold the precious land their forebears had bled and died for since the Civil War.

No wonder they were unwilling to consider that option.

"I know who the raider is," Clay said.

"Why the hell didn't you say so?" Blackjack said.

An expectant hush fell on the room. Jocelyn held her breath, wondering who the anonymous corporate raider could be.

When Clay took another slow swallow of whiskey instead of divulging the name of their nemesis, Summer prodded, "Please, Clay. Who is it?"

"North Grayhawk."

Jocelyn gasped, then covered her mouth and looked through the crack in the door to see if she'd been discovered.

No one was paying any attention to her. The Blackthorne and Coburn men stared at Clay through narrowed eyes, their jaws locked and their hands fisted in anger. The women reached out to restrain their enraged husbands, but their bodies were no less tense, their anger no less palpable.

"I should have known," Blackjack said. "Those damned Grayhawks have been the bane of my existence since—"

Jocelyn saw him cut himself off as he glanced over his shoulder at his wife, who caressed the hair at his nape and said, "I'm so sorry, Jackson."

"It's not your fault," he said gruffly. He reached a

hand up toward his wife and she grasped it, as their eyes met and held.

Jocelyn felt her throat swell with emotion at the look that passed between them. She wondered what it would be like to be loved like that. In the stories she'd heard, Blackjack and Ren were star-crossed lovers who'd married other people—Eve DeWitt and Jesse Creed, respectively—and raised families who'd become mortal enemies.

After Ren's husband was shot and killed under suspicious circumstances, Blackjack had offered to give up everything he owned, including the land that was the source of contention now, to marry Lauren Creed, the woman he'd always loved. Eve's untimely death had made the sacrifice unnecessary.

Blackjack turned back to his family and said, "If anyone's to blame for this mess—"

"It's the Grayhawks," Summer interjected. "King's behind this, Daddy. He must be."

"I'm not so sure King Grayhawk is the villain this time," Clay said.

"He hates Daddy," Summer said.

"So does North," Clay said. "And he's the man my shark watcher says is our anonymous corporate raider."

"I don't disagree that North hates us," Blackjack said. "I just don't understand why that pup has taken up his daddy's fight like it was his own."

"He blames you for his mother's divorce from his father, her suicide, and the succession of stepmothers that came and went because King could never find a replacement for Eve DeWitt. The woman you stole from him. The only woman he ever loved," Clay said.

"How could you possibly know something like that?" Summer asked.

"Libby told me."

Jocelyn felt her heart skip a beat at the mention of North Grayhawk's sister Libby, the woman she knew Clay had loved once upon a time. The woman he might have chosen to marry instead of her, but hadn't. Libby Grayhawk was closer to Clay's age, and they had a history—and a daughter—together. Jocelyn had tried to convince herself that Libby was no threat to her future happiness. She hadn't been entirely successful.

Two years ago, Jocelyn had spent day after day at her sister's bedside while Giselle's body was being slowly eaten away by cancer, listening to stories of Giselle and Clay's life together. Libby Grayhawk's name had come up surprisingly often. Clay had definitely loved her. The only reason he hadn't married her twenty years ago, when she was pregnant with his child, was because King Grayhawk had forbidden it.

A year ago, Libby and Clay had met again in Jackson Hole, Wyoming, when their eighteen-year-old daughter Kate was kidnapped. Jocelyn wasn't sure what had been said, but something had changed between them. Some dormant ember had sparked to life.

Jocelyn had been worried that she might lose Clay to his former love. So she'd admitted to Libby that she'd fallen in love with Clay before he'd ever met her sister Giselle. That she'd been so jealous of her sister, when Clay had chosen Giselle over Jocelyn, that she'd stayed away for years—until Giselle had gotten sick with cancer.

She'd revealed to Libby a secret she'd previously told no one. As her sister lay dying, Giselle had begged Jocelyn to take care of Clay and to love him. And that she did love Clay . . . and hoped to marry him.

Jocelyn didn't know if her speech to Libby had made a difference. But when the summer was over, Clay had proposed to her—not Libby.

Jocelyn had discovered over the past year that she was engaged to a far different man than Giselle had married. The Clay Blackthorne her sister had married had been groomed his whole life to become president of the United States.

That dream was gone. Dead. Killed by scandal.

It had turned out that Kate's kidnapping was a ruse to get Clay from Washington, D.C., to Jackson Hole, Wyoming. Once there, a villain hoping to blackmail Clay into using his position as U.S. attorney general to push through an illegal oil deal had framed him for murder.

Clay had been cleared of the charge, but the scandal had resulted in his resignation as U.S. attorney general. And ended his political career. In a world dominated by appearances, there would always be people who believed he'd literally "gotten away with murder."

Clay's life had turned in a new direction with his appointment as a federal judge in the Western District of Texas. Jocelyn was still in culture shock with the sudden move from Washington, D.C., to what felt like the Wild, Wild West. But she was ready to be Clay's wife, even if it meant living in a world of cowboys and cattle.

The one good thing to come out of Clay's resignation from politics was that he'd been able to publicly acknowledge his illegitimate daughter. Clay had made it clear that once he and Jocelyn were married, Kate would become a part of their family. Jocelyn was hoping they'd have children of their own, as well.

Her thoughts were interrupted by Blackjack's brusque voice.

"All right. We know the worst. What do we do about it?" he said, his gaze moving from face to face in the room and finally focusing on Clay.

"What do we have that North wants?" Trace asked on the speakerphone. "What could we give him to entice him to walk away?"

"What can we possibly offer him that he doesn't already have?" Summer said derisively. "He's rich as Croesus."

"He doesn't even need Bitter Creek," Owen pointed out, setting his empty whiskey glass on the bar and pouring himself another drink. "He already owns a ranch in the hill country west of Austin."

"This is vengeance, pure and simple," Billy said.

"Like it or not, he's beaten us," Clay said in a quiet voice.

"I'm not giving up," Billy retorted. "I'll never give up."

"Me neither!" Summer said.

"Easy to say," Trace said on the speakerphone. "But how do we fight back?"

"I can always shoot the bastard," Blackjack muttered.

An uneasy silence settled on the room.

Jocelyn wasn't sure whether Blackjack was serious or not. The family had a history of violence that made his threat seem all the more provocative.

Jocelyn felt her stomach clench when she realized that she knew something North Grayhawk wanted, something that might even assuage his need for revenge.

Me. He wants me in his bed.

Jocelyn inched away from the door and stood with her back against the wall, her heart pounding in her chest. Suddenly, she saw a way she could provide the help Clay had refused earlier in the day. When she'd begged him to let her help, he'd replied, "There's nothing anyone, including you, can say or do that will make a difference. That bastard has no heart, no soul. This is my fault. My responsibility. Just stay away. I don't want you there!"

Jocelyn had felt terribly wounded by Clay's rejection of her offer to stand by his side. She'd felt sure he would have allowed Giselle to be there. What was it her sister had been able to offer him that he didn't seem to find in her? She'd wondered how she could ever prove that she was as capable of providing love and support as Giselle.

And now this opportunity had fallen into her lap.

What if she could persuade North Grayhawk to part with his Bitter Creek stock in exchange for having Clay Blackthorne's woman in his bed?

How are you going to get Clay to take you back after you've made the ultimate sacrifice? a little voice asked.

She couldn't think about that right now. Right now she had to focus on what she must do to save Bitter Creek. She had to prove to Clay she loved him every bit as much—indeed, much more—than Giselle ever had.

If she told Clay what she was thinking, he would probably forbid her to act. She couldn't bear to be shut out again. She wanted to help. She was determined to help. Her idea might be a little crazy, but it was just crazy enough to work.

EAST MOLINE PUBLIC LIBRARY

She tiptoed away from the door, then hurried up the stairs to her bedroom. She threw a few things into an overnight bag, grabbed her purse, and headed back downstairs, easing past the library, afraid that if she thought too much about what she was about to do, she might revert to her normal, sensible behavior—and chicken out.

She left a note for Clay in his bedroom, telling him that she had something *very important* she had to do—for both their sakes—that she was borrowing his car, and that he shouldn't follow her. She promised to call him when she got where she was going. Jocelyn didn't intend to make that call until she was sure it was too late for Clay to interfere.

She was determined not to fail. Too much depended on her success. And she had no other way to prove her love for Clay. No other way to convince Clay that she could offer him something her sister never had.

Jocelyn could hear arguing behind her as she headed down the hall toward the back door. The lunch dishes had been washed and put away, and she could smell dinner already roasting in the oven, but luckily, the housekeeper wasn't in the kitchen. She took the keys to Clay's car from the rack by the back door and stepped outside, easing the screen door closed behind her.

It was early May, but the sunny, mid-morning heat

was stifling. Jocelyn realized she was dressed all wrong for the trip she was about to make. Her navy skirt and matching jacket, long-sleeved, white silk blouse that tied in a bow at the neck, spiked high heels, and nylons were de rigueur in Washington, D.C., but they weren't very functional in South Texas.

She could already feel the sweat—her mother would have said perspiration—pooling under her arms and inching down the center of her back. She'd bought herself a cotton western shirt, denim jeans, and cowboy boots after she'd arrived at Bitter Creek, but she felt like she was dressing in a Halloween costume every time she put them on.

She'd packed them for this trip.

Jocelyn opened the door to Clay's Mercedes SUV and slid onto the seat, biting back a yelp when the hot black leather hit the backs of her nylon-clad legs. She sat forward to get her legs off the seat, keyed the ignition, and turned the air-conditioning up full blast.

She headed the SUV around the magnolia-lined circular drive that led ten miles back to the state highway. She would have to keep her foot on the accelerator if she wanted to get to North Grayhawk's hill country ranch before dark.

She started to punch off the country-and-western song on the radio, but the melancholy lyrics of a love affair gone wrong caught her ear. And made her think twice about what she was about to do.

The impulse to confront North Grayhawk and offer her body in exchange for his controlling interest in Bitter Creek stock suddenly seemed silly. Why should he listen to a word she had to say? More to the point, what if she was wrong? Perhaps she'd misunderstood North when they'd had their confrontation at his cabin in Jackson Hole a year ago. Maybe he hadn't meant what he'd said.

Jocelyn flushed. He'd meant it, all right.

Libby had introduced her to North in the living room of his cabin and then gone into the kitchen to get coffee. Jocelyn had immediately felt a frisson of fear run down her spine, as though she'd been left alone with a predatory wolf.

She was five foot eleven in her bare feet, but even to her, North Grayhawk looked big. He had to be six foot five, with enormous, rippling shoulders narrowing to a lean waist and hips.

Jocelyn knew how to handle men in suits, but North was dressed in jeans that molded his masculinity, and the sleeves of his plaid wool shirt had been folded up to reveal strong, sinewy forearms. His shiny black hair hung over both his brow and his collar, and a day's growth of dark beard made him look unkempt and . . . dangerous.

She'd felt edgy and had surreptitiously backed as far away from him as the room allowed, until she reached the crackling fire in the stone fireplace. She'd faced him with her hands knotted behind her and tried to ease the tension by smiling, which had been amazingly difficult, and saying something innocuous. "You have a lovely home."

He'd focused his ice blue eyes on her as he closed the distance between them until they were only a breath apart. She'd been mesmerized, unable to look away. She'd felt the heat of his body and caught the musky odor of a man who'd just been chopping wood. She found herself imagining his muscles flexing, swinging a heavy ax, and the sharp crack of splitting wood.

Without warning, he'd reached out and brushed her breast with his big, callused hand.

Her nipple instantly peaked.

Her breath caught in a gasp of disbelief at his effrontery, and her heart actually skipped a beat as she jerked backward a step. She ran into the fireplace mantel and lost her balance.

He rescued her by snaking a powerful arm around her waist and pulling her close. So close that she became unmistakably aware of his arousal. She trembled in his embrace, aware of her own body's equally unmistakable response, to a man she'd only met sixty seconds before. A man who was rude and arrogant and disturbing and cocksure. A man she *hated* without knowing a single thing more about him than what he made her feel.

Hot. Achy. Wet with desire.

He spoke in a low, grating voice that rasped over her flesh, making the hairs stand on end. "I want to lay you down and put myself inside you so deep—"

She hadn't heard the rest of what North Grayhawk wanted, because that was when she'd slapped him.

And fled the room like the hounds of hell were after her. She'd found Libby in the kitchen and sputtered and stuttered and been unable to get her to leave before *he* showed up in the doorway—with the white imprint of her hand still starkly visible on his reddened face.

She wasn't proud of having slapped North Grayhawk. But she wasn't sorry, either. He'd deserved it. She was a perfect stranger, for heaven's sake! She was a lady. And pure as the driven snow.

Although North couldn't be expected to know that. What twenty-four-year-old woman in this day and age was a virgin? She wondered what it was about her behavior that had led him to think he could act on his desires.

It was only later that she'd figured out he must have acted boorishly on purpose, to scare her away, unwilling to endure his sister's matchmaking attempt.

And matchmaking, she'd realized, was exactly what Libby had tried to do. She'd introduced Jocelyn to her brother North in hopes that North would distract Jocelyn from Clay.

It hadn't worked.

Jocelyn had put the incident completely out of her mind and focused on Clay, the man she'd loved from the first moment she'd set eyes on him.

The man who'd married her sister instead of her.

Which made Jocelyn wonder again what it was about her that had made the right man reject her— and the wrong one desire her. She supposed she should count her blessings. If she was right and North really did want her, despite the scene he'd acted out to scare her off, she had a bargaining tool that might save Bitter Creek.

Jocelyn was certain the Blackthornes would never go down on bended knee before their enemy, but perhaps she could persuade North to show mercy. Or negotiate with him to do so. After all, he was so wealthy, he didn't need another piece of property in Texas. Especially one the size of Rhode Island.

She gnawed her lower lip, uncertain whether her sexual inexperience was going to be an asset or a liability. Would North want an accomplished lover? Someone who could give him pleasure? Or would he find satisfaction in knowing he'd stolen her virginity from Clay Blackthorne?

Jocelyn blushed at the mere thought of what North might want her to do. She wasn't ignorant. Just innocent. Which was more the result of a lack of opportunity than a lack of interest. She'd been in France with her father, the ambassador, most of her youth, and should have experimented. But her mother had told her she should seek love before sharing her body with a man.

She simply hadn't fallen in love.

That is, until she'd met Clay Blackthorne. There hadn't been another man after that, because she hadn't been able to fall out of love with Clay, even when he was married to her sister.

Jocelyn didn't let herself consider whether Clay would approve of the proposition she planned to make to North. There were some things a woman in love had to do for the man she loved. If the loss of her virginity would satisfy North Grayhawk's need for revenge against the Blackthornes, it was a sacrifice she was willing to make.

Besides, Clay didn't know she was a virgin.

It might have seemed odd that they hadn't made love yet, but they'd been separated for much of their year-long engagement. She'd needed to act as hostess for her father in Connecticut, and Clay had traveled between Texas, Wyoming, and Washington, D.C., tying up loose ends and meeting with family.

And there was the awkwardness of being his former wife's sister. The first time she and Clay had been alone after their engagement, she hadn't been able to give herself to him. She'd been surprised at her reluctance, and confused and distressed. This was the man she loved, she'd told herself. It was all right to have sex with him.

But she hadn't been able to go through with it.

Clay had been understanding, but she'd been careful never to let things go so far again. She'd convinced herself it would be better to wait for their wedding night, when they truly belonged to each other.

Jocelyn had the fleeting thought that it might not be that easy to have sex with North Grayhawk, either. But she couldn't afford to get cold feet. If he demanded sex from her, she would grit her teeth and bear it. She would make sure there was nothing in her bargain with him that said she had to enjoy it!

Jocelyn nearly turned back several times during the hours-long drive from South Texas to the hill country west of Austin. She knew where North lived because she'd dropped Kate off to visit her uncle North one weekend. She had no trouble finding the ranch.

Her cell phone had rung several times during the day, but she hadn't answered it, unwilling to argue with Clay over the phone. When it rang again, she picked it up and punched the button to take Clay's call. She was close to her destination, and it was too late for him to stop her.

"Where are you?" he asked. "Why haven't you answered my calls? I've been worried."

His voice was anxious, not angry, and she answered, "I borrowed your car. I hope you don't mind."

"Where are you?" he asked again.

"Just west of Austin."

Silence. And then he said, "What are you doing, Jocelyn?"

"Something I have to do," she replied.

"Listen to me, Jocelyn. Whatever you're thinking—"

"Don't try to find me, Clay. Don't follow me. I'll get in touch . . . when I can."

"Don't do anything foolish," Clay said. "Come back to Bitter Creek. To me."

Jocelyn put her foot on the brake at the pleading sound of his voice. But it was far too late to turn around and go home. She was stopped at North's back door.

The back porch light flipped on.

"I'm hanging up now, Clay," she said.

"Jocelyn, please don't—"

She closed the flip phone and turned off the ignition. She'd long since removed her jacket and thrown it into the backseat, but with the air conditioner off, she already felt uncomfortably warm. Jocelyn never appeared in public when she didn't look perfectly put together. But it was hot. And she knew North would be just as happy if she showed up stark naked. She left the jacket where it was, opened the door, and stepped out into the sultry night air.

The countryside was amazingly dark, with no sign of civilization for miles around. There was no moon and very few stars. She could hear crickets. And cattle lowing. And the wind rustling through the live oaks that shrouded the house.

She could see a half-naked male figure in the kitchen doorway. He pushed open the screen door and stood there.

It was North.

Jocelyn felt her heart begin to batter frantically against her chest, like a frightened bird in a cage. She was terrified he would send her away before she had a chance to speak. Everything she'd imagined saying fled her mind, and she halted, staring at the figure in the doorway. Surely once she looked into his eyes, the right words would come. She started toward him, but the dirt driveway was rutted, and her high heels made her stumble.

She saw his hand go over his brow to shade his eyes from the bright porch light, trying to figure out who she was.

Her high heels wobbled again on the rutted dirt road, and she balanced herself with a hand on the warm hood of the SUV until she reached the end of it. The last ten feet to the door, she kept her eyes focused on the uneven ground.

When she looked up again, North had backed up a step and the screen door had closed. She could see him silhouetted by a light beyond the dark kitchen. Moths and mosquitoes were buzzing the porch light,

EAST MOLINE PUBLIC LIBRARY

and she waved her hands to keep them out of her face as she stepped onto the back porch.

She looked up at him and opened her mouth to speak.

He shut the door in her face. And flipped off the light.

2

Jocelyn felt her face flame in anger. How dare he shut the door in her face! After she'd driven so far to— A second wave of heat shimmered up her throat, as shame washed over her. She was well repaid for her arrogance. How stupid to think she could ever manipulate a man like North Grayhawk with sex! The whole idea had been foolish from the start. She'd simply been too desperate to help Clay to see it.

As she stared at the closed door, a hysterical bubble of laughter escaped. The situation was that ridiculous. How could she have been so wrong? If North really had been attracted to her, he wouldn't have slammed the door in her face. Which he had. She opened the screen door, still furious enough—at both him and herself—to bang on the closed wooden door, demanding to be let in. Instead, she stared at her fisted hand and laughed again.

Suddenly, the porch light came on and the door opened.

Once her eyes had adjusted to the stark light, Jocelyn found herself facing a man every bit as tall and imposing as she remembered. His cold blue eyes were distant and unapproachable. His rangy body was deceptively relaxed, but she had the impression of a wild animal, ready to pounce.

He was barefoot and wearing a western shirt that he'd apparently just pulled on, because it wasn't snapped or tucked into his jeans. Which weren't snapped either.

Her eyes locked on the hair-dusted strip of tanned, muscular abs and chest in front of her and arrowed down to jeans that fit like a glove. She flushed and forced her gaze back up to North's face.

His eyes had narrowed, and his lips had twisted in a cynical smile. "Still shopping for a man? Or you finally ready to buy?"

Jocelyn ignored the taunt and waited for an invitation to come in. It wasn't forthcoming. Finally she asked, "May I come in?"

North stepped back, but not very far, and Jocelyn's breasts brushed against his naked chest as she edged into the shadowy kitchen, lit only by the spill of light from the hallway and the porch. She was flustered, but a quick glance upward revealed that North wasn't as unaffected, or uninterested, as he wanted her to believe.

Jocelyn watched as his gaze left her face and slowly dropped to her nipples, which had visibly peaked beneath her silk blouse. She felt a frisson of desire shiver up her spine and caught her lower lip in her teeth to keep from moaning.

He did want her. She could do this. She had to do this. Clay's happiness, his family's future, depended on her success.

"Like what you see?" she asked in a disturbingly breathless voice.

His eyes moved back up her body slowly until they were focused on hers. Then, in a whiskey-rough voice, he said, "Yes."

Jocelyn realized she'd been hoping North would proposition her, so that all she had to do was agree. But his full lips remained sealed as his avid gaze roamed her face.

"We're going to let the moths in," she said at last, as she eased the screen door closed.

At the same moment, North turned out the porch light.

Jocelyn felt trapped with him in the darkness. She didn't move. Couldn't breathe. Her breasts felt achy and her body clenched in sudden desire as she felt his hand close around her breast.

She gasped.

"This is what you came for, isn't it?" he said in a voice that resonated deep in his throat. He backed her against the door, his hips thrusting against hers, so there could be no mistaking what he wanted from

05105 6801

her. He was hard and hot, and her body trembled with fear and desire.

"Yes," she whispered.

And then, as though someone had thrown a pail of cold water on her, she realized where she was and what she was doing and what she'd said.

"I mean no," she said hastily, putting her hands to his shoulders and looking up at eyes that glittered dangerously in the meager light from the hallway. "I mean yes, but—"

"Make up your mind, honey. I haven't got all night."

Jocelyn had never heard such brutally frank—and unflattering—language from a man. It shocked her. And angered her. "Get away from me," she said through bared teeth. "Before I—"

She was free before she could say what awful carnage she would wreak on him for the insult she'd suffered.

"I'm going to bed," he said, heading for the hallway. "Shut the door when you leave."

"Wait!" she cried.

He stopped, glanced at her over his shoulder, and said, "What for?"

"We need to talk."

"Talk isn't what I want from you."

Jocelyn held out her hands in supplication. "Please. I only need a few minutes of your time. This is important."

"There's only one thing you have that I want, honey. Unless you've changed your mind—"

"That's what I want to talk to you about," Jocelyn said.

He turned around and crossed his arms and spread his long, bare feet wide. "I'm listening."

He looked as unassailable as a brick wall. And equally unsympathetic. She was anxious and nervous and afraid that what she was offering wouldn't be enough to sway him. She searched her mind for something to say that might postpone the inevitable discussion. "I've been driving for hours. I could use something cold to drink."

"Glasses are in the cupboard. Tea is in the fridge. Ice is in the door. Help yourself."

Jocelyn knew better than to ask "Which cupboard?" She simply moved to the most logical place where glasses might be kept, opened the cupboard and found one there. "Would you like some, too?" she asked.

"Nope."

She took out a glass, crossed to the refrigerator door, which had an automatic ice dispenser, then opened the fridge and stood there in the cool air and welcome light while she poured herself a glass of tea from a half-gallon jug. She closed the door and turned to him and tried to smile. And failed dismally. "Thank you," she said as she swallowed a sip.

"Can we sit down?" she asked, gesturing toward a round table in the corner of the kitchen.

"I'm waiting," he said in response.

"Yes. Well. The thing is—" She looked across the room and found North's spread-legged stance as intimidating as she was sure he intended it to be. Two could play that game. She set the glass down on the counter and moved toward him. She stopped six inches away. Definitely in his space. She put her hands on his crossed forearms and felt the muscles bunch under her fingers.

"I'm here to ask a favor," she said.

A muscle worked in his jaw, but he remained silent.

She took a deep breath and said, "I want you to sell your controlling shares of the Bitter Creek Cattle Company back to the Blackthornes."

"Why would I want to do that?"

"Because you don't need Bitter Creek."

North snorted.

"And because I'm offering you something more valuable in exchange."

"Nothing on earth could match the feeling of satisfaction I'm going to get from owning Bitter Creek," North said savagely.

"You can have me in your bed," Jocelyn said. "Willing. And eager."

"What makes you think I care?"

Jocelyn lowered her eyes along his body until she reached the abundant proof cupped lovingly by his butter-soft jeans. She let her hand follow where her eyes led, until her fingertips had outlined the width and warmth of him.

Then she met his gaze and said, "I think you care a great deal." Her voice caressed as her hand caressed.

"I want revenge more," he said curtly, grabbing both her wrists and holding them in front of him tight enough to hurt.

"You can still have your revenge," she argued. "Just in a different way."

"What way is that?"

"You can steal me from Clay, the way Blackjack stole Eve from your father. Wonderful symmetry, don't you think?"

He paused so long she thought for sure she'd found an argument he would buy. But he said, "I don't want a wife."

"Fine," she said, smarting from his dismissal. "You can have me for as long as—"

"I'll take you just long enough to make him suffer," North interrupted. "That's all I want."

"Our wedding day is June 4. I—"

"Call it off," he said. "That's my price."

Jocelyn couldn't speak past the sudden lump in her throat. She swallowed painfully, and said in a soft voice, "Very well. It's done." The ache in her throat made it hard to speak, and she whispered, "Now what?"

He let go of one wrist, but held onto the other and headed out of the kitchen and down the hallway, pulling her along behind him. Her high heels clacked on the wooden floor.

"Where are we going?" she asked.

"To bed."

"No. Wait!" Jocelyn stuck her hand out to brace herself on a passing doorway, but it was no use. He was too strong, and she lost her balance in the high heels and careened after him. "Please. I don't think I can—"

He turned so suddenly her breasts flattened against his chest when she ran into him, and his arms circled her to hold them both upright. She could see his eyes just fine now, and they were as cold as Arctic ice.

"You trying to wriggle out of the deal already?"

"You don't have to drag me along like a cat on its way to a bath," she snapped. "You could leave me a little dignity."

"There's nothing dignified about sex. It's hot and sweaty and coarse and vulgar and about as primitive as life gets."

Jocelyn gaped. She was too stunned to breathe. "I don't even know you. We're strangers. Surely you can't want—"

"I want you, honey," he said. "Or there wouldn't have been a deal. You coming? Or not?"

"I need time—"

"This is a one-time offer," he said. "Take it or leave it."

"How do I know you'll do what you say after you have what you want from me?" she countered.

His eyes narrowed. "I killed the last man who called me a liar."

Jocelyn would have thought he was exaggerating, except his voice had been too soft—and menacing. "I'm not a man," she said. "I can't meet you with six-shooters at dawn. I need some sort of—"

"My word has always been good," he growled.

"I want it in writing."

He took her by the hand this time and headed down a different hall. He didn't stop until he was standing in front of an oak rolltop desk. He let go of her and grabbed a pen and a piece of paper and wrote something, then thrust it at her. "Here's your damned paper."

On it he'd written:

In exchange for sex with Jocelyn Montrose for as long as I want her, I hereby agree to sell my shares of the Bitter Creek Cattle Company.

He'd dated it and signed his name.

"This won't work," she said.

"What the hell's wrong with it?"

She reached for the pen he'd dropped on the desk and crossed out *for as long as I want her* and wrote in *until September 1* and added language to say that he would sell his shares *to Clay Blackthorne no later than that date.* She thrust the paper back into his hands and said, "Initial the changes."

He read it and said, "I'm not getting much for what I'm giving up."

Jocelyn held onto her temper, refusing to respond to the provocative insult. "Then don't initial the changes. I can always walk back out to my car and drive away."

His lips quirked on one side, and he laid the paper on the desk and initialed the changes she'd made. He then added another sentence and handed it back to her.

Jocelyn read his words with dismay. She looked up at North and said, "But I have to tell him why I've done this. Otherwise, he'll think—"

"Let him think what he wants. That's my offer. Take it or leave it."

Jocelyn's jaw was locked as she laid the paper on the desk and initialed the line that read, *Clay Blackthorne will not be told the terms of this agreement.* Then she folded it up into a very small square and stuck it in the pocket of her skirt. "I hope you're happy now!"

He headed for the door and said, "Follow me."

Jocelyn couldn't believe it was going to be this easy. Would North do as he'd promised? Was Bitter Creek really out of danger? What if he didn't follow through? Was the document he'd signed enforceable in court? After all, she was exchanging sex for . . . It wasn't prostitution. It wasn't. It was a favor in exchange for a favor.

She and North were on their way back down the first hall when they heard pounding on the back door. "Are you expecting someone?" Jocelyn asked, her eyes wide.

"No," he said.

North was still moving toward the bedroom, but Jocelyn had stopped and was looking toward the back door, where the banging had gotten louder. "Don't you want to answer that?"

He shot her a crooked smile and said, "Honey, there's only one thing on my mind right now. And it isn't company."

"Jocelyn! I know you're in there!"

"That's Clay!" Jocelyn exclaimed.

She heard North mutter a series of profanities before he strode past her on his way back to the kitchen door. He grabbed her wrist as he passed and said, "Come with me."

He didn't leave her any choice. He dragged her behind him, then swung her around and settled his arm around her waist, just beneath her breasts, with her buttocks molded into his hips.

Jocelyn realized what this posture would look like

to Clay, and she was terrified of what he might do. And of what North might do in response. She struggled to get free. "Don't! I don't want Clay to see me like this."

"Why not? You're mine now."

"Until September," she shot back.

"The wedding sure as hell is off. The sooner he knows it, the better," North said.

"He'll kill you," Jocelyn said, horrified at what she'd set in motion.

"He's welcome to try," North said in a steely voice.

Jocelyn gripped the arm he'd tightened around her with both hands and said, "Please don't provoke him."

North's laugh was terrifying. "You should have thought of that before you showed up at my door."

"I was thinking of Clay. I'm doing this for him. Because I love him," she said.

"You sure have a funny way of showing love, honey."

Before she could retort, he'd flipped on the back porch light, yanked open the back door and shoved past the screen.

She was greeted by Clay's shocked face.

"This isn't what it looks like," she hurried to explain. "I mean, it is, but there's a—" North's arm tightened enough to cut off her air, and she realized she'd been about to make the explanation she'd been forbidden to make.

"Let go of her, North," Clay said through tight jaws.

"She's here of her own free will," North said. "Find yourself another Mrs. Blackthorne. Jocelyn is mine."

Jocelyn's stomach knotted as she watched Clay's face twist in a snarl of rage.

"I don't believe you," he said. "Jocelyn would never agree—"

"I don't give a damn what you believe," North interrupted. "Now get off my land."

Jocelyn watched Clay's hands bunch into fists as his feet spread in a fighting stance. Any moment violence was going to erupt. She had to stop this, even if Bitter Creek was forfeit. A piece of land wasn't worth dying for.

And then she realized that, of course it was worth dying for. Generations of Blackthornes had died—and killed others—to keep Bitter Creek. Clay wouldn't hesitate to make the ultimate sacrifice. She had to stop him from doing that.

"What are you doing here?" she asked brusquely. "How did you find me?"

"There's a tracking device in the car in case it's stolen. I've been following you most of the day. What are you doing here, Jocelyn? If this has anything to do with this bastard trying to steal the Bitter Creek Cattle Company—"

"I'm here for my own reasons, Clay," Jocelyn said. "You shouldn't have come."

"I . . ."

At that moment, North started to release her. She drew a relieved breath and then realized why he'd loosened his hold. His hand eased up to cup her breast.

She gasped and stared down at the offending gesture. And then looked at Clay, who was already charging North.

She held up both hands and cried, "Clay! Stop!"

He barely managed to rein himself in, stopping when her extended hands caught his shoulders. "What the hell is going on, Jocelyn?" he demanded. "I want to know why you're here."

"I came here because I . . ." She realized that if she didn't come up with a convincing story, the two men would end up fighting—until one of them was dead. "Last summer Libby introduced me to North and I . . . I felt something different for him than what I'd experienced with you. With the wedding coming up—and after the way you shut me out this morning— I . . . I wanted to see if what I felt was real."

"What are you saying?" Clay asked.

She saw the hurt on his face, proof that he believed the lie she was concocting. She couldn't say more, afraid of closing all doors to reconciliation when September came. "I can't marry you, Clay. Not right now. I need to find out—"

"He won't ever love you, Jocelyn," Clay said. "He's

incapable of love. Like all his kind. He'll only use you, hurt you. For your sister's sake, come home with me, please."

The invocation of her sister's name was like a stab to the heart. Jocelyn was not so hysterical that she didn't realize what Clay had failed to say. That *he* loved her. That *he* would cherish her. But they'd never said those three words to each other. They'd simply been understood.

Now she might never hear Clay say "I love you." Or be able to say those precious words to him. Why had she waited? Ever since her sister's illness, she'd been aware that time was fleeting. She put a fist to her chest to counter the hurt inside.

"I have to stay, Clay," she said. "I need to know if . . . if I'm making the right choice."

"I won't take you back when he's done with you," Clay shot back.

Jocelyn's vision blurred and her nose pinched with tears. "I'm sorry, Clay. I have to stay."

"You heard her, Blackthorne. Get moving."

"Come with me, Jocelyn," Clay pleaded. "It's not too late. I need you."

Jocelyn wondered if she would have ripped herself from North's arms if Clay had said *I love you* instead. She could hardly blame Clay, though, for not baring his heart in front of his mortal enemy. She was no better. She'd never told Clay how much she loved him.

She opened her mouth to say it now and realized it was the wrong time for such a confession. It could only result in pain for Clay if she stayed with North, and danger if he decided to fight North for her.

"Good-bye, Clay," she said.

He stared at her for another moment, his heart in his eyes, before he turned and marched to his car without looking back.

Jocelyn's nose burned and she felt a hot tear slide down her cheek. "Oh, God," she whispered. "What have I done?"

The porch light went out and a strong arm pulled her back from the kitchen door as it closed. She sagged against North's arm, and when his hold loosened, jerked free. She ran for the door and yanked at the knob. "Clay!" she cried. "Come back!"

But North's hand was there to cover hers and keep the door closed. She could hear Clay's tires spinning on the gravelly dirt road as he tore away from North's ranch house.

"Let me go!" she cried. "I want to go!"

When he stepped back, she yanked open the door. But it was too late. Clay was gone.

"Leave if you want," North said, coming up behind her. "It's no skin off my nose."

She whirled on him and pounded on his chest. "You're the most ruthless, inhuman—"

"You made the deal, honey," he snapped back,

catching her wrists and holding them tight. "I just went along for the ride."

"I love him!" she cried. "I love him, and now he's going to hate me."

"Good!" North said savagely. "Revenge is a dish I like hot and smoking."

"I've changed my mind," she snarled at him. "I wouldn't sleep with you now—"

She was off her feet and in his arms so fast, she grabbed hold of his neck to have something to hang onto. "What do you think you're doing?" she shrieked.

"We have a bargain, honey. And I'm going to collect on it."

Jocelyn grabbed two handfuls of his hair and yanked as hard as she could.

"Ow!" he said. "That hurts!"

"Put me down," she said in a feral voice. "Right now. Or I'll do worse."

He set her on her feet and took a step back. They stared at each other with narrowed eyes, chests heaving.

"I never thought you'd have the guts to go through with it," he mocked. "That's why I agreed to the deal."

Jocelyn felt an unbearable ache in her chest. She'd ruined everything. Now, not only would Clay hate her, but his family would lose Bitter Creek. North was right. She was a coward. But she didn't see how she could make love—*have sex*—with a virtual stranger.

Someone who clearly disliked her as a person as much as he desired her as a woman.

But if she didn't follow through on her bargain, the consequences would be terrible and irreversible.

Jocelyn was not, in fact, a courageous person, but she did know how to make sacrifices. She'd been doing it all her life. For her father. And her sister. And now for Clay.

"I'm not afraid of you," she said.

"Prove it."

"I don't have to prove anything."

"Then you're reneging on the deal?"

She looked him in the eye and said, "Where's the bedroom?"

3

〜⧜〜

Jocelyn gasped, and then couldn't seem to catch her breath, as North scooped her back up into his arms. The house was larger than it looked from the outside, and North had stalked his way down several corridors before he passed into an earth-toned room so spartan she knew it must be his. He hit the light switch at the doorway with his elbow and soft lights came on near the bed and the chest.

A patchwork quilt covered an old four-poster, which looked too small for North, let alone the two of them. He crossed to the bed, ripped the quilt and top sheet away and dropped her onto the bed so she bounced twice.

Jocelyn realized with horror that there would be no way to hide her virgin's blood on North's pure white sheets. Maybe, if the room was dark, he wouldn't notice, and she could change the sheets before he discovered the truth.

She braced herself for his weight, but he merely

stood beside the bed staring down at her. For an instant, she allowed herself to believe that he'd changed his mind about wanting her. That she was going to get a reprieve.

Then he reached for the zipper on his jeans.

"Wait," she said, reaching out a hand in supplication.

"For what?" But the zipper stayed where it was.

She stared in fascination as he shrugged out of his shirt instead, revealing a perfectly sculpted body, except for his left shoulder, where the artist's chisel had slipped and left a raking scar. As he reached for the zipper again, she quickly scooted off the bed and stood facing him.

"Shouldn't we talk first?" she asked, keeping her eyes focused on his face. That wasn't altogether satisfactory, because his gaze was heavy-lidded, his lips full. He was clearly ready to do what he'd brought her here to do.

"What else is there to say?" he said, reaching out to tug on one of the ties at her throat, releasing the bow. "This must be choking you."

"It's fine." Jocelyn reached up to stop him, but he'd already released the button at her throat and the one after that, and her hand met bare skin. The next two buttons were undone before she had the presence of mind to cover his hand with her own. She flushed as she realized he was staring at her bra—her incredibly provocative Victoria's Secret bra—which covered just enough to titillate the imagination.

His lips formed a smirk as he lifted his gaze to meet hers. "The way you had that bow tied so tight at your throat—and that fiery hair of yours all bound up like that—I wouldn't have figured you for sexy underwear."

Jocelyn flushed hotly and reached up self-consciously to smooth her auburn hair back into its elegant French twist. But as usual, not a hair was out of place. "What's wrong with my hair?"

He reached behind her and began pulling out pins. She batted at his hands uselessly, and a moment later, heavy curls fell past her shoulders. She opened her mouth to rail at him and stopped short when she saw the look of shock—and awe—on his face.

"There's not a damned thing wrong with your hair. Now." He reached out a reverent hand and caressed a silky curl.

She quivered as his knuckle brushed her breast.

He rubbed her hair between his fingers as though it were spun copper silk. "I can't imagine why you'd hide something so glorious."

Jocelyn had needed to be adept at hiding her charms. A political hostess wasn't a sexual being. Or at least shouldn't be. She was appalled to think what North would say when he saw her pristine white garter belt with the silk bows, her lacy white underwear and her silk nylons. It didn't make sense to wear something so utterly feminine, so specifically intended to arouse the male libido, when she had no intention of undressing in front of anyone.

But she'd never been brave enough for overt misbehavior. Unconventional underwear had become her rebellion against all the rules of proper behavior she'd so circumspectly followed her entire life.

Her secret was about to be revealed. In a very big way.

North eased the blouse out of her skirt, his hands going around her, making her aware of the height and breadth of him, as he pulled the fabric out in back. She held her breath until his hands no longer surrounded her. He took his own sweet time unbuttoning the last few buttons.

She was still clutching the sides of the blouse around her middle. He eased it off her shoulders and then tugged it out of her grasp and dropped it onto the floor, leaving her standing before him in a white demi-cup bra that lifted her breasts up as though they were dessert on a plate.

It seemed he was intent on having the main course first, because a moment later, her breasts were nestled against his chest, as he reached around her to undo the button on her skirt. She held her breath as he eased the zipper down. Before she realized what he intended, his lips tenderly caressed her bare shoulder.

The kiss was surprisingly sensuous, and she shivered in excitement at the damp touch of his mouth.

"Are you cold?" he asked, lifting his head to look into her eyes.

She lowered her gaze, ashamed to admit the bald truth. Instead she said, "A little."

"Let's get you undressed and under the covers."

"I—"

As her skirt slid down to her ankles, he took a half step back and muttered a profanity.

She stepped out of the skirt and stood before him with her hands at her sides, resisting the urge to cover herself. She couldn't bear to meet his gaze, but he didn't give her any choice when he put a finger under her chin and said, "Look at me, Joss."

Her head jerked up at his use of the shortened name, and she was surprised to see him frowning. "What's wrong?" she asked.

"How long have you been planning this?"

"Planning what?"

"To seduce me in exchange for selling Clay my stock."

"I didn't plan anything," she protested. "I heard Clay's family arguing about how they were going to lose Bitter Creek and decided on the spur of the moment to come here and—"

"I don't believe you."

"It's the truth!"

"You expect me to believe you get up every morning and put on stuff like this—" He snapped one of the garters against her leg. "—under those prim clothes you wear?"

"Believe what you want," she said, feeling the heat of another blush on her throat.

His lips curved in a sardonic smile. "Maybe there's more to you than meets the eye, Miss Montrose."

"What is that supposed to mean?"

"It means I'm very much looking forward to finding out what other surprises you might have in store for me."

A lump of cold dread lodged in Jocelyn's stomach. If North was talking about sexual acrobatics in bed, he was far off the mark. She was willing to go along with whatever he wanted from her, because that had been the deal, but she couldn't guarantee she'd be the kind of lover he wanted. Certainly not, if he was expecting someone experienced in providing physical pleasure.

"You can get rid of the heels," he said. "And the rest of that getup. My tastes don't run that way."

Jocelyn wasn't sure what way he meant, but she hurriedly stepped out of her high heels and reached down to undo the garter that held up her left stocking.

"On second thought, I'll take care of that myself," he said.

As he bent over, Jocelyn braced one hand on his

shoulder, feeling the play of muscle under her hand. She caught her breath at the brush of his callused hand against her thighs as he released both garters front and back.

To her surprise, he picked her up again and set her gently on the bed, then knelt on the old-fashioned tied-rag rug beside the bed to skim the nylons off her legs, discarding them on the floor behind him.

"You have big feet," he said, holding one in his hand.

Jocelyn laughed, embarrassed, and tried to pull free. "What do you suggest I do about it?"

He held onto her foot, looked up at her and said, "I like the fact you're tall. You'll fit me better. And you need feet this big to balance the rest of you." He let go of her foot, stood, put his hands on her waist and stood her upright once more. "Let's get rid of this," he said, his hands on the garter belt.

Jocelyn was still trembling with shock at the feel of his powerful hands on her bare flesh as she reached for the hooks at the back. "I'll take it off."

"Easier for me to do it," he said, reaching around her to release it. He held it out for a moment, shook his head, and tossed it away as he had the other garments.

Jocelyn wished she hadn't worn such tiny bikini panties. It would have been nice to be wearing granny cotton ones right now, because North's glance focused on her navel, then slid down to the right, to something else no man had ever seen.

"What's this?" he said, laying his hand on her hip, so that what he was looking at was framed by his thumb and forefinger against her skin.

"Exactly what it looks like," Jocelyn said.

He met her gaze and smiled. "I didn't figure you for the kind of woman who'd have a tatt, either."

The tiny blue and yellow butterfly tattoo had been yet another defiant impulse, something she'd done after her father had chastised her for being too friendly with one of the younger diplomats who'd attended a dinner party at their home. As with every other gesture of mutiny in her life, it had been invisible to anyone except her.

She lifted her chin and said, "I like it."

He grinned and said, "I do, too."

The boyish grin disappeared so quickly Jocelyn thought she must have imagined it.

North's face was completely sober as he reached for his zipper once again. This time, Jocelyn heard the rasp of it coming down. He'd already hooked his thumbs in the top of his jeans and underwear when she jumped into bed, turned away from him and pulled the covers up over her shoulder. She heard the rustle of denim coming to rest in a heap and then North's bare feet padding on the wooden floor.

She realized he was moving to the opposite side of

the bed and lay back flat with her eyes squeezed tight and the covers pulled to her chin.

"Don't be coy, honey," he said in a harsh voice. "I haven't got anything you haven't seen before."

Jocelyn barely managed to avoid blurting, "Oh, yes, you do!" Instead she said, "Would you please turn out the lights?"

"Not on your life," he retorted. "I intend to see what I've paid for."

He gave one good hard yank, and Jocelyn was left lying totally exposed on the bed wearing only her bra and panties. She felt North sit on the side of the bed and waited with bated breath, eyes squeezed tightly closed, for whatever came next.

To her surprise, she felt his hand playing with one of the auburn curls on her shoulder. She finally had to breathe, and exhaled as quietly as she could before gasping another lungful of air.

"Open your eyes, Joss. I want you to know it's me making love to you. Not some other man."

Considering no other man had ever made love to her, Jocelyn wasn't going to be making any comparisons. But North didn't know that, and she wasn't about to give him any more ammunition to make fun of her—or make his revenge against Clay that much sweeter. She could get through this without North ever finding out she'd come to him a virgin. She just had to endure.

And wash the sheets before he got a good look at them.

She opened her eyes and stared up at him, relieved that she couldn't see anything that might have caused her to blush and expose her ignorance—and innocence. She was startled to realize his blue eyes no longer looked icy. They reminded her now of the sea off some sandy island beach, light and warm and inviting.

"You're very beautiful," he said. "But you know that."

No one had ever told her so. She hadn't realized how erotic such words could be. She felt even more tense. And her insides were twisted up, doing something they'd never done before.

North's fingers continued playing with her hair, but his eyes were focused on her mouth. She opened her lips slightly and realized they were dry and slid her tongue around to wet them.

She heard him make a little sound in his throat, before he shook his head and smiled. "That's good, honey. More of that."

"More of what?" she said, confused.

He wrapped his hand around her hair until his fist was bunched against her cheek. "You don't need tricks to make me want you, honey. Just lying there is enough to—"

"I wouldn't know how—"

That was all she got out before his mouth covered hers. She clenched her teeth instinctively, and his other hand came up to force her mouth open for his intrusion.

She felt a frisson of unexpected desire as his tongue teased along the crease of her mouth, before sliding inside. She hadn't expected to like it. She hadn't expected to be aroused by it.

He sat up abruptly, and she stared up at him, her breathing erratic, her mouth open to gasp air. His hand loosened in her hair and once again played with it. He reached for her shoulders and sat her upright. She was frozen with embarrassment as he released the front clasp of her bra and slid it off her arms.

She could feel her nipples forming into rigid peaks and thought it must be the cold air, although she felt unbelievably warm.

North slid a gentle hand under her chin and lifted it and searched her face. She knew she was blushing again. She watched his glance slip to her breasts and then back to her face.

"You're exquisite."

His hand left her chin and trailed down her chest until he cupped one of her breasts. She'd never imagined her belly would clench at his touch. Never imagined how good his rough, callused hand could feel against her smooth flesh.

His thumb brushed the stiff nipple, and she caught her lip in her teeth to bite back a groan of pleasure.

"So responsive," he said in a guttural voice. He lowered his head and caught her nipple in his mouth and suckled it.

Her hands grasped his hair, unsure whether she wanted to push him away or pull him closer.

Before she could do either, his mouth returned to hers. This time it opened wide for his tongue, and she returned the favor, eliciting an animal sound in his throat. His hands were busy doing something unbearably wonderful to her breasts, and she felt herself arching toward his touch.

Abruptly he released her, and she stared into his eyes, which had changed again. This time they were stormy blue seas. Turbulent. Troubled.

He hooked a finger in the tiny bikini panties and slid them down her long legs, then gave her shoulders a slight push. She fell slowly backward, her eyes caught on his, as he covered her with his body, his knees forcing her legs wide.

She felt a moment of panic, realizing how vulnerable she was, realizing what must come next, and begged, "Please. Will you turn off the light?"

"No."

Just that one guttural word. No apology. No mercy.

He eased himself into the cradle of her thighs, bearing most of his weight on his elbows.

She tensed like a bowstring as she felt the heat and the utterly strange—and frightening—hardness of him against her nakedness.

"Relax," he crooned as his mouth began to play across her shoulders and throat. And then he was whispering in her ear. Words she'd never expected to hear from so ruthless a man.

"You smell like a woman should. Like a fragrant blossom whose scent is set free by the summer sun."

He made her feel beautiful. He made her feel desired. He made her feel . . . terrified.

He thought she knew what came next. He thought she wanted to play. He thought she'd only teased him to excite him more.

His hand reached down between her legs, and she pressed her legs tightly together and reached down to grasp his wrist. No man had ever—

"Don't," she gasped.

Her breath caught in her throat as he pressed his palm against the heart of her. When he looked at her in question, her mind raced for a way to put off the inevitable.

"Not yet," she said in a voice that was breathless— with fear, rather than passion, although he could have no way of knowing that.

He smiled and said, "Anticipation is always a good thing."

The smile made her relax.

And he slid a finger deep inside her.

"Ohmigod," she said. And tensed around his finger.

He looked into her eyes, and she saw the first signs

of confusion. She wondered if there was any way he could know she was a virgin. She didn't want him to know. Would never give him that satisfaction. There had to be some way to keep him from discovering the truth.

She traced the scar on his shoulder with her fingertip and felt him shudder. "How did you get this?" she asked.

"Childhood wound," he replied in a brusque voice.

She looked into his eyes and saw the wound was more than skin deep. And that it had never really healed. She heard him draw in a hiss of air as she kissed her way down the length of the scar.

Then she put her hands around his neck and kissed his throat. And his ear. And his cheek. And his closed eyes. And one side of his mouth and the other. His mouth opened wide, and she slid her tongue inside, tasting him, feeling the textures of him.

He made a sound of satisfaction deep in his throat and withdrew his finger from inside her. She was congratulating herself on distracting him, when he grasped her hips and spread her legs wider with his knees. She looked down and saw the size of him.

He was too big. He would never fit!

And she panicked.

"No!" she cried. She began to kick at him and beat at him with her hands. "No!" And then she burst into tears.

He looked furious. He caught both her wrists in one of his hands, and pressed her legs flat beneath his own. He was bigger and stronger, and there was no way she could stop him, if he chose to fulfill their bargain, as it seemed he intended to do.

It was only when he had her completely within his power that he caught her chin in his other hand and said, "What the hell is going on? Stop that blubbering and talk."

His eyes were icy again. Absolutely frigid. Remote. Dangerous.

"This was a mistake," she said.

"You've got that right," he retorted. "I've got no patience with a cocktease."

"I'm not a . . . what you said," she said between hiccups and sobs, uncomfortable even repeating the word.

"Then what the hell are you?"

"I'm a virgin."

He let go of her hands as though she'd said she had leprosy, shoved himself off her and stalked naked around the bed to pick up his jeans and yank them on. When he had them zipped, he turned to her and said, "Cover yourself up!"

She sobbed again and reached for the sheet and pulled it up tight under her arms, pulling her knees to her chest. She looked up at him and saw that his eyes had narrowed.

"How do I know you're telling the truth?" he said.

"Why would I lie?"

"So I'll take pity on you, and say it's all right if you don't keep your end of the bargain," he shot back.

"I meant to go through with it."

"Sure you did, honey," he said, his voice filled with sarcasm. "And a bear doesn't shit in the woods."

"I did! I do," she said defiantly.

He lifted a mocking brow. "Fine. Lie down. Get rid of the sheet. Let's get to it."

She looked at him in horror. "Right now?"

He crossed his arms and said, "Is there a better time?"

"When I know you better."

"I've only got you till September. I want to get full value for my bargain."

"I need time," she pleaded. "You're a stranger. This is . . . it feels like . . ." Like she'd sold herself for money. She just couldn't do it. She looked at him and saw there wasn't a shred of mercy in his soul. Which was why she'd put herself in his clutches in the first place. He would have stolen the Blackthornes' heritage and never looked back.

"You've got a week," he said. "You fulfill your part of the bargain by then, or the deal's off." He lifted a brow and said, "Unless you want to call it off right now."

"I would love to call this off!" she snarled. "I don't

like you. I don't respect you. I think you're a heartless man without a care for anything or anyone. But—"

"But you want to save your precious fiancé," he snarled back at her. "You've got a reprieve for seven days, honey. Not one day more!"

He whirled and headed for the door without another word. When he reached it, he looked back at her and said, "You can have the room down the hall. If you're still here when I get back, I'll figure you've decided to finish our bargain tonight."

She was out of bed with the sheet wrapped around her before he'd slammed the door behind him.

North balled his hands into fists because they were trembling so badly. Joss had been a Venus lying beneath him, and he'd been harder and hotter than he could remember being since he was a teenage boy fantasizing about what sex would be like with his first woman. Until she'd dropped that little bomb.

I'm a virgin.

Sonofabitch. He still ached—hurt—with wanting her.

He paced the length and width of his study, wondering whether he should go back down the hall and kick her out of his house right now. This was going to end badly. For him. And for her.

He shouldn't have listened to that sob story Kate had told him about how her mother and father were fated to be together. He must have been mad to come up with this particular scheme to stop Clay's wedding. Buying up a controlling interest in Bitter Creek stock had only been possible because Libby had insisted North be one of the trustees for Kate's trust, which held shares of Bitter Creek that Clay had given to his daughter, and for which North controlled the voting power.

North had figured that Clay would be the one to come crawling on his knees begging for mercy. He'd planned to sell the stock back to the Blackthornes in exchange for Clay calling off his wedding.

Jocelyn had shown up instead.

He should have sent her away. He wanted her too much. Had wanted her ever since Libby had thrown her at him a year ago in Wyoming. He'd come away from that encounter admiring Jocelyn's refusal to submit to him—and her willingness to defend herself.

His hand went reflexively to the cheek she'd slapped. He had a feeling the oh-so-proper Jocelyn Montrose didn't often resort to violence. But the instantaneous attraction between them had been undeniable, and she must have recognized in him the same threat he'd seen in her. The power of this one person, above all others, to destroy everything he believed about himself.

Which was why he'd done everything he could to scare her off. He'd tried to forget about her, but the feel of her skin, the fragrance of her hair, the possibility of a life with her, had crept into his dreams. He'd imagined touching her. Holding her. Putting himself inside her.

None of which required getting emotionally involved with her. He'd seen how love had ruined his father's life. He was never giving a woman that sort of power over him. But last year, when he'd turned thirty-five, he'd decided it was time to marry. He wanted children. He wanted their laughter and the pleasure of raising them in a house where there was joy.

He'd been looking for the right woman to be his partner when his sister had brought Jocelyn Montrose through the front door of his Jackson Hole cabin. She was exactly the type of female he liked, with her generous bosom and long legs. She was undeniably beautiful, with a porcelain complexion, aquiline nose, and full lips.

He'd felt like he'd been poleaxed when he'd looked into her eyes, which reminded him of the bluebonnets that covered the hills of his Texas ranch in spring. Like bluebonnets, her eyes were a soft lavender, rather than blue, as their name suggested. He'd felt his body come alive. Felt his insides quiver with anticipation. In a different place and time, he would have fought tooth and claw to make her his mate.

Perhaps it was his feral, animal response to her presence that had raised her hackles and made her instinctively wary.

What he hadn't liked was the way she'd looked down her nose at him, as though he were some alien beast, with *beast* being the operative word. He'd been chopping wood, and granted, he probably hadn't smelled as clean as the men who showed up at her diplomatic dining table. But when she'd pulled her coat closed to keep him from looking at her breasts, and he admitted he'd leered to goad her, the tight leash he usually kept on himself had broken free.

He'd moved into her space, stalking in a tight circle around her, brushing against her, feeling her flinch, seeing her nose wrinkle when she caught the odor of hardworking man. He'd made provocative suggestions about what he'd like to do with her—and to her. He'd felt her body tense, saw her look toward the door and escape.

But he was much too aroused by then to let her go. And angry at her for making him want her, when it was so obvious to him that she was the very last sort of woman he needed in his life. *The kind of woman he could come to crave.* Like his father had craved the woman who'd been stolen away from him by Jackson Blackthorne. The woman who'd obsessed his father and made him a bad husband to the three women—or four, depending on whether you counted his annulled marriage— he'd subsequently made his wives.

North's intent had been to cow Jocelyn. To prove that she was too weak ever to stand up to him, and therefore an unfit mother for his children. So, after he'd taunted her into releasing her coat, he'd reached out and touched her breast.

But she hadn't run. She'd attacked, like a wild animal with its back to the wall, that knows its very life is at stake.

He'd taken a step back after she'd slapped him and gestured toward the doorway, smirking. She'd hesitated for a moment and opened her mouth to speak, then turned and fled. He'd wondered for a long time afterward what she'd wanted to say.

Unfortunately, although she'd walked away from him without looking back, she'd never left his thoughts. He hadn't slept well that night, and many that followed, dreaming of her. Her fancy northeastern name, Jocelyn, had been shortened to a more casual western Joss in his dream encounters. And, he'd woken up hot and bothered by his dream woman too many times to count.

He'd refused to go after her. He wasn't going to repeat his father's mistake. He wasn't going to attach himself to a woman who occupied so much of his mind. And he'd never let her get near his heart.

But he'd found out a lot about her over the past year. And somehow, even the whisper of her name had the power to make him dream of what might have been. When she'd shown up at his door tonight, looking up at him with those stunning violet eyes, so

wide and innocent, he hadn't been able to send her
away.

Shit. He should have known she was a virgin. The
truth had been there all along, staring him in the face.
Her hair pinned up to within an inch of its life against
her head. Her clothes tying her up like a package not
to be opened before Christmas.

Tonight he'd discovered the real woman she'd kept
so carefully hidden. With her amazing copper hair.
And her delicate tatt. And her incredibly arousing lin-
gerie. All of which only made him want her more.
And made him even more determined not to let her
get under his skin.

His body tightened as he remembered how Joss
had looked at him when he'd touched her. In wonder.
And delight. And passion. She'd been aroused. He
was sure of it.

But she'd only offered herself as a virgin sacrifice
for the sake of the man she loved. *Damn her!* He was a
fool to let her stay. A fool to go through with this lopsided bargain.

But if he let Joss leave, she would go back to Clay.
And Libby would never have the chance to make
amends with the man she'd always loved. Kate would
be disappointed. And Libby would be devastated. He
owed it to both of them to keep Jocelyn here.

So, even though he might want to throw her out on
her exquisite fanny, Joss couldn't leave. He had to

keep the virgin temptress here with him. At least until after her June 4 wedding date to Clay had come and gone.

He might as well take advantage of the opportunity he'd been given to scratch the irritating itch she'd become. Maybe if he could quench this unendurable physical hunger, he could rid himself once and for all of this unwelcome yearning for . . . her.

She must have some fatal flaws, personality quirks that would reveal her for the conniving Jezebel she was. What kind of woman could do—would do—what she'd done tonight? Who was Jocelyn Montrose, really?

North didn't know. But starting tomorrow morning, he intended to find out.

4

Jocelyn felt nauseated. For the better part of the day, she'd endured the panicked bawling of cattle as they were castrated and a red-hot brand was pressed against their hides. The sickening smell of blood and burning flesh had become overwhelming in the heat of the day.

She was grateful not to have been asked to perform either of those jobs, but she'd been posted at a cattle chute to inoculate cows with a vaccinating gun. Her back ached and her feet hurt. She was sweaty and dirty. And starving.

Which was her own fault.

She'd cried half the night and tossed and turned the other half, so she'd been less than happy when North flipped on the guest bedroom light while it was still dark outside. He'd *ordered* her out of bed, insisting she had to work to earn her keep, and gave her *five minutes* to get to the breakfast table.

She'd taken a very quick shower and then put on

the "costume" she'd brought with her, a beautiful tailored white western shirt with a blue yoke and pearl snaps, designer jeans, a black belt decorated with silver conchas, and expensive black ostrich cowboy boots. She'd put her hair up in an elegant French twist and swiped on some lipstick.

When she'd arrived *twelve minutes* later in the kitchen, she discovered North had already fed her breakfast to a couple of dogs loitering at the screen door.

"Breakfast is over and done," he said. "You want to stay, you do a full day's work. That's the deal."

Six hours later, Jocelyn was still seething at North's arrogant behavior that morning, but hell would freeze over before she'd complain to that *brute*!

She squinted at the afternoon sun, then pulled off the battered felt cowboy hat North had lent her and dabbed delicately at the sweat on her forehead with the already dirty cuff of her yoked western shirt. Her brand-new boots had been stepped on by cows and were coated with a fine layer of dust. Her designer jeans were dotted with cow slobber.

She needed a long, cool bath. The sooner, the better.

"Put your hat back on. Your nose is pink."

She jerked at the sound of North's voice and nearly dropped the vaccinating gun. She looked up with narrowed eyes into the stony face of her nemesis. "It's my nose."

"Just don't come crying to me later."

Before they'd left the house, she'd asked North for sunscreen. Instead, he'd tossed her the brown felt hat, with its grimy sweat stains along the band. Not only was it dirty, it didn't match her outfit.

"You expect me to wear this?" she'd asked.

"Your choice. But we're going to be outside most of the day."

Without sunblock, her pale complexion would roast in the hot Texas sun. "I'll have to take my hair down," she'd protested.

He'd shrugged and said, "Day's wasting." A moment later she was staring at his back, as the screen door slammed behind him.

She'd yanked the pins from her hair and tossed them onto the kitchen table where she could find them later, then hurried after him.

Hungry as she'd become during the endless morning, she'd never said a word about food. But her stomach was growling, it was so empty. "When do we eat?" she asked, cringing as she eased the sweat-wet hat back on, tugging it down low on her forehead, the way North wore his.

"You quitting already?" North said.

"I'm not quitting," she said. "I'm just hungry."

"We'll stop when the job's done."

"When will that be?"

"Another half hour."

By then it would be one o'clock. They'd trailered horses here, which was another half-hour drive. By the time they got back to the house, she'd be famished.

At that moment her stomach made a loud, undignified cry for sustenance.

"Chuck wagon's on the far side of the corral. If you can't wait, ask Cookie to give you something now."

"I'm fine," she said. Her arm might fall off from holding the vaccinating gun, and she might never walk again after she got out of these high-heeled boots, but as far as North Grayhawk was concerned, she was just dandy. Especially if all she had to do to find food was make it to the other side of the corral.

"What I really need is a bath," she said, as she laid down the vaccinating gun, pulled off the too-large, sweaty buckskin gloves North had also lent her and looked at her blistered hands.

"There's a pond not far from here. We can take a swim when we're done."

"I prefer a bath. Alone."

"The swim you can have after lunch. The bath would have to wait until dark."

She wrinkled her nose. She couldn't wait until dark. She needed to rinse off this sweat and dust, and the offer of cool water sounded too inviting to resist. There was only one problem.

"What am I supposed to wear for a bathing suit?"

He grinned and said, "Who needs a suit?"

"Where are you going to be while I'm taking this swim?"

"It's a big pond."

At that moment, one of North's cowhands called to him. He turned away, as though the matter were settled, and headed back to the branding fire.

It took another forty-five minutes to finish the job, and for the last fifteen, Jocelyn was functioning on sheer grit. She handed the vaccinating gun over to one of the cowhands when the triangle at the chuck wagon clanged, signaling everyone to come and eat.

She was surprised at how courteous the cowboys were, each one tipping his hat to her and saying "Ma'am" as though she were the Queen of Sheba. All except North, who handed her a tin plate and said, "Food's being served for the next fifteen minutes."

She realized it was a warning, and she hastened to the dutch oven simmering over the fire, where Cookie had created a hearty beef stew and added dumplings on top. She found a seat on one of the logs that had been situated around the fire, set her plate in her lap and concentrated on the meal until it was gone. Nothing Jocelyn had ever eaten had tasted so good.

When the late lunch was over, she stood by as North sent his cowhands off to do other chores around the ranch. She waited, her shoulders aching, to see what he expected from her next.

"You ready for that swim?" he said.

"I told you, I don't have a suit."

He shrugged. "Your choice. There's some barbed wire fence needs to be—"

"I'll go for the swim," she interrupted. She wouldn't put it past North to force her to spend the afternoon manhandling barbed wire.

"Fine. Can you ride?" he asked.

"Of course." She'd starting riding almost as soon as she could walk.

"Then we'll ride to the pond," he said.

Jocelyn would have ridden all the way to Connecticut if that's what it took to remove the smug look from North Grayhawk's face. "No problem," she replied.

Except she hadn't been on a horse since she was fourteen and had broken her leg in a fall while jumping a high stone wall. Her father had taken the family to Paris before she was well again, and the opportunity hadn't arisen for more than a year for her to get back on a horse. When the opportunity had come, for some reason she couldn't explain, she hadn't taken advantage of it. Then her mother had died, and spending all her free time on the back of a horse had no longer been an option.

As she followed North to where two saddled horses

were tethered, she realized her heart was pounding and her palms were damp. She couldn't possibly be afraid. That was ridiculous. She'd spent most of her youth on a horse.

North gestured to a fat white gelding and said, "Whitey's friendly. Mount up and I'll check the stirrups."

Whitey was a far cry from the sleek thoroughbred hunters she'd ridden as a child. Even so, she shivered as she contemplated getting back on a horse, even one as tame as this. "Whitey looks like he should have retired a few years ago," she muttered.

"You say something?" North asked.

She patted the docile gelding. "Whitey and I will get along just fine." Jocelyn grimaced at the western saddle, with its horn in front and high cantle in back. It was far more bulky than the English saddles on which she'd ridden in her youth.

"Problem?" North said.

"No problem," she said, as she placed her foot in the stirrup and mounted. Even if there was, she would never admit it to him.

Her heartbeat immediately ratcheted up a notch. *I'm not afraid*, she told herself. Nevertheless, her hands began to tremble. She took a deep breath and blew it out, trying to expel the anxiety she felt.

She jerked when North removed her left foot from

the stirrup and stared down at him. "What are you doing?"

"Your stirrups are too short," he said.

By the time he'd lengthened both stirrups, Jocelyn was feeling decidedly uneasy. She'd seen enough western movies to know that cowboys didn't post—that is, rise in the stirrups and sit in the saddle in rhythm with a trotting horse—the way English riders did. The stirrups were now too long to do that, anyway. She felt awkward and out-of-place, which was unusual for a diplomat's daughter like herself.

"You okay?" North asked.

She stared at the hand he'd placed on her thigh and tensed as her flesh warmed beneath his touch. She was sure the gesture was intended to comfort her, but it was only making things worse. "I'm fine," she said, pulling her knee away.

A moment later he was on his horse, a big black stallion, and kicked him into a canter. She watched in admiration as the man and the horse moved in one fluid motion, before she kicked Whitey in the ribs and said, "Let's go."

To her surprise, the placid animal went from standing still to a lope in a matter of seconds. Instead of feeling joy at the sensation of the wind in her hair once again, she felt scared. She grabbed the horn and tugged on the reins to slow her horse down. The animal was so responsive, he sat back on his haunches, bringing him to a sudden stop. She slid up onto Whitey's neck, grabbing hold with both hands to keep from going over his head.

It reminded her vividly of her long-ago accident, when her horse had refused a fence, and she'd taken such a terrible fall. She was breathing heavily and trembling horribly and wanted *off* this horse. *Now.* But she couldn't move. She was clinging to Whitey's neck for dear life and frozen with fear.

She heard hooves thundering back in her direction and looked up to see North pull his horse to a stop and frown at her.

"I thought you said you could ride."

"I can. I . . ."

Before she could say another word, a powerful arm circled her waist, and North lifted her off Whitey and held her tight against his side. His voice was right in her ear as he said, "Do you think you could swing your leg over my horse's back and sit behind me?"

Jocelyn would have done anything that got her left breast out of contact with North's chest. She took a deep breath to gather herself and said, "Sure."

North wrapped the reins around the horn and used both hands to help her make the transition. She whimpered when the stallion sidestepped, but he gripped her tighter and said, "I've got you."

After a little maneuvering, Jocelyn found herself

sitting comfortably on the stallion's back behind North. Once she was in place, he pulled her hands around his waist and said, "Hang on."

She was afraid he'd kick his horse into a lope, so she grabbed hold of his waist. But her fears were groundless, because he gathered the reins and his mount stepped out in an easy walk. She couldn't let go even then, because it would have been obvious that she was afraid of him.

Jocelyn cringed as he whistled sharply, calling to one of his cowhands, "Take Whitey. We won't be needing him."

She waited for North to chastise or criticize her, but he remained silent. Jocelyn was grateful for the slow tempo of the ride, but she had too much time to be aware of the play of muscle and sinew under her hands and the not unpleasant hardworking-man smell of North's shirt.

"We're here," he announced at last, halting his stallion. "You ready to get down?"

She was more than ready, but still embarrassed by the whole incident with Whitey. "Yes," she mumbled to his back.

She watched from the corner of her eye as he wrapped the reins around the saddle horn, lifted one leg over the saddle, and slid to the ground. Then he turned and grabbed her waist with both hands and pulled her off the horse, letting her slide down his body.

She backed up so quickly she stumbled, and he reached out and steadied her. Jocelyn wished she'd never agreed to a stupid swim. As she stood there, embarrassed by her gaucheness, he turned away and ground-tied his horse, which was already lipping the tall, green grass.

Jocelyn turned her back on him and found herself suddenly entranced by the idyllic setting. Tall cottonwoods surrounded the pond and the branch of an enormous live oak extended out over the water with a rope attached to it that was obviously used as a swing from which to drop into the water.

"This is beautiful," she said.

"I've always thought so," he replied.

The water was surprisingly clear, and Jocelyn could see small fish swimming in it. Large flat rocks edged the pond, making a convenient place to lie in the sun, and a turtle was sunning itself on the bank.

When she turned to face North, she realized he'd already pulled his boots off and was working on his belt buckle. She quickly turned her back and heard the continuing sound of clothing being removed. She struggled to keep her voice calm as she asked, "Are you really going to swim in the nude?"

"Last one in's a rotten egg," he said.

She could hear the laughter in North's voice, and then a loud splash. When she turned, she saw his feet disappearing into the water. She waited a long time for him to reappear, long enough to become anxious.

When he did come up, he erupted from the water grinning, and swiped his hair back from his raw-boned face. "You gonna stand there all day?"

The water looked wonderfully inviting. If only she had something to wear! Then she realized that just because North had removed every stitch of clothing didn't mean she had to do the same. She took a deep breath and began to unsnap the fancy western shirt. "You could turn around," she said.

"I could. But I'm not going to," he replied, paddling to keep himself in place in the water.

She stopped, the shirt unsnapped, but not pulled from her jeans. "Why not?"

"You figure it out."

He wanted to see what he'd paid for, she realized. Well, he was going to be disappointed. Jocelyn pulled the shirt from her jeans, unsnapped the cuffs, and pulled the shirt off, folding it neatly and laying it on a nearby flat, hip-high rock.

Then she sat on the rock and pulled off her boots and socks. She stood with her back to the pond while she unbuckled her belt and unzipped her jeans and shimmied out of them, picking them up and folding them equally neatly and setting them on the rock. She looked ruefully at the lacy white bra and white silk bikini panties she was wearing—she didn't own anything less provocative—and strode into the water.

"As you can see," she said, "I'm not skinny-dipping with you. All the important parts are completely— This is ice cold!" she protested, stopping knee-deep in the pond.

"It's spring-fed," he said. "It'll feel good once you're in."

Jocelyn held her breath and took the plunge. She burst out of the water laughing and shivering. "It feels amazing. I'm—" She stopped abruptly when North appeared right in front of her, grinned, and splashed water in her face.

Her mouth was open in shock, and she swallowed a good deal of it before she recovered enough to put her hands on his shoulders and kick herself high enough out of the water to get the leverage to shove him under. She felt his hands on her bare waist as he went down and then felt herself coming up out of the water as though she were being propelled by a porpoise. She went sailing high in the air and landed in the water with a gigantic splash.

She had the forethought to close her mouth this time, but she opened her eyes and went searching underwater for North, to pay him back. She caught sight of his naked butt and realized the water was far too clear for modesty. But she owed him, and she pinched the inviting portion of his anatomy before she sped away.

She came up in time to hear him yelp and grab his behind. "Serves you right," she said, laughing.

And then he came after her.

She shrieked with laughter, something she hadn't done since she was seven, and tried to race away, but he caught her ankle and walked his hands up her leg until he had her by the waist and could turn her into his arms. She was laughing and shoving at his chest, still trying to get away, when he caught a handful of her wet hair. She stilled immediately, caught by the look of desire in his eyes.

She had known—feared—this moment was coming since North had invited her to come swimming with him. She was aware of the heat of his body tangled with hers. Her underwear was no protection at all. She could feel his heart pounding under her hand, feel his breath against her cheek, and watched as his eyes turned warm again, like Caribbean waters.

She waited for the kiss she knew was coming. Waited. And wanted.

He swam them closer to the edge of the pond until he could stand. Her feet were still off the ground, so she had to depend on him to keep her afloat.

She watched his eyes as he lowered his mouth toward hers and saw the demand for surrender. And the promise of pleasure beyond bearing. She would have fought the first, but she wanted the second. Had wished for it all her life. Had dreamed of it, but never felt it.

His lips were warm and soft, and she opened her mouth as his tongue came searching. She slid her arms around his neck and held on for dear life as he pulled her close, until her breasts were crushed against the muscular wall of his chest.

The sensations were marvelous. Amazing. Overwhelming.

She wasn't aware he'd even touched the back clasp of her bra before he separated them and pulled her bra off and threw it onto the bank. She didn't have a moment to protest before his mouth was back on hers, and her breasts were nestled against the coarse hairs on his chest. She rubbed herself against him, wanting the feelings that came with the friction of her smooth female skin against his hairy male body.

And heard him groan.

She stared at him in wonder, suddenly aware of a female power that had never dawned on her before. She could bring this powerful man to his knees with . . . a touch? She grasped a handful of his hair and pulled hard enough that he broke the kiss and stared into her eyes.

His look was feral. And avid beyond imagining. He wanted her. Desperately. That much was clear.

She put a hand against his cheek and felt the rough dark beard that had already grown since morning. She kissed his eyelids and his cheeks. Kissed his throat and felt the pulse beating frantically there. Nipped at the scar on his shoulder and felt his body tense. She looked into his eyes again and saw the warm blue had turned darker. Like storm clouds. Compelling in a way she found very hard to resist.

She felt her body twist inside. Felt her breasts fill and become achy. Felt her throat swell with emotion. Felt her heart beat a fast tattoo of fright and desire.

Not a word had been spoken between them, but she knew what he wanted. All that remained was for her to decide whether she was willing. He'd given her a seven-day respite. But Jocelyn suddenly realized it would be unbearable to wait so long, knowing she must inevitably give herself to him. She let her eyes and hands speak for her.

And North got the message.

Jocelyn felt the fragile strip of cloth at the edge of her silk panties give way under his hand, and felt them slide away, replaced by his callused fingertips against her bare bottom. Her breath rasped against his cheek as he turned his face and captured her mouth with his.

The moment of no return had come. If she wanted her seven days of grace—only six of which remained— she had to act now. This instant.

She found herself unwilling to let go. Unwilling to cry off. There was no turning back. She wanted him. Desperately.

Both of his hands were on her bottom, lifting her, and then she felt the head of his shaft against her, seeking entrance, pushing, and the feeling was exquisite. She shoved against him, and felt him grunt and tighten his hold until he realized she was reaching down to position him, to help him accomplish his goal.

Their eyes met, as his body slid into hers. She was aroused enough to ease his entrance, but he was big, and she winced as he broke through the proof of her virginity. Once he was fully seated inside her, she hid her face against his neck, unwilling to let him see the surprising tears that had appeared in her eyes.

"You okay?" he asked gruffly.

She nodded, because she couldn't speak. She felt his hand on the back of her head, soothing her. His lips were warm and gentle against her neck. And reawakened her desire.

She moved her hips and heard him make a sound in his throat. Then his hands were on her hips again, pulling her up so her legs clasped his hips. Her hands circled his neck as they moved together, seeking the pleasure that came from being joined, man and woman together, as nature had meant them to be.

Jocelyn had a fleeting thought that she wasn't protected, but it came and went, obscured by the enormous pleasure of what he was doing to her. His mouth had captured hers, and his tongue was mimicking the action of their bodies below, while one of his hands was stimulating a spot between them that made her moan and writhe in his arms.

She could feel herself moving toward a precipice, and North's throaty voice urging her toward it, asking her to embrace the danger, to take the risk. And then she was over the edge, crying out and clinging to him, as he thrust one last time inside her and made a guttural sound of triumph and exultation.

Jocelyn felt completely limp afterward, and her cheek fell on North's shoulder as she clung to him, their bodies heaving as they gasped air to keep them alive. Her hips were cramping, and as she moved to ease them, he helped her straighten her legs and walked closer to the bank until she could stand.

Even then, she clung to him, since her knees threatened to buckle. "I had no—" She had to clear her throat to finish her sentence. "I had no idea . . ."

She heard him chuckle.

It was amusing, she supposed, that she could have stayed so ignorant for so many years. And he surely must feel proud of himself for having seduced her so quickly after she'd demanded time to get to know him. It was embarrassing to realize what an easy target she'd been. A little skinny-dipping. A little playfulness.

And she'd allowed North Grayhawk to take what she'd given to no other man. And now could never offer to the man she loved.

Jocelyn realized the enormity of what she'd done. And felt ashamed. And humiliated. And furious.

She covered her breasts as she stepped back, unwilling to expose herself to the villain who'd seduced her. She looked him in the eye as she said, "You've gotten what you wanted. The sooner you transfer the stock to Clay the better."

His eyes, which had been warm a moment ago, were suddenly frigid again. "You're one cold-blooded bitch. I'll say that for you."

She was stung by the insult but still wounded enough to want to hurt him back. "You get what you pay for."

"That's the truth!" he shot back. "The deal was September first. I'll transfer the stock then, not one day sooner. At least that way I can be sure you'll hang around to service me until then."

Jocelyn was mortified. And terribly hurt. But why should he trust her? They were strangers, who happened to be lovers, because of the devil's bargain they'd made.

North turned his back on her and stalked from the water. He was obviously agitated, muttering to himself.

Jocelyn had the sinking feeling that he'd been disappointed by the sex. What did he expect, when she'd been a virgin? She wiped the unwanted tears from her eyes and realized she'd only made it easier to see his nakedness. He was a magnificent male animal, with long, strong legs, lean buttocks, and a broad, powerful back. And no more compassion in his soul than the most merciless of beasts.

He grabbed his clothes from the ground, glanced at her over his shoulder, and said, "We're done here. Get dressed." Then he turned his back on her and headed for a secluded area of the pond.

Jocelyn was too hurt and angry to retort. She was glad North wasn't there when she reached the bank, because she wasn't sure what she would have said—or done. She picked up her bra, but it was sopping wet, and her underwear was nowhere to be found. She yanked on her socks and jeans and snapped on her shirt, then stuffed her bra into her pocket before pulling on her boots.

Just as she finished, North showed up at her side. "Let's go," he said. "Day's wasting."

She laid a hand on his arm to stop him, but he jerked free and turned to face her, his jaw set, his eyes like icebergs ready to crack and splash in the cold Arctic sea.

"What the hell do you want now?" he snarled.

She wanted to apologize. To go back and act like a sophisticated adult, instead of a spoiled, antagonistic child. She wanted to take back the unkind things she'd said and explain how wonderful he'd made her first experience with sex. She wanted to tell him she was confused by her feelings—feelings she hadn't expected to have when they scarcely knew each other.

And she wanted to make peace with him because, whether he believed it or not, she intended to keep her part of the bargain. It was terrifying to imagine those cold, disdainful eyes impaling her every time he looked in her direction.

"I asked you a question," he said. "What the hell do you want?"

All she could get past the lump in her throat was, "Nothing."

5

"Uncle Owen!" Kate called, waving vigorously. "Over here!"

Kate watched as her father's twin made his way around the sawhorses that had been set up to make a police barricade to traffic on Eighth Street in front of the federal courthouse in downtown Austin. Kate recognized a reporter from KVUE, the local NBC affiliate, one of many TV reporters standing within the barrier holding a microphone and talking, with a camcraman facing her. Satellite vans from every TV station in Texas—and many from out of state, Kate was sure—crowded the adjoining streets around the courthouse, where someone had to constantly feed parking meters.

U.S. marshals and deputy marshals were thick on the ground, along with local police and some FBI, whom Kate recognized only because she'd seen enough movies to know they were the ones in the dark suits. And of course, at least one Texas Ranger was on hand, her uncle Owen. He was wearing the only "uniform" the Rangers had, a white shirt and dark trousers, with a Stetson and cowboy boots. He wore his SIG P226 on his hip and his silver Texas Ranger badge on his shirt pocket.

What surprised—and worried—Kate were the sharp-shooters clearly visible on the nearby roofs. When her uncle reached her, the first question she asked was, "Are those sharpshooters really necessary?"

"Just a precaution," Owen said. "Harold Hastings Brown—Bomber Brown—is a guy with friends, and without a conscience. These days, judges are fair game. You want your dad to be safe, don't you?"

Kate searched the crowds worriedly. "You really think there might be someone out there who wants to hurt Daddy?"

"Better safe than sorry, Kitten," her uncle said, using the endearment her father favored.

"Will Daddy be safe?" Kate persisted.

"As safe as a personal bodyguard—provided by the marshal's office, a cordon of policemen and FBI, sharpshooters, a magnetometer at the door, personal security searches, visible and concealed cameras—also monitored by the marshal's office, bomb-sniffing dogs and a concerned brother, who's also a Texas Ranger, can make him."

Kate laughed. "No one's getting through security like that." But she felt an inward quiver of foreboding at the thought of how dangerous the threat must be, to have so much manpower there to guard her father and the courthouse building.

"I thought you had classes this morning," her uncle said.

"Not until this afternoon," Kate said. "But I wouldn't have missed Daddy's first day in court for anything. Are you going to watch, too?"

"Sorry, Kitten. I'm working."

"There are plenty of cops here to—"

"I'm still looking for whoever might have helped Harold Hastings Brown blow up the federal courthouse in downtown Houston," he said.

"I thought he acted alone. That's what the newspapers said."

"Maybe he did, and maybe he didn't," Owen said. "I'm not taking any chances with your dad's life."

Blackthornes stick together, Kate thought.

Of course, Uncle Owen had a special reason to watch out for her father. They were identical twins. Even though they hadn't spent much time together over the past twenty-five years, Kate had often seen them communicate without words. Now, at the age of forty-six, they no longer resembled each other as closely as they once had. They might still be mistaken for one another at a distance, but up close, it was easy to see the harsh lines that the brutal Texas sun and wind had etched on Uncle Owen's face as he went about his duties as a Texas Ranger.

"You be careful, too," Kate said, putting a hand over her uncle's heart.

"I'm always careful," he said with a grin.

Kate looked at the noisy mass of humanity waiting to get through the brass-lined glass doors of the courthouse and past security. "Will I have trouble getting inside?"

"The trial's open to the public," Owen said, "so long as they're willing to go through all the security checkpoints. It's first come, first served on the seating, though, and the courtroom's not large enough for everyone who wants inside."

"I'd better get moving, then."

Before Kate could head up the stairs, a gray-haired reporter stuck a microphone in her face and said, "Aren't you Judge Blackthorne's daughter?"

Kate was astonished to be recognized by the media, even though her relationship to her father was no longer a secret.

"Move along," Owen said in a voice that expected to be obeyed.

But the reporter was used to brushing past obstacles. "Can you tell us why your father postponed his wedding?" he asked, following Kate. "Does it have anything to do with his presiding at such a high-profile trial?"

"Back off," Owen said, stepping between the reporter and Kate.

There was no getting past her uncle this time, and Kate shot him a grin and a wave as she headed up the courthouse steps. "Thanks, Uncle Owen."

As she stood in the long line waiting for security, Kate mused that she had no idea why her father had "postponed" his wedding. She'd been stunned—and elated—when she'd gotten her father's call telling her that his wedding had been delayed until he and Jocelyn could "work a few things out." When she'd hung up the phone, her mind was already racing with thoughts about how to get her parents together during her father's wedding hiatus.

The first, and biggest, problem was how to get her mother down here to Texas from Wyoming when she was busy getting things ready for her summer guide season in Jackson Hole. Maybe something would come to her while she was standing in this interminable line.

At last, Kate was through security. But, as with latecomers at church, the only seats left in the bench gallery of the Austin courtroom were all down in front. That wasn't a bad thing, because that way she'd have a good seat to observe the Honorable Clayton Blackthorne presiding at his first criminal trial. She felt anxious and excited and proud, as she settled herself between a young man and an older woman in the second row to wait for her father to appear.

Just as the bailiff opened his mouth to call the

courtroom to order, a tall, broad-shouldered man stepped into her aisle and wedged himself between her and the older woman. She pulled her book bag from the bench between them and set it on the floor, to make more room, then offered him a tentative smile. He didn't smile back.

By then the bailiff was saying "All rise," and her attention moved to the door from which her father would be making his entrance. When he stepped onto the dais in his black robe and took his place behind the bench, a radiant smile broke out on her face. She was so happy for him. And relieved.

She'd felt terribly guilty for her part in the events of the previous year that had led to her father's resignation as U.S. attorney general. She'd wondered what he would find to do with his life, since his dream of becoming president of the United States had come to an end. Then, something wonderful had happened. The president had nominated him to fill this vacancy as a federal judge in the Western District of Texas.

Federal judges were appointed for life, and it was only the tragedy of the previous judge's death in a small plane accident a month ago that had made all this possible. What was all the more incredible was the notoriety of her father's first case. The defendant, Harold Hastings Brown, dubbed by the newspapers "Bomber Brown," was accused of blowing up the federal courthouse in downtown Houston eight months ago, killing seventy-two innocent people.

The Fifth Circuit Court of Appeals had decided, despite defense counsel's pleas to move it elsewhere, that the trial should stay in Texas. The urgency of selecting a judge to take over the case had meant her father's quick approval by the Senate. Everything had happened so fast, it was hard to believe it was real.

Kate felt a thrill when her father's gray eyes met hers and he gave the slightest of nods. She was delighted that he'd been assigned to an Austin courtroom, not far from the UT campus. For a girl who'd been deprived of seeing her father most of her life, this was her dream come true. She planned to come here often to observe him at work, and she hoped to fit in a few lunches and dinners along the way.

As everyone sat down again, she leaned over to the young man at her left and whispered, "That's my dad up there."

The young man gave her an odd look and said, "That's my dad over there."

Kate frowned and looked where he'd gestured with his chin, toward the defendant's table. "He's one of the lawyers?"

"He's the defendant. My name's Donnie Brown."

"Oh." Kate didn't know what else to say. She couldn't see any way out of the introduction without being rude, so she said, "I'm Kate." She didn't tell him her name was Grayhawk, not Blackthorne. The fact her parents had never been married was none of his business.

Her father held the power of life and death over this young man's father. He would be making the decisions, like whether incriminating evidence could be admitted, that might mean the difference between conviction or the charges being dismissed.

Then she realized how lucky this young man was, because her father was as honest as the day was long. Harold Hastings Brown would get the fairest trial any man could get. And since he'd blown up a federal courthouse, killing judges who'd been the friends of every other federal judge in Texas, her newly appointed father was the perfect man to preside over his trial.

Then she had another thought. "Why aren't you sitting over there, behind your dad?"

"Because my mom's over there, and my older brother Bobby John."

"You don't get along with them?" Kate asked.

"We have our differences," Donnie said.

Donnie must not agree with, or support, what his father had done, Kate decided. It must be hard not to side with your father, even though, in this case, his father was the one in the wrong.

She glanced up at her father, chagrined that she

still hadn't figured out a way to get her mother to Texas, so her parents could realize they belonged together. Uncle North had been no help at all. As far as she could tell, he'd stuck pretty close to his hill country ranch for the past couple of weeks.

Kate chewed on her thumbnail, or what was left of it, completely forgetting the courtroom, totally focused on figuring out a way to get her mother to Texas in a hurry, to take advantage of the postponement of her father's wedding.

Donnie bumped her elbow and whispered, "I do that, too. It doesn't help." He held out a masculine hand where the fingernails were chewed to the quick.

"You must be very worried," she said.

"Shh!" the man to her right said.

Kate shot him a dirty look. It was her father's courtroom, after all, and she was the last person who was going to interrupt the proceedings. And honestly, Donnie Brown needed all the sympathy he could get. Everything Kate had read indicated that the government's case was airtight. Harold Hastings Brown was very likely going to be convicted and sentenced to death.

She pointedly turned to Donnie and said, a little louder than necessary, "Are you a student at UT, too?"

"Yeah, but I dropped out when all this happened," he said.

Kate put a comforting hand over Donnie's poor,

chewed fingers, which were resting on his thigh. "Must be tough."

"Yeah, it is."

A shoulder bumped hers rather hard from the other side, and she turned to confront the obnoxious man on her right. When she tried to get his attention, he ignored her. She turned to follow his gaze and realized his eyes were focused on her father, who was refusing to delay Brown's trial and ordering jury selection to begin the next day at 9:01.

She smiled as she recognized this tactic of her father's for making sure things happened on time. Setting a specific minute meant courtroom proceedings would start *exactly* at 9:01, and not one minute later. It had always kept her father's meetings on time, and it was sure to keep this case on schedule.

A moment later they were all rising again, so the judge could leave the courtroom. Kate reached down to grab her backpack, intent on getting to her father's chambers to talk with him.

Donnie put a hand on her arm and said, "Would you like to get some coffee, or maybe have lunch? I could use someone to talk to."

Kate immediately wondered if it was some kind of conflict of interest for the judge's daughter to spend time with the defendant's son.

Then she was struck with a brilliant thought. Getting involved with Bomber Brown's son would get her mother down here from Wyoming in a big hurry. But was it safe? The young man, with his wide-set blue eyes and short-cropped sandy hair and freckles, looked harmless. Kate chewed a hangnail, debating her options.

He was a UT student just like herself, whose father might have—all right, probably had—committed a criminal act. Donnie certainly wasn't guilty of anything. Apparently, he didn't agree with what his father had done, to the point of sitting on the prosecution's side of the courtroom.

But her mother wouldn't know that. The fact Kate was dating Bomber Brown's son would scare her mother to death, especially since Kate had been kidnapped by just such an innocent-looking man last year. She didn't relish frightening her mother, but something had to be done to get her hardheaded parents together. It was an added bonus that her father was as likely to be upset by the situation as her mother. It was all just too perfect for words.

"I'd love to have lunch with you," she said to Donnie with a bright smile.

"May I join you?" a voice said from over her shoulder.

Kate was annoyed at the interruption and turned to tell the obnoxious man on her right to get lost. For the first time, she got a good look at his face. Her jaw dropped, and she gaped like a teenager at a convention of rock stars.

"You're Jack McKinley," she said with awe.

"Guilty," he said, flashing her a smile so charming, and so incredibly white against his tanned skin, that she could see how he'd become the playboy he reputedly was.

"I'm Kate Grayhawk," Kate volunteered.

"I know your uncle North," Jack said. "We played football together at UT."

"I know," Kate said. But she'd never seen Jack McKinley in the flesh. Flustered, she gestured toward Donnie and said, "This is Donnie Brown." Kate debated whether to mention Donnie was Bomber Brown's son but decided against it. By then, Jack and Donnie had shaken hands.

Kate couldn't seem to stop staring at Jack. He was wearing an open-throated, starched white cotton shirt with a black suit coat, a pair of creased jeans, a black leather belt and black alligator cowboy boots. He looked powerful and confident and good enough to eat.

But Kate wasn't sure whether she ought to be nice to him because when Jack had become the quarterback for the Texas Longhorns his freshman year at UT, he'd done so by taking the job away from her uncle. Uncle North had mentored the kid who'd stolen his position, and Jack had later thanked North publicly for his help. But North had ended up going home to Jackson Hole after graduation, while Jack went on to play professional football.

Jack must be thirty-two, since he was four years younger than Uncle North, and she knew from the game stats that he was six foot three. He looked just as lean and strong as he must have been when he'd played professional football ten years ago. He had sun-streaked chestnut hair and inscrutable dark brown eyes that were watching her so intently, she felt flustered.

Then Kate remembered the other important fact she knew about Jack McKinley. He'd retired at the peak of his career due to a gambling scandal—right after his team lost the Super Bowl. Accusations had flown that Jack had thrown the game. It was said his teammates refused to play with him again. Nothing had ever been proven, and no charges had ever been brought.

"Are we going, or not?" Donnie said.

"Why don't we all go?" Jack suggested. "You can have lunch on me at my place."

"Your place?" Kate said.

"I own a sports bar not far from here."

Kate was dying of curiosity about Jack, and not just because he made her heart rate kick into another gear. She was sure Uncle North would want to know what he was doing these days. She turned to Donnie and said, "You don't mind, do you?"

Donnie hesitated. "Having lunch with Jack McKinley? I guess not." He looked at Jack. "You're famous, man."

Kate saw Jack's high cheekbones flush and realized that he must be as famous for the scandal as he was for his prowess on the football field. To her surprise, she felt sorry for him. "It looks like we're all agreed," she said. "Let's go."

Jack's place was called the Longhorn Grille and it seemed pretty upscale for a sports bar, with white table-cloths and crystal glasses and fancy silverware. Kate re-alized it was close enough to the state capitol to cater to the political crowd for lunch during the week. In fact, as they entered, Jack greeted the lieutenant governor and a number of state senators and congressmen.

Kate could see Donnie was as impressed as she was. The hostess ushered them to a table by the front window, which had a view of the pink marble capitol building, and a waitress appeared at Jack's elbow a moment later.

Jack ordered a beer for himself and asked, "What will you folks have?"

Donnie said, "I'll have a beer, too."

"How old are you?" Jack asked.

"Twenty-two," Donnie said.

Jack looked at him askance. "You have ID?"

Donnie smiled and ducked his head shyly. "All right, so I'm nineteen. I figured you own the place, so—"

"So I don't want to lose my liquor license," Jack said. "No beer."

Donnie shrugged and said. "Sure, I understand," then told the waitress, "I'll have a Sprite."

"I'll have a Diet Coke," Kate said.

"You don't need to diet," Donnie said gallantly, his admiration obvious.

Kate blushed and said, "Thank you, Donnie." However blatant it was, Donnie's attention gave her hope that he might ask her for a date. She needed that date to convince her parents she was considering a relationship with Bomber Brown's son.

A moment later, Donnie's attention was focused on Jack as he asked, "So tell me, did you do it?"

Kate saw the tension in Jack's shoulders and watched his jaw muscles flex. She waited with bated breath for the answer to a question she would never have dared to ask.

At that moment they were interrupted by the waitress, who'd returned with their drinks. After she left the table, Donnie said, "Well?"

"I don't answer that question," Jack replied.

"Not even to deny it?" Kate asked.

"I shouldn't have to deny it," Jack said.

Kate realized the slight flush had returned to his cheekbones.

"My dad knows exactly how it feels to be accused of

something and not be able to prove you're innocent," Donnie said before taking a swallow of his Sprite.

Kate watched Jack's hand ball into a fist on the table, but he didn't try to defend himself or explain himself. She supposed he must have learned over the years that people were going to believe what they wanted to believe, and there was nothing he could say that was going to change their minds.

"I guess it took a lot of money to set up a nice place like this," Donnie said, looking around.

Jack didn't answer what hadn't really been a question, but Kate watched that muscle in his jaw work again. "Is this what you've been doing since you retired from football?" she asked. "I've wondered what a pro football player does with his life once he's done playing."

"Everyone finds his own way of moving on," Jack said. "This is mine."

Kate looked at the sports memorabilia hanging all around them on the walls, jerseys signed by Hall of Fame players and everything from football helmets to hockey sticks. "Pretty impressive," she said. "Do you know all these guys?"

Jack shrugged. "Some of them. The rest I bought from collectors."

"I'll bet your signature is worth a lot," Donnie said. "You being so notorious and all."

"I don't do autographs," Jack said.

"That would make having one even more valuable," Donnie said with an engaging grin. He took a small notebook and pen from his shirt pocket and thrust them toward Jack. "How about it?"

"No." Just that one word, spoken in a voice that would have chilled the blood of anyone less oblivious than Donnie seemed to be.

Kate picked up the notebook and pen and handed them back to Donnie with a smile meant to soften the blow. "You heard the man. No autographs. He's picking up the tab for lunch. That ought to be enough."

For a moment, Kate thought Donnie would protest. Instead, he picked up his Sprite and drained it. When he set it down, he reached into his pocket for a couple of dollars and threw them down on the table. Then he looked Jack in the eye and said, "It was really great meeting you, and I'd really like to stick around for lunch, but I don't want anyone accused of shaving points buying anything for me. You know what they say about birds of a feather. I have to be careful. The press is watching everything I do. You ready to go, Kate?"

Kate was surprised by Donnie's remarks and his sudden decision to leave. Until it dawned on her that Donnie hadn't been as interested or excited about the fact that Jack was *famous* so much as the fact that he was *notorious*. She supposed the son of an accused bomber probably did have to be careful about what kind of people he consorted with, for fear of being tarred with the same brush that had blackened his father's name.

Kate realized she ought to go with Donnie, if she wanted to establish a relationship that would rattle her parents. But she felt sick at the look that flashed in Jack's eyes. So she said, "I think I'll stay."

"Your choice," Donnie said as he rose and threw his cloth napkin onto the table. "See you in court."

Kate realized she very likely would see him in court. And that they weren't likely to be friends when they met, if she stayed with Jack. Which probably meant a date was out of the question.

"Damn," she muttered as Donnie headed for the door. "I needed him!"

"A kid like that's not worth your time and trouble," Jack said.

"I still needed him."

Jack shot her a quizzical look. "What for?"

"I can't explain. It's too complicated."

"I've got nowhere else to be," Jack said, taking a sip of his beer. "And I've got broad shoulders."

He certainly did, Kate thought. And slim hips and very long legs. And a face that was hewed in stone and could have belonged to a Greek god. But who was looking? She certainly couldn't hope to attract someone as sophisticated and worldly as Jack McKinley. Even though she found him breathtakingly attractive.

"I wanted to date him because I was sure my mom and dad would disapprove," she said.

Jack laughed. "I'm not sure I understand."

"Like I said, it's complicated."

"I'm listening."

Kate was glad that being illegitimate didn't have the same stigma these days that it had in days gone by. And yet, she was surprisingly reluctant to admit to this attractive and compelling man that her parents had never been married. Her secret had been well kept because of the threat to her father's political career if the truth of her birth ever came out. Now that he'd retired from politics, that was no longer necessary.

"Do you know who I am? I mean, that I'm Clay Blackthorne's daughter?"

"And Libby Grayhawk's daughter," he said. "I recognized you from a picture North has at his ranch. He told me about your parents. That's a bum deal for you."

Kate was surprised North would have shared that information with Jack. "North only bought that ranch a couple of years ago," Kate said. "When were you there?"

"Actually, I've been hanging out there quite a bit the past couple of weeks."

"I was with North two weeks ago," Kate said. "I didn't see you."

"I've been hiding out at the foreman's house," Jack admitted.

"Hiding out?" Kate said with alarm. "From what?"

Jack shot her one of those charming grins and said, "The tax man."

"You're hiding from the IRS?"

Jack shrugged. "They're claiming some discrepancies between what they say I earned and what I paid in taxes." He looked around and said, "They want to take this place from me to pay back taxes plus some serious penalties and interest."

Kate could see how Jack's past wouldn't exactly help him in a situation like this. Donnie's reaction was very likely typical. If you'd cheated once, you'd probably cheat again. "It must be awful," she said.

Jack didn't even pretend that he didn't know what she was talking about. He simply said, "It is."

She didn't insult him by asking if he'd cheated on his taxes. Somehow she knew he hadn't. Which made no sense, because the whole world believed he'd shaved points in the Super Bowl.

Then she realized why she believed in Jack's honesty. Because he had been—still was, apparently—North's friend. It was impossible to believe her infallible uncle could be fooled by anyone.

It was the man's charm that worried her. Maybe he had North—and a lot of other people—bamboozled. Because, despite his tarnished reputation, Jack had managed to run a successful sports bar where the political powers of the state felt comfortable having lunch. She would have given a great deal to know whether he was honest or not.

"I didn't know you and North kept in touch," Kate said.

"We didn't," Jack said. "This situation just came up and we happened to cross paths and he offered to help me out."

"You can't really hide from the IRS, can you?" Kate said.

"Not for long," Jack conceded. "I just need time to collect some documentation to help me prove my case." He smiled again and said, "You let me get distracted from your problem. How can I help?"

"How are you at performing miracles?" she asked.

"I did it all the time on the football field," he said. "I was famous for it."

Kate grimaced. "I don't think my problem can be solved by throwing a touchdown pass. I need some disaster—not a real one—to get my mother, who lives in Jackson Hole, down here, something that requires her to talk to my father."

"Will I do?"

Kate's brow furrowed in confusion. "What do you mean?"

"You were going to date Bomber Boy. How about me, instead?"

She eyed Jack suspiciously. "Did my uncle send

you to that courtroom today? I mean, that's pretty co-incidental, you showing up like you did."

"Believe me, I'd never volunteer to baby-sit," Jack said with a laugh.

"Baby-sit? I'm hardly a baby," Kate retorted.

"More like a babe in the woods," Jack said.

Kate rose and threw down her napkin. "I don't need anyone to take care of me. I can take care of myself."

Jack rose and put a hand on her arm to keep her from fleeing. "I thought the point here was to find a way to get your parents back together. Walking out on me isn't going to solve your problem."

Kate felt angry and frustrated but was still enough in control of herself to realize he was right. She jerked her arm free and sank back into her chair, as he sank back into his. She crossed her arms and said, "I'm listening."

"I think I fit the bill," he said. "I mean, as someone your parents would *not* approve of."

Kate stared at him, her eyes going wide as she realized he was right. Not only was Jack McKinley a known playboy, his life was tainted by scandal, and he was running from the tax man. To top it off, he was *much* older and North's friend, both of which were sure to upset her father. "You're perfect!" she said.

She heard Jack breathe what she thought was a sigh of relief but knew that couldn't be right. She frowned and said, "Why are you so willing to help me out?"

"Let's just say I owe your uncle a favor he would never let me repay."

"I really can use your help," she said, "but I'm not exactly sure how we should go about this."

"I'm up for anything. So long as I don't end up at the altar in a shotgun wedding," he added, flashing her that charming grin.

"Don't worry," Kate reassured him. "That isn't going to happen."

He met her gaze and said, "Where Blackthornes and Grayhawks are involved, I wouldn't bet the farm on anything."

"I promise I won't agree to marry you, even if they're holding a gun to your head," Kate said wryly.

Jack laughed and said, "I can't tell you what a comfort that is."

Kate laughed with him and realized that she liked him far more than she should, considering the fact that he was only a pawn in a game they were playing. "Where do we start?" she asked.

"I think I should take you home," he said.

"I can walk," Kate said. "It's not far."

"We can walk together," he said as he rose.

"The sooner I call my mother with the bad news, the better," Kate said as Jack helped her to her feet, took her book bag from her and put it on his shoulder.

"Do you want me to be there when you do?" he asked.

"That's not a bad idea," Kate said. "You can introduce yourself, so she'll know I'm not making this up. After all, it's pretty amazing, when you think about it. Me with someone like you."

The flush was back on Jack's cheekbones, and Kate wanted to tell him that she hadn't meant someone dishonest and scandalous. She'd meant someone so much *older*—and handsome and charming and successful. But she knew if she tried to explain herself, she would only make it worse, so she held her tongue.

Kate was living at the Westgate, a condominium situated across the street from the imposing domed state capitol building, not far from the Longhorn Grille. The conversation between them was so easy, the walk felt surprisingly short. She wondered if Jack was trying to charm her, or whether it just came naturally.

"This is my place," she said as she unlocked the door and let him into her fifth floor apartment. Her father was footing the bill, or she never would have been able to afford it, but it was furnished with secondhand furniture she'd bought herself.

Kate loved everything about the West, and her decor showed it. A leather couch. An ancient wooden rocker. A cowhide rug. A standing lamp that had been fashioned from a wooden hanes, the horse collar used to pull a wagon.

The door made a solid *thunk* sound when Jack closed it behind him. Kate suddenly felt nervous, way out of her depth. Which was silly, because it was pretty obvious that a man who felt like spending time with her was "baby-sitting" wasn't likely to have designs on her person.

"Would you like something to drink?" she asked. The sun had been warm on their backs during their walk.

"Iced tea if you've got it," he said. "Otherwise, water will be fine."

Kate made herself busy in the kitchen, watching from the corner of her eye as Jack toured her living room, picking up various objects and inspecting them and putting them back down.

"Nice antlers," he said, as he inspected half of a five-point rack of deer antlers that decorated her coffee table.

"I found them when I was hiking on North's ranch," she said, as she crossed and handed him a glass of iced tea.

She held up her own glass and said, "Here's to marriage. My parents' marriage," she quickly corrected.

"I'll drink to that," Jack said, clinking his glass against hers. "You ready to make that call?"

"Not really," Kate said. "But I guess it has to be done." She didn't like deceiving her parents, but she was doing this for their own good. This wasn't as crazy as some of the stunts she'd suggested to Uncle North in the barn a couple of weeks ago. But it was close.

"Hi, Mom," she said, looking into Jack's dark eyes as she made contact with her mother. "I'm fine," she said. "I have some news."

Jack stepped close enough that she could smell some faint scent of piney male cologne, while she held her cell phone a little away from her ear so he could hear the other side of the conversation.

"Good news, I hope," her mother said.

"Wonderful news!" Kate said, her eyes once more locked with Jack's. "I have a new boyfriend."

"That is wonderful news," her mother said. "Tell me about him."

"It's Jack McKinley," Kate said.

Kate was looking into Jack's eyes and saw the resignation in them at her mother's awed silence.

"*The* Jack McKinley?" her mother said. "The football player?"

"Yes, Mom. He's the most amazing man. So handsome—"

Jack rolled his eyes.

"And charming—"

Jack flashed his smile.

"And . . ." Kate searched for a word that would describe what she felt when she looked into Jack McKinley's eyes. "And kind, Mother. Thoughtful and kind."

Jack turned his back on her and headed for the picture window that revealed a stunning view of the pink marble state capitol and the lovely park that fronted it. Kate stared at his back as she listened to her mother caution her about getting involved with someone so much older.

"He's not that old, Mom. Only thirty-two."

"Does your father know about this?" her mother asked.

"I haven't told Daddy," Kate said. "I was kind of hoping you would be here to support me when I do."

After a pause, her mother said, "You do realize how inappropriate this young man is for you."

"I'm crazy about him, Mom."

Jack turned around, his mouth twisted in a grimace.

"I want you to meet him, Mom," Kate continued, her eyes pleading with Jack to accept the necessity for such lies. "I need you to be here when I introduce him to Daddy. Please say you'll come."

Kate couldn't help the grin that spread on her face when her mother agreed. She met Jack's gaze with sparkling gray eyes as she said, "I'm so glad, Mom. When can you get here? You're coming tomorrow? Great!"

Her mother said she would rent a car at the airport and to see if Jack could join the two of them for dinner.

Kate turned to Jack and said, "Can you make dinner tomorrow night?"

Jack nodded.

"Yes, he's right here," she said to her mom. She held out the phone and said, "She wants to talk to you."

Jack took the phone as though she were passing him a rattlesnake by the tail, and said, "Hello, Ms. Grayhawk." And then, "We've been seeing each other for a while." He gestured for Kate to come up with some amount of time, and she held out five fingers.

"A week or so," he said.

Kate turned the phone in her direction, laughed into the receiver and said, "Jack means a week or so of pretty constant time together. We actually met about five weeks ago. We're looking forward to seeing you, too, Mom. Love you, too. Bye."

The instant she closed the flip phone, a hysterical bubble of laughter escaped. "Five days?"

"That's longer than most of my relationships," Jack said with a wry smile.

"You almost blew the whole thing."

"Five days makes more sense than five weeks. How are we going to convince your mom and dad we've known each other that long?" Jack said.

"We'll just have to compare notes and exchange information."

"We've only got twenty-four hours," Jack pointed out.

"Then we'd better get started."

"Hell. We might as well get this out of the way first," he said.

Kate wasn't sure what Jack meant, until he took her in his arms. "Whoa! What are you doing?"

"I guarantee you if we'd been dating for five weeks, we'd have done a lot more than kiss. I figured we should get this first kiss over with."

"*Over with?*" Kate said. "You make it sound like the mumps!"

"Those weren't much fun, either," Jack said.

"You can turn around and head for the door right now, for all I—"

Kate never finished her sentence because Jack was kissing her. His mouth captured hers as he pulled her close. At first, she struggled in his arms, because she wasn't done arguing. When his tongue probed the seam of her lips, she opened her mouth to protest, and he slid his tongue inside. She grabbed his hair, intending to pull it, but he shoved his right leg between hers and pulled her up high on his thigh.

Kate gasped at the pleasurable contact and pressed her tongue deep in Jack's mouth. He groaned, and hands that had held hunks of his silky hair threaded through it and drew his head down to hers. The kiss was tumultuous, a war of wills—and tongues—that left them both breathing hard.

She was hanging onto Jack's neck for dear life when they were done, and his hands still grasped her waist to hold her close. She felt her insides twist as she looked up into his dark, heavy-lidded eyes.

"Thank God that's over with," he said, shoving her off his leg.

"Yeah," she agreed, her knees wobbling as she struggled to stay on her feet. She shoved her hair away from her face and said, "Now we can focus on the details."

"Yeah, like your favorite ice cream."

"Strawberry," she said.

"Chocolate," he said. "And your favorite drink?"

"I'm not legally old enough to drink alcohol," she said.

"Yeah. Right. I could use a strong drink right now," he said, raking both hands through his hair and leaving it standing on end. "Where were we?"

She leaned toward him, and as though some unseen force drew them together, his mouth found hers again. Infinitely tender. Unbelievably needy. Undeniably sweet.

He ended the kiss abruptly, frowning down into her face.

Kate stared up into his dark, questioning eyes, feeling like she'd been poleaxed. "This is . . . strange," she said. "I didn't think this sort of instantaneous physical attraction happened."

"It doesn't," he said flatly. "I wanted to make sure we could convince your parents this is for real."

"Are you telling me you were *faking* what just happened between us?" she said incredulously.

"It was all for show. Every bit of it."

"You're lying," she accused.

"Sweetheart, the woman hasn't been born that can get under my skin."

She stared at him for a moment and said, "We'll see about that."

"Don't waste your time. It can't be done."

"Why are you suddenly acting like a bastard?" Kate said.

"I thought that was the point. To convince your parents you've made a bad choice."

"I think you should leave now," she said, confused by the sudden change in Jack's demeanor.

"Sure. Fine. I'll come by tomorrow, when I have some free time, to finish this up. We need to make sure we have all our facts straight before I meet your mother."

When she turned a troubled face to bid him farewell, he was already gone.

The instant Jack was out the door, he opened his flip phone and hit two. When the call was picked up, he said, "I've made contact. Don't worry. She isn't going anywhere without me from now on. When you want her out of the way, just say the word, and I'll take care of it."

He listened for a moment, then made a growling sound in his throat. "You call it. But I'm telling you right now, as far as I'm concerned, the sooner the better."

6

Kate was still in bed, half asleep, when she heard someone pounding on her front door. "I'm coming," she called out. She felt waterlogged, like she was coming up from deep below the surface. She glanced at the clock and bolted upright. "Eleven? That's impossible!" She'd missed both of her Friday morning classes, and her mother was due to arrive in a matter of hours.

She fell backward, covered her head with the second pillow on her queen-size bed and groaned. It was *his* fault she'd overslept. She'd had serious second thoughts about revealing any more of herself than she already had to a scoundrel like Jack McKinley. And she'd spent half the night worrying about the plan she'd set in motion. There were too many things that could go wrong.

What if her mother changed her mind and decided not to come? What if her father didn't have time, with his busy new schedule, to spend with her mother?

What if they talked and talked and talked without ever admitting that what they really needed was to spend the rest of their lives together?

People in love, she'd discovered, could be amazingly obtuse.

"I'm coming!" she yelled at the top of her lungs, pushing her way out of bed. She raced barefoot to the front door and pulled it open, glaring at the frustratingly attractive man she found standing there. "I overslept. I should be in class right now."

"But you're not," Jack pointed out. "After I left here yesterday, I had a great idea how to get your parents together."

"Better than mine? I doubt it."

"Do you want to hear it or not?"

"Not."

"I thought you wanted to get your parents together."

"I do."

He leaned an arm against the door frame high above his head, so she was treated to the sight of his entire rangy body looking deliciously sexy. He focused his dark, chocolate brown eyes—which, she suddenly noticed, were framed by ridiculously long eyelashes—on her and said, "Are you going to let me in?"

She had visions of the two of them intertwined. Naked. "I'd rather not."

He pushed his way inside and closed the door behind him, pacing the width of her apartment as he spoke, his masculine presence filling the room.

Kate was suddenly aware of how mussed her nearly waist-length black hair must be, and that there wasn't a drop of makeup on her face, because she'd washed it all off last night. She was glad she slept in a tank T-shirt and drawstring pajama bottoms. This could have been awkward if she were a Victoria's Secret sort of girl.

Then she saw his eyes had locked on the front of her T-shirt. She looked down and saw her nipples had peaked beneath the soft white cotton. It must be the air-conditioning. She crossed her arms to cover the offending body parts and said, "So what's your big plan?"

She heard Jack swallow hard before his eyes met hers.

"We need to make sure your mom realizes this isn't a passing phase. That we're serious. You can say you're planning to quit school to be with me. Of course, we have no plans to marry."

"That would drive her nuts, all right," Kate said.

"You should ask your mom—actually, your mom and dad—to meet you at the foreman's house on North's ranch. That way they can see we're living together."

Kate gaped. "We're *living* together?"

"I don't know a better way to make the point that we're really a couple," Jack said.

Kate shook her head and said, "It won't work."

"Why not?"

"Uncle North will never allow it."

"North isn't going to interfere," Jack said.

Kate's eyes narrowed. "How can you be sure?"

"The foreman's house is a half mile down the road from the main ranch house, so he isn't even going to know you're there unless he stops by to see me. Which he won't. When he gave me the key, he promised he wouldn't bother me unless I called him first. Which I won't. Besides, he's got his own problems to deal with. He isn't going to be paying any attention to us."

"I don't think—"

"You don't need to think, just get dressed and pack some clothes so we can get out of here," Jack said. "How long before your mom arrives?"

"Any time now," Kate said.

"Then we'd better get a move on."

When Libby got off the plane in Austin there was a message on her cell phone telling her that Kate wasn't at home, that "Dad will know where I am," and that she should go directly to the federal courthouse, "where Daddy is working now. Surprise!"

Libby had heard nothing about Clay going back to work after leaving the U.S. attorney general's office, and she wondered what kind of job he'd gotten that took him to the federal courthouse. Was he a federal prosecutor? He would be good at it, she knew. But it was a big step down from aspirations to the presidency.

Libby tried to reach Clay on his cell phone before she left the airport, to ask where Kate was, but the call went directly to voice mail. She tried Kate's cell phone again and got the same result.

When she arrived at the courthouse, she was surprised at the tight security, until she realized the Bomber Brown trial was in progress inside. King had known two of the judges who'd died in the Houston courthouse bombing. She asked where she could find Clay Blackthorne, and was told, "Judge Blackthorne is in his courtroom."

Libby barely managed to keep her jaw from dropping. Clay was a federal judge? Why hadn't someone told her? How had she missed hearing about it on the news? How wonderful for him!

And how awful for her.

Her life was based in Jackson Hole, where she took city folks on backpacking trips into the wilderness with Doc, Magnum and Snoopy, the three hounds she'd left in the care of a friend. Clay's appointment as a federal judge in Austin was for life. How were they supposed to end up together when their jobs would keep them at opposite ends of the country?

Libby slipped into the courtroom and realized there weren't any seats left in the back. Which meant she could either leave or head up to the front. She moved as unobtrusively as she could down the center aisle, shivering when she felt Clay's eyes on her. His gaze narrowed on her briefly, then shifted back to the defense attorney.

Libby had to move to the center of the third row to find an empty seat. To her dismay, Clay's father, Jackson Blackthorne, and his stepmother, Lauren Creed Blackthorne, were sitting directly in front of her. Ren turned and smiled at her, but Blackjack kept his eyes on his son, the judge.

Libby didn't know Ren Blackthorne very well, since Blackjack had been married to Eve DeWitt all those years ago, when Libby had been pregnant and unwed and very much in love with Clay, who'd only wanted to marry her, she believed, to "do the right thing."

The more contact she'd had with Eve, the more Libby had realized what a blessing it was that Blackjack had stolen her away from King. It was Eve, Libby believed, more than Blackjack, who'd been opposed to Clay marrying her. Eve had made it clear that her son—the future U.S. president—deserved better than a harlot, a word Libby had never heard before and had needed to look up afterward.

She'd flushed beet red at what she'd found: härlət\'har-lot\n[ME, fr. OF *herlot* rouge](15c): PROSTITUTE.

Her own mother had been long dead by the time

all this happened. It was her mother's death, of sorrow, after her father had divorced her, that had prompted Libby to seek revenge against the Blackthornes. And she'd had no one with whom she could discuss the depths of her despair when everything had gone so terribly wrong. She'd started out to avenge her mother's death and ended up in love with the enemy.

And pregnant with his child.

Her father's response to the situation, to forbid her marriage to Clay and threaten dire consequences to her lover if she tried to run away with him, had been particularly heartbreaking.

Here she was, twenty years later, still in love with a man who'd never been able to forgive her for refusing to marry him. Even after he'd learned that she'd been blackmailed by her father into turning him away. Even after he'd learned that she still had feelings for him. Even after he'd admitted that he still had feelings for her.

Instead of nursing the long dormant love between them to life, he'd turned his back on her and gotten engaged to his former wife's sister.

Suddenly, Libby had been thrown back into the arena with the lion. Because they shared a daughter. And their daughter was in yet another scrape.

She heard Clay say that court would resume at 1:16, and then everyone around her was rising. She stood and waited for Clay to exit the courtroom, anxious to be gone before she had to speak to his parents.

That hope was lost when Ren turned around, extended her hand and said, "Libby! It's so wonderful to see you." She turned to Blackjack and said, "Isn't it wonderful, Jackson?"

Blackjack was saved from lying when Ren continued, "Clay asked us to meet him in his chambers at the noon recess. Won't you join us?"

That was the last thing Libby wanted to do, but it seemed the quickest way to get to Clay and find out what had happened to Kate.

Clay had barely greeted his parents when he rounded on Libby and said, "How long have you known about Kate and that felon?"

"I don't believe he was actually convicted of—" Libby began.

"How long?" Clay interrupted brusquely.

"Kate called me last night."

"Did you know they're living together?" Clay said.

"What?" Libby was reeling from Clay's attack and shocked at what he'd said. Her daughter was living with a man? "Where are they—"

"At North's ranch," Clay snarled. "In the foreman's house."

Libby was stunned into silence.

"That no-good bastard," Blackjack muttered.

"Do you know Jack McKinley, Mr. Blackthorne?" Libby asked.

"Hell, no. I was referring to your brother North."

Libby bristled. "My brother—"

"Is doing his level best to steal the Bitter Creek Cattle Company right out from under us," Blackjack said.

Libby turned to Clay. "What is he talking about?"

"That can wait, Dad," Clay said.

"Not for long," Blackjack said. "I don't know why North hasn't called for a vote to kick us off the ranch. Probably just enjoys watching us swinging in the wind."

Libby looked at Clay uncertainly.

"Save it, Dad," Clay said.

"I'd like to hear more," Libby said.

"How about if we talk more at lunch?" Ren said. "Your father and I—"

"I can't leave. I'm sorry," Clay said.

"Another time then," Ren said. "Jackson?"

"I suppose we can finish our discussion later, Clay," Blackjack said. "I'm very proud of you, son."

Libby was surprised by the open compliment, and when she glanced at Clay's face, saw he was equally surprised. Then she saw how Ren was beaming at Jackson and realized she must have encouraged him to say something.

"Thank you, Dad," Clay said.

"We'll see you soon, Clay. Nice to see you, Libby," Ren said.

Blackjack slid a protective arm around Ren and ushered her from the room.

Alone with the lion, Libby took a deep breath and said, "Would you mind explaining what your father was talking about? What, exactly, has North done that has him so upset?"

"I thought you knew," Clay said. "North owns enough Bitter Creek stock to throw us out, lock, stock and smoking barrel."

"Oh, no!," Libby said.

"Right," Clay agreed. "It's driving my father crazy waiting for the ax to fall. You have any idea what North's got in mind?"

Libby shook her head. She had no idea what her older brother was thinking. But his machinations, which once again pitted the Blackthornes and Grayhawks against each other, boded no good for her efforts to reconcile with Clay.

"Damn this awful, disgusting horrible feud," Libby said under her breath. But she didn't apologize for what North had done. He was her brother, and when it came to choosing between Blackthornes and Grayhawks, she owed him her loyalty.

But because he was Kate's uncle, she was righteously furious with her brother. "I can't imagine what North was thinking, letting Kate stay with Jack at his ranch," she said, deftly changing the subject.

Clay grimaced and said, "Kate told me she's planning to quit college at the end of the term to be with Jack. Of course, they have no plans to marry."

Libby groaned. "What can we do?"

"I'm going to break his neck," Clay said.

Libby shot Clay a look that said, *Be serious.* Then she realized he was his father's son, and if he'd had Jack McKinley in his grasp, he might very well have wrung his neck. Or tried to. From what she'd heard, Jack McKinley was a powerful man himself. "There must be something we can do," she said.

"I'm going to start by calling Owen to see if the Texas Rangers can find an excuse to arrest him."

"You can't do that, Clay," Libby said.

"Why not?" he said angrily. "That bastard is sleeping with my daughter and has no intention of making an honest woman of her."

"He isn't doing anything you didn't do," Libby said.

The silence was awesome. And painful.

"I loved you," Clay said into the silence.

Libby felt her heart wrench in her chest. *Loved.* Past tense. "Maybe he loves Kate. Don't you think we should give him the benefit of the doubt?"

"I'd like to give him the sole of my boot in his ass," Clay retorted. "That sonofabitch is going to break Kate's heart."

"We don't know that," Libby said. "I think we should talk with him. With them. I don't approve of what North did, but there must be something redeeming in Jack's character for my brother to make the foreman's house at his ranch available to them."

"North should be shot for allowing it."

Libby stared at him in disgust. "I understand where you learned that sort of hyperbole," she said. "But I don't appreciate it. North is my brother. And you should trust Kate to know her own heart."

"She's an innocent lamb and that lone wolf is going to eat her alive and leave a bleeding carcass when he's done."

"Now you're exaggerating," Libby chided. "I'll go out there this afternoon and—"

"No."

"No?" she said, eyes flashing at his audacity in forbidding her to do anything, when there was nothing binding them to each other. "Since when do you tell me—"

"I think we should go together and present a united front, and I can't leave until this evening."

"Do you really think that will make a difference?"

"I don't know," Clay said. "But so long as you're here, it's worth a try. Will you wait for me? I can be ready to go by six."

This time it was more a request than a demand. Libby conceded he might be right. Two parents were better than one when confronting Kate and Jack. "Sure. Fine. That'll give me a chance to see you in action in your courtroom this afternoon." She picked up a wooden gavel from his desk, turned to him and said,

"I never realized you were considering a future on the bench."

"This opportunity just fell in my lap," Clay said. "But I have to admit I'm enjoying the work."

"You're not worried about adjudicating such a high-profile case your first time out?" Libby asked.

"No. But . . ."

Libby raised her eyebrows, encouraging him to finish his thought.

"There's evidence the plane crash that killed the previous judge was no accident."

"Do the authorities believe his death had anything to do with his involvement in this case?" Libby asked, controlling her speech so Clay wouldn't see the fear that had suddenly stolen her breath.

"Criminal judges deal with some pretty shady characters day in and day out. Bomber Brown seems to be worse than most. It's possible the previous judge was assassinated."

"And you still want this job?"

Clay met her gaze and said, "I feel like I'm doing something worthwhile with my life."

She listened for self-pity in his voice, but didn't hear any. "I'm sorry you're never going to be—"

"This is enough," Clay interrupted. "And I'm safer than you might think. After what happened to the last judge, I've been assigned a bodyguard. You must have seen the deputy marshal outside the door to my chambers."

"He's certainly big enough," Libby said. "Does he follow you everywhere? I mean, are you in danger all the time?"

"My condo has good security, so he usually follows me as far as the door. But whenever I'm in the courthouse, he's my shadow."

Libby tried to hide the horror she felt, but Clay must have seen what she was feeling because he said, "It won't always be like this. I mean, security this tight. It's only this trial, because the defendant is charged with having targeted the judiciary once before."

"Kate seemed so excited about spending time with you. But under the circumstances, I don't think—"

"I've told Kate I don't want her in my courtroom. Of course, she's ignored me. If she insists on coming, I'll ask the marshal's service to have a bodyguard assigned to her, too."

"Oh, my God," Libby said. "This is insane."

"It would be good if you could coax her back to Jackson Hole at the end of the semester."

"I will. That is," Libby said, her brow furrowing, "if she's not married to Jack McKinley by then."

"What on earth was she thinking, getting involved with a character like McKinley?"

Libby ignored the question, which had no good answer, and said, "Will this new job interfere with your honeymoon?"

"There isn't going to be any honeymoon," Clay said bitterly.

Libby stared at him, her mouth agape, unable to hide her astonishment. "Why not?"

"Because there isn't going to be any marriage," he said in a harsh voice.

Libby's heart was pounding. She was afraid to acknowledge what she was feeling, because it felt suspiciously like hope. "What happened?"

"Ask your brother North."

"What does North have to do with anything?" Libby asked.

"He's got her there. At his ranch."

Libby was totally confused. "He's got who at his ranch?"

"Jocelyn. North has Jocelyn living with him at his ranch."

Libby was dumbfounded. "How did that happen?"

"I don't want to talk about it."

"So. My brother is not only trying to take over your family's ranch, he's stolen your fiancée."

Clay's silence spoke volumes.

Libby barely stopped herself from saying, "I'm sorry." That would be a blatant lie. She felt a surge of gladness that took her by surprise. She'd long since conceded the loss of the man she loved to another woman. Suddenly he was free again because North had taken Jocelyn Montrose out of the picture. The future was full of possibilities.

Or would have been, if she and Clay had not been born to families who hated each other. The hostility between Blackthornes and Grayhawks had lain dormant for years. Until North had roused the beast from its lair. Here was the monster, fully formed once more, filled with malice and hate, rearing its ugly head.

Clay reached out to touch Libby's elbow, to escort her out the door, and she jerked at the jolt of electricity that passed between them. She exchanged a stricken look with Clay. It was still there. The sexual spark that arced between them every time they touched.

"Sorry about that. It's friction from this damned carpet," Clay said as he ushered her through the door, this time hands off. "The previous judge was a Longhorn fan, and he's got that Texas burnt orange everywhere, carpet to courtroom."

Libby didn't contradict Clay's contention that it was static electricity they'd felt. "Where do you want me to meet you later?" she asked.

"Here in my chambers at six," he said, stepping back to make more space between them.

"Fine. I'll be here."

Libby didn't look back as she headed down the courthouse steps. She'd spent a lot of time reconciling herself to a life without Clay Blackthorne, and she'd learned to cope with disappointment. She'd felt sorry for him when the woman he'd been engaged to after their liaison was murdered a day before his wedding. And lived through a marriage of her own and a subsequent broken engagement while he'd been married to Giselle Montrose. No matter how discontented she'd been, life had to be lived.

Her hopes had risen high last year when Clay had come to Jackson Hole, a widower of a year. Their first kiss after nearly twenty years had resulted in a not altogether welcome revelation. Whatever magic had been there between them a lifetime ago was still there. They belonged together. Always had, always would.

But Libby was too proud to ask him to take her back. He had to want her. He had to come to her and forgive her and ask on bended knee for her hand.

That simply hadn't happened.

Libby realized she should have known better. The last place you would find a Blackthorne was on bended knee. Sure enough, Clay had gotten engaged to Jocelyn Montrose last fall, rather than deal with the baggage he and Libby had carried around for twenty years.

Now Jocelyn was out of the picture, and Libby couldn't help thinking this might be their last chance, and the man she loved was just too stubborn to see it. Tears welled in her eyes, and she stopped in the middle of the sidewalk, because she couldn't see where she was going.

Why, oh why, couldn't she stop hoping? Stop caring? Stop dreaming about a man who was too much his mother's son ever to be able to forgive her that one trespass? Why couldn't he realize that she'd done it for him? That she'd believed her father when he'd threatened to put Clay in jail. That she'd loved him enough to live her life without him.

Libby realized, as she stood on a scorching sidewalk in Austin, that she'd reached her Waterloo. This was where she would plant her feet and fight her battle for the future. It was now or never. And she meant *never*.

There was more than Kate's relationship with Jack that would be decided by their trip to North's ranch. Libby intended to confront Clay and discover once and for all whether they were destincd to have a future together.

She felt exultant at the possibilities that existed. And an awful fear that within thc next twenty-four hours all hope would be lost.

7

~~~~~

"Mom and Dad are here," Kate said excitedly, as she looked out the window over the sink in the kitchen. She threw the towel she was using to wipe her hands onto the counter and hurried to the screen door to observe the approaching vehicle.

The bright sun was low in the sky, but by shading her eyes, she recognized the black Mercedes SUV coming down the oak-lined dirt road to the foreman's house. She turned and smiled happily at Jack, who was sitting at a wooden trestle table set for four, and said, "They came together in Dad's car."

"I guess the first part of your plan worked," he said. "They've joined forces to check out the monster you're dating."

Kate made a face at him. "You're not a monster. In fact, you're my knight in shining armor." She glanced toward the door, then back at him, and frowned.

"What's wrong?" he asked.

"I think I should be sitting on your lap when they come in."

"Is that really necessary?"

"Actions speak louder than words," Kate said. "Please, Jack?"

His chair screeched as he shoved it back on the aged hardwood floor, making space for her. "You're the boss."

Kate glanced one last time at the oncoming car. She hadn't seen her mother since spring break, and she hadn't spent time with her dad for eons. She wanted to run out the door and hug them and kiss them and tell them how much she loved them. But this wasn't about what she needed. It was about making sure the two of them realized they needed each other.

She crossed quickly to Jack and plopped onto his lap, looping her arms around his neck.

"Not like that," he said. "Stand up."

She stood and he scooted the chair a little farther away from the table and said, "Straddle my lap."

She was the one who'd wanted to set a loving scene for her parents, but Jack's suggestion made her insides clench. "That's a little provocative, don't you think?"

"We're lovers, remember?" He guided her spread legs onto his lap, then circled his hands around her hips and pulled her close as she sat down, so the heart of her was nestled close to the heat of him.

She stared down at the intimate contact, then searched his dark eyes to see if he was as affected as she was. She felt the growing evidence of his arousal. And knew he was.

"Maybe we should be kissing," she murmured as she stared at his long lashes.

"Go ahead," he said, his voice low and rough. "Better make it quick. I can hear them opening their car doors."

It was daunting to be the one making the first move. Nervous, she said, "I'm not sure what to do with my hands."

"Put them around my neck," he instructed. "Better yet, thread them through my hair."

Kate did as she was told, marveling once again at the silkiness of his sun-streaked brown hair, relieved that they'd gotten their first—and second—kiss over with yesterday, because she was already feeling overwhelmed by all this physical contact. She still wasn't prepared for the sensations that moved through her as his soft lips rubbed against hers.

She made a satisfied sound in her throat as his mouth covered hers for the third time. She sank into the kiss, completely losing herself in the taste and feel of him.

"What the hell do you think you're doing!"

Kate would have lurched out of Jack's arms if he hadn't gripped her waist and held her in place. She turned her head, her eyes unfocused and her breath sketchy, and found her parents staring at her with incredulous faces. She took a deep breath to rejuvenate her suffering lungs, shot them a lopsided grin and said, "Hi, Mom. Hi, Dad. This is Jack."

By then, Jack was rising, scooting her off his lap and holding her hands to help her stand, easy as you please, as though her father hadn't yelled at them to end their loverlike pose.

Jack smiled his charming smile, reached out a hand to her father and said, "Nice to meet you, Judge Blackthorne."

It quickly became apparent that her father wasn't going to take Jack's hand. Her mother reached out and took it instead, saying, "I'm glad to meet you, Jack."

Her father said, "I'd rather not be meeting you, McKinley. Especially under these circumstances."

Despite the telltale flush high on Jack's cheekbones that revealed he was aware of the cut he'd been given by her father, Jack took her mother's hand in both of his and leaned over to kiss her on the cheek. "I can see where Kate gets her good looks."

The comment surprised Kate, because she and her mother were total opposites. Kate was tall like her father, with his black hair and gray eyes. Her mother was petite, with blue eyes and short blond curls.

EAST MOLINE PUBLIC LIBRARY

"Kate has your nose and chin," Jack said. "And your smile."

Kate realized her mother was smiling, which was nothing short of amazing, considering the situation. Her father was not. He was scowling at all the attention Jack was paying her mother. Which was when she realized that Jack was only a couple of years younger than her mother. And her father was jealous.

That had to be a good sign, wasn't it?

Kate might have been jealous herself, except it was ludicrous to imagine someone like Jack McKinley taking a second look at someone like her, in the ordinary course of things. Which made her wonder, suddenly, what he owed North that justified him doing this favor for her.

It occurred to Kate that she should have questioned Jack's motives sooner. She'd simply been too glad to have a willing accomplice to wonder whether Jack had some hidden agenda. As she watched him with her mother, she wondered whether her uncle North might have asked Jack to make her father jealous.

Except that wasn't possible. Her initial meeting with Jack had been an accident, hadn't it? If not, what was Jack hoping to get out of all of this? Kate looked at him with eyes suddenly willing to see what she'd shut out in her anxiety to get her parents together. Jack McKinley was charming her mother. And infuriating her father. And all he'd done so far was say hello.

She crossed past Jack and hugged her father, wanting to comfort him, then took the two steps to bring her mother close. "I'm so glad you're both here." She stepped back to look at her parents and felt Jack's hands settle at her waist. He stepped close enough for her to feel the length of his body along her back. She could almost see her father's neck hairs hackle.

"I hope the two of you can stay for the weekend," Kate said.

She saw her parents exchange a surprised look, before her father said, "I didn't plan on it."

"Neither did I," her mother said. "But I don't see why I couldn't, if you've got an extra toothbrush."

"I'm your mother's ride, so I suppose I have to hang around as long as she does," her father said, eyeing Jack suspiciously. "Where did you plan to put us?"

"There are three bedrooms," Kate said. "Mom and Dad, you can each have one of the guest rooms. Jack and I are sharing the master."

Kate felt Jack's hands tighten at her waist and could almost feel his body stiffen in disapproval. She didn't know what he was so upset about. Like everything else they'd done today, it would only be pretend.

She hadn't previously discussed the sleeping arrangements with Jack, because she hadn't planned to ask her parents to stay. She'd made the decision on impulse. But there were only three bedrooms, and if

she and Jack weren't sharing a bedroom it would end
the illusion that they were lovers.

"I don't approve of this relationship," her father
said. "Or these sleeping arrangements."

"I'm a grown woman, Daddy," Kate said.

"What's the deal here, McKinley?" her father said,
ignoring her and confronting Jack. "What is it you
want? Money to get out of her life? You've got it.
Name your price."

"Daddy!" Kate said, shocked to the core by her father's attack. "Jack doesn't want anything from you."

"You're wrong, Kate," Jack said, his arm tightening
around her.

Alarmed, Kate tried to turn around to look into
Jack's eyes, but he had too strong a grasp on her. She
could feel his body quivering with anger and heard
the menace in his voice when he said to her father,
"There is something I want, Blackthorne. For you to
butt out of my business!"

"I know about you, McKinley," her father retorted.
"My daughter deserves better."

"She's made her choice," Jack said.

"Daddy, please," Kate said. "Don't judge Jack before you get to know him."

"I know his kind," her father said. "No-good riffraff.
A rolling stone that won't stop for anything or anyone.
An opportunistic—"

"Daddy, don't—" Kate cried.

"That's enough, Clay," her mother said. She turned to Kate and said, "Maybe we shouldn't stay."

Kate looked from her mother to her father and back again, seeing all hope of a reconciliation between them turning to dust. "Please, Mom. Please, Daddy. Once you get to know Jack like I do, you'll understand why I . . . I love him."

Kate felt Jack's hands tighten painfully at her waist and knew he hadn't liked that bold admission either. Well, she could explain everything once they were alone. She focused her eyes on her mother and said, "I want you to stay."

"Of course I'll stay, if you want me here," her mother said. She turned to Kate's father and said, "Clay?"

"I'm not going to pass up the chance to spend some time with you, Kitten."

"Then it's settled," Kate said with a glowing smile. "We waited supper for you. I made a pot roast. Are you hungry?"

"Starved," her mother said.

Her father said nothing, and Kate had to tug free of Jack's hold to direct her parents to their seats. "Daddy, you can sit at that end of the table, and Mom you can sit across from me. Jack's at the other end of the table."

"Is there anything I can help with?" her mother asked.

"It's all ready to go," Kate said. "You and Dad just sit. Jack, will you pour the iced tea, while I serve the plates?"

They moved together like silent dancers in a ballet. Pouring. Serving. Sitting.

Once they were all seated with food in front of them, Kate said to her father, "How long are you postponing your wedding?"

Her father choked, and he grabbed for his glass of tea.

"Are you okay?" Kate asked.

Her father swallowed a gulp of tea and said, "Jocelyn and I haven't decided on another date. Why do you ask?"

"I just wondered if the trial is going to interfere with your wedding preparations now."

"I think the trial will probably be over before we head to the altar."

Kate felt a sudden lurch of hope. The trial might take months. Her parents were committed to spending the weekend together, and by some miracle, Jocelyn Montrose was no longer standing between them. All Kate had to do was make sure her mom and dad were thrown together in romantic circumstances. Love would do the rest.

She knew she ought to offer sympathy for her father's loss, but she could barely resist shouting "Hallelujah!"

"You're going to find out," her father said, "so I

might as well be the one to tell you. Jocelyn is staying with North."

Kate felt her stomach do a joyful somersault. Oh, her wonderful *devious* uncle! But her voice was neutral when she asked, "How did that happen?"

"I think it's my fault," her mother said in a low voice. "I introduced them last year in Wyoming, and it seems there was some attraction that neither of them acknowledged at the time."

"She's living with him here. At the ranch," her father said.

"Here?" Kate said. "I can't believe it. I just visited Uncle North two weeks ago and—"

"She moved in two weeks ago," her father said.

Right after her visit with Uncle North, Kate realized. He had been listening. He had cared. And he'd somehow manipulated the situation so Jocelyn had called off the wedding. Kate wanted to find her uncle and give him a big hug. But there was work to do here. Uncle North had set the stage. It was her job to make sure the actors played their parts.

She rose and carried her empty plate and her mother's to the sink. "I'm sorry, Daddy," she said. "But you wouldn't have had time for a honeymoon right now anyway with this big trial."

Her mother started to rise, but Kate said, "Don't get up, Mom. Jack and I can handle the dishes. Coffee, Daddy? Tea, Mom?"

"Yes," they both said almost in unison. They smiled at each other, and Kate felt her heart give a sudden lurch. Oh, this could work. It could. She set about making tea for her mother and coffee for her father.

"Coffee, Jack?" she asked.

"None for me after dinner," Jack said as he rose with his plate and collected her father's plate to bring them to the sink.

Kate saw her father's gaze shooting from her to Jack and back again. She searched for what she'd said that was wrong and realized her mistake. Surely, if she and Jack had known each other for so long, she would know Jack didn't drink coffee after dinner. It was a very small faux pas, but her father was a very smart man.

Kate needed a distraction. When Jack reached the sink with his handful of dishes, she met his gaze and flushed at the temerity of what she was about to do. "Thank you, sweetheart," she said. Then she reached up on tiptoe and kissed his mouth, whispering, "Daddy's suspicious. Do something!"

Jack said, "You're welcome, dear." He took the coffee and teacups she handed him to the table to serve her mother and father, then returned to Kate's side at the sink, leaning back against the counter next to her as she stacked dishes in the dishwasher, and asked her father, "How's the trial going?"

Kate saw her father eye Jack speculatively before he said, "I'd rather talk about something else."

"'Bomber Brown's trial is the biggest news around,'" Jack said.

Her father's eyes narrowed slightly before he said, "I saw in the paper that you're in a little trouble yourself."

Jack flushed but said nothing.

"I don't understand," Kate's mother said. "What kind of trouble are you in, Jack?"

"A little disagreement in numbers between me and the IRS, Ms. Grayhawk," Jack said.

From the corner of her eye, Kate watched her mother melt under Jack's charming smile. "Please call me Libby," her mother said. "It must be very perturbing after all these years to have your life still bruited about in the newspaper."

"It is," Jack said.

"Where did you grow up, Jack?" Kate's mother asked.

"I was born and raised in San Antonio, ma'am."

"Libby," her mother corrected. "Do you have brothers and sisters?"

Kate listened attentively for Jack's answer, since this was all news to her.

"My older sister died when I was in high school. I have two younger sisters living in San Antonio, not far from my parents."

"What have you been doing with yourself since you were drummed out of football?" her father asked.

Again, the telltale flush, but no other evidence that Jack found her father's question offensive. Kate felt offended on his behalf and said, "Jack's got a really great restaurant in downtown Austin, Daddy, the Longhorn Grille."

She saw the surprise on her father's face before he said, "My father's been trying to get me to meet him at the Grille for dinner. He says you make an exceptional steak Oscar."

"I've got a good—by good I mean expensive—chef," Jack said. "I made up my mind that if I was going to open a restaurant, it was going to be the best one in Austin. I'm not quite there yet. But I will be."

Kate leaned over to kiss Jack's cheek, where it was still flushed, then turned to her father and said, "Jack's going to be the best husband, too."

"That remains to be seen," her father retorted.

"I'm looking forward to watching the trial, Daddy," Kate said as she closed the dishwasher and turned to slide her arm around Jack's waist. She was a little surprised, but grateful, when he did the same to her.

"I've told you I don't want you there," her father replied.

Kate frowned. "I hardly ever get to see you. I thought we'd be able to have lunch together once in a while during your noon recesses."

Kate watched her father eye Jack's hand, which had slid up from her waist to a sensitive spot just below her breast, before he said to her, "The plane crash that killed the judge who previously presided over this case was probably the result of sabotage."

Kate saw her mother's hand was trembling and watched with wonder and elation as her father reached out to take her hand and comfort her.

"I know you don't want me in the courtroom," she said. "But that would mean I'd have to wait until this trial is over to see you. And I'm not willing to do that."

She watched as her father exchanged an exasperated glance with her mother. "It's not safe."

"I'll be careful, Daddy. I promise. Besides, I'm writing a paper on the effects of violence on governmental limitations on personal freedom and I need to see as much of the trial as I can to do a really good job. And you're forgetting, I'll have Jack to look out for me."

"Somehow that makes me feel more alarmed than reassured," her father said.

"Daddy!" Kate said, shocked at his rudeness. "Jack is a very responsible person."

"Who just happened to arouse the scrutiny of the IRS."

Kate felt mortified for Jack. "Jack just needs to collect some documentation—"

"I don't need you to defend me, Kate," Jack interrupted. His dark eyes bored into her father's as he said, "And I don't owe you an explanation."

"Like father, like son," her father said quietly.

Jack moved so fast he knocked over a glass on the counter behind him, which fell into the sink with a crash of breaking glass. He stood feet widespread, fisted hands clenched at his sides as he said, "I'm *nothing* like my father!"

Her father had moved equally fast, rising from his chair so quickly it clattered to the floor behind him.

Kate grabbed Jack's arm at almost the same moment she saw her mother take hold of her father's. "What's he talking about, Jack?" Kate asked.

She flinched when he jerked himself free. His jaw was clamped and his steady glare never wavered from her father's face. Kate turned to her father and said, "What are you talking about, Daddy?"

Before her father could speak, Jack said, "My father's a gambler. He's addicted to it. Craves it like an alcoholic craves gin, or a drug addict craves crack cocaine. Incapable of stopping. Always making one more bet. Taking one more risk in hopes of finally cashing in. But always losing. Losing everything."

The kitchen was silent except for the sound of Jack's raspy breathing. She looked at Jack, her heart in her eyes. How devastating it must have been for him to be forced out of football because of a gambling scandal. Kate suddenly felt sure Jack had never shaved a point in football. Not with his history. Not when it was so obvious how much he hated gambling for what it had done to his father.

Kate sought for some way to break the awful tension in the room and said, "Why don't we take a walk down to the river. Mom, you and Dad go on ahead. I'll stay here with Jack just long enough to clear up this broken glass. There should still be plenty of light to see where you're going."

Her father turned to her mother and said, "Libby?"

"That sounds lovely."

Kate stayed between her father and Jack, to be sure there was no chance for them to come to blows, and said, "We'll join you in a few minutes."

Her father narrowed his eyes at Jack, but her mother said, "I know the way, Clay," and led him out of the house and down the dirt path toward the river.

The instant they were out of hearing, Jack turned Kate so she was facing him and said in a harsh voice, "What the hell were you thinking?"

Kate frowned in confusion. "What has you so upset?"

"Your father hates my guts. I can't believe you asked him—both of them—to spend the night, and then set it up so we have to sleep in the same room."

"He doesn't hate you."

Jack snorted. "Right."

"Anyway, it's only pretend."

"Tell me that when we're alone in the dark in the same bed," he countered harshly.

She shivered at the dangerous look in his dark eyes. "But—"

She was interrupted by her mother, who yanked open the screen door and said, "I'm sorry, Kate, but I have to leave."

"But you can't!" she protested, flummoxed by her mother's abrupt return.

Her mother met her gaze, blue eyes brimming with unshed tears, and said, "Your father and I—"

Kate felt her stomach clenching as she realized that all her well-laid plans were falling apart. "But, Mom, you and Daddy—"

"Are at loggerheads again," her mother said with a wan smile, as she stepped inside.

At that moment her father entered the kitchen, his own face dark as a thundercloud. She watched as her mother took a step away from him. Kate was appalled at this evidence that they'd already argued. What had her father said to upset her mother so quickly and so badly?

Then she looked at her father's strained face and realized he was as distressed by whatever had been said as her mother was. "I need to get back to Austin," he said in a tight voice. "We won't be able—"

"No!" Kate interrupted in a panicked voice. "I'm not going to let you go, Daddy. Or you, either, Mom. I

hardly see either one of you, and I was looking forward to all of us going riding tomorrow morning. You
have to stay!"

She knew her parents loved her, even if they
couldn't comfortably spend time together. She saw
the guilt that flashed in her father's eyes, and the em-
pathy and pain in her mother's. She watched as they
exchanged a glance of mutual consternation.

"May I add my own encouragement that you stay?"
Jack said. "Kate has been so excited to see you. I very
selfishly want to make her happy."

Kate felt her jaw drop at Jack's short speech and
quickly closed her mouth. She turned back to her parents to see what effect his plea might have.

It was her mother who gave in first. She tried to
smile, failed, then tried again and succeeded. "It will
be nice to ride together again."

Kate shifted her gaze to her father, whose lips were
pressed in a flat line. She didn't beg. Grayhawks didn't
beg. Besides, Blackthornes had no mercy.

But what she felt must have been plain in her eyes,
because her father's mouth twisted wryly before he
said, "I haven't been on a horse in a while."

Kate grinned, realizing her father had agreed to
stay. "I'll make sure you get a gentle mount," she said.

Her father snorted, and she laughed. Her parents
were both excellent riders. In fact, they'd met on
horseback. She was hoping this ride would remind

them of that long-ago day. And of their long-ago feelings.

"I've had an exhausting day traveling," her mother said. "I hope you won't mind if I retire early."

"No problem, Mom," Kate said. "I can loan you something to sleep in. Jack, maybe you can find something for Daddy—"

"I'll be fine," her father said, the scowl back on his face as he looked at Jack. "I brought some work with me. It's in the car. I'll go get it."

By the time Kate returned from getting her mother settled, her father had closed himself inside the second bedroom. She looked around for Jack and found him standing at the screen door.

"I think we'd better take that walk," he said soberly.

Kate realized he wanted to argue, and that he didn't want her parents to hear. She wasn't about to give him the chance to yell at her. "I'm tired, too," she said. "I think I'll go to bed."

To her dismay, he followed close on her heels. She could feel his masculine presence, the heat of him at her back. The moment she was inside the master bedroom, he closed the door behind her.

She turned to face him, trembling with some emotion she couldn't name. But she wasn't about to cower. Grayhawks weren't afraid of anyone. She crossed her arms over her chest in defiance and said, "You're going to ruin everything if you start yelling at me."

"I have no intention of arguing with you," Jack said.

She watched, appalled, as he unsnapped his cuffs, and with a single yank, unsnapped his western shirt and tugged it out of his jeans. He wasn't wearing an undershirt, exposing a broad chest covered with dark curls. She quivered at the rattle of his belt being un- buckled and heard the slide of leather as he pulled it free.

When he reached for the button of his jeans, she turned her back abruptly. "You could at least respect my modesty."

"You're the one who set this up. What did you ex- pect me to do?"

"You could sleep in your clothes."

He snorted in disgust. "I should never have agreed to baby-sit—"

She whirled on him, incensed at his dismissal of her and stopped short as she realized she could see his white briefs in the V where his jeans had been un- zipped. She forced her eyes to his face and said fiercely—but softly, "I'm not a kid!"

"Get undressed and get in the damned bed," he said.

"Where are you going to sleep?"

"On the floor."

"That's not necessary," she said, eyeing the king- size bed. "There's plenty of room for both of us."

"We're not married. We're not engaged. Hell, I don't even like you. I went along with this ridiculous scheme because—" He cut himself off, and Kate wondered what he'd stopped himself from saying. He looked at her, his mouth a thin, disgusted line, and said, "I'll be damned if I get tricked into marriage by some spoiled brat."

She was toe-to-toe with him a moment later, keeping her voice down, but surprisingly hurt and furiously angry. "Don't worry! I wouldn't marry you if you were the last man in the universe. I can't believe I asked you to help me get my parents together. You can have the bed. *I'll* take the floor! I wouldn't want you to lose any sleep!"

"A gentleman doesn't—"

"I'm no lady, remember? Just a kid."

"I never—"

Kate blinked back the tears that were blurring her vision. She wasn't about to cry and confirm his belief that she was a child. She'd show him! She was nineteen. And a woman.

She reached for the buttons on her shirt.

"What are you doing?" Jack said.

"Getting undressed." She waited for him to say something, anything, that would give her an idea what he was thinking. But he remained silent as she unbuttoned her tailored white shirt, pulled it from her jeans and let it slide down her shoulders onto the floor. She didn't bother turning her back. She simply reached for the button on her jeans—she wasn't wearing a belt—and began to unzip them.

"Whoa," Jack said, putting out a hand. "What do you think you're doing?"

"I've already told you," she said, sitting on the edge of the bed to yank off her boots and socks. She lifted her hips and pulled off her jeans. Then she stood before him, wearing only her white bra and a pair of colorful bikini bottoms.

His eyes surveyed her from head to toe. He lifted an eyebrow, but he looked distinctly . . . unimpressed.

Kate was seething inside at his dismissal of her charms, but she'd be damned if she let him know it. She retrieved a pillow from the top of the bed and a blanket from the foot and made herself a pallet on the rug.

"I said I'd take the floor," Jack said in a biting voice.

"And I said that isn't necessary,"

"You're being ridiculous."

"Well, we children have a tendency to do that," she replied saracastically. She turned to glare at him, and found herself arrested by what she saw.

His butter-soft jeans didn't leave much to the imagination. She'd been wrong. He *had* noticed how grown up she was. Her eyes shot to his face, but he looked annoyed, rather than aroused. He was clearly determined to ignore her.

Well. She'd see about that. Kate didn't know what imp provoked her to test his self-control. She shoved her hands up into her hair as though it was heavy on her shoulders and let it fall across her breasts, then reached behind her to unsnap her bra and let it fall to the floor.

Kate felt herself flushing when she realized her hair had not covered her breasts as she'd hoped. Her peaked nipples protruded. She resisted the urge to re-arrange her hair to cover them. Instead, she lifted her eyes to meet Jack's and moved toward him slowly, one bare foot in front of the other, wondering what would happen when she reached him.

"Stop right there," he said in a guttural voice.

She stood a mere foot from him, but she could feel the tension arcing between them and smell some masculine scent that made her body prickle. The hairs on her arms stood up, and her belly curled with unmistakable desire. Jack's eyes were heavy-lidded, dark and lambent. He focused on her mouth before moving to her breasts, and then her belly, where the last of her dark tresses curled against the hem of her bikini panties.

She felt an irresistable urge to move into Jack's em-brace, but her feet were rooted to the floor. The look on his face was terrifying. And exhilarating. She'd wanted to prove to him that he wasn't as cool and calm and collected as he thought he was. And she'd suc-

ceeded. She'd peeled away the thin veneer of civilization that covered his base animal lust, but she wasn't
sure what to do with the savage beast she'd set free.

She heard Jack swallow audibly. She met his gaze
and felt frightened by his dark, inscrutable eyes.

She was surprised at how quickly he moved, how
tightly he held her arms in his powerful grasp, and
how fast his mouth captured her own. His tongue
thrust deep and the sound he made in his throat
caused her insides to twist with an agony of pleasure.
She moaned as she reached out for him. But he had
too tight a hold on her and kept their bodies
separated.

A moment later, he wrenched their mouths apart.
He stared down into her eyes, his own glittering with
a need so fierce it stopped her breath. "Get in that
bed," he said in a harsh, guttural voice. "Before I put
you there."

It only took a moment for her to divine what he
meant. She could get into bed—and sleep there by
herself. Or she could wait for him to put her there—
and join her.

Kate usually responded to threats with defiance.
But she could see his body quivering and knew that
whatever leash he had on himself was within a hairs-
breadth of breaking. She opened her mouth to say she
wanted him as much as he wanted her, and suddenly
remembered why they were in this room together.

It was all pretend. For the purpose of getting her
parents together. He was a playboy, a gambler, and,
for all the world knew, a cheat. He might want her
body, but that was all. He didn't even know who she
was, not really.

Kate waited for him to release her. When he didn't,
she realized that he'd gone beyond that point. If she
wanted to be free, she would have to make the first
move. She met his gaze, raised her chin, and said,
"Let me go."

The instant she spoke, his hands released her. She
almost stumbled backward. He reached out to catch
her, but she stepped beyond his reach, certain that if
he touched her again, she might surrender to his desire. And regret it the rest of her life.

"I'll take the bed," she said in a shaky voice. She
barely managed to swallow the sob that threatened to
prove what a child she really was.

He reached for his shirt and threw it to her. "Put
that on."

Her hands were shaking too much to find the arm-
holes, but he didn't offer to help. He stared at her, his
dark eyes hard and dangerous, until she finally managed to get her arms into the shirt and pulled it over
her shoulders.

She could hear his harsh breathing, feel a bestial
need emanating from him, almost smell the harsh
scent of sexual desire.

She tried to snap the shirt, but her hands were trembling too badly for her to get the two pieces of metal to meet. Abruptly, his large hands appeared under her nose. As she stared up at him, he snapped the top two snaps, then took a step back and said in a rough, scornful voice, "Get in bed."

She stared at him a moment, wishing she could get the tongue off the roof of her mouth to speak. But it was stuck there. She climbed into bed, shivering as the cold sheets hit her bare legs, then watched, wide-eyed, as he turned away without another word and settled onto the pallet she'd arranged on the rug. As a final insult, he turned his back on her and pulled the blanket up over his shoulder, shutting her completely out.

Kate glared at him, then realized he couldn't see her disdain. Just in case he looked back in her direction, she turned her back on him and pulled the covers up over her shoulders. She realized the light was still on, but she was afraid to move to turn it off. Besides, she felt safer with the light on.

A moment later, however, she heard the light behind her click off. She shivered again in the dark, and pulled the covers tighter around her. She'd had a narrow escape.

Kate tried to sleep, but sleep evaded her. She listened for Jack's breathing and realized he wasn't asleep either.

"I'm sorry I got us into this," she said.

"You should be," he shot back.

She sat up, perturbed at his ungracious response. "I'm not sorry I put us in the same room," she clarified. "I'm only sorry I started playing games once I got here."

"You should be," he repeated just as brusquely.

"That's not fair, Jack," she said. "You're as much to blame—"

That was as far as she got before the light clicked on and she found herself staring up at a very intimidating male figure. She clutched the sheet to her chest, aware that she was half naked.

"Don't you know better than to do that sort of striptease in front of man?" he demanded.

"I never thought—"

"That's right," he said, "You don't think! You're an impulsive—"

She was on her knees facing him in an instant, holding the covers with one hand, poking his chest with a finger of the other. "This was supposed to be *pretend!* You're the one who made it into something else."

"I suggest we forget what happened here tonight and get back to the original plan."

"Fine," Kate spat.

"Fine," he retorted.

They glared at each other for another moment, before Jack reached over and turned out the light.

Kate was left staring into the darkness. She could hear him settling back onto the floor and, grumbling to herself, curled onto her side, her back to him, wondering how she could ever go on with the game they were playing. Wanting Jack suddenly felt very real.

"I'm only doing this because I love my parents and want to see them together," she whispered into the darkness.

Jack didn't reply.

Jack was careful not to make a sound as he snuck out of the house to make a call on his cell phone.

"You'll never guess who's sleeping under my roof," he said when the call was answered. "That's right. The judge himself. And the girl and her mother."

He listened, then said, "Now is not the time. I think it's better if we wait."

The wind soughed through trees, making them rustle as he listened. Finally, he said, "I'd better get back inside. I can't count on any of them staying put all night, and I don't want to have to do any explaining. I'll talk to you soon."

Donnie watched as his brother Bobby John closed his cell phone. Donnie hated his brother. And his mother, whose eyes were squinted into narrow slits as she leaned her head back to avoid the smoke curling up from the filtered cigarette between her bony fingers. The two of them were deep in conversation. They expected him to think the way they did. But he never would. Not if he lived to be a hundred and three.

The two of them were sitting across the smoky bar from Donnie, in a corner booth with an old-time lantern that shed scant light. Donnie picked up his beer—nobody here had questioned his age—and took a deep, satisfying drink, wiping the foam from his lips with his sleeve.

"So, Donnie," the reporter from *The Weekly Herald*, the newspaper serving the suburb closest to their farm, said, "I haven't seen a Letter to the Editor from you in a long time."

Donnie glowered at the middle-aged man, with his close-cropped hair and clean-shaven face, sitting across from him and said, "I've been a little busy."

The sound of wailing violins and a mournful country voice on the jukebox made it hard to hear each other, even across the table.

"When can I expect to print something?" the man persisted.

Donnie scowled. "Give me a chance to get my thoughts together. I'll get in touch with you when I have something."

The gray-headed man picked up his Stetson, which had been sitting crown down on the table between them and settled it very carefully and evenly on his head. "Not much time left before the trial is over," he said.

Donnie shot a murderous glance toward his brother and mother, whose heads were close together. He watched as his brother laughed. "You'd never know it to look at the two of them," he said bitterly.

"You know I'm there whenever you need me," the reporter said.

"You always have been," Donnie said. "And I appreciate it. I'll be in touch with you. Very soon."

8

Libby sat with her arms circling her knees, wrapped up snug in a quilt, on a wooden swing on the front porch of the foreman's house, wishing she'd stayed in bed. At least there she'd had a chance at sleep. For the past hour, she'd been listening to the soothing night sounds—the cicada, the occasional lowing of cattle, the rustle of the live oak in the wind—but she felt no less disturbed.

It seemed lately that whenever she and Clay were alone together, one or the other of them said something hurtful. The sad thing was, it hadn't always been that way. During the years Kate was growing up, they'd somehow managed to be civil. Ever since Kate had been kidnapped last year, and Clay had kissed Libby for the first time in twenty-odd years, the gloves had come off.

Tonight, she'd been the one who'd said something scathing. She tried to remember exactly what Clay had said to provoke her, something like, "Kate's acting as crazy as you did at her age." It hadn't taken much to push her over the edge.

She hadn't been able to contain the bitterness she felt that, despite everything she and Clay had been through over the past twenty years raising a child together, and the never-extinguished sexual sizzle that last year's kiss had revealed, Clay was still so *god-damned* unforgiving of that long-ago betrayal.

"I see you couldn't sleep either."

Clay's quiet voice startled her. Libby would have jumped to her feet, but she got tangled in the patchwork quilt. Before she could get free, Clay was already sitting beside her on the swing. She felt at a disadvantage, because he was dressed in a UT sweatshirt and jeans, while under the blanket, she was wearing only a set of skimpy baby doll pajamas Kate had lent her.

"What time is it?" she asked.

"Four. Five. Too close to morning for me to lie in bed anymore. How long have you been sitting out here?"

"Not long," she lied.

As he set the swing moving with one booted foot, she pulled her bare toes farther beneath the blanket.

She waited for Clay to speak, but he seemed content merely to sit with her and watch the gold and pink beginnings of the dawn. Libby was very aware of him, of his body heat, his musky smell, the way his too-long-for-a-judge black hair settled over his brow and nape. His silent closeness, and her heightened awareness of him, reminded her of the last wonderful night they'd made love, more than twenty years ago.

And the devastating morning that had followed.

They'd fallen asleep on a blanket in the grass beneath a willow on Clay's Wyoming ranch. Libby couldn't remember who'd woken first, but she remembered feeling anxious and guilty when she'd looked into Clay's gray eyes, which looked back at her with tenderness in the early morning light.

In that precious predawn moment, she'd been very aware that she loved Clay Blackthorne. And that she'd lied to him.

Libby was terrified of what Clay would do when he found out the truth. That she was only sixteen, not twenty-one, as she'd told him. That she was the daughter of his father's mortal enemy, King Grayhawk. And that she was pregnant.

She'd known she owed him an explanation. But after the exquisite night of lovemaking just past—which might very well be their last, considering what she was about to tell him—it was hard to confess what she'd done.

"Clay . . ." She heard a gurgle as she swallowed over the painful lump in her throat.

His forefinger smoothed the furrow between her eyes. He smiled at her as he said in a gruff, early-morning voice, "What's this frown all about?"

"I have something I need to tell you."

He grinned and said, "That sounds serious."

"It is."

He sobered, leaned forward and kissed her lips gently, and said, "What can I do to help, sweetheart?"

Her throat ached from the deceit she'd practiced on the man she loved. Her heart was pounding with fear of what Clay would do when he knew the truth.

"I'm pregnant," she blurted.

She saw surprise flare in his eyes, before they narrowed. He sat up and pulled her up with him. She grabbed at the wool blanket to cover her nakedness, suddenly ashamed, like Eve in the Garden of Eden.

"You said you were on the pill."

She glanced at him from beneath lowered lashes, needing to hide her guilt, and said, "I'm not."

He grabbed her arms and said, "Look at me, Libby."

She forced herself to meet his gaze and saw the sudden wariness in his eyes.

"What's going on?" he asked between tight jaws.

"I thought you'd be able to tell," she said quietly.

"Tell what?" he said irritably. When she didn't answer, he shook her and said, "Talk to me!"

"That I was a virgin when you and I—"

"Are you telling me—" He let her go abruptly. "That's not possible. There was no barrier to—"

"There was!" She'd felt something the first time

he'd broached her, but whatever barrier had been there had apparently been broken without Clay being aware of it.

His hands fisted on his thighs as he stared suspiciously into her eyes. "Why didn't you say something?"

How could she explain that she'd never intended to have sex with him? That she'd only planned to tease him and leave him high and dry? But that she'd loved what she felt when he touched her, adored his kisses even more, and she hadn't wanted him to stop.

It had just . . . happened.

She hadn't wanted to tell him the truth about herself, because she hadn't wanted this amazing interlude to end. As she'd known it would, as soon as he found out who she really was.

"I'm sorry," she said in a low, trembling voice, focusing her gaze on her knees.

"Sorry isn't going to cut it!" he shot back. "What are you going to do?"

She stared up at him, confused. "What do you mean?"

"About the baby."

She continued to stare.

"Are you keeping it?" he snapped.

"Of course I'm keeping it!" she retorted, appalled that he could think anything else.

He let out a breath and said in a voice so low she wasn't sure she'd heard him right, "Thank God."

"I didn't mean for this to happen," she said miserably. *For any of it to happen.*

He reached out and twined his hand with hers and looked into her eyes and said, "I would rather have waited for kids, but I can't say I'm sorry."

Her eyes opened wide. "You're not?"

He grinned and said, "I didn't plan to fall in love with you. But I have. A politician needs a wife. I suppose we'll just have to marry a little sooner than I'd planned and with a little less pomp and circumstance."

"You want to marry me?" she said, her jaw gaping.

In the moment he opened his mouth to speak, they heard hoofbeats.

Libby leapt to her feet at the sight of the four riders loping in their direction and dropped the blanket to scramble into her clothes. Clay was laughing at her, telling her not to worry, that he'd make sure that whoever it was didn't bother them. He dragged on his briefs and jeans and stepped out bare-chested from beneath the willow that had protected them.

And found himself confronting King Grayhawk, backed up by three of his cowhands.

"You're trespassing on my land," Clay said. "You can turn your horses around and—"

"Where's my daughter?" King demanded.

"How the hell should I know where your daughter is?" Clay retorted.

"I'm here, Daddy," Libby said, stepping from beneath the concealing branches of the tree.

If she lived to be ninety-nine, Libby would never forget the look of utter horror on Clay's face as he turned to face her. "You said your name was Henderson."

She shook her head.

"King Grayhawk is your father?"

Libby flushed with shame and once again lowered her gaze, unable to endure the shock and confusion in Clay's eyes. "Yes," she whispered past her constricted throat.

"My sixteen-year-old daughter," King said.

She heard Clay suck in a breath of air and waited for him to release it. She reached out to him, wanting to explain, but he jerked away as though she were something unclean and expelled his breath in a rush. When she reached out her hands to him in supplication, he shook his head, his gray eyes remote, as though a wall had gone up to keep her from seeing inside.

"Saddle my daughter's horse," King ordered one of his cowhands.

"I can do it, Daddy," Libby said.

"Get your clothes on," he said curtly.

Libby realized she was still barefoot, and that her blouse wasn't tucked into her jeans and her belt was still unbuckled. She shoved her long blond hair behind her ear and felt a piece of grass, which she quickly plucked out and threw away. She turned her back on her father and his men and tucked in her blouse and rezipped her jeans and buckled her belt, then stood one-legged while she pulled on her socks and boots.

"Let's go," King ordered.

She didn't look at Clay. She didn't speak to him. But before she'd taken two steps toward her horse he snagged her arm and said, "Wait."

"Let go of my daughter," King ordered.

Clay looked up at him and said through tight jaws, "She and I have things we need to discuss."

"No, you don't," King said implacably.

Clay turned to her and said, "I'll come see you at your father's house, and we'll talk."

She glanced up at him long enough to see the warmth was gone from his eyes, then hurried to mount her horse.

Behind her she heard her father say, "Don't bother coming to Kingdom Come. You won't be welcome."

"I'm coming. Do what you have to do," Clay said.

"You set one foot on my property, and I'll shoot you for the lowdown coyote you are!" her father said.

"Send your men away," Clay said eyeing the three cowboys. "So we can talk."

Libby was mounted by then and rode toward her father, stopping at Clay's side. "I'll talk to him, Clay. I'll tell him . . . everything."

"I'll come tonight," Clay said. But he didn't touch her.

Libby felt tears sting her eyes and nose.

"Get home, girl," her father said.

Libby had kicked her mount into a lope. She hadn't despaired, because she thought perhaps Clay was the one man who could talk her father around. Clay loved her.

Or had before he found out the truth.

She was carrying his child. A child he'd wanted.

Or had before he found out the truth.

All would be well, she thought. She would explain everything and he would forgive her and they would be together forever.

She couldn't have been more wrong.

Libby glanced sideways to the man sitting next to her twenty years later, moving the swing with his booted foot, wondering if Clay ever thought about that long-ago dawn. And the darkness that had followed it.

"I'm worried about Kate," he said.

Libby felt a stab of hopelessness that his first words were not about the two of them, but about their daughter. It was a blessing that he cared so much about Kate, under the circumstances. But she wanted . . . the impossible.

Clay Blackthorne was his mother's son, all right. Eve Blackthorne had never forgiven Clay's father for loving another woman. And Clay was never going to forgive her for deceiving him. She was tired of longing for a doomed love. Maybe it was time to give up. Maybe, ha! It was long past time to give up.

But they had a daughter together. And she was in trouble. Her own concerns would have to wait.

"I'm worried about Kate, too," Libby said. "Jack's a great deal older than her. And his reputation is . . . not the best."

"I wish there were some way to convince her what a big mistake she's making," Clay said.

"How do you know it is a mistake?" Libby asked. "She seems very much in love with him."

"He doesn't seem equally smitten."

"That would be a problem if it were ture," Libby said. She looked at Clay and asked, "What makes you think Jack doesn't love Kate?"

Clay's brow furrowed. "I can't put my finger on anything specific."

"The physical attraction is certainly evident," Libby said.

Clay smiled ruefully. "It's hard to tell her not to have sex before marriage when it's so obvious her parents did it."

"And did it well." Libby bit her lip. She had to forget dreams of what might have been. Or wishes for what might be. She had to stay focused on Kate.

She shivered as a tendril of morning mist settled

onto her bare shoulder, where the quilt had fallen away.

"You're cold." Clay pulled the quilt higher on her shoulder and settled his arm around her, drawing her close.

It would have been awkward to try to hold her head upright, so Libby gave in to the urge to lean against Clay's shoulder, to pretend that they were the *happily married* parents of an exuberant, willful child—who might be headed for heartbreak.

She listened to the steady thump of Clay's heart for a moment before she asked, "How are we going to convince Kate to slow down?"

"I don't know," Clay said. His other arm joined the one that was on her shoulder, so she was being held in his embrace. They sat silently for a long while, as the sun moved higher in the sky. Libby would have given a great deal to know what was going on in Clay's head, but she didn't want to interrupt this moment of truce and solace.

"If North wasn't busy stealing Bitter Creek from you, we could ask him," Libby said. "Kate always listens to him."

She felt Clay's body tense beneath her cheek before he said, "I don't think North is going to be much help with Kate. He's got someone much more interesting to keep him busy. My fiancée. Or should I say former fiancée."

Libby leaned back abruptly, pulling out of Clay's embrace. "The choice was Jocelyn's, wasn't it?"

"Was it? Don't tell me you don't know what your big brother's been up to," Clay said.

"I don't!" Libby protested.

"The same day my family had its powwow and discovered that North was the corporate raider who'd bought up all our stock, Jocelyn decided to move in with your brother."

Libby frowned. "And you think the timing of their liaison isn't coincidental."

"I think it's entirely intentional. I think Jocelyn went to North's ranch to talk him out of taking Bitter Creek away from us."

"Why would he listen to her?"

Clay's eyes narrowed and his lips flattened before he said, "I think she sold herself to him—in exchange for holding off on doing anything with Bitter Creek."

Libby stared at Clay, wondering how he'd made such a leap in logic. "What makes you think she'd do something like that? Or that North would accept such an offer?"

"Why else would she call off the wedding so suddenly?" Clay said. "And jump into bed with a man she hardly knows?"

"Maybe Jocelyn wasn't sure she loved you and—"

"She loves me," Clay said certainly. "Giselle told me so."

"Your late *wife* told you her *sister* loves you?" Libby said in disbelief.

Clay rubbed a self-conscious hand across his nape. "Giselle and I talked a lot before she died. She wanted to make sure I'd be happy when she was gone. She knew Jocelyn loved me and wanted to make sure I wouldn't dismiss the possibility of a relationship just because Jocelyn was her sister."

"And you fell in love with Jocelyn," Libby said flatly. "Right on cue."

"It wasn't like that," Clay said.

"What was it like?" Libby said, feeling her face flush at the realization that she'd never had a chance with Clay, that his future wife had been selected even before Giselle had died.

"Jocelyn is a wonderful political hostess. She—"

"A role I never would have filled comfortably," Libby said caustically.

"She's easy to get along with."

"And I'm not?" Libby flared.

"She's beautiful and—"

"Good in bed?" Libby snarled.

"That's enough," Clay said quietly.

It infuriated Libby when Clay got calmer as she got angrier. She supposed it was something he'd learned as a politician, but it never failed to make her lose her temper. "I want to hear more about how your *precious*

Jocelyn sold herself into sexual slavery to my brother to save your *precious* Bitter Creek," she flared.

"I don't know that for certain. It's just something I suspect," Clay said.

"And you forgive her, I suppose, for betraying you, because her motives are so self-sacrificing and noble?"

"Yes, I do. If she'd have me, I'd take her back in a heartbeat."

Libby leapt to her feet, dumping the quilt on the porch, her body flooded with heat, despite the fact she was practically naked. "I can't believe what I'm hearing! You can forgive her for leaving you for another man, for lying to you, and 'understand' she never meant to hurt you. Yet you've never forgiven me for the lies I told. I'm a fallen woman who can never be raised up. I'm a hated Grayhawk who got the better of a Blackthorne, and you're going to make me pay for it the rest of my life! Is that it?"

Clay was also on his feet, his gray eyes stormy, his hands fisted, his legs spread wide. "There's a big god-damn difference in the two situations," he said. "I loved you! You tore out my soul, Libby. How am I supposed to forgive you for that?"

Libby's eyes were blurred with tears, and her throat so painfully swollen she could hardly speak. But speak she did. "You were supposed to forgive me *because* you loved me. You were supposed to realize that all those things I told you when you came to Kingdom Come were lies! That I only said I hated you because I didn't want you to be hurt the way my father was threatening to hurt you."

"You father was powerless to hurt me!"

"How was I supposed to know that? I was sixteen and pregnant—and you'd gotten me that way. My father said it was statutory rape, that you'd go to prison. And he was—is—such a powerful man that—"

"My father was—is—just as powerful," Clay retorted. "You should have had faith in me!"

Libby moaned and covered her face. "Oh, God." She forced herself to raise her eyes to Clay. "You should have had faith in me, Clay. That I loved you. That I wanted you. That I *needed* you. But you stalked away like a wounded buffalo—"

"You told me to get out!" he shouted. "Of your house and your life!"

"You should have known I didn't mean it!"

"How, Libby?" he said, furiously quiet again. "How was I supposed to know?"

"Because," she sobbed.

"*Because.* Right. That's a hell of a reason," Clay said, shoving a hand through his hair.

"How can you forgive Jocelyn and not me?" she said, her chest physically painful with the hurt she felt. "How can you believe her motives are virtuous and that mine weren't?"

His hands uncurled and lay limp at his sides. He shook his head. "Damn it, Libby. Why are you doing this? I thought this was all water under the bridge. Why does it matter—"

"I loved you, too," she interrupted. "So much that I haven't been able to have a relationship with another man. I kept hoping that somehow, someday, you'd see the light."

He stared at her, stricken.

She lifted beleaguered eyes to him, laughed softly, and said, "I've just realized that while you've always been the love of my life, it's obvious I've never been the love of yours. I can't believe I've been waiting around for you to wake up and realize that anytime these past twenty years, when we were both single, we could have had back what we lost because of a young girl's foolishness and a young man's pride."

Her lips curled in a sneer. "That ends now. Today. You had your chance, Clay. You had a hundred chances, but you blew them all. As of right now, I'm over you. The moment, the *instant*, our daughter is out of the mess she's in, I never want to see you again!"

At that moment, the screen door was shoved open and Kate stepped onto the porch. She was wearing a man's terry cloth robe, and Jack was right behind her. "What's wrong, Mom? Daddy? I heard shouting."

"Nothing's wrong, sweetheart," Libby said with a

wobbly smile, as she grabbed for the quilt and awkwardly settled it around her shoulders.

"Then why are you crying?" Kate demanded.

Libby swiped at her eyes with her wrists and said, "I was reminiscing with your father." She forced her smile wider and said, "How about some breakfast? I need to get back to Austin."

"I wanted us all to go horseback riding this morning," Kate said, looking from one parent to the other.

"I'm afraid I have to get back to the city, too," Clay said.

"Please, Daddy. Please, Mom," Kate begged. "Just a short ride. I have something I need to discuss with you both."

Libby reminded herself that their entire purpose in being here was to ensure their daughter didn't make a mistake that would ruin her life. She exchanged a quick glance with Clay, who nodded slightly. Then she said, "All right, Kate. A quick breakfast and a short ride. Then your dad and I need to head back to Austin."

Libby was the last to leave the porch. She stared at the door through which Clay had passed, realizing what she'd done. It was hard, so very hard, to let go of a dream. But she'd finally woken up.

Now she just had to figure out how to face the future without the man she loved.

*   *   *

Clay sat in the backseat of Jack's extended-cab pickup with Libby as they drove to North's stable from the foreman's house, but she spoke only to Kate and Jack. When they arrived, she refused his offer to saddle her horse with an abrupt, "I can do it myself."

Once the four of them were mounted up, they followed an old wagon trail over the rolling hills dotted with mesquite and live oaks, Kate chattering a mile a minute to fill the thundering silence between Clay and Libby.

Clay stared at Libby's back, which was all she'd shown him all morning, wondering if this would be the extent of their relationship from now on. He blessed his daughter for keeping the stream of conversation going, or this horseback ride would have been more than a little awkward. On the other hand, Kate's monologue was giving him far too much time to think. And feel.

Clay couldn't remember the last time he'd been provoked into raising his voice or using profanity. He never shouted and he rarely swore. He was proud of the self-discipline, the absolute control, that had made him such a good politician. But Libby knew all the right buttons to push. This morning, she'd yanked the tight rein he kept on his emotions right out of his hands.

He wondered if Libby had recognized the slip he'd made—the admission that the difference between his willingness to forgive Jocelyn, and his unwillingness to forgive her, was that he *loved* Libby.

Did that mean he didn't really love Jocelyn? That he'd kept blinders on his eyes, so he wouldn't realize the truth? And what was the truth?

Clay grimaced. The truth was, he'd been so frightened by his powerful attraction to Libby last year that he'd gotten himself engaged to Jocelyn as fast as he could, to make sure he didn't do anything about it. The truth was, he'd never stopped loving Libby. And never stopped being furious with her for robbing him of his own "happily ever after."

He could remember his mother's reaction when he'd said he would simply wait two years until Libby was eighteen and then marry her, when King couldn't stop them.

"Do you think no one will notice that you're marrying a *child*—and one with a babe in arms?" his mother had said. "The tabloids will find out the truth. Count on it. And that will be the end of your political career."

"I don't care," he'd said. "I love her."

"You can't afford that luxury," his mother replied.

"I can live without becoming president," Clay said.

"It's been your dream—"

"It's been *your* dream," Clay interrupted. "Not mine."

"Don't delude yourself," his mother said. "You're

ambitious. And driven. And determined. What will you do with your life if you give up your dreams for a woman who lied to you, who betrayed you, who only wanted vengeance?"

"It wasn't like that," Clay said. But his face was flushed, and his heart was beating hard. He'd tried to convince himself that Libby's cruel dismissal of him when he'd gone to see her after they'd been discovered by her father had been forced on her by her father. But his stomach rolled when he remembered the scorn on her face as she told him how she'd used him. How she'd always planned to discard him. How her father's interruption of their interlude had only hastened the inevitable.

"She's her father's daughter," his mother continued. "She used you, Clay. She's a viper, who'll poison your life. Let her go."

"I can't!" he'd cried. She was his life, the other half of his soul. And she carried his child.

Clay had tried to see Libby, to tell her he didn't believe her, that he knew she loved him. That she could trust him to take care of her. To tell her he'd fight King, hell, he'd fight the whole world, if he had to, to spend his life with her.

But when she'd finally agreed to see him—so he'd go away and leave her alone—she merely repeated the foul slander he'd heard the first time, her eyes even more heartless, her voice even more venomous.

To survive the devastation, he'd had to believe Libby was what his mother had called her—a viper who'd poisoned his life. The only way to survive was to suck out that poison. And stay away from Elsbeth Grayhawk in the future.

He'd stayed away for six long years. But that had meant denying himself his daughter, too. At long last, he'd gone to see Libby. And lost his heart to his daughter.

After that, there had been no question of staying away.

Clay wasn't sure when he'd realized that his first instincts had been correct. That Libby had lied, probably to protect him from threats her father must have made against him. That she must have loved him as much as he'd loved her. But she was engaged by then, so there was no reason to confront her and demand the truth.

As the years passed, he'd nursed the grievous hurt he felt at what Libby's cowardice had cost them. And continued to blame her for causing them to spend their lives apart. If only she'd trusted him. If only she hadn't lied when he'd come to her. If only she'd had a little faith in him, they might have had their happily ever after.

This morning Libby had forced Clay to admit his part in their broken fairy tale. His unwillingness to forgive. His unwillingness to take the chance of letting anyone, especially Libby, tear his heart in two again.

So where did that leave them?

He was willing to admit, now that Libby made it clear she wanted nothing more to do with him, that he'd never stopped loving her. But it was too late now to go back and undo the damage of the past.

Libby had done him a big favor after all. No one could say he didn't learn from his mistakes. He wouldn't wait for things to play out between Jocelyn and North. He wasn't going to make the same mistake twice. He would go to Jocelyn and tell her what he suspected about her sacrifice, and that he was there for her if she ever wanted him back.

It wasn't only gratitude that made him determined to have her, if he could. Jocelyn had social skills she'd learned practically from the cradle. She was supportive and loyal, giving and loving. She very much wanted children, and she would be a good mother. To add icing to the cake, she was extraordinarily beautiful. In short, she was everything he'd ever wished for in a wife.

And if Jocelyn didn't want him back? If he was free of his engagement to her? What then?

Clay didn't let himself think that far ahead. It was too late to make amends with Libby. It was too late for the fairy tale.

Wasn't it?

"What do you think, Daddy?"

Clay hadn't been paying attention and said, "I'm sorry, Kate. I didn't hear what you said."

"About Jack and me getting married this summer."

Clay thought this about-face—this sudden suggestion of marriage—was more alarming than the situation where his daughter and Jack McKinley had no plans to wed. "I think marriage is a bad idea," he said. "You're too young to know what you want. You need to get a college education, choose a profession you enjoy, and figure out what life is all about, before you even start to think about marriage. Jack should know better—"

"Don't say anything bad about Jack, Daddy. Please. I won't be able to stand it if you do."

Clay couldn't bear the wounded look on his daughter's face. He exchanged a *What do we do now?* glance with Libby behind Kate's back.

"Why don't you and I ride ahead, Kate," Libby said, "so Daddy and Jack have a chance to talk and get to know each other better."

Kate looked warily at her father, then leaned over to kiss Jack on the lips before she said, "Be nice, Daddy."

"I'm always nice," her father replied. A moment later, Kate and Libby kicked their mounts and loped away, and he was alone with Jack McKinley. He turned to the ex-quarterback accused of throwing the

Super Bowl and said, "I'll give you twenty-five thousand dollars to walk away from her."

Jack lifted an eyebrow and said, "Is that all your
daughter's worth to you?"

Clay felt his throat flush with heat and realized he
was angry on his daughter's behalf that she'd gotten
herself involved with such a scoundrel. "Fifty thousand. Take it and get yourself out of my sight."

"I don't want your money," Jack said.

"What will it take to get you out of Kate's life?"
Clay demanded.

"I'm not going anywhere, Judge Blackthorne," Jack
said. "Except down the aisle with your daughter."

"Over my dead body."

The smile on Jack's face made the hairs stand up
on Clay's nape. He resisted the urge to grab Jack by
his throat and squeeze the life out of him. "All Kate's
money is in trust. She won't get a penny till she's
twenty-five. Long before then, she'll have seen you for
what you are."

"I don't want her money, either," Jack said.

"What do you want?" Clay asked through tight
jaws.

"For you to back off. For you to let Kate decide
what she wants."

"She's too young to know what she wants," Clay retorted. "She needs to be protected."

"It seems to me," Jack said in a voice more quiet

than Clay's, "that you haven't done such a good job of that in the past."

Clay thought of Kate's kidnapping last year. How she'd been held hostage and only barely escaped with her life. He met Jack's gaze and said, "Last year—"

"What about right now?" Jack said. "I've heard plenty of speculation at the Grille that Brown didn't bomb that courthouse in Houston on his own. That Judge Kuykendall was executed—pure and simple. These guys mean business, and they don't care who gets hurt. Kate isn't safe when she's anywhere near that courthouse—or you. She needs someone to keep an eye on her."

"I suppose you're applying for the job," Clay said sarcastically.

"A deputy marshal will do just fine." Jack looked him in the eye and said, "It doesn't take a genius to figure out that you could be next."

"Killing the judge—again—isn't going to stop the trial."

"But it's going to leave Kate without a father," Jack said. "Keeping Kate safe and happy is my one goal in life right now. So I suggest you pay attention to your business, and let me take care of mine."

Clay was left sitting his horse alone when Jack spurred his mount and disappeared over the next hill. Clay frowned as he stared after the young man. Jack McKinley was going to be a harder nut to crack than he'd suspected. He and Libby were going to have to put their heads together to figure out how to free Kate from his clutches. He might even ask Owen to investigate Kate's boyfriend. Maybe his brother could find a reason to lock him up.

Jack didn't immediately rejoin Libby and Kate. He rode just far enough to be out of Clay's sight over a hill, then stopped his horse where he was hidden by the massive trunk of an ancient live oak. He pulled out his cell phone, punched the button to call a programmed number, and waited for it to be answered.

When it was, he said, "I want to take the girl out of the equation now. She's a problem that's only going to get worse. I think you ought—"

Jack's jaw tightened. "All right. I'll hold off. For now. But you'd better do something. And soon."

9

Jocelyn dumped the last of her coffee in the sink and turned to North, who was leaning against the kitchen counter, cup in hand. "Another cup?" she asked.

"No time," he said.

Jocelyn flushed. They were late getting started because he'd woken up wanting her. And she'd provided the service she'd agreed to provide until September. He'd lingered over the matter, taking the time to arouse her fully, taking the time to make sure she was incoherent with pleasure before finally taking his own.

It was Saturday, but one of the first things Jocelyn had learned was that there was very little leisure time on a ranch. There was too much to do. In addition, North had other businesses here and in Wyoming he was managing. She wondered sometimes how he handled all the responsibilities she saw resting on his shoulders. But he never complained. And he certainly never asked for help. From anyone.

Within the first few days of moving in with him, she'd offered to help, but he'd refused. Jocelyn wasn't sure why she persisted in spending her days with him, when he never asked for her company. But North already had a housekeeper and cook, neither of whom he'd been willing to let go, since her stay was only "temporary." And she needed to be doing something useful.

Jocelyn found herself enjoying the time she spent outdoors with North. She loved everything about the ranching life, especially starting the day when it was still dark outside, so she got to watch the sunrise every morning. The work was constant and endless, and she was always amazed at how well North managed the ebb and flow of maintaining so much land and so many animals.

She glanced at North's broad shoulders, remembering how he'd looked yesterday with his shirt off, straining with a ratchet to pull a strand of barbed wire tight, his powerful muscles moving beneath smooth flesh, his back glistening with sweat in the sunshine. She'd wanted to lick his skin, to see if it was as salty as it looked.

Jocelyn flushed guiltily at her thoughts, glad North couldn't read her mind. She might be committed to stay with him for the summer, but she had a life to return to when this episode was over. And a man she loved.

She was rinsing out her cup when she heard a

knock on the screen door. She leaned back to see past North, but the rising sun obscured whoever was outside the door. She glanced at North and flushed again when she realized his gray eyes were focused on her, letting her know that he didn't care if they kept the whole world waiting outside.

Jocelyn shivered as her body reacted to his. They'd been living and sleeping together—having sex—for two weeks, and the tension between them was worse now than it had been the day North had opened his door to her. Oh, yes, her body wanted his. Craved it, despite so many nights of lovemaking.

But Jocelyn had yet to see a sign of compassion in the man, a sign of vulnerability, anything that would allow her to believe that he cared for her—or anyone else in this world. She was merely a pawn in a despicable game between Blackthornes and Grayhawks.

"Expecting company?" he asked.

Jocelyn shook her head. "No one knows I'm here." Except Clay, of course, and it wasn't likely he would have knocked politely.

North called out, "Who's there?"

No one answered. The knock came again, more insistent.

"I'll see who it is," Jocelyn said, heading for the door.

"I'll go," North said, setting down his coffee cup.

Jocelyn reached the screen door the same time he

did. She was about to push it open, when he grasped her wrist and stayed her hand.

"What the hell are you doing here, Sassy?" North said brusquely.

Jocelyn stared through the screen door at a young, very pretty, model-tall blue-eyed blond. She was wearing three-inch heels and a tailored pink suit cut in a deep V to reveal generous cleavage. For a devastating moment, Jocelyn thought the woman must be one of North's paramours.

"I've been hunting you for a week, North," the tall blond said. "The least you could do is tell people where you're going to be."

"What do you want, Sassy?"

"Who are you?" the woman asked Jocelyn.

"She's none of your business," North said.

"I'm Sassy Grayhawk," the woman said to Jocelyn. "North's stepmother. His middle stepmother, I should say. I came between Leonora and Jill. Although I don't think King—or anyone else—ever counts Leonora, since that marriage was annulled, on account of—"

"Sassy!" North interrupted.

Jocelyn's diplomatic training stood her in good stead, and neither her voice nor her face showed her shock at the young woman's revelation. Sassy Grayhawk didn't look a day over thirty. A second look revealed a tautness to her skin, beneath very carefully applied makeup, that suggested plastic surgery.

Although the day had just begun, Jocelyn recognized the smell of gin on the woman's breath. Then she noticed how tightly Sassy was clutching her pink snakeskin purse against her substantial bosom. Whatever the woman wanted, it hadn't been easy coming here to ask for it.

Jocelyn took one look at the stony, indifferent face North presented to his stepmother, and her heart went out to the woman. "Would you like to come in?" she asked, pushing open the screen door with the hand North wasn't holding.

"I don't have time to visit," Sassy said, actually taking a step back. "I only came to ask a favor."

Jocelyn felt North's body tense beside her.

"How much do you want?" he said in a flat voice.

"I don't need your money," Sassy replied indignantly.

North stared at his stepmother, who stared back only a moment before her glance wavered and finally slid toward something to her right.

Jocelyn turned at the same time as North to see what had caught Sassy's attention. Standing just beyond the open screen door was a lanky teenage boy, with too-long, raven black hair. His strange, almost silver eyes were sullen, his chin jutting. He was posed with his hip cocked and his arms crossed defiantly—or protectively—across his narrow chest. His bronze skin, sharp cheekbones, and blade of nose reminded Jocelyn of some long-ago Sioux warrior.

As though Sassy had read her mind, she said, "This is my son Breed. King's son Breed, I should say. He named the boy the first time he laid eyes on him. And started divorce proceedings before I was out of the hospital," she said bitterly.

Jocelyn could see how the boy's odd silver eyes and deeply bronzed skin might make King Grayhawk question whether he was the boy's father. But, Jocelyn realized, the law would not have allowed King to disown a son born in wedlock. It seemed cruel, however, to have branded the boy Breed, apparently a shortened form of "half-breed," at birth. Especially when the child was innocent. Even if his mother was not.

"What do you want, Sassy?" North repeated.

"I want you to keep Breed. Only for a little while," she said, holding up a hand to forestall North's refusal. "I'm going into alcohol rehab—"

"Again?" North interrupted harshly.

"Again," Sassy said in a high-pitched voice on the edge of control. "I'm going to make it stick this time, North. Really, I am. But I don't have anywhere I can leave Breed. My family disowned me when— And your father— And my last husband—There's just nowhere else I can turn. I thought since you had this ranch, and Breed is so good with horses, well, maybe you could find a place for him here. In a bunkhouse. Or the barn. Or . . . somewhere."

"I can take care of myself," the boy muttered.

"You're only fourteen," his mother said. "You need—"

"I don't need anyone or anything!" the boy shot back. He glared at North and said, "Especially not charity from some half brother whose father doesn't claim me as kin."

"It wouldn't be charity," Jocelyn said. "You're family."

"That's debatable," North said.

Jocelyn turned on North and said, "His name is Breed Grayhawk. That makes him your brother." She pushed the screen door farther open and said, "Please come in, Breed. Have you had breakfast?"

"He can stay in the barn," North said. "There's a room for the hired hand who mucks out the stalls." He turned to Breed and said, "That is, if you want the job."

"A job?" Breed said.

Jocelyn saw the wary hope that lit the boy's silver eyes.

"You said you didn't want charity," North said. "I'm offering you a job. Take it or leave it."

The lowest kind of job, Jocelyn thought. Most cowboys wouldn't do work that couldn't be done from the back of a horse. North had offered his brother a place in his barn—shoveling manure.

All the same, Jocelyn held her breath, and saw Sassy was doing the same, waiting to see whether the boy would accept North's grudging offer.

"I'll take it," Breed said.

North offered his hand. "Then we have a deal."

The boy shook North's hand, then took a step back as though to announce that taking a job did not mean giving up his independence. Taking a job did not mean relying on anyone or anything. Taking a job did not mean he intended to give up keeping himself aloof and alone.

At that moment, he reminded Jocelyn very much of North.

"Good. That's settled," Sassy said with a relieved, gin-scented sigh. She turned to Breed and reached out to pick at the too-small, not-quite-clean T-shirt the boy was wearing, rearranging it over his narrow chest. "Be good," she said. "Don't give North any trouble. I'll be back soon."

Jocelyn watched the boy's eyes brighten suspiciously and his valiant struggle to blink back unmanly tears.

He swallowed hard, and his Adam's apple bobbed up and down, before he spoke in a voice that grated like a rusty gate. "You won't forget about me. Like last time."

Jocelyn watched as he swallowed again, his eyes miserable as they pored over his mother's face, as though he were seeing her for the very last time. Jocelyn wondered how long ago it had been since Breed had been left like this. And how long it had taken his mother to return for him.

"I promise I won't get romantically involved with anyone in rehab this time," she told the boy. "I won't . . ." Her smile wobbled. "I promise I'll be back for you soon, Breed. And I'll be sober when I come."

"You said that the last time," he accused. "And the time before that."

"This time I mean it." She turned to North and said, "Thank you. I won't forget this."

"We'll take good care of him," Jocelyn said.

Sassy frowned, as though just noticing Jocelyn, and once again asked, "Who are you?"

"I'm—"

"My mistress," North interrupted. "For the rest of the summer, anyway."

"That figures," Sassy said to North. She turned to Jocelyn and said, "Just don't give him your heart, honey. Grayhawks are murder on hearts."

Without another word, she turned and headed for her car, a black Jaguar convertible. The three of them stood without moving until the car was hidden by the tail of dust flying up behind it.

"You got any boots?" North said as he glanced at the worn high-tops Breed was wearing with his jeans. "Or a hat?"

"No, sir," Breed replied. The "sir" seemed to be automatic, which suggested the boy had been taught respect. But the look on his face, his posture, his tone of voice toward North, was pure defiance.

Which was better than fear or self-pity, Jocelyn thought. What must it be like to be left without recourse with someone who, even though he had the same name, was so obviously a forbidding stranger? In the ordinary course of things, this boy, with his too-small T-shirt and his worn jeans and his teenage high-top sneakers, should have been able to stay with his father at Kingdom Come. Instead, he was an outcast.

"Time for work," North said.

"What about breakfast for Breed?" Jocelyn turned to the teenager and asked, "Are you hungry?"

"No."

North shot the boy a look, and the kid added belatedly, "Ma'am."

"Please call me Joss," Jocelyn said.

North rolled his eyes. Probably because she'd made such a point of telling him her name was *Jocelyn* whenever he'd tried to use the diminutive term over the past two weeks.

"I've got some blueberry muffins left over from dinner last night," she said. "I can warm them up in the microwave and slap some butter on them in no time flat."

She could almost see Breed's mouth water, but his lips remained sealed.

"Make it quick," North said, backing into the kitchen. "Come on in, boy, and shut the door. You're letting in the flies."

Breed stayed just inside the door while Jocelyn hurried to retrieve the extra muffins from the freezer, then wrapped them in a paper towel and microwaved them for a few seconds. She'd left the butter on the counter to soften before breakfast, and it was still there.

She didn't ask what Breed wanted to drink. Growing boys needed milk. She pulled the half-gallon dairy carton from the refrigerator, poured him a large glass and set it on the table.

The boy stood at the door with his hip cocked in a pose that was intended to be nonchalant. "Go ahead and sit," she said, gesturing toward the place where she'd set the glass.

North crossed to the sink and leaned back with his arms crossed, staring at the boy, not masking his irritation at the delay.

Jocelyn saw the boy's hand shaking as he reached for the glass of milk. She frowned ferociously at North, who was clearly intimidating the boy with his presence, and said, "Don't you have somewhere you need to be?"

"Nope."

She pulled two muffins from the microwave when it dinged, sliced them, buttered all four halves and set them on a plate, which she dropped in front of Breed. "Don't feel like you have to hurry on our—"

By the time she'd gotten that far, the boy had inhaled three of the four muffin halves. He took a long swallow of milk to wet them down, swallowed everything in his mouth, then stuffed the last piece of muffin in his mouth and swallowed that, too. Then he inhaled the rest of the glass of milk, set it on the table, shoved the chair back, stood and said, "I'm done."

Jocelyn was appalled. Could Breed really have been that hungry? Or had North simply made him too anxious to sit and eat at a more normal pace? She frowned again at North, who ignored her and said, "Come on, kid. I'll show you where your room is in the barn, and where you can find a wheelbarrow and pitchfork. You know how to muck a stall?"

"I've done it before," the boy said.

Jocelyn followed behind them as the tall man and the lanky boy walked side by side toward the stable, the boy hop-skipping to match his stride to that of the man. Jocelyn wondered how the son of someone as wealthy as King Grayhawk knew so much about mucking out stalls. But if his mother's abandonment of him this morning was any example, the kid had led a tough life.

They had just arrived at the stable when Jocelyn heard the sound of hoofbeats. She turned and recognized three of the four people approaching on horseback. Her heartbeat ratcheted up a notch. She glanced at North and said, "I didn't know Libby and Clay and Kate had come for a visit."

"They aren't here to see me," North said. "They must be visiting Jack. He's staying at the foreman's house for a while."

"Jack?" she said.

"Jack McKinley," North said.

"The quarterback?" Breed said, his eyes wide. He turned to stare at the four people on horseback. "Hi, Kate!" he called out, waving to his cousin.

"Breed!" she cried, jumping off her horse and running toward him. "What are you doing here?"

The boy suffered Kate's hug, then backed off and said, "Mom's in rehab again."

Kate crossed to her uncle and gave him a hug. Jocelyn was interested to note that North's eyes never left Clay's as he hugged his niece. He watched his rival as though Clay were a renegade wolf that posed a threat to life and limb.

Jack dismounted and crossed to shake North's hand. "How's it going?"

North lifted a brow and said, "Fine. How about you?"

"I'm in love," Jack said.

Jocelyn watched North's eyes narrow as Jack slid an arm around Kate's waist and pulled her close.

"I took one look at her and fell head over heels," Jack said, his gaze focused on Kate, whose face blushed rosily.

"I hope we're not intruding, Uncle North," Kate said, eyeing Jocelyn warily. "Mom and Dad came out from Austin last night to meet Jack, and I asked them to stay over so we could ride this morning."

"Hello, North," Libby said, stepping off her horse and crossing toward her brother.

Jack and Kate stepped back, so Libby could greet her brother without crossing Jocclyn's path.

"Clay and I are still adjusting to Kate's news."

"What news is that?" North asked.

"We're thinking about getting married this summer," Kate said.

North's brow lifted again as his gaze slid back to Jack. "Really?"

"That's what we're thinking," Jack said.

"Take care of the horses," North said to Breed.

"I'll help you," Kate said as Breed moved to retrieve the reins of the four horses they'd ridden and headed for the stable door.

"I'll come with you," Jack said, slinging an arm casually around Kate's shoulder.

"I'd like to talk with you before we take off," Libby said to North, sliding her arm through his and walking him away from the others.

Clay was the last to dismount. Jocelyn felt awkward when she realized that not only were his eyes focused on her, he was headed straight for her, without apparent regard for North's presence. Jocelyn shot a quick glance in North's direction and was relieved to see he'd been distracted by Libby.

She took a few steps in the other direction, to put a little more distance between the two men, uncertain how to handle the situation. She watched North's retreating back as he walked away with Libby, expecting him to glance over his shoulder at any moment and realize that another man was poaching on his territory. She started when Clay touched her shoulder.

She had never felt so uncomfortable in her life. She managed a tremulous smile and said, "Hello, Clay."

"I think we need to talk."

Jocelyn shot another anxious look in North's direction, but his attention was focused intently on his sister. "I don't think we have anything to say to each other that hasn't already been said."

"I know what you've done. What you're doing," he corrected.

"What do you mean?" she asked, feeling a shiver of alarm skirt up her spine.

"I never realized you cared so much." He caught her hand and squeezed it. "That you'd be willing to sacrifice yourself like this for me. And for my family."

"I don't know what you're talking about," Jocelyn said, pulling her hand free and turning away, no longer able to bear his intense scrutiny.

He stepped up behind her, his breath on her neck and said, "I think you offered yourself to North in exchange for his not taking Bitter Creek away from us."

"I don't know why you'd think—"

He took her elbow and turned her to face him. "Tell me I'm wrong."

She couldn't. She glanced up at him, then dropped her gaze. Because of the written contract she'd signed with North, there was no way she could confirm or deny Clay's deductions. But that didn't seem to be necessary.

"I can't tell you how much I admire you for what you've done," he said. "And how much my family is in your debt."

"There's no debt," she said, then bit her lower lip. She'd done what she'd done for love. There could be no debt where there was love.

"I'll wait for you," he whispered in her ear. "However long it takes for that bastard to get his pound of flesh from you. You deserve my loyalty. And you have it."

Jocelyn closed her eyes. *Admiration. Debt. Loyalty.*

But no word of love. Did Clay love her? Could he still love her after she'd given herself to a man he hated? Or was she asking the impossible? There was no way she could question him about his feelings right now. It was enough, she supposed, that he would be waiting for her when this strange interlude was over.

And then he gave her the reassurance she'd sought. He took both of her hands in his, lifted each one to his lips to kiss it, and said, "I want to spend my life with you, Jocelyn. I want us to raise a family and grow old together. Please give us a chance."

Before she could reply, Kate and Jack stepped into her line of vision. She quickly pulled her hands free and stuck them in the back pockets of her jeans.

Clay turned with her to watch the approaching couple. "There's a misalliance that defies understanding."

"Maybe she loves him," Jocelyn said as she observed the couple walking toward them hand-in-hand. Breed had stayed in the stable, apparently still busy with the horses.

"I have no doubt she thinks she loves him," Clay said. "But what does he want from her?"

"Isn't it possible that he's in love with her?" Jocelyn asked.

"In lust, more likely," Clay said. "They have nothing in common. Nothing on which to base a real relationship. She's a kid. He's too experienced to be involved with someone like her."

"And yet, you see them laughing together," Jocelyn said softly. She was jealous of Jack and Kate's easy rapport. She'd never laughed like that with Clay. And there was nothing easy about her relationship with North.

Jocelyn glanced uneasily at North, who was still deep in conversation with his sister. She watched as

Libby's face flushed, and her lips pressed flat. North's body was rigid with anger. Obviously the discussion was not going well. She wondered what they could be arguing about.

"Hey, Mom!" Kate called. "You ready to go?"

For a moment Libby didn't respond. She said something else to North, whose jaw tightened in response. Then Libby turned and smiled brightly—too brightly—at her daughter and said, "I'm coming."

When Libby reached them, Clay said, "I need to be heading back to Austin."

Jack looked down at Kate and said, "You'd better think about heading back, too. You've got early classes tomorrow."

Kate made a face at him and said, "I was hoping we'd have more time together today."

"I've got work to do this afternoon," Jack said.

"How are you getting back to town?" Clay asked his daughter.

"I rode out with Jack," Kate said. "Do you suppose I could get a ride back with you and Mom?"

Jocelyn watched Clay and Libby exchange a look of total understanding that made her heart sink. She'd known it would be hard to leave Clay for the summer. She'd just never expected him to have Libby Grayhawk for company while she was gone. Despite Clay's declared willingness to wait for her, he shared a history with Libby, and he had a powerful attraction to her that might flare to sudden life. Thank goodness Kate would be with them on the ride back to Austin to chaperone.

North slid a possessive arm around Jocelyn's waist when he rejoined her. But Clay never noticed, because he was too busy opening the back door to Jack's pickup to usher Libby inside.

Kate rolled down the passenger's side window and waved to North as they drove away.

Jocelyn felt North's arm tighten around her waist as the pickup disappeared down the road. She had never felt so much like a prisoner.

She looked up at him, searching his face and asked, "Is all this really necessary?"

His brow furrowed as he watched the disappearing pickup. "I thought it was. To separate you from him. Apparently, I was mistaken."

She frowned. *To separate you from him. To separate her from Clay? Was that what North meant? What did that have to do with anything? This arrangement was about separating the Blackthornes from Bitter Creek, wasn't it?* "I'm confused."

He shoved his free hand through his hair and down across his face. "So am I."

"What are we talking about?" Jocelyn asked.

"Nothing." He let go of her and headed for the stable.

She hurried after him and grabbed his arm to stop him. "Talk to me!"

"You can go anytime you want. I'm done with you."

She stared at him, her jaw agape. "What?"

"You heard me."

"I can leave? Today? Right now? Is that what you're saying?"

"That's what I'm saying. Plain as a barn painted red. You can go," he said brusquely.

"What's happened? What's changed?" she asked.

"I don't need you anymore."

"What about the Bitter Creek stock? Have you sold it back to the Blackthornes?"

"Not yet."

"You want me to leave so you can renege on our agreement," Jocelyn said angrily. "That's not going to happen. I'm not going anywhere!"

He turned on her, his hands clenched into fists, his shoulders tense, his legs spread wide. "I told you to get out."

"No, you said you didn't need me anymore. Since you never *needed* me in the first place, nothing has changed. I'm staying right here until September." She stabbed his broad chest with a pointed finger and said, "I expect you to transfer that stock on September first. Don't even think about reneging. Because I'll make you sorry if you do."

He suddenly looked amused. He shrugged, although she could see it was a gesture that took some effort. "Fine," he said. "Do what you want. Makes no difference to me."

Jocelyn couldn't help feeling insulted at his suggestion that whether she stayed as his bedmate for the next three months or left in the next three minutes, it didn't matter to him.

She laid a hand on his chest and felt his heartbeat immediately accelerate. She looked up into his eyes and saw his pupils dilate as he looked down at her. He still wanted her. There was no question of that. So why was he so willing to let her go?

It didn't really matter. The important thing was that she had no intention of leaving him until their bargain was complete. Especially now that she knew Clay would be waiting for her when her obligation to North Grayhawk had been fulfilled.

"You're stuck with me," she said. "Until September. Live with it."

With that, she turned her back on North and headed toward the stable. "I'm going to help your brother." Over her shoulder she said, "See you tonight. In bed."

10

"Hasn't that boy done enough work for one day?" Jocelyn asked.

"He'll be done when I say he's done," North replied.

Jocelyn stepped in front of North, hands on hips, and glared into his wintry eyes. "When will that be? When he's fallen down with exhaustion? You've been working him like a mule for a month."

"He looks fine to me," North said, eyeing Breed, who was digging postholes, a job most cowboys looked on as punishment. Only his protruding hip bones kept the lanky boy's jeans from sliding on down, and his bare, bronzed torso glistened. The brim of the battered straw hat North had lent him was dark with sweat.

"He's as stubborn as you are, that's for sure," Jocelyn said. "Don't you see he'd sooner die than quit? You've pushed him hard all day, and he's never once complained. What are you trying to prove? That he's no Grayhawk? Well, he's not! Your father made that clear when he named the boy."

"Sassy swears he is," North said.

"Is what?" Jocelyn queried, when North didn't continue.

"A Grayhawk. She says she never slept with another man when she was married to King."

Jocelyn followed North's narrowed gaze and studied the black-haired, silver-eyed, bronze-skinned boy. "How is that possible?"

"It's a long story."

"I've got time," Jocelyn said.

North tugged off his leather gloves as he spoke and tucked them into his back pocket. "One of my ancestors was an English nobleman, the earl of Grayhawk. The earl was some sort of black sheep and came west before the Civil War hunting his fortune. When folks started calling him 'Mister' Grayhawk, he didn't correct them."

"How do you know all this?" Jocelyn asked.

"Mom was into genealogy. She figured out 'Mister' Grayhawk must have been Christopher Kingsford, the fifth earl of Grayhawk. His younger twin brother inherited the title."

"So you come from good English stock," Jocelyn said. "I don't see how Breed—"

"I'm not finished," North interrupted.

Jocelyn lifted a brow, telling him to go ahead.

North's lips curled sardonically before he continued. " 'Mister' Grayhawk married a Sioux woman in Montana and settled with her in Wyoming. They had four sons. Only one of them looked Indian, but they all carried her blood. It's there, all right. Which is why Breed looks the way he does."

"Are you saying Breed really could be your father's son?" Jocelyn asked incredulously.

North shrugged. "Doesn't matter. King can't repudiate him. He'll inherit along with the rest of us, so what's the difference?"

"The difference is that he's grown up with the stigma of being a bastard. The difference is that his father rejected him at birth. Does Breed know?"

"Know what?"

"That he might actually be King's son?"

North shrugged again. "That Sioux great-great-grandmother of ours is no secret."

"Then why would King deny Breed is his son?"

North looked at her and smirked. "I think it has something to do with Sassy flaunting her indiscretions in King's face before the boy was born."

"I thought you said she never slept with anyone else."

"That's what she admitted to me. That's not what she told my father. She was mad at King for ignoring her, and she figured if she made him believe other men desired her, it would pique his interest. It didn't quite work out that way."

"It seems so unfair that Breed has to pay the price for his parents' stupidity," Jocelyn said. "Hasn't anyone ever suggested that the boy get a blood test to prove his paternity?"

"Sure," North said.

"What happened?"

"Breed wouldn't do it," North said.

"Why not?"

"Said it didn't matter," North said.

"I will never understand the male of the species," Jocelyn said, shaking her head.

She watched Breed drop the posthole digger and grab one of the mesquite timbers to replace the rotted post that had been discarded and set it in the hole he'd dug.

"Are you going to stand here, or are you going to go help that boy?" Jocelyn asked.

North grinned. "You sure can be feisty. I like that in a woman."

Jocelyn felt her insides quiver.

He left her and crossed to help the boy finish setting the post and then connect it to the nearest posts with three strands of barbed wire. North didn't remove his shirt, and when he was done it was stuck to his back and chest with perspiration.

He removed his hat, swiped his forehead with his sleeve, then tugged the hat back down. "How about a swim?" he called to Jocelyn.

When they'd left the house after lunch, Jocelyn had anticipated exactly this situation. She was wearing a bikini bathing suit under her jeans and shirt, and she'd brought along some cut-off jeans for Breed and North.

"Sure," she said.

When they arrived at the pond, she untied the pack from behind her saddle and dropped the cut-offs on the flat, hip-high rock near the two men, who were busy stripping down. She turned her back quickly and said, "Put those on please."

"Aw, North—" Breed began.

To her surprise, North said, "Do as the lady asks."

The next thing she heard was two almost simultaneous splashes. She quickly pulled off her own boots and clothes and turned to see that the two brothers had come up in the middle of the pond, grinning and blinking to clear water from their eyes and eyelashes, their dark wet hair flat against their foreheads.

Jocelyn slid into the water at the edge of the pond and watched, her heart in her throat, as they played like sleek otters, shoving each other under, diving and lunging and splashing their way back and forth across the pond. She wanted to join in, but they were roughhousing, fighting for dominance in the water, and there was no way she could compete physically.

As she watched, she realized North was moderating his strength so the battle would be more even. The boy seemed always on the verge of winning, though he never did. Suddenly, Breed caught North off guard and sent him under. As North came up sputtering, Breed laughed aloud, a joyous sound.

Jocelyn waited with bated breath to see how North would react. Her heart turned over when North grinned and then joined Breed's laughter, before swimming after the boy once more. Breed eluded him momentarily, but eventually got dunked and came up laughing again.

"Look at Joss," North said to Breed as they swiped water and hair from their faces. "She's hardly even wet."

"I'm fine," Jocelyn said, feeling a skitter of nerves at the thought of frolicking in the water with North. "You guys just keep on with what you're doing."

"We don't want to exclude you from all the fun," North said, swimming in her direction.

Jocelyn stood up and started backpedaling out of the pond. "No. Really. I'm fine."

"Don't let her get away, Breed," North said, as he lunged at Jocelyn.

"I've got her covered," Breed said, as he suddenly appeared behind Jocelyn.

"Where did you come from?" she squeaked.

Breed laughed and grabbed her arm on one side as North grasped the other. There was no way to dig in her heels in the pebbly bottom as they tugged her inexorably deeper into the pond.

"I don't want to get my hair wet," she protested.

"She doesn't want to get her hair wet," North said.

Jocelyn knew a moment of relief that North understood she didn't want to roughhouse with them, before he scooped her up in his arms. She grabbed at his shoulders as he swung her one way, threatening to drop her.

She shrieked like a ten-year-old.

He laughed down into her face, then swung her the other way. She actually felt herself falling before he caught her in his arms again.

Giggling, she grappled for a hold on broad, wet, sun-warmed shoulders and cried, "Don't drop me!"

North grinned and let go.

Jocelyn shrieked again as her bottom got wet, before she was scooped up again in North's embrace.

North exchanged a conspiratorial look with Breed and said, "How about it? Middle of the pond?"

"Think you can throw her that far?" Breed asked.

"Don't you dare!" Jocelyn said. "I don't want to get my hair—"

With all his considerable strength, North threw her up and out. She felt herself flying, her arms waving frantically in thin air, mouth open in a scream, but so frightened, there was no breath to make a sound. After

what seemed like an endless fall, she landed with a re-
sounding splash in the center of the pond.

Jocelyn managed to gasp a lifesaving breath of air
and shut her mouth only an instant before water covered her head. She started to shoot up out of the
water, madder than a wet hen, ready to seek
vengeance. And then had what she thought was a
much better idea.

She didn't come up.

Among Jocelyn's many talents was the ability to
hold her breath for a very long time. She swam away
underwater from the spot where she'd been dropped
and then stayed underwater at the far edge of the
pond beneath a willow. She wondered if she could
still hold her breath for ninety seconds.

She started counting.

Jocelyn got to ninety-three before she finally had to
come up for air. She came up slowly, half hidden by
the willow and turned to locate North and Breed. She
was smirking. She bet they were going crazy wondering what had happened to her. It served them right for
treating her like a helpless babe in the woods.

She intended to gloat fully in her triumph.

Jocelyn couldn't see North, but she found Breed
paddling in the center of the pond staring at the spot
where she'd gone underwater.

She started to shout out to him and stopped when
she noticed how pale and wide-eyed he looked. Sud-

denly, she realized North was nowhere to be seen. Had something happened to him? Her heart was in her throat, as she swam hurriedly toward the center of the pond.

"Where's North?" she called to Breed.

The boy spun in the water, obviously startled, and stared at her as though he were seeing a ghost. "Are you all right? Where were you? What happened to you?"

"I'm fine. I was teaching you a lesson."

"You scared the crap out of us!"

At that moment, North surfaced, his face drawn, his brow furrowed, his eyes agonized. And then he spotted her.

An instant later Jocelyn was being crushed in his embrace. His cheek pressed hard against hers, so she could almost feel the bones beneath his skin.

North's arms tightened around her, so she could feel the hair on his chest rough against her breasts. His breathing was harsh, and she heard a raspy "Thank God!"

She saw the stark look on Breed's face over North's shoulder and realized she'd made a terrible miscalculation when she'd pretended to drown. North's arms constricted, as though he hoped to keep her safe by keeping her very, very close.

"I can't breathe," she managed to croak.

He released her enough to take her by the arms

and look into her eyes. "Are you all right?" The whole time his eyes devoured her face, his hands frantically roamed her body, as though to reassure himself that she was there, whole and well, and not a figment of his imagination.

"I'm fine. I was teaching you a lesson."

Jocelyn realized the flip response was a mistake before the words had faded. But it was too late to take them back. And impossible, in any event, to speak, because she was being shaken within an inch of her life.

"I thought you were dead! I thought I'd killed you!"

"North, stop!" Breed hollered. "You're hurting her!"

She saw Breed from the corner of her eye, his eyes wide with terror, reaching toward her, and his reflexive jerk backward when North turned on him with teeth bared like a feral wolf.

"Get out!" he snarled at the boy. "Go home." And when the boy hesitated, "Get the hell out of here! Now!"

Jocelyn heard the splash of water as Breed raced to the edge of the pond and the drip of water against stone as he collected his clothes. Her eyes were still riveted on North's face, which had turned hard as granite, and his eyes, which had become shards of ice.

"I never wanted you here," he said through gritted teeth. "I never asked you to come. This was all your doing. I knew this would happen. I knew it!"

Jocelyn studied his face, wondering what he meant. He knew *what* would happen? "What are you so steamed up about?" she said, angry at being so roughly manhandled. "All I did was play a harmless little trick on you. A ninety-three-second trick!"

His hands tightened so hard on her arms that she knew she would have bruises later. His nostrils flared and his eyes narrowed. "You don't get it, do you?"

"Get what?" she said in exasperation.

"I thought you were *dead*. I thought you were gone from my life forever."

The words seemed wrenched from him. She couldn't believe what they seemed to imply. So she made another mistake. She made light of them.

She tried a half-hearted laugh and said, "I'm sure you've wished me gone from your life any number of times—"

There was nothing tender about the way he captured her mouth. It was all about possession. A man staking his claim on his woman. His tongue came stroking as his fingers broke the narrow strap between her breasts, leaving them naked for his hands, which grasped them hard and pushed them upward. His mouth broke free from her mouth and captured one taut nipple.

Jocelyn moaned as he suckled her, feeling her knees turn to weak reeds. He must have felt her falling, because he gathered her up in his arms and stalked to the edge of the pond, where he laid her in the grass. He broke the strings on her bikini bottom and threw it aside, then stripped himself.

"You're mine," he muttered against her mouth, as he spread her legs wide with his knees and thrust inside. "Mine."

The sound was guttural, his lovemaking raw and savage. Jocelyn realized it for what it was—a reaffirmation of life. He had believed her dead. She was reborn in his arms.

Their passion was violent. Sweaty and primitive. Tumultuous. To her shame, she was as hot for him as he was for her, and they both cried out at the moment of climax.

When he was done, he rolled away from her onto his back in the grass beside the pond and covered his eyes with his forearm. Jocelyn saw his throat working and heard him swallow loudly several times. He seemed to be fighting some great emotion.

She reached out a hand to comfort him, but he shoved it away.

"Don't touch me!"

He sat up facing the pond, with his back to her.

Jocelyn turned her face away, confused and hurt. She sat up, wanting to cover herself, wanting to be away from this man with his strange moods and stranger behavior. She stood, naked, and walked to the flat rock where she'd left her shirt and jeans.

He glanced at her over his shoulder, watching her as she dressed. "When we get back to the house I want you gone."

She pulled her shirt over her shoulders and turned to him as she buttoned it, noticing that his eyes slid down her body to the apex of her thighs, and that he liked what he saw.

She felt hurt by his rejection. And confused by it. Especially after their tempestuous lovemaking. "Where is it you'd like me to go?" she asked in as calm a voice as she could manage.

"I don't give a shit. I just want you gone."

She flushed at his use of such crude language. It was a sign he wasn't as much in control of himself as he wanted her to believe. "I'm not going anywhere," she said.

He stood and crossed to the rock where he'd left his clothes, revealing his lean flanks and hard buttocks. Jocelyn felt the ache between her legs at the remembered pleasure of this man inside her, of the feel of his flesh beneath her hands.

He pulled up his shorts and then his jeans while she stared, unmoving. He glanced at her over his shoulder, scowling.

She flushed and turned to reach for the thong she'd tucked into her jeans pocket for use after she'd taken off her wet suit. She bent to step into it, wondering how much she was revealing as she felt her shirt slip up over her fanny. Her buttocks remained bare even after she'd pulled the tiny scrap of material into place.

She reached quickly for her jeans and felt North's large hands cup her bottom. And then the caress of his callused fingertips. His mouth nuzzled her shirt away from her shoulder so his lips could reach bare skin.

Here was the tenderness that had been missing during their recent exchange of passion. Here was the show of love that she hadn't even known she'd been yearning for until he'd offered it.

She angled her head away to give North greater access to her throat, as he kissed the sensitive skin beneath her ear and then tugged gently on her earlobe with his teeth.

Then she heard his voice, rough as sandpaper and heavy with need. "I want you again."

His hands made short work of the thong, and he unsnapped and unzipped his jeans and freed his arousal. He bent her over the flat rock and thrust himself inside her from behind.

Jocelyn was shocked. And unbearably aroused.

Her palms were flat against the hot rock, and she felt North's hands come around to tease her nipples as his teeth and tongue caught at the skin at her neck, sending shivers through her. His hands slid down until they found the tiny nubbin that ached with want.

Jocelyn moaned.

North groaned.

She felt her body tightening, felt her legs tremble as they threatened to buckle, felt North's hand flatten against her belly as he held her upright through the tremors that rocked her. She closed her eyes and gritted her teeth, fighting against letting go, because she was afraid she would lose herself if she gave him what he seemed to be asking for.

He never asked in words. He only kept up the steady rhythm of his body in hers, driving her toward the precipice, willing her to leap into the chasm. Until finally, there was no escape.

Jocelyn cried out, and heard North's guttural shout in her ear, as they leapt into the abyss together.

She was trembling too much to stand, and for some reason, she was crying in great gulping sobs. North separated their bodies and turned her into his arms and pulled her tight against him, cocooning her against his chest.

"You see why you have to go," he said in a harsh voice.

"No, I don't see," Jocelyn sobbed. "I don't understand any of this."

He took a step back, and without his support Jocelyn wavered, before she sank onto her jeans, which were draped over the abrasive rock. She looked up at him, searching for answers to this enigmatic man.

"I will never love you," he said brusquely. "I can never love any woman."

Suddenly, she understood. He cared for her. Or thought he did. And he didn't like it one bit.

"You mean you don't choose to love me—or any woman," she countered.

"Use whatever words you want. It means the same thing. I want you out of my house. Out of my life."

"I'll be glad to leave."

She saw the flicker of regret that flashed across his face before she continued, "In September."

"Goddammit, Joss. I want you gone *today*!"

"That's too bad," Jocelyn said. "We have an agreement. I'm not going to let you say I welshed on the deal when I'm not here in September."

"I absolve you of any and all—"

"No need, when I'm not going anywhere."

"Goddammit, Joss—"

"I would appreciate it if you wouldn't swear so much."

Jocelyn watched as his lips pressed flat and his eyes narrowed. She stood on wobbly legs and reached for her jeans, putting her buttocks—her very enticing buttocks, she hoped—in North's way. "You'll just have to cope," she said as she pulled on her jeans and zipped them.

His fisted hands hit his hips and his bare toe tapped

as she slowly and carefully sat down on the rock and pulled on her socks and boots.

At last she stood and said, "I'm ready to go home now."

"You won't leave?" he said.

"Not until September."

"I'll transfer the damned stock today. Will that satisfy you?"

"Do whatever you want," she shot back. "The deal was, I'd stay till September. So I'm staying!"

He grabbed his boots and socks and stalked away toward the horses, leaving her behind. She stared after him with a furrow of worry between her eyes. Why hadn't she taken advantage of the opportunity to be free? Why hadn't she rushed back to Clay's waiting embrace? North clearly didn't want anything to do with her. He'd admitted he was incapable of loving anyone. What was wrong with her?

"Oh, God," she whispered.

There was a very good reason why she didn't want to leave North Grayhawk. She was in love with him.

North had ridden back to the house with Joss, but he'd driven away immediately afterward in his Dodge Ram without giving her any explanation where he was going or when he'd be back. He'd needed time to think. Time to figure out what he was going to do

about her. Because somehow she'd gotten under his
skin. Maybe even burrowed her way into his heart.
Like a virus. Or a tapeworm. Something that had to be
gotten over. Or gotten out.

He didn't trust love. It had made his father a miserable man when the woman he loved had chosen
someone else. King had made the four women he'd
subsequently taken as wives equally miserable when
he wasn't able to give them the love he was squander-
ing on another man's wife.

North could see a horrible symmetry in his infatuation—that's all it could be—with Jocelyn Montrose.
She'd been engaged to another man when she'd come
to him. Under the terms of their agreement she was
going to leave him in September. Only a fool would
fall in love with a woman under those circumstances.

North was no fool.

He'd meant it when he'd told Joss he wanted her
out of the house. Frankly, he'd been surprised that she
hadn't grabbed at the opportunity to leave. But that
could be corrected. He could be a mean sonofabitch.
He was sure he could drive her away.

It wouldn't be easy. He was vulnerable to her tears.
Hell, it wouldn't even take tears. His gut wrenched
whenever she was unhappy or uncomfortable. He'd
found himself moving heaven and earth to please her,
and her smile made him feel good inside.

North grimaced at the realization that he'd run

away from his own home this afternoon because he was afraid to face a slip of a woman to whom he owed nothing. How had she stolen past his defenses? What was it about this woman that made him think about her even when she wasn't around? What made him want her even after he'd just made love to her? What made him wonder what she was thinking, and lie in bed in the dark listening as each slow and steady breath left her body, thinking of ways to please her?

He felt a sense of dread at the thought of what the rest of his life would be like without her. And a sense of doom when he thought of how vulnerable he would be if he let her under his guard. If he let himself love her.

How many times had he heard his father say, *Women never stick around for long. They love money, not men. They're only good for two things: sex and sons.*

Rationally, he knew his father's attitude toward women was chauvinistic, to say the least. But he had his own experience with his mother, and a series of stepmothers who'd come and gone in his life, who'd seemed to care more about their divorce settlements than about their children, whom they'd happily abandoned in his father's home to yet another stepmother.

Except for Breed, of course, who'd gone with Sassy.

He saw a light on in the barn and remembered the boy was there. He felt a spurt of guilt that he hadn't let the kid into the house. But he hadn't wanted Breed to see him touching and kissing Joss, as he often did when the mood struck him. He had no intention of curbing his behavior. And he didn't want to have to worry about sounds carrying from the bedroom.

That room in the barn hadn't been used for a while, and North remembered it had been in pretty bad shape. He stopped his truck. He might as well make sure the kid was okay.

North's eyebrows rose when he stepped inside the room he'd offered to Breed. It had looked nothing like this a month ago when the boy had moved in. He knew better than to remark on the changes. The kid was sitting up in bed on top of the covers with two pillows arranged behind him, wearing a T-shirt and print boxer shorts, reading a fantasy novel with a buxom woman on the cover holding off a dragon with a sword.

"You okay?" North asked.

"What do you think?" Breed swept his arm around the room, forcing North to focus on the clean, shiny wooden floors, the cowhide decorating the area beside the iron bed, the clean white sheets and pillowcases, and a colorful patchwork quilt he recognized from his own bedroom. The antler lamp beside the bed had been in the living room of the house. He saw a painting of a nineteenth-century cattle drive on the wall that he knew had been in the guest room.

North realized who was responsible for the transformation when he saw the bowl of Indian paintbrush and black-eyed Susans on the chest of drawers. She'd done the same damn thing to his house. Put flowers all over. Added little feminine touches that neither his housekeeper nor his cook had ever suggested.

"I see Joss's hand here," North said.

"I told her there was no need, that I was used to a lot worse," Breed said. He grinned, one man to another, and added, "She was horrified."

North found himself grinning back. "You watch out, or she'll have you putting down the toilet seat and squeezing the toothpaste tube from the bottom instead of the middle."

Breed laughed. "Sounds like she's got you hog-tied."

North sobered. "No woman's gonna throw a lasso on me. Ever."

Breed set down his book and dropped his feet over the edge of the bed. "She's nice, North. She's not like Sassy."

North snorted. "That's for sure."

"She cares," Breed continued. "And she doesn't know me from Adam."

North had noticed the same thing. Joss had a heart that was wide open to any and everybody. She'd given the cook the week off when the woman had given her some sob story about a niece who needed help with her new baby, and ended up having to do the cooking, along with all the other work she did with North.

He'd been surprised and pleased when Joss had turned out to be some sort of gourmet. Apparently, she'd taken cooking classes in France when her father was ambassador. North had eaten in five-star restaurants where the food wasn't as good as the meals Joss had prepared.

"I'll admit Joss grows on you," North said.

"You should marry her."

North snorted again. "Why would I want to do that?"

"She'd be a great mother."

North looked at the youth who'd spent his life doing more caring for Sassy than the other way around. "Fortunately," North said, "I don't need a mother."

Breed flushed. "I mean for your kids."

North opened his mouth to say he wasn't having any kids and shut it again. The truth was, he wanted kids. And they were going to need a mother. He'd planned to marry someday. He just hadn't planned to love the woman. He'd intended to choose a wife with his mind, not his heart.

He imagined Joss with his child at her breast. The image made his breath catch and brought a lump to his throat. He focused on the cattle drive on the wall until he could speak again. "Joss is leaving."

Breed was instantly on his feet confronting North. "Don't you chase her away!"

He was surprised by the boy's vehemence and felt his neck hairs hackle when he realized the kid was probably half in love with her himself. "What I do with Joss is my business."

"You made her cry."

"What are you talking about?"

"I saw her in the kitchen window when she was washing dishes tonight. There were tears on her face. You put them there."

The accusation stung. "Joss doesn't need you for a champion. She can take care of herself."

"But you made her cry," Breed persisted.

"What happens between a man and a woman—"

"You know you can be mean, North. I've seen you do it when you don't like someone. When you want your way. Like King."

North was pretty sure that was about the worst insult Breed knew to hurl at him. Breed despised King. Equating North with King was like comparing him to slime.

"You don't always act like King," Breed conceded when North stared at the boy, daring him to say more. To say worse.

In the end, Breed's chin came up and he added, "But sometimes you do. Joss isn't as strong as you or me. Don't hurt her."

There was more demand than plea in what the boy said. But North wasn't about to explain or excuse himself to his maybe-brother, who was here only because he didn't have anywhere else to go. He didn't need a conscience. He wasn't going to let this boy be one. Tomorrow, next week, whenever Sassy gave up on rehab and found another man to support her, Breed would be gone. He didn't owe the boy an answer. He didn't owe the kid a thing.

"We've got a lot to do tomorrow. Don't read all night," he said.

Then he turned on his heel and left.

The house was dark and quiet when he let himself into the kitchen. He flipped on a light and felt his throat tighten when he saw the note from Joss on the table telling him his dinner was in the fridge and giving him instructions how to warm it.

He wasn't hungry. At least for food. He wanted Joss.

He felt a gnawing fear that she wasn't in the house, that she'd cooked him one last supper and disappeared, that his "meanness," as Breed had described it, had driven her away.

He headed down the hall to his bedroom, not just wanting but needing to hold her in his arms, needing to smell the flowery shampoo she used in her hair, needing to feel her warm breath against his throat.

No light showed under the bedroom door. He hesitated, his heart pounding, as he reached for the knob and quietly eased the door open. He could see her figure in the moonlight and exhaled a breath he hadn't realized he'd been holding.

She was wearing a short white cotton sleeveless nightgown. It was his favorite. It had a little pink bow in front that was all that held the top together. One tug and the material fell away to reveal tempting flesh. She was lying on her side, one knee drawn up, her long, silky hair spread across her pillow.

North fought against the raging desire that had made him rock hard, fought against wanting—against needing, like he needed air to live—the woman lying in his bed in the dark.

And lost.

11

North woke suddenly, aware something was wrong. He groaned when he saw daylight through the window and rubbed his eyes. He rarely overslept. But he'd kept Joss awake half the night, and been awake himself, making love to her, dozing lightly before reaching for her again. He'd recognized his desperation for what it was, but he'd been unable to stop himself.

He knew before he looked that Joss wasn't in bed beside him. The room felt empty. He felt bereft. He hated admitting, even to himself, the effect she had on him. But the plain truth was, the sky was bluer when she was near, and even a sunny day didn't feel as bright when she wasn't.

He could smell coffee. She was probably in the kitchen making breakfast. He couldn't believe he'd slept through her shower. He felt like he was moving through deep water as he rose from the bed and headed for the shower himself.

Ten minutes later, North stopped cold in the

kitchen doorway and stared. "What the hell are you doing in here?"

"Waiting for you to wake up," Breed said. "I made coffee."

"Where's Joss?"

"She left."

North felt his stomach flip-flop. He kept his voice even as he asked, "When did she leave? Where did she go?"

Breed rose and crossed to the coffeemaker, poured North a cup of coffee and shoved it into his hands. "She drove to Austin. Said she had to see someone."

"Did she say if—when—she'll be back?"

"You want her back?" Breed asked angrily. "You'd never know it from the way you treat her. She left in one damned big hurry this morning. What did you do to her?"

North slammed the coffee cup on the counter and jerked back when hot coffee splashed his blue chambray western shirt. He walked out without another word.

Breed ran along beside him, pestering him with questions for which North had no answers. He had no idea why Joss had left. Unless it had something to do with what had happened between them last night. But she'd never turned him away. And she'd enjoyed the slow and tender lovemaking the third time as much as she'd participated in the hunger of the first and the passion of the second.

"Where are you going?" Breed asked when North pulled open the door to his pickup.

"You've got chores to do," North said. "Get to them."

"Bring her back," Breed shouted after him, as North gunned the engine. "Bring her back!"

North tried to imagine who Joss might need to see in Austin. Only one name came to mind.

"He's not getting her back," North vowed. "He had his chance and he didn't fight for her. I'd never let a woman I loved give herself to another man."

North realized what he'd said and made a growling sound in his throat. *I don't love her. But she's mine until September. And I keep what's mine.*

He went straight to the federal courthouse in Austin, because that's where he thought Joss would have the best chance of finding Clay Blackthorne. He sat in the back of the courtroom and listened to some expert testifying about the sophistication of the bomb that had been used to destroy the federal courthouse in Houston.

His eyes searched the courtroom for Joss. He worried that he'd made a mistake when he didn't see her. And then he did. She was sitting in the second row next to his sister and his niece. He was wondering how long it would be before the court took a break and he could talk to her, when Clay called a break for lunch, and everybody stood to allow him to leave the courtroom.

North searched the milling crowd for Joss. He watched as Libby, Kate, and Joss disappeared out a door near the bench and suspected they were headed for Clay's chambers. The question was whether he should join them, or wait for Joss to come back out. As he headed toward the front of the courtroom, he saw there were two deputies standing on either side of the door the women had passed through. But North had spent his life confronting trouble head-on. He wasn't about to stop now.

All Jocelyn had wanted when she'd left North's ranch was a chance to talk with Clay alone. It hadn't turned out to be as easy as she'd hoped. He'd been unavailable before court started for the day, so she'd found herself a seat in the second row. To her amazement, she'd been joined by an exuberant Kate Grayhawk, who was with her mother, giving Jocelyn and Libby no choice except to greet each other. Fortunately, the court session began before Jocelyn needed to say much more than hello.

Jocelyn had been surprised when Libby returned to Wyoming a month ago—alone. To North's disgust, and her parents' dismay, Kate had signed up for summer classes, instead of returning to Wyoming with her mother after the spring semester ended.

According to North, Kate had coaxed Libby back to Texas this weekend, in the middle of her mother's short, busy season of guide trips, with a request to help her shop for a wedding dress.

When court recessed, Jocelyn had been swept along with Kate and Libby toward Clay's chambers.

"We're only going to be with Daddy for a few minutes," Kate said. "Mom is here to help me buy a dress and plan my wedding."

"'I didn't know you'd set a wedding date."

"We haven't yet," Kate said airily. "We don't have to worry about reserving a church at the last minute because we can be married at Bitter Creek any time we want. But the wedding is definitely on. Because really, when you find the love of your life, what's the point of waiting?"

Jocelyn realized the girl was lying. She'd been to enough embassy parties to recognize the signs. The staccato speech, the nervous flicker of her eyes, and the fidgeting hands all revealed Kate was uncomfortable with her story.

Jocelyn glanced at Libby to see if she knew her daughter was prevaricating. She found a frown of concern on Libby's brow. She didn't think Kate—or Libby—would welcome her help but she offered it anyway. "I'd be happy to help, if there's anything I can do."

"There is something," Kate piped up. "You can help me convince Mom and Daddy to come to Bitter Creek this weekend with Jack and me. Mom thinks

the Blackthornes won't want her at Bitter Creek—
because of Uncle North's buying up their stock and
then just *sitting* on it, making them all wait and wonder when the ax is going to fall."

Kate turned to Jocelyn and said, "Has North said
anything to you about what he plans to do? I mean,
about when—or whether—he's going to force the
Blackthornes off the ranch?"

Jocelyn was surprised to be so suddenly confronted
with such a loaded question. "I can't speak for North,"
she said. "Maybe you should ask him."

Kate grinned and shrugged. "I have. He won't tell
me. But the very fact he's hesitated, and is holding his
cards so close to the vest, must mean he's reconsider-
ing his options, don't you think?"

Jocelyn laughed uncomfortably. "With North, anything is possible."

Kate turned to her mother and said, "No one at Bitter Creek is going to be mad at you for something
North hasn't done yet."

"I wouldn't be comfortable just showing up without an invitation, Kate."

"But *I'm* inviting you. And Daddy will be there."
Kate put her arm through her mother's and said, "Aw,
Mom. Come spend some time with me and Jack. It'll
be fun."

"I'll think about it," Libby said.

By then they'd reached Clay's chambers. Kate

walked right into her father's open arms and got a hug.

"You were great again, Daddy," Kate said as she stepped back. "Overruled, overruled, overruled. I thought the defendant's attorney was going to choke when you wouldn't allow any of his objections to that expert witness's testimony."

Jocelyn watched Clay closely as he turned to greet Libby. "It's good to have you back in Texas," he said.

Libby smiled slightly and said "Kate didn't give me much choice."

Then their eyes met, and as though someone had flipped a switch, Jocelyn suddenly became uncomfortably aware of the sexual tension arcing between them.

"I know you're not free for lunch, Daddy," Kate said. "I just came by to see if you can get away this weekend to come down to Bitter Creek with me and Jack. And Mom."

"Kate, I haven't agreed to go," Libby said.

"I'd love to come," Clay said at the same time. Then Clay turned to Libby and said, "I hope you'll join us, Libby."

"Please come, Mom. Pretty please? With sugar on it?"

Libby laughed and shook her head at Kate's juvenile antics, then met Clay's gaze and said, "I've always wanted to see the Castle. Do you really think I'd be welcome?"

"You'll be with me. I'll run interference, if neces-sary."

"All right," Libby said. "I'll go."

"Great!" Kate said. "Then it's all settled. Jack and I are driving down together. Can you give Mom a ride?" she asked her father.

"We can fly down," Clay said, never taking his eyes off Libby.

Kate put an arm through her mother's and tugged her toward the door. "See you tomorrow night, Daddy," she said as the door closed behind them.

An awkward silence descended once the two Gray-hawk women were gone. Jocelyn finally broke it by saying, "I'm glad to see you and Libby are on good terms."

Clay picked up the gavel from his desk and turned it back and forth in his hands. "Yes. Well. We've spent a lot of nights over the past month talking about how to stop this wedding."

Jocelyn thought they must have discussed their re-lationship as well, they seemed so attuned to each other. She felt a surge of relief, knowing her defection would be less painful to Clay.

She opened her mouth to confess her change of feelings toward Clay and chickened out. Instead she said, "You still don't approve of Kate getting married?"

He pitched the gavel back onto his desk with a clat-ter. "No. I don't approve. Neither does Libby."

"Maybe you can use the time with Kate and Jack this weekend to convince them to wait."

"Maybe," Clay said with a rueful smile. "Kate seems pretty sure of what she wants."

Jocelyn remembered her perception that Kate hadn't been telling the truth when she'd rattled on about her wonderful relationship with Jack. Maybe Libby and Clay would be more successful in talking her out of this marriage than Clay thought.

"It's nice to see you," Clay said, interrupting her thoughts. "I have to admit I'm surprised. Where's North?"

"You get right to the point, don't you?" Jocelyn said.

Clay shrugged. "He made it pretty plain you were his property."

"It isn't like that," Jocelyn protested. "In fact," she said, plucking up her courage, "that's why I came to see you."

Clay leaned back against his desk and crossed his arms. "I'm listening."

"I don't want you to wait for me, Clay."

He stood again and unfolded his arms. "I owe you—"

"That's exactly it," Jocelyn hurried to say. "I don't want you to feel obligated to marry me."

Clay took a step toward her and said, "Don't give up on us now, Jocelyn. Just wait until September when—"

"Don't!" Jocelyn said, cutting him off. "The truth is, my feelings have changed." She took a breath and added, "I no longer want to marry you."

Clay crossed to the window and looked out. "You're in love with him," he said flatly.

"More to the point, I'm not in love with you," Jocelyn said. She didn't add that she might never have been in love with him after her first infatuation, only jealous of her sister's loving relationship with a man she'd wanted for herself. Jocelyn wasn't proud of that realization, but she'd come to terms with it.

Clay turned to face her. "Does North know how you feel?"

"No."

Clay made a disgusted sound in his throat. "I wasn't kidding when I said he can't love you. He isn't capable of it."

"That's not really your problem, is it?" she said gently.

"It is if you're ruling out any chance of us being together in the future."

Jocelyn didn't want to argue. So she didn't say anything.

"What happens now?"

"You go on with your life. I go on with mine."

"That doesn't work for me."

"Clay, I—"

He grasped her shoulders and said, "I want more,

Jocelyn. I want what you're offering North. I'm not going to let you walk away. I'm going to be standing right here when North gets tired of you—and he will. You'll never be happy with him."

"And I will be with you?" Jocelyn said heatedly. "I'm only an *obligation* to you!"

"No. No," Clay said, pulling her into his arms and holding her close. "That's not true."

Jocelyn laid her head against his beating heart. She was confused. Was Clay right? Would North tire of her? He'd already tried to send her away—more than once. She leaned back and looked deep into Clay's gray eyes, searching for the answers she sought.

And was amazed at what she found. *Hope.*

She laid a palm against his cheek. "Thank you, Clay, for caring so much."

"It's more than—"

She put her fingertips against his lips. "No. Don't say any more."

"Just be careful, Jocelyn," Clay said. "North can't—"

"Can't what?" an irritated voice said from the doorway.

North tried to shut the door behind him, but a huge deputy caught it with both his hand and his foot and said, "You okay with this guy, Judge Blackthorne?"

"Yes, Harvey. Thanks," Clay replied.

The deputy backed out, and North shoved the door closed behind him before turning to confront Clay.

Jocelyn felt her pulse speed as Clay released her. She realized their embrace probably appeared more intimate to North than it was.

"What brings you here, North?" Clay said.

"I came to get Joss."

"If I'm not mistaken, Jocelyn drove herself here," Clay said. "I'm sure she can—"

"She's coming with me," North said.

"Why don't we end this farce, so Jocelyn's free to go when she wants and with whom she wants," Clay said. "Why don't you sell that Bitter Creek stock back to me right here. Right now."

North shot Jocelyn a look that asked whether she'd betrayed him.

"I haven't said a word," she said.

"She didn't need to tell me what's going on," Clay said. "I figured it out for myself. After all, why else would any woman willingly put herself in the way of a bastard like you?"

Jocelyn gasped, afraid Clay's fighting words might actually provoke violence.

To her amazement, although North's jaw muscles worked furiously, he merely turned to her and said, "Let's go, Joss."

"Don't go, Jocelyn," Clay said. "I can tell you stories about King Grayhawk that would make your hair stand on end. And it's obvious the apple hasn't fallen far from the tree. Blackmail. Coercion. The destruction of lives and fortunes."

North's hands fisted, and he took a step toward Clay as he said, "Go to hell, Blackthorne."

"That's enough," Jocelyn said, as the two men glared at each other. She turned her back on North and said, "Thank you, Clay. Think about what we discussed." Then she turned to North and said, "I'm done here."

She could see the tension in North's body, the dangerous shards of ice in his blue eyes, but she had no intention of allowing two men she cared about to pound each other to a pulp.

"Stay away from her," North said, pointing a finger at Clay over Jocelyn's shoulder.

Jocelyn shot Clay a look warning him not to retaliate, which kept him silent. Then she grabbed North by the hand and reached for the doorknob. "Let's go," she said.

For a moment, North resisted. Then he followed her out the door.

Jocelyn wasn't sure how she felt about the fact North had followed her to Austin. She eyed him sideways as they left the courthouse, wondering whether he'd been motivated simply by a sense of possessiveness, or whether deeper feelings, feelings Clay had said North would never—could never—exhibit might be involved.

"I told Breed to tell you I'd be back after lunch," Jocelyn said.

"Apparently, he didn't believe you."

"Why wouldn't I come back?"

North stopped suddenly on the sidewalk and turned her toward him, grasping her arms. "Because of last night."

Jocelyn blushed and lowered her eyes. "I loved what happened last night."

North abruptly released her. "I thought . . ."

Jocelyn looked up at his face, which might have been made of granite, for all the emotion it revealed. "What did you think, North?"

"It doesn't matter," he said.

"It does to me."

"I thought maybe you didn't want—"

She put her fingertips over his mouth. "I wanted you. I always wanted you."

She saw his blue eyes flare, saw the muscle flex in his cheek, and became aware of a sudden tension between them.

She ran her finger across his lower lip, her eyes sparkling with laughter. "In the middle of the sidewalk in downtown Austin?"

He grabbed her hand away from his mouth and

dragged her down the street after him. "Don't push me, Joss. I had work to do this morning that didn't get done."

Jocelyn dug in her high heels, causing North to stop and turn toward her, irritation now written plain on his face.

"Yesterday you wanted me gone," she said. "What's changed? Why did you 'waste' your morning driving to Austin coming after me?"

If she'd hoped North would reveal any softer emotion toward her, she was doomed to disappointment.

"I offered you your freedom," he said in a harsh voice. "You threw it back in my face. Now I'm holding you to our bargain. You're mine until September."

"I don't like the way you make that sound," Jocelyn said. "You don't own me."

"You don't have to like it," North said. "You just have to stick to our agreement."

Jocelyn felt like crying, but she'd be damned if she'd give North the satisfaction of seeing her fall apart. Clay had warned her. She knew she was fighting an uphill battle. But she'd been there last night when North had turned to her not once, not twice, but three times.

It hadn't been about the sex, although the sex had been wonderful. It had been about a man and a woman needing each other, wanting each other, finding solace in each other. And yes, she thought, loving each other. Even if North would never admit it.

"I've got my car," she said. "I'll drive myself."

He opened his mouth to speak, then seemed to change his mind. "I'll follow you," he said finally.

"I want to do some shopping first."

He grimaced. "I'll go with you."

Jocelyn pursed her lips. She couldn't believe North was going to make the ultimate sacrifice. "I thought you had work to do."

"It can wait."

Jocelyn couldn't hold back a smile. "Fine. Let's go."

North reached for her hand, and she gave it to him. His grasp tightened and he started down the sidewalk. The sunlight felt warm on her face. And the skies had never looked so blue.

12

Kate was coming out the door of the courthouse when she saw Donnie Brown standing near the sawhorse police barricade blocking Eighth Street to traffic, arguing with his mother. Donnie's head was hung low, his eyes on the ground, and his mother seemed to be haranguing him about something, punctuating her speech by stabbing her cigarette at him. Then Kate saw his mother storm away.

Jack had more than once told her she should steer clear of Bomber Brown's son. Which, of course, only made Kate go out of her way to be nice to him. Today, she felt downright sorry for him. "Hi, Donnie," she said. "How's it going?"

"You should know," he said, crushing out his mother's cigarette stub with his booted foot. "You were sitting there when your dad let in all that evidence against my dad."

Kate ignored the edge in Donnie's voice, attributing it to his recent tongue-lashing from his mother, and said, "He only did what he had to do."

"Donnie Brown!" A TV newsman stuck a microphone practically up Donnie's nose and said, "How do you think the trial's going?"

Donnie said nothing, simply put his third finger up in front of the TV camera.

"Cut!" the newsman said to his cameraman, making a cutting motion across his throat. He turned back to Donnie and said, "I've been trying to get a quote from you for the past month, kid. When are you going to give me something I can use?"

"When hell freezes over," Donnie said.

The reporter shook his head, then moved off to easier prey.

Kate understood Donnie's frustration with the constant press attention. She felt the same way about the bodyguard who never left her alone. She'd forgotten what privacy felt like.

"You going back in?" Donnie asked.

"No, I'm going shopping with my mom." She glanced over her shoulder at her mother, who'd stopped at the top of the steps to answer her cell phone. "How 'bout you?" Kate said.

"Yeah. Might as well see how this all plays out. I heard the lawyers are going to do their summations tomorrow. I dread facing that all alone. I mean, my mother and brother are no comfort at all."

"Want some company?" Kate asked.

"That would be great," Donnie said. "I'd really like to have you there to hold my hand. Not really hold it, I mean, just be there for support."

"You can count on me to be there." She might even manage to come without her bodyguard, whose enormous gun, she knew, made Donnie nervous. She could tell her bodyguard that her uncle Owen was going to keep an eye on her. She'd done that a couple of times in the past.

Kate looked into Donnie's relieved, freckled face and said, "See you at 9:01."

Kate had always enjoyed shopping with her mother, but she felt guilty as she began trying on wedding gowns. She came out of the dressing room wearing a strapless white creation that was beaded with pearls across the bodice and fell in an A-line to the floor. She was also wearing a simple net veil that dropped to her waist in back, held in place by a crown decorated with pearls.

"Ta-da!" she said as she twirled in a circle before the mirrors that dominated the showroom. "What do you think, Mom?"

She turned to her mother, who was sitting on a couch nearby, and realized her mother's eyes were brimming with tears.

"Don't cry, Mom," Kate said, hurrying to her

mother and stooping down so they could see eye to eye.

"You're so beautiful," her mother said, stroking Kate's hair where it fell away from her bare shoulders. "I can't believe my baby is going to be a bride."

Kate's heart sank. She felt a surge of guilt so strong she nearly blurted out the truth. She reminded herself of her ultimate goal—to get her mother into a wedding gown—and remained silent. "Thank you, Mom." She smiled mischievously and said, "But to tell you the truth, this dress pinches!"

Her mother laughed through her tears. "Then I guess you better go try on something else."

Kate came out next in a gown with puffy sleeves and a full skirt with a thousand layers of net that made her feel like a fairy-tale princess. She twirled for her mother and said, "Jack would have to be waiting for me at the altar wearing a suit of shining armor if I showed up in this."

"Jack won't even see your dress," her mother said. "He'll only be looking at you."

Kate forced a laugh. "I had no idea you were such a romantic."

"Once upon a time—" Her mother stopped and laughed awkwardly. "Is there anything else back there you'd like to show me?"

Kate tried on several more dresses, but seeing how her mother was affected by the whole experience made it one of the most uncomfortable hours she'd ever spent. She managed to get through it by remembering the way her father had looked at her mother that morning in his chambers. And by reminding herself that, because of her charade as a bride, her parents had agreed to spend an entire weekend together at Bitter Creek. Surely once they were alone together, nature would take its course.

As she and her mother were leaving the bridal shop, Kate said, "Actually, Jack and I aren't staying with you and Daddy at Bitter Creek."

"Oh?" her mother said warily.

They'd arrived at her mother's rental car, and after she unlocked the door and opened it to let the heat out, her mother stood looking across the hood of the car waiting for Kate's explanation.

Kate filled her voice with enthusiasm and said, "There's this really neat cabin on Bitter Creek where President Eisenhower once slept, and I thought you'd love it, so I talked Summer and Billy into putting you and Daddy there."

Libby's lips flattened. "So I'm not welcome after all."

"They weren't overjoyed that I wanted you to come," Kate admitted, which was a whopper of an understatement. Grandpa Blackjack had nearly had a cow. "I just thought having you and Daddy stay at the cabin would make it easier on everyone.

"I see." Her mother slipped into the driver's side

and turned on the ignition to get the AC started. She waited for Kate to slip into the passenger's seat and asked, "Where will you and Jack be staying?"

"We'll be at the Castle," Kate said. The main ranch house at Bitter Creek was so enormous that someone had dubbed it the Castle. Kate thought the name fit, because like a castle in England, there were lots of old things—paintings and furniture and silverware and chandeliers and knickknacks—that had been accumulated over more than a century by the Blackthornes living there.

Her mother turned sideways in her seat so she was facing Kate and said, "How far is the house where Clay and I are staying from the Castle?"

Kate found it hard to hold her mother's stern gaze. Since the ranch was the size of a small northeastern state, it was possible for all of them to be on Bitter Creek land, yet staying some distance from each other. "Twenty-five miles," she admitted at last.

"I don't like being manipulated, Kate."

Kate felt her heart squeeze. She swallowed hard over the painful lump that suddenly constricted her throat. "What are you going to do?"

"I'm not going to sidle up to the Blackthornes with my head hung low in shame for what the beastly Grayhawks have done to the poor, helpless Blackthornes—and then run off to some cabin with my tail between my legs!"

Kate sat in a miserable huddle on her side of the car, as her mother shoved the car into gear and drove her back to her condo. She'd been telling herself like a mantra that everything she did was aimed at her mother and father's ultimate happiness, that they belonged together, that all she needed to do was give them a nudge in the right direction and they'd find true love again.

The truth was, Kate didn't really know whether her parents wanted to be together. Neither of them had ever confided in her. For the very first time, she felt a niggle of doubt about the plans she'd set in motion.

When her mother reached the Westgate, she put the car in park, then reached out and cupped Kate's chin, turning her face so they were eye to eye. "After your wedding I'll be returning to Wyoming. And I'll be staying there. There isn't going to be any reconciliation between me and your father."

Kate jerked free. "Mom, why not?"

"It won't work, Kate. I gave your father every chance—"

"But, Mom," Kate pleaded, scooting forward in her seat toward her mother, "you and Daddy are meant to be together. I know it!"

"You have to let your father and me find our own way, sweetheart. Right now, our lives are taking us in different directions. I have my guide trips in the mountains around Jackson Hole, and your father has his work in the courtroom here in Austin."

Her mother brushed Kate's hair away from her face, a gesture meant to soothe her, to calm her, to make her accept facts that Kate found totally unacceptable.

"Then why did you agree to go to Bitter Creek this weekend?" Kate demanded, sitting back and crossing her arms so all contact between her and her mother was broken.

"Honestly? For your sake."

"What?" Kate exclaimed.

"Your father and I are both worried that you may be making a mistake with Jack."

"I'm not! I'm not," she said, knowing that she was protesting too much, but too agitated to shut up. "Really, Mom. You're so wrong. Jack is a wonderful man. He's . . . He's . . ."

Kate realized she didn't know much more about Jack McKinley than her parents had gotten him to reveal over dinner a month ago. She knew he'd once been accused of cheating, was in some kind of trouble with the IRS, and had agreed to participate in this charade with her. Which suggested he didn't have much trouble lying. Which could hardly be considered a positive attribute she could tout to her mother.

Her mother gave her a sympathetic, loving look that made Kate's stomach churn. She resisted blurting that she and Jack weren't getting married, that she wasn't even sure Jack *liked* her, and he sure as hell didn't *love* her, so her mom could just tuck her tail between her legs and run back to Wyoming and spend the rest of her life alone, like a bitter old spinster, for all Kate cared.

The meanness of her thoughts horrified Kate.

She lurched across the seat and put her arms around her mother and said, "I'm so sorry, Mom."

"There's no need for you to be sorry, Kate. Your heart has always been in the right place."

Since her mother didn't know what she'd been thinking, and Kate had no intention of telling her, she simply hugged her mother tighter and said, "I love you, Mom."

"This will all work out, Kate," her mother said, patting her back, as she had when Kate had been a small child. "Please don't worry about this weekend. Your father and I are on better terms now than we have been for a very long time. I'm sure we can manage to get through a couple of days with a crowd of nasty old Blackthornes."

Kate laughed, then sat back and brushed at the unaccustomed tears that threatened to squeeze past her guard. "You mean you're still going? I thought—"

"Wild horses couldn't keep me away," her mother said. "I'm not about to miss the chance to look every single one of those goddamn Blackthornes right in the eye and *dare* them to say a harsh word against me or any of mine!"

Kate stared at her mother, astonished at her outburst. Until she remembered how much hurt her mother must have suffered over the years. She couldn't wait to see the look on Grandpa Blackjack's face when Libby Grayhawk showed up on his doorstep.

As quickly as her mother's rant began, it was over. Her mother put the car in gear, then turned to Kate and said, "Just, please, don't do any more finagling."

Kate didn't respond, which kept her from having to lie. Anything could happen if her parents were together for an entire weekend. She'd seen herself how cacti could blossom in the desert.

Kate had a Thursday afternoon class she couldn't miss, so as her mother headed back to her room at the Four Seasons, Kate hurried inside to pick up her books.

Kate changed out of her cowboy boots into tennis shoes, slipped her book bag onto her back, and started out the door—where she literally ran into Jack, her breasts coming into contact with what turned out to be a very muscular chest.

"What are you doing here?" she asked, feeling a physical awareness of Jack McKinley that irritated her, because he seemed so totally unaffected himself. "Why didn't you knock?"

"We need to talk," he said.

"I have class," she told him. "You can walk with me if you like, and we can talk on the way." She tugged on a baseball cap and headed down the hall.

"The campus is a long walk from here," Jack said, striding beside her. "Let me give you a ride. That way we can talk in private."

"I need the exercise," Kate said, hitting the elevator button to take her back downstairs. They were on the sidewalk a moment later, Kate setting a fast pace so she wouldn't be late.

"Something's come up, and I can't go with you this weekend."

Kate stopped in her tracks and turned to face Jack. "You're not going this weekend?"

"No."

"Why not?"

"This game was fun while it lasted, kid, but I've got work to do."

Kate's whole body turned to ice. A pretty good trick when the temperature was in the eighties. She wanted to speak, but her tongue seemed to be stuck to the roof of her mouth. "So you really have been baby-sitting me," Kate murmured, her face suddenly flushing with heat as the blood began to flow again.

"I wouldn't call it baby-sitting, exactly," Jack said uncomfortably.

"What would you call it? Exactly?" Kate said, her hands on her hips.

"Being nice to a friend's niece."

Kate's chest ached, and she wasn't sure why. She was well aware her relationship with Jack had never been anything but a sham. But it still hurt to have him point out how shallow it really was.

"Sorry, kid. I never meant for this to go on so long. But I didn't think you could handle—"

"I can handle anything!" Kate said, poking Jack in his muscular chest with her forefinger. "Despite what you and Uncle North might think, I'm not a child. Not even close to being a child. I'm totally grown up!" Kate swiped at the tears that brimmed in her eyes, furious with herself because she was, in fact, losing control like some kid having a tantrum.

"Aw, hell." Jack slid an arm around her shoulders and, despite her resistance, urged her into a nearby alley, where they wouldn't be so visible to passersby. When she jerked free and started to run, he caught her and pulled her into his embrace. Kate struggled, but it was clear she wasn't going to get away until he let her go. She finally gave up and stood rigid in the circle of Jack's arms.

It was shady and cool in the alley. Kate swallowed once over the lump in her throat, but it hurt. She couldn't believe how much she'd indulged in the fantasy she'd created. She couldn't believe how much she'd wished it was real.

She looked up at Jack, but his face was only a blur

through her tears. She felt his large hand slide through her hair as he pressed her cheek against his chest. She couldn't summon the will to fight. Instead, she closed her eyes and listened to the steady thump of his heart.

"I'm sorry, kid," he said.

Kate swallowed a sob. He thought she was a *kid*. He'd never been the least bit attracted to her. She'd been a fool. She'd been an *idiot*.

Kate shoved at Jack's shoulders, and he let her go. He stood with his hands at his sides, looking almost as miserable as she felt. She wiped at her tears with her sleeves. Jack handed her a folded handkerchief and she blew her nose. She offered it back to him and he said, "Keep it."

She sniffed and said, "What's so important that you can't come with me this weekend?"

"My business is private."

Kate lifted a brow. "So your problems with the IRS—"

"Are none of your business."

"You must owe North a great deal of money to have taken time out from your busy schedule to baby-sit me," Kate said, disgusted by the self-pity she heard in her voice.

"I owe North more than I can ever repay," Jack said.

"I'll bet," Kate muttered.

THE NEXT MRS. BLACKTHORNE 271

"There's been a development. I've got to follow up on it this weekend."

"It doesn't matter," Kate said with a sigh. "As long as Mom and Daddy don't find out we aren't going to Bitter Creek until after they're already there."

"You never give up, do you?" Jack said.

"They belong together," Kate said fiercely. "They always have, and they always will."

"I guess this is good-bye," Jack said.

"You've said it. Now go." Kate didn't know how much longer she could hang on to her composure.

"I do have one last piece of advice," Jack said.

"What's that?"

"Stay away from Bomber Boy."

"I asked you not to call Donnie that. He's not—"

"—like his father," Jack finished for her. "The point is, this Bomber Brown character hates the world, and he's got friends out there somewhere who would be happy to kill your father, or hurt him by hurting you."

"But Donnie's nothing like his father," Kate repeated. "He doesn't agree with what his father did."

Jack shot her a strange look. "How do you know that? Did he say something to you?"

"No. But he never sits near his father. He never talks to him—or to his brother or mother—who *do* sit with his father."

"Just do me a favor and stay away from him," Jack said.

"But Donnie asked me—"

Jack grabbed her arms roughly and pulled her up on her toes. "Weren't you listening to me? The kid's dangerous."

"You aren't my mother, my father, or my fiancé," Kate retorted through clenched teeth. "You can't tell me what to do!"

"If I have to, I'll tell your uncle you're consorting with Bomber Boy and see what he has to say."

"You wouldn't dare!"

"Try me."

They stared at each other, both angry, both determined, until the tenor of their looks changed. Kate felt it. The shift from anger to desire happened so quickly she hadn't realized it was happening.

Jack stiffened. And let go of her like she'd caught fire.

Kate stumbled as her feet landed back on the sidewalk. Jack reached out to steady her, but she jerked backward and almost fell over. A second later he was holding her close again. She looked up at him, saw the flare of desire in his eyes, felt the heat and hardness of his body and realized he was fighting what he felt.

"Don't go near him," he said.

"You say that like you expect me to obey you."

"I do."

Kate was glad she hadn't told Jack she would be sitting with Donnie Brown in court in the morning. She wasn't about to give him the satisfaction of agreeing to stay away, even if what he'd said made her doubt the wisdom of what she'd agreed to do. There would be plenty of cops around if she needed to call for help.

He let go of her as though it was the hardest thing he'd ever done. Once again, Kate was standing on her own two—wobbly—feet.

"What I'm asking is for your own safety, Kate."

Kate shot him a mulish look.

Jack sighed. "It's obvious you aren't going to listen to me. We'll see if your uncle—or your father—can talk some sense into you."

He started to stalk away, and Kate grabbed his arm. "No. Wait! You can't go to Daddy. If you do, he'll know the truth about us, and he'll cancel the trip to Bitter Creek this weekend."

"This isn't a game you're playing, Kate. This is a matter of life and death."

"My parents' future together is a matter of life and death to me," Kate said. "Please don't talk to Daddy. I'll be careful. I promise."

"You'll stay away from Donnie Brown?"

"What if he's in court the same time as I am?"

"Stay away from your father's court."

"If it's so dangerous, why doesn't everyone have to stay away? I mean, if it's so dangerous, why is the trial still open to the public?" Kate demanded.

For a moment, she didn't think Jack would answer. Finally, he said, "I suppose because nobody actually has found proof—yet—that Bomber Brown didn't act alone."

"Why are you so sure he did have help?" Kate asked.

"My gut tells me I'm right."

"And my gut tells me that Donnie's okay," Kate said.

"Dammit, Kate, I—"

"I've got to go," she said. "I'm going to be late for class." Kate turned and started jogging.

"Kate!" Jack called after her.

She turned and jogged backward, so she could face him. "What?" she called back.

"Be careful."

13

Late Friday morning, Kate glanced surreptitiously around her father's courtroom. She'd managed to slip away from her bodyguard, but she felt surprisingly uneasy. Unsafe. Which was all Jack's fault, filling her head with all that talk of conspiracy and accomplices. But there was definitely something to be said for having a very large man with a very big gun following you around.

Kate felt a little safer knowing everyone in the courthouse had to go through tight security to get inside. Surely Bomber Brown's accomplice, if he existed, wasn't going to set off a bomb while Mr. Brown was sitting here.

And there were armed deputy marshals to guard Mr. Brown when he came to and from the courtroom. So what were the chances a terrorist would turn up in their midst?

Zero to none, Kate decided. So there was no reason for her to be feeling so antsy. While she waited for

Donnie to arrive, Kate thought about her encounter with her father in his chambers earlier that morning.

The challenge had been to convince her dad to spend the weekend with her mom, even though Kate and Jack weren't going to be there. Because really, Kate had decided, what was the point of her going to Bitter Creek, if Jack wasn't?

She'd seen her father's surprise, followed quickly by pleasure, when he'd noticed her from behind his desk.

He'd risen and crossed to meet her in the middle of the burnt orange carpet and given her a hard hug. "Hello, Kitten," he'd said. "What brings you here?"

"I just wanted to see you, Daddy," she'd said. "After all the years when I couldn't drop in like this, it seems so wonderful to be able to walk right in and say good morning."

He smiled and said, "Good morning. Now, what can I do for you?"

She laughed and looked up at him shyly from beneath dark lashes. "Well, there is something."

He chuckled and said, "Cough it up, Kitten."

As though she had a hairball or something! How could she connive to get her parents together, when her father was so watchful of her motives in coming to see him?

"Actually, Daddy, I have a confession to make."

This time he laughed and made a gesture with his hands to encourage her to speak.

"Jack and I aren't going this weekend. It'll be just you and Mom."

Once upon a time, Kate might have been cowed by the frown that appeared on her father's face and the way his arms crossed over his body in his judicial robes, to make him a more prepossessing figure. But she'd learned that where she was concerned, her father was far more bark than bite. She crossed to him and put her hands on his crossed arms and peered up into his gray eyes with her most plaintive look.

"Jack has to work, Daddy." Which was the truth, so far as it went. "And I could use the time to study."

Her father snorted, because he'd seen how many Bs she'd gotten the previous semester and knew that if she'd studied at all they would have been As.

Kate debated whether to warn her father about the reception he and her mother were likely to get from the Blackthornes—and how agitated her mother had been about having to confront his family. But she realized her parents would probably discuss the whole thing on the flight to Bitter Creek. Besides, no matter how bad things got, her father would be able to handle it.

"Mom really wants to see the Castle, and I thought you guys might enjoy the time alone together. So I wanted to ask you not to cancel, even though Jack and I aren't going."

Her father looked away, so she couldn't see what he

was thinking. He often did the same thing in the courtroom before a ruling. Her heart made a heavier thump when he met her gaze again.

"You know your mom's planning to return to Wyoming after your wedding," he said.

Kate nodded. "She told me."

"So there isn't going to be any 'happily ever after' between her and me."

"And why is that, Daddy? I've got eyes. I saw how you looked at Mom when she was in here yesterday. Why are you letting her walk away?"

"I have a responsibility to Jocelyn that—"

"Listen to yourself! *Responsibility?* Daddy, you and Mom were inseparable for an entire summer. You must have felt something for her. Why are you so afraid to follow your heart? At least use the weekend together to find out how you really feel."

When she was finished speaking, Kate waited with bated breath to hear her father's verdict.

At last he said, "Does your mom know you and Jack aren't going?"

"I haven't told her. And I wasn't going to tell her."

"Why not?" her father asked.

"Because I think she might not go if I did," Kate admitted.

"I think you're right," her father said quietly. The corner of his mouth lifted before he said, "So maybe we better not tell her."

Kate wasn't sure she'd heard her father right. "You're not going to tell her?"

He smiled and said, "I could use the vacation before I give jury instructions next week. And your mom's good company."

"Thanks, Daddy," Kate said, throwing her arms around him and giving him an excited hug. "Just remember what I said."

"So what are you really going to be doing this weekend?" he asked, as he tugged her arms from around his neck.

She gave him an indignant look. "Studying!"

He laughed and swiped a finger down her nose. "Thanks, Kitten."

"For what?" she said.

"You know for what."

Against all odds, her father suddenly seemed excited about spending the weekend with her mom. She studied his face and said, "Did you love her, Daddy? I mean, when you made me, did you—"

"Yes," he said. "More than life."

Kate was embarrassed by the ferocity of his answer. He seemed to be, too, because he hustled her out of his chambers.

Kate had spent the rest of the morning sitting in the back of the courtroom beside Donnie Brown. She glanced at him and saw he was chewing a fingernail. Again.

She could understand why. Kate thought the prosecuting attorney had done a masterful, surprisingly brief, job of summing up the case against Donnie's father. So far, the defense attorney hadn't been nearly so effective. Of course, he had less helpful evidence to make his argument for acquittal.

As sure as God made little green apples, Kate thought, Donnie's dad was going to be convicted.

She turned to Donnie and whispered, "How are you doing?"

"It's looking pretty bad," he mumbled. "Let's get out of here."

"You don't want to wait until your dad's lawyer is finished?"

"Naw," he said. "I've heard enough."

Kate tried to catch her father's eye before she left, but his gaze was focused intently on the attorney speaking to the jury. "Ugh. It's hot," she said as she stepped outside with Donnie. She was wearing a white T-shirt with a black tailored jacket, jeans, and boots, which had been fine inside but was too warm on the street.

"Let's go get something cold to drink," Donnie said.

Kate glanced at Bomber Brown's son, whose forehead was already dotted with sweat, and realized he must have been perspiring even before they'd left the courtroom. Probably due to worry over his father's dire situation, she decided. "Something cold sounds wonderful." And thanks to Jack, she didn't have anywhere else to be.

"I've got my car around the corner," Donnie said.

Kate followed Donnie to his car, which turned out to be a brand-new Cadillac Escalade. "Wow," she said, running her hand along the silver pearlized finish. "Pretty fancy."

"It's my dad's," he said.

As Kate stepped up into the expensive car and sat in the soft leather seat, she glanced sideways at Donnie. She never thought of terrorists as having a lot of money. "What did your dad do before . . . before?"

"Before he got arrested?" Donnie finished for her, as he started the car and headed down the street.

"Yeah," Kate said with a shrug.

"We farmed. That is, before the government decided we couldn't use the fertilizer we needed to get our crops to grow, and the pesticides we needed to keep the critters from eating everything before the harvest. They said we were polluting the water."

"A river runs through your land?" Kate asked, thinking how Bitter Creek was named after a creek tht ran across the ranch and was never dry, even in the driest years.

"No. No water at all. We had to irrigate." Donnie turned a look on Kate that made her shiver. His eyes looked strange, lit with some fervent light.

Kate suddenly heard Jack's warning voice in her ear. And realized she'd left the courthouse—and the multitude of cops with guns—behind. Then she told herself she was seeing things that weren't there. Donnie hadn't said or done a thing that was remotely suspicious. She moved her hand away from the door handle and set it in her lap.

Donnie's gaze turned back to the road as he continued, "It seems our land is right on top of some deep cavern or something where groundwater collects. And everything we put on our crops was seeping down, contaminating the water down below. The government said we could keep farming, as long as we didn't use chemicals of any kind. No fertilizer. No pesticides."

"So you became organic farmers?" Kate said.

Donnie shot her a look that made her want to reach for the door handle. "We went to court to fight the government. But we lost. We had to sell the farm to pay the lawyers. But we got them all back."

"Them?" Kate said faintly.

"The judges, the lawyers, and the government."

Kate realized they'd left the downtown area and were on the parkway headed west at too high a speed for her to jump out of the car. Way too late, she realized Jack was right. Which was very cold comfort now. "Where are we going?" she asked in as calm a voice as she could manage. No sense warning Donnie

THE NEXT MRS. BLACKTHORNE   283

that she was scared to death and was busy planning her escape.

"There's a place on the north side of town I like to go to for lunch."

"I thought we were just going to get a drink somewhere downtown."

"I'm hungry," Donnie said. "I didn't think you'd mind."

Kate shot him a tremulous smile to cover up the terror she felt and said, "Sure. No problem."

Kate wondered if Donnie realized what he'd said. *We got them all back. We.* She stared at the sandy-haired boy with the innocent-looking freckles. It must be the sight of the skinny boy sitting behind the wheel of a big, powerful car that made him suddenly seem sinister.

Or the inclusion of himself when he described the vengeance that had been visited on judges, lawyers, and the government.

Even with everything he'd said, Kate was still having trouble believing that Donnie was some kind of terrorist. Surely the FBI had investigated the entire Brown family thoroughly before they'd finally arrested Donnie's father. How had Donnie flown so far beneath their radar?

Or maybe he hadn't. Maybe Donnie had been suspected all along. And all that was missing was proof.

Kate felt a shiver run down her spine. Her gut was

telling her that she'd made a terrible mistake getting in the car with Donnie Brown. The very next time Donnie slowed the car, she was going to make a run for it. Time enough later to be embarrassed if this was all a horrible misunderstanding.

When Donnie got off the parkway he kept the car moving above the posted speed, and made a sudden, hair-raising turn down a rural road. He stopped in front of what seemed to be an abandoned house that was virtually hidden by overgrown azaleas and forsythia, which were in wild, beautiful bloom. The house, which had boarded-up windows, looked way too much like something from a bad horror movie. Kate's stomach was genuinely upset.

"Donnie, where are we?" she asked.

"Oh. This is where I live."

Kate wondered if Donnie's mother and brother were in the house—the two family members who'd always sat behind his father in court. "Why did you bring me here?" Kate asked.

"I've got to pick something up before we go to lunch."

"I'm not getting out of the car," Kate said decisively.

"Suit yourself. I'll just be a minute." To Kate's dismay, Donnie turned off the ignition and took the Escalade key ring, which he shook in Kate's face, several keys jangling against each other. "Need them for the front door."

Kate stared at the door to the ramshackle house, which was lucky to still be on its hinges, let alone locked. More likely, Donnie suspected she was on to him and didn't want her to be able to drive away in his car.

She unbuckled her seat belt as soon as Donnie was far enough away from the car to not be able to see what she was doing. The instant he stepped inside the house, Kate shoved open the car door and ran like a bat out of hell.

She followed the road they'd come in on, thinking that was the fastest way back to civilization and help. She'd almost made it back to the highway when she saw another car coming. Since there were other houses along the road, she took a chance and flagged it down.

The middle-aged man with short-cropped gray hair who stepped out of the Chevy pickup looked wonderfully normal.

"I need your help!" she said, panting and holding her side, which ached. "There's someone after me!"

"Slow down," the man said, putting his hand on her shoulder. "Who's after you?"

Kate heard Donnie shouting her name. She looked down the road and saw he was heading her way. "Help me, please! I have to get away." Kate jerked to free herself.

But the man held on.

"Not so fast," he said, grabbing both her arms.

Kate kicked him hard in the shin and jerked her shoulders to free herself, but he was surprisingly strong. She glanced over her shoulder and could see Donnie running hard toward her.

"Let-me-go!" she said, digging her fingernails into the man's shirt, and kicking with her feet.

"Cut that out, you silly bitch," the gray-haired man said.

Kate was so shocked, she hesitated for a single instant, staring at him.

At that moment, Donnie pressed a rag against her face so hard he cut off her air. Kate automatically inhaled—and realized she couldn't breathe. Donnie had put something on the rag. Kate fought hard, scratching and kicking, but not for long. She had to take another breath, and she got another dose of whatever drug Donnie had poured on the cloth.

As she began to lose consciousness, she heard the middle-aged man say, "I decoded your Letter to the Editor. I'm glad to see your father was right. You are the Chosen One."

Kate couldn't believe she'd been so stupid. She thought of her parents—and Jack—as the blackness closed in around her. And realized that not one of them had any reason to come looking for her before Monday.

14

Ever since she was sixteen, pregnant and alone, Libby had wondered—and imagined—what it would be like to step across the threshold of the Castle. Today, that long-ago dream was going to become reality.

She'd seen pictures of the Castle in *Southern Living*, and *Architectural Digest*, which had featured the elegant two-story mansion, with its uppper and lower gallery porches and its circular driveway lined with towering magnolias. Libby had always smiled at the inevitable comment made by the author of each article touting the Castle's magnificence, that Bitter Creek was comprised of 745,000 acres of prime ranchland, and there were *ten miles* of pavement maintained by the Blackthornes between the nearest Texas state road and the Castle.

The mansion contained priceless Tiffany lamps and original Chippendale furniture and too many first editions in the Blackthorne library to count. But Libby had always loved the sturdy ranch furniture made of wood and horn and hide that had survived a hundred and fifty years of Blackthornes in residence.

Clay had landed his Citation jet on a Bitter Creek airstrip near the cabin where President Eisenhower had once slept. Libby was surprised that, although an SUV had been left for them at the airstrip, no one from the Blackthorne family had been there to greet them personally

"I have to confess, I'm a little anxious about spending this weekend with your family," she said to Clay once they were headed for the Castle.

Clay reached over and put a hand on her knee, smiled and said, "I won't let the dragons eat you."

Libby arched a brow and replied, "You're expecting dragons?"

"Everybody's been on edge since North bought that controlling interest in Bitter Creek stock," Clay said. "You might find one or two folks breathing fire. But I'll be there to protect you."

As he hadn't been twenty years before.

When they reached the circular drive lined with magnolias, Clay stopped to give Libby her first up-close and personal look at the Castle.

"What do you think?" he asked.

"It's . . . majestic. Like a grand old dame," Libby said with reverence, as she slowly perused the house.

Instead of stopping, Clay drove past the front entrance and headed toward the back of the house.

Libby felt a spurt of pleasure. Only strangers, and those attending funerals, entered the front door of a ranch house. Friends and family were welcomed at the back door.

Clay pulled the SUV into a spot next to several other SUVs and pickups beside the back porch. He turned to her and said, "Welcome to the Castle, Libby."

Libby felt a smile curve her lips. "Thank you, Clay."

It was dusk, but Libby could see Blackjack and Ren sitting in side-by-side rockers on the left side of the back porch. Clay's younger sister Summer, whom Libby recognized from pictures taken with Kate, sat on the right, on a porch swing that hung from the second story gallery.

Summer was barefoot, with her legs crossed in front of her on the seat of the white wooden swing. Her husband Billy was sitting on a porch rail nearby, and gave the swing a push to keep it moving.

There was no screen around the porch, and moths fluttered around oil lanterns that gave off a soft yellow light. A trellis of morning glories, which had closed for the night, enclosed the right end of the porch. Tall glasses containing a dark liquid, bearing a sprig of something green and dripping condensation, sat on nearby end tables. Libby imagined the many generations of Blackthornes who must have lingered here to enjoy the sunset at the end of a hard day riding herd on their cattle.

Her stomach was filled with nervous butterflies. She turned to Clay and said, "I can't believe I'm actually here. After all these years."

"It's about time, don't you think?"

"I wonder where Jack and Kate are. I thought they'd get here before us."

"There's been a slight complication," Clay said.

Libby shot him a concerned look. "Are they both all right?"

"As far as I know," Clay said. "I'll explain later," he said, when she prompted him with a raised eyebrow for details. "Let's leave our bags in the car while we go say hello and get ourselves one of those mint juleps."

Libby eyed Clay askance, wondering if he was leaving the bags in the car because he wasn't sure whether they would be welcome. She felt her stomach knot. She wasn't looking forward to the next few minutes. But, as she'd told Kate, she wasn't going to run.

Libby had debated what to wear tonight and opted for a simple white blouse belted into jeans and cowboy boots. She wiped her sweaty palms on her Levi's before she stepped out of the car. She waited for Clay to join her, and they walked the short distance to the porch together.

"Hello, everybody," Clay said as he stepped onto the porch.

Libby's anxiety shot up a notch when not a single person on the porch made a move to acknowledge their arrival, as though she were an insect beneath their notice.

Clay slid an arm around her waist to draw her close and turned them both to face his younger sister and her husband. "Summer, I don't think you've ever actually met Libby. Libby, this is my sister Summer and her husband Billy Coburn. They manage the ranch."

Libby pasted on her brightest smile and said, "I'm so glad to meet you both at last."

Summer's face was openly hostile as she uncrossed her legs and dropped her bare feet to the wooden porch, but she said nothing, and Billy made no move to reach out and greet Libby. From the corner of her eye, Libby saw Ren lay a restraining hand on Blackjack's arm to keep him from saying whatever ugly thing she was sure he'd been about to say.

Libby felt the hair on her arms stand up.

Clay had led her to believe he'd smoothed the way for her visit. But it was obvious that no one on the porch wanted her here.

She'd been bushwhacked.

But a lot of years had passed since Libby Grayhawk had been a powerless sixteen-year-old girl and allowed her brash, bullying father to intimidate her. She wasn't about to bow her head or bend her back to a bunch of Blackthornes.

She turned and nodded her head to Blackjack and Ren and said, "I envy you the rich heritage of your home."

"Which won't be ours much longer, if your brother gets his way," Summer retorted. She stood, and Billy moved to her side—to check her, Libby realized, when he slid an arm around her shoulders.

"No thieving Grayhawk is crossing the threshold of this house," Summer said heatedly. "Not while I'm alive and kicking."

Libby cocked a disdainful brow in response to Summer's hyperbole. She hadn't stolen a thing. And neither had North. Yet.

Clay's response was more direct. "Cut the crap, Summer. Libby's not responsible for what her brother does. And Kate's been in and out of this house all her life, so there's already been a Grayhawk over the threshold."

Summer was clearly embarrassed at being corrected but uncowed by her older brother. "You know what I mean, Clay. I don't want *her* in my house."

"It isn't your house," Clay replied with brutal frankness. "Bitter Creek belongs to all of us. Now stop being a horse's ass and welcome Libby."

"You hate the Grayhawks as much as I do," Summer said. "Maybe even more!"

"I have no fondness for King. And I'm mad as hell

that North managed to put us in this position. But Libby is the mother of my child, and I won't see her treated rudely by my family."

Libby's heart swelled as she listened to Clay defend her. Was this what it would have been like if she'd told him the truth about how much she'd loved him twenty years ago? Clay not backing down? Clay shielding her from his family's animosity?

It was a lovely thought.

But Clay's defense of her had done nothing to soften his family's feelings toward her. If she spent the night in this house, it would be over the objections of the four people sitting on this porch. The expression on Ren's face wasn't antagonistic, but it was clear her loyalty was to Blackjack, and that she wasn't going to greet Libby until Blackjack did. And Libby was pretty sure Blackjack wouldn't.

"You know, Clay," Libby said, as she looked from face to face on the porch, meeting the unfriendly eyes of first Billy, then Summer, and finally Blackjack, "I've always wanted to sleep under the same roof as a president. Why don't we stay at the cabin?"

Clay was clearly startled by her about-face. "You don't want to stay here?"

Libby met his gaze with shining eyes and said, "No. I've already got what I wanted from this visit. Let's go."

Clay had defended her against his family. Chosen

her over his family. It meant more to her than she could ever tell him in words. But she could show him, if they were alone. Suddenly, she wanted to be away from here. "Come on," she said, reaching for Clay's hand. "Show me the bed where Eisenhower slept."

Libby watched as Clay shot everyone on the porch a look of disdain. "You're my family. I expected better of you than this."

Summer broke first under his stare. "Clay, I—"

"We'll be at the cabin," he said, cutting her off. "Don't bother us. We don't want your company."

Libby turned quickly, before Clay's family could see the satisfaction she felt at how he'd turned the tables on them. Then she felt Clay's warm, protective arm around her shoulder, escorting her away from the Castle.

Libby had always thought that crossing the legendary threshold of the Castle would be a life-altering event. It would mean the demons of the past had been conquered. That she could banish them from memory.

Tonight, she hadn't set one foot inside the Castle, and yet, Clay had slain all her dragons. Maybe she was never supposed to cross the fabled threshold. Maybe she was destined to find the inner peace she'd been seeking in a pair of fierce gray eyes.

"This is it," Clay said as he stepped into his family's hunting cabin ahead of Libby and turned on the lights. He set down his overnight bag and hers, and turned to see her reaction to the two-story log home in the middle of the South Texas prairie. Filled with leather and wood and antlers, the walls lined with glass and wood cases filled with guns of all kinds, it seemed more like something built in the 1850s than the 1950s.

The cabin was equipped with state-of-the-art security devices to ensure the safety of dignitaries, including the president of the United States, who'd stayed there. Since the shoot-out at the cabin several years past, between Blackthornes and Creeds and a rogue FBI agent, it had been used primarily as a family retreat.

"I wondered what we would find behind all that concealing shrubbery," Libby said with a smile. "It's . . . quaint."

Clay smiled and headed for the fireplace, where Summer and Billy kept a fire laid, and set a match to it. Then he and Libby removed the sheets that covered the furniture when the house wasn't in use. Clay settled into the brass-studded leather sofa centered before the fire and patted the seat beside him. "Come sit down."

Libby hesitated, then joined him.

"I was proud of what you did," Clay said.

Libby arched a brow. "Attacking your family?"

"Standing up for yourself," Clay said. "it made me wonder . . ."

"What might have been?

"Yeah," Clay admitted.

"Me, too," she said quietly.

A comfortable silence descended as they watched the fire begin to crackle and spit.

Clay hadn't tried to make conversation during the short flight in his Citation from Austin to the family airstrip near the cabin, and Libby had seemed content to remain silent. He hadn't wanted to take the chance that she would ask him about Kate and Jack. He didn't want to lie to her, and he thought there was a good chance she would cancel if she realized their trip to Bitter Creek had turned into a weekend on their own. But he couldn't put it off much longer.

Libby had to be told that when she'd chosen the cabin over the Castle, it meant she'd be spending the entire weekend alone with him.

Clay looked at the woman who'd held his heart in her keeping all these years and wondered what it was about Libby Grayhawk that had so captured his imagination. She wasn't beautiful. Her eyes were spaced too wide apart, and her chin was too pointed. She had a nice figure, with a small waist and trim hips, but she lacked the long legs he'd admired in both his late wife and his former fiancée.

But something indefinable about Libby had appealed to him from the first moment he'd laid eyes on her. Was it her feistiness? The sound of her bubbling laughter? Her enthusiasm for life? Her fearlessness? Or perhaps it was the fact that, like him, she was a survivor. Someone who would never shrink from life, but meet it head-on, fighting back against adversity and never giving up.

Physically, she'd changed over the past twenty years. There were lines from squinting against a strong sun sprayed at the corners of her eyes and brackets around her mouth where she smiled. And there were tiny wrinkles in her forehead, from worry, he supposed. All of which only made her more attractive in his eyes.

She started when she caught him staring at her.

"You're beautiful, Libby."

She seemed flustered for a moment, then thwarted his attempt to make the conversation personal by abruptly changing the subject. "I was surprised you decided to fly down here, after what happened to the last judge who presided over this trial."

Clay smiled and said, "I had my mechanics check everything carefully and then keep a close eye on the plane."

"So you might be in danger, after all?" Libby asked as she edged toward the opposite end of the couch, as far from him as she could get.

"I've made a lot of enemies as a prosecutor, and then as the attorney general for Texas and U.S. attorney general," Clay said, turning his body to face hers. "If I let threats worry me, I wouldn't be able to leave the house."

Libby looked around and said, "This cabin is so isolated we're either very safe or a very vulnerable target."

Clay pointed to the windows and said, "Bullet-proof glass." He pointed to the guns on the wall and said, "Plenty of ammunition to go with these."

Libby laughed. "I wonder if Kate arranged for us to stay here to make sure you'd be safe."

"I wouldn't put it past her," Clay admitted.

"Do you suppose she and Jack have arrived by now? Should we call them?"

The moment of truth had come. Clay took a deep breath and said, "Jack had to work this weekend. So Kate decided to stay in Austin."

Libby sat forward on the edge of the couch. Clay thought she looked ready to bolt and felt his stomach lurch. He hadn't realized until this moment how much he wanted this time with her. He wasn't sure what he hoped would happen over the weekend. But he was pretty sure if he let Libby walk out of his life this time, it would be forever.

She sat perched tensely on the couch, her blue eyes never leaving his. "You came knowing Kate and Jack wouldn't be here?"

Clay nodded, cleared his throat and said, "Yeah."

"Why?"

Clay hadn't expected to be asked for an explanation, and he gave the excuse that seemed most logical.

"We still need to figure out how to separate those two."

Libby dropped her gaze so he couldn't see what she was thinking. He realized that if they were going to have any sort of chance to resolve things between them over the weekend, he was going to have to take the first step, so he added, "And I wanted to spend time with you."

He held his breath waiting for her to look up. When she finally did, what he saw in her eyes was distress.

"I haven't changed my mind, Clay. I'm not going to fall into your arms. Or into your bed."

Clay flushed. He'd been imagining exactly that scenario. In the past, he was sure, all he would have needed to do was beckon, and Libby would have come running. He'd certainly been holding all the cards. Things had definitely changed. Now he was the one wanting a relationship, and she'd put up a stone wall to keep him out.

He knew he ought to apologize for his past behavior, clear the air, make a clean breast of the things he'd realized about himself, explain why he'd been so unwilling to forgive. But it was so unusual for him to apologize—for anything—that he found the words "I'm sorry" caught in his throat.

"I was hoping you'd reconsider," he said instead.

Libby rose and crossed to the fireplace, putting her hands out to catch the warmth from the fire. "No."

Clay crossed to stand behind her. He put his hands on her shoulders and felt her tense. "I want another chance, Libby."

She eased herself free and turned to face him, her blond curls bouncing on her shoulders as she shook her head. "I'm not going to let you hurt me again, Clay."

"I don't want to hurt you. I've never wanted to hurt you."

She laughed scornfully. "Right."

"Maybe I did once upon a time," he corrected.

She crossed her arms and lifted her chin.

"A long time ago."

She tilted her head and glared up into his face.

"Maybe even more recently," he conceded. "But I had good reason."

Libby threw her hands up in apparent frustration. "Good reason? I was sixteen years old when I hurt you. I was in love. I thought being with me would ruin your life, so I lied to you. I've paid dearly for it every day since."

"I know."

"You know? You *know*?" Libby said, her voice sharp. Clay flinched.

She stepped deeper into his space, and Clay had to force himself to stand his ground. He resisted the urge to take hold of her arms, to keep her at a distance. He had to let her in. Finally. At last. If he wanted any kind of future with her, he had to hear what she had to say. And let himself feel her pain.

Except he had no idea how he was supposed to do that. He'd been catered to all his life, so he had no experience being empathetic. Partly, it was because he'd been his mother's spoiled, favorite child. Partly, it was because he was and always had been rich and hadn't needed to pander. Partly, it was because from a very early age he'd been in a position of power. People answered to him. He didn't answer to them.

How could he begin to comprehend what Libby had been through over the past twenty years? How could he expect her to forgive him for walking away from her? How was he going to convince her that he'd never stopped loving her even when he'd been married to one woman and gotten engaged to another? All he could do was try.

"I'm listening," he said.

Libby opened her mouth to speak and shut it again. "Talking isn't going to solve anything." She backed up two steps, then crossed to where he'd dropped the two overnight bags, picked hers up and slung the strap over her shoulder. "Will you fly me out of here? Or shall I take the car?"

"Don't leave. Please. We won't talk about us. I won't even mention us. We'll focus on Kate and Jack."

Libby pursed her lips. "I don't want you thinking that if I stay here I'm capitulating to—"

"I wouldn't think that," Clay said. But he now had some idea exactly how thick and how high she'd built that stone wall to keep him out.

"I am concerned about Kate," she said. "Did you know I went with her to try on wedding dresses?"

"I'll bet she was beautiful."

Libby frowned. "Beautiful. And flippant."

"Flippant?" Clay crossed and slipped the luggage strap from Libby's shoulder and set the bag back on the ground. "By the way, how about something to drink? There's a bar here with anything you want, and I'm sure Summer and Billy keep the refrigerator stocked."

"Something hot," Libby said, rubbing her arms against an apparent chill.

With another woman, Clay would have stepped closer and warmed her himself. But Libby had set boundaries he had to respect. Boundaries he had to hope she would relax as the weekend progressed. He thought of all the pressure he normally brought to bear when he wanted something and was determined to have it. None of those tried-and-true methods were going to work with Libby.

He was going to have to humble himself. He was going to have to grovel—if necessary. He was going to have to give Libby the chance to hurt him as badly as he'd hurt her all those years ago. And pray that he could free the love she'd once felt for him from whatever deep, dark place she'd buried it.

Clay felt his stomach turn over. So much was at stake. He felt like he was walking through a minefield, and any wrong move could end in disaster. He headed for the kitchen to get something hot for Libby to drink, and she followed after him.

"Hot tea? Coffee? Cocoa?" he said, as he looked through the cupboards.

"Cocoa sounds great," she said. "Let me help."

Clay was surprised how easily they moved around the kitchen together, searching through cupboards and drawers to find what they needed to make the packages of instant cocoa he'd found.

"Porch swing?" he asked when they each had a cup of cocoa in hand.

"Sure," she replied.

She followed him to the wide back porch, which had a second-story veranda above it, from which hung a white wooden swing. He didn't turn on a porch light, so the only light came through the screen door from the kitchen. He sat down on the swing, setting his cocoa on a nearby table, and waited for her to sit beside him. Instead, she settled in one of a pair of pecan rockers that were situated nearby.

Clay told himself he couldn't expect miracles. That he had to be patient, even though patience wasn't one of his virtues. He had to consider Libby's wants and needs—and her fear that he would hurt her again. Maybe the best thing was to keep the focus of any discussion on Kate and Jack and let things between the two of them happen as they would.

"Tell me about the wedding dresses," he said.

Libby balanced her cocoa in both hands and set the rocker in motion with her foot before she spoke. "I know she's a grown-up. She's in college, after all. But when I saw her in those wedding gowns, I couldn't ignore the fact that she isn't my little girl anymore. Soon she'll be married and on her own."

"And you'll be all alone," Clay said, when she didn't say it herself.

"My life is very satisfying," Libby said.

"Even without a man in it," Clay finished again.

"Yes. Infinitely more comfortable, I think, than yours without a woman in it."

Clay smiled. "Touché. Tell me about Kate being flippant when she was trying on dresses. What was that all about?"

"Trying on wedding gowns should be fun," Libby said, keeping the rocker moving, making a pleasant creaking sound against the wooden porch. "But Kate didn't seem to really care whether she found a dress she liked or not."

"Which means what?" Clay asked.

"I think she was flippant about trying on dresses because she's having second thoughts about getting married."

"That's good news," Clay said. "Isn't it?"

"Maybe. What if Jack didn't have to work this weekend? What if they've decided to spend the weekend together in Austin, and they let us come here because they didn't want us around?"

"There's another scenario that also works," Clay said. "What if Jack having to work is an excuse Kate gave us because she was too embarrassed to admit he opted out of a weekend with her and her parents?"

"That's certainly a possibility," Libby said. "I just wish we knew which scenario is the right one. I hate to think of Kate being hurt, but I'd rather Jack dumped her now than after they're married."

"I hate to think of my daughter being a fling for some playboy ex–football hero," Clay said.

"Would you rather he married her?" Libby said wryly.

Clay grimaced. "I suppose when you put it that way, a fling has its merits."

Libby laughed. "I can't believe we're discussing our daughter's love life."

"Better hers than ours." Clay hadn't meant to sound embittered, but he was having a hard time biting his tongue. He was a man of action. It was hard to pretend there was nothing wrong, hard to pretend they were just two ordinary parents discussing their child.

The silence grew until Clay realized he could hear the cicadas and the rustle of the wind through the bushes and the distant lowing of the Santa Gertrudis cattle his family raised on the ranch.

He rose from the swing and crossed the porch to sit on the railing that surrounded it, closer to Libby. "I miss being here."

"Didn't you tell me you left Bitter Creek to go to college and never came back? If you liked it so much—"

"Not being the eldest son, there was never any chance I was going to be the one running Bitter Creek," he said. "Trace was always destined for that role. It's ironic that he ended up running a cattle station in Australia and Summer, the youngest of us, and the only girl, ended up in charge of the ranch."

"Would you have wanted to be a cattleman?" Libby asked.

"I might have enjoyed it. As I said, I wasn't given much choice."

"You could have found a job that would keep you in Levi's and boots," Libby said. "Owen became a Texas Ranger."

Clay had sometimes envied his twin. He certainly respected him. "My mother had different plans for me."

"I never think of you as someone who would let someone else run his life."

"I don't think I realized my becoming president was her dream and not mine, until I was a long way down the road to achieving that goal," Clay admitted.

"I never wanted to become a mother," Libby said into the silence. "I did enough mothering as a child in my father's household to last me a lifetime."

Clay worked to keep the shock off his face. Before he could figure out how to respond to such a momentous statement, she was speaking again.

"I mean, there was never a mother figure in my life to make me think that being a mother was a good thing. King married my mother, a woman he didn't love, and she presented him with two offspring, North and me. When she died—of heartbreak, I sometimes think—he married his second wife.

"Lenora didn't last long. Once she realized King wasn't going to open his wallet for her, and that he expected her to take care of two little kids, she asked for an annulment. King married Sassy next, and you know how that turned out. She took Breed with her when she left.

"King's third wife, Jill—or fourth, depending on how you count—presented him with three children in five years, my half brothers and sister, Taylor, Gray, and Victoria. But King's eye was already wandering, and Jill decided in a fit of pique to divorce him. Of course, she didn't want anything to do with King's Brats, who'd become infamous in the neighborhood for causing trouble. She left them behind when she hit the road with a big divorce settlement.

"I stepped into the role of mother. Until I met you, and had a daughter of my own."

"Why didn't your father hire a nurse or a nanny or whatever people do—"

"When they don't want anything to do with their children?" Libby said.

Clay shrugged. "People who can't be home with their kids need outside help. There's no crime in—"

"I know that," Libby interrupted. "King did hire a nanny. But there's a big difference between a caretaker and a mother."

Clay arched a brow, "So the nanny was the caretaker, and you became the mother?"

"Someone had to love them!" she said fiercely.

"Who loved you?" Clay said quietly.

It took her a while to answer. "King loved us all . . . in his own way. When he married Sassy, I thought maybe I'd been given a reprieve. Before Sassy started drinking, she was a wonderful mother to all of us. Then Breed was born, and that was the end of that."

Libby fell silent.

Clay tried to imagine how awful it must have been for Libby to lose her own mother so young, and then have King divorce the only one of his wives who seemed interested in mothering. "I'm sorry you—"

"It's all water under the dam," Libby interrupted. "I didn't tell you all that so you'd feel sorry for me."

Clay wondered how he'd managed to spend the better part of a summer with Libby twenty years ago and never understand the kind of life she'd led before she'd entered his. "Then why are you telling me all this now?"

"I want you to understand why I hated you—your family, all Blackthornes—so much. Why I seduced you. How I could plot and plan and manipulate to make you fall in love with me, knowing every minute I was with you that I intended to walk away, leaving you brokenhearted—if such a thing was possible. I didn't know if you even had a heart."

Libby set her untouched cocoa down on a small table between the two rockers and scooted forward in the rocker. "Jackson Blackthorne had stolen Eve De-Witt away without a care for the heartbreak he left behind. I blamed Blackjack—North and I blamed him—for how unhappy our mother was. And for the succession of mothers that came and went, women with whom King couldn't be happy, because they weren't Eve DeWitt."

"I still don't understand why the Blackthornes are to blame for King's behavior," Clay said.

"Don't you see? Your father never loved Eve De-Witt, even when he married her," Libby accused.

"And she committed suicide when she realized your father was going to leave her for the woman he'd loved since the day he married her. The only time I ever saw King cry was the day he heard Eve was dead."

"Lots of people don't end up with the one they love," Clay said. "Look at us."

"Yes, look at us," Libby said. "You certainly went on with your life without a thought of me."

"That's not fair," Clay said. He hesitated, then added, "And it's not true."

Libby's brow furrowed. "If I'm not mistaken, the only thing that kept you from getting married within months of our separation was the bride getting murdered before the wedding."

Clay swore.

Libby covered her face with her hands. "I can't believe I said that."

"It's true," Clay said through tight jaws. "And it's true I married Giselle, and it's true I got engaged to her sister, Jocelyn. That doesn't mean I stopped loving you."

"Oh, please!" Libby said, rising from her rocker and standing with her hands on her hips confronting Clay.

He rose and met her toe-to-toe, his hands on his hips. "You wanted to break my heart? Well, goddammit, you did! There, are you happy?"

Libby looked stunned. "You went on with your life. You got married. You—"

"So did King. So did my father. That doesn't mean we didn't love other women the whole time."

Libby put a hand to her brow, as though she were dizzy. Clay reached out a tentative hand to support her and was suprised when she took a step forward and leaned her cheek against his chest. He felt a swell of emotion in his throat when her hands went around his waist and she held him tight. He could feel she was trembling. His arms circled her and he pulled her close, offering the comfort that he hadn't been able to give her twenty years before.

"This is all such a mess," she murmured. "What are we doing here this weekend, Clay? It isn't possible to go back."

"We can go forward," Clay said.

Libby leaned back and looked up at him, searching his features for something he hoped she would find there. "In what world?" she asked. "My home and my work is in Wyoming. Your home and your work is in Texas."

"I don't have to be a federal judge. I can quit."

"I'd never ask you to do that."

"Does that mean you'd be willing to move to Austin?"

"What would I do with myself?"

Clay knew what he wanted to say, but he didn't have the courage to say it. *We could have more children. We could raise them together.* Instead he said, "Be my wife."

She pulled herself from his arms and took a step back. "I think we've already established that I wouldn't be happy passing canapes."

"I don't want a hostess. I want a wife."

"I need something to keep me busy. I need—"

"What about more children? We could—"

"Are you out of your mind? I'm thirty-five years old."

"Last I heard, women your age are still bearing children."

Even in the scant stream of light from the kitchen doorway, Clay could see her face was beet red.

"Who says I want more kids?" Libby demanded.

"I don't know if you do or you don't," Clay said. "But I'd like a chance to raise kids with you."

Libby shook her head. "It wouldn't work, Clay."

He took the steps necessary to catch her up in his arms and pull her close. He looked down into her up-turned face and said, "Why not?"

"We don't even know if we can live together. By the time we find that out, I *will* be too old—"

"The only thing that kept us apart all these years was my stubborn pride," Clay said. "Even though we haven't lived together, even though I wasn't able to be with you when Kate was born, we've managed to get along all these years. Even if we decided never to see each other again, we'd always have Kate to bind us together. So why shouldn't we reach for

the gold ring, Libby? Why shouldn't we make ourselves happy?"

"Marrying me would make you happy?" she asked
skeptically.

"I know this is sudden—"

Libby barked a sarcastic laugh. "Unbelievable, is
more like it."

She shifted to be free, and he let her go.

"We were always good together, Libby. What was
there between us twenty years ago is still there."

"I doubt that," she said.

"Let me prove it."

She lifted a brow. "You want to make love to me?"

He was dying to make love to her. But he didn't
think eagerness was going to help his argument any.
"Yes."

"And this will prove what, exactly?"

That we're soul mates. Clay thought it, but he felt
foolish saying it. He wasn't a romantic. He didn't believe in romantic nonsense. He was too practical a
man for that. But he had the example of men around
him—his own father and King Grayhawk came to
mind—who had loved one woman, and one woman
only, for the entirety of their lives. He'd never been
able to stop wanting Libby, even when he'd hated her
for deceiving him. And he'd long since admitted that
it was only because he'd loved her so much that he'd
been so devastated by her betrayal.

"Let me make love to you," he said. "Afterward, if you still think there's no hope for us, I'll take you back to Austin."

He watched her face to see what she thought of his proposal. She seemed wary, skeptical, perhaps fearful. He felt his heart sink, because none of those emotions suggested the answer he wanted to hear. "Well, Libby? What's your answer?"

"Take me to bed, Clay."

15

The more Libby had listened to Clay, the more desolate she'd felt. He'd said he wanted another chance with her. He'd said he wanted to have children with her and raise them together. If Clay had recognized the truth and forgiven her—or if she hadn't been so immature—twenty years ago, she would have run pell-mell into his arms. But so much of her life had been lived alone, Libby wasn't sure she could go back and pick up where they'd left off. She was older now. And wiser. More cynical. Less trusting.

She was also aware of what was at risk. What if she'd been yearning all these years for a relationship that had died a natural death when Clay had walked away? Would they be able at this late date to forge a life together? More to the immediate point, could Clay's lovemaking possibly be as wonderful now as it was in her memories?

Libby had been a virgin when she'd lain with Clay the first time. What if she'd glorified their time together? What if the special something that had existed between them during those youthful, halcyon days had been extinguished over time?

She glanced sideways at Clay, looking for the physical changes time had wrought. His body was still lean and strong, his shoulders broad and powerful. But the silver in his hair, the deep parentheses that bracketed his mouth, and the crow's feet at the corners of his eyes attested to the years that had passed.

What if making love to him disappointed her? Or—she shuddered at the thought—disappointed him? That would be a great laugh, the two of them languishing for each other when the spark that had brought them together had long since gone out. They'd hurt each other so badly then. Could they come together with love now?

It was frightening to make herself vulnerable. Had Clay truly forgiven her in his heart? Could she forgive him?

"Twenty years is a long time," she said as Clay led her upstairs and down the hall.

"Too long," he said. He opened the door to a moonlit bedroom with twelve-foot ceilings and an enormous canopied four-poster bed.

When Clay reached for the light switch inside the door, Libby put her hand over his. "No lights."

"I want to see you," he said.

Libby laughed softly and repeated, "Twenty years is a long time."

He smiled and said, "There are candles on the mantel. How about if I light them?"

Candlelight sounded very forgiving. "All right," she said.

Libby waited by the door as Clay made his way across the shadowy bedroom and lit a half dozen candles of odd sizes on the wooden mantel. He also bent to set a match to the fire that had been laid in the stone fireplace.

Libby waited at the doorway until Clay returned and stood before her. The flickering candlelight made the moment seem too romantic, too fraught with expectations. "I don't think I can do this," she said.

"We won't know until we try."

"Does that mean you're as nervous—as scared—as I am?"

"I thought Grayhawks were fearless," he said as he tucked a blond curl behind her ear. "Blackthornes don't fear anything."

"Kiss me, Clay."

His lips were soft against hers, but his hands grasped her waist as though he was afraid she would run.

Libby gripped Clay's forearms, feeling the power of muscle and sinew, and the trembling that revealed he recognized the danger in what they were doing. How awful to replace treasured memories with an awkward coupling. And what were the chances they could match the wonder of those summertime afternoons when they were young and carefree and so much in love?

Libby broke the kiss and said, "Wait."

"For what?" Clay asked, his breathing unsteady. "I never expected this to be easy."

Libby was surprised to hear Clay acknowledge the trepidation that she felt. "Then why don't we wait until—"

"I don't think waiting—"

Libby put her fingertips to Clay's lips, astonished at the quiver of feeling even that small touch caused. Maybe this was possible. But she still wanted more time. "I'd like to spend the night with you in that bed. But I don't want to do more than talk."

She saw the crinkles form at the corners of Clay's eyes as he smiled, and felt his lips curve under her fingertips. "Agreed. With one condition."

"What's that?" Libby said warily.

"We do it naked."

"What's the point of that?" Libby asked.

"It'll give you a chance to get over any shyness you might feel about—"

"Fine," Libby interrupted, flushing at the thought of exposing her thirty-five-year-old body to Clay's gaze.

Clay lifted an eyebrow. "I expected you to argue more."

"I want to see you. I might even want to touch."

"Uh-uh," Clay said. "No touching, unless you remove the ban on sex."

Libby wrinkled her nose. "We used to be able to touch without having sex. We used to kiss for hours—"

"I was a younger and stronger man," Clay said with a wry smile.

"Are you suggesting you don't have the stamina—"

"All right. Fine. But if you can touch, I can touch."

"No intercourse," Libby said firmly.

"How are we defining intercourse?" Clay asked. "Is this the presidential definition or—"

Libby laughed. "It's anything likely to produce—"

"An orgasm?"

"A baby," Libby said.

"That leaves a lot of room for . . . play."

"Oh, I hope so," Libby said with a teasing smile.

When Clay started to unbutton his shirt, Libby stepped forward and moved his hands away. "I want to do it."

His breathing became ragged as she stepped closer, brushing her hands across his bare flesh as she shoved the crisp white button-down Oxford-cloth shirt off his shoulders. Libby reached for Clay's tooled western belt, unbuckled it, and slowly pulled it free. When she reached for the snap on his jeans, he caught her wrists and said, "My turn."

Libby held out her arms as Clay unbuttoned her cuffs, then her blouse, before shoving it off her shoulders and down her arms. She wasn't wearing a belt, and when he reached for the button on her jeans, she said, "Boots first."

"You're right," he agreed.

A pair of wing chairs were arranged in front of the fire, and Clay gestured toward them. Libby sat down in one, and Clay gestured for her to give him her foot. He pulled off one boot, then the other, dropping each of them onto the cowhide that covered the wood floor.

"Your turn," Libby said. Clay sat and Libby took the booted foot he extended, straddled his leg with her back to him, then hooked her palms around the heel and pulled. When the first boot was off, she followed the same procedure with the other, except Clay put his socked foot on her rump and gave a little shove to help.

She dumped the boot, then turned, and as Clay was rising, pressed a flattened hand against his furred chest to push him back into the chair. She sat on his lap, her folded legs on either side of his hips. She sat back far enough that there was no direct contact where Clay might have wanted it most.

She shoved her hands through his springy hair, eas-

ing a curl off his forehead. "I've been wanting to do
that for ages."

He wrapped his hands in her shoulder-length hair
and pulled her face down to his. "Ditto."

Their mouths were close enough that Libby could
feel Clay's breath against her cheek.

"Kiss me, Libby," he said.

His voice sounded like a rusty gate. His eyes invited
her to take a chance, and Libby closed her eyes and
leaned close until her lips touched his.

"Ouch!" she said, jumping back as a painful elec-
trical spark arced between them.

Clay laughed and said, "I guess the spark's still
there."

"Scientific phenomenon," she said. "Socks brushing cowhide, creating friction which—"

Clay captured her nape and pulled her down so his
mouth covered hers. Libby felt like she'd dived into
warm, welcoming waters. It was an easy kiss, without
demands, a "How are you? I'm feeling fine," kind of
kiss. She broke it to gasp a breath and sat up to stare
down into Clay's eyes. His gaze was interested, but not
aroused.

"What would you like to talk about?" he asked, his
hands settling high on her jean-clad hips.

Libby rested her hands on his shoulders, because
she wanted to feel the play of muscle and bone, and
said, "Do you think Bomber Brown is guilty?"

Clay laughed and shook his head. "You know I can't discuss that."

"If we were together, if we were a couple, you'd be coming home to me after a day in court, and I'd expect you to let off steam. How do you usually do that?"

"I usually play a game of squash," Clay said. "After I whack the ball around for an hour, I don't feel so much like bashing heads together."

"And you feel like that—like bashing heads—after a day in court?"

"Not so much as a judge," Clay said. "I just listen to the evidence. I don't have to develop it against a defendant. But yes, work as a prosecutor was stressful."

"How much of your life would you be able to share with me?" Libby asked, finding the curve of Clay's ear fascinating. She traced it with her fingertips and tasted the lobe with her lips and teeth. "I mean, if we lived in the same house."

"Ah," Clay groaned.

Libby stopped what she was doing and met Clay's gaze. "Ah? That much, huh?"

Her smile was cut off when his hands slid around to her buttocks and he pulled her close, so her heat was pressed tight against his hardness. She framed his cheeks with her palms, then leaned down and pressed her lips to his. It was a close-mouthed kiss, a simple meeting of warm flesh. And yet she felt butterflies take delighted flight in her stomach.

"I've been thinking about what work I could do here in Texas," she murmured against his lips.

He put his hands on her shoulders and eased her back so they could look into one another's eyes. "I'm listening."

"There are lots of hunting leases on ranches around here—for deer and turkey and javelinas. I think some of those businessmen from back east coming out here to Texas might enjoy having a guide."

"You've lived in Wyoming your whole life," Clay said. "Can you be happy waking up without the Tetons?"

"All I would need to wake up to is you."

"Ah," Clay said again.

Libby rubbed her silk bra against Clay's chest, purring in her throat, like a cat with a bowl of cream.

"How about if we get rid of this?" Clay said as he unsnapped the front clasp of her bra and slid it down her arms.

Libby felt self-conscious. She lowered her gaze shyly. These weren't the perky breasts she'd had at sixteen. Then she felt Clay's warm hands cup her breasts and watched her nipples peak, amazingly perky, as he brushed them with his thumbs.

"Ah," she purred. Libby rubbed herself against him, feeling the rough hairs on his chest against her tender breasts. She wrapped her arms around his neck and found his mouth with hers.

Clay made her welcome, opening his mouth to her intrusion, and returning the favor. She remembered this. How they fit together. How good he tasted, how right. How he seemed to know where to touch her with his hands, as he made love to her with his mouth. She felt passion rising between them, and wanted more. Needed more.

She felt his hands gentling her, his mouth disengaging to give their struggling lungs a chance to catch up.

"Wow," he said, with a breathless laugh. "That brings back memories."

"Good ones, I hope."

"The best." Clay nestled her body against his, tucking her head under his chin and said, "I have a question for you."

"Shoot," she said on a gust of air.

"When did you know you loved me? I mean, the summer we met. You obviously plotted to seduce me and leave me high and dry. When did your plans change?"

Libby tried to lift her head, but Clay captured her nape and kept her tucked close.

"I'm not trying to put you on the spot," he said in a voice that rumbled against her ear. "I'm just curious."

"I don't know, exactly," she said at last. "One moment I was planning the destruction of a Blackthorne. The next, I was willing to go against everything I'd al-

ways known was true just to be with you. I can't believe you never suspected how young I was."

She heard Clay make a sound in his throat before
he said, "I was surprised by your virginity, that's for
damned sure. The way you flirted, the way you kissed,
I never suspected you were untouched. When we
made love, when everything I did seemed to surprise
you, that's when I began to wonder if you might be
younger than you'd told me."

"Why didn't you confront me?" Libby asked. "I
would have caved, I think, and spilled the beans, if
you'd acted the least bit suspicious."

"I don't think I wanted to know," Clay admitted. "I
think I was already in love with you."

This time when Libby raised her head to look into
Clay's eyes, he released her to do so.

"You loved me?" she said, searching his eyes for the
truth.

"If you'll recall, I was willing to marry you when
you told me you were pregnant."

"I thought that was just—"

"That wasn't nobility or responsibility or even political self-preservation. That was me wanting to spend
the rest of my life with you. Believe it or not, I was
thinking dynasty," Clay said with a self-deprecating
smile. "I had visions of little girls with your golden
curls. And little boys who looked like me."

"Kate has your gray eyes. And your dark hair. And your height. It's always been hard for me to look at her without thinking of you."

"She's you," Clay said, smoothing his hand over Libby's head and then twirling a curl around his finger. "Her fearlessness, her sense of adventure, her willingness to tackle anything—she got all that from you."

"I suppose, like any child, she's both of us," Libby conceded.

"The best of us," Clay amended.

"We were lucky. Maybe we should quit while we're ahead," Libby said, her lips quirking.

"I don't need to have more children," Clay said. "I just thought it would be something we would both enjoy."

"I always wanted a little boy. And I would love to have another little girl," Libby said.

"How do you think Kate would feel about a sister or brother?" Clay asked.

A tiny V appeared between Libby's brows. "I think she'd be ecstatic if we got married. I'm not sure what she'd think of us having children."

"She'll be too busy with her own family, if she ends up marrying Jack, to worry about us," Clay predicted.

"Oh," Libby said in a startled voice. "I just realized we're probably going to be grandparents about the time you're thinking of us becoming parents again."

"Like I said, kids are something I'd like, not something I have to have. What I have to have is you. In my life."

He put a finger under Libby's chin and lifted her face so he could kiss her. Libby enthusiastically returned the kiss, and it was some minutes later before they continued their conversation.

Libby's nose was pressed against Clay's skin, and she inhaled the scent of him, something dark and masculine. She slid her hands into the hair on his chest and said, "A month ago you were engaged to Jocelyn Montrose and planning to spend the rest of your life with her. What's changed between us to make you want me in your life?"

"When Jocelyn left, I was forced to take a hard look at why I'd gotten engaged to her in the first place."

"Aside from the fact she's stunningly beautiful?" Libby said sardonically.

"She is beautiful," Clay said. "And intelligent and charming. And marriage to me is the repayment she deserves for the sacrifice she's making for my family. But I can't do it. You see, I don't love her, and I never have. The person I love is you."

Libby inhaled sharply.

"Last year, when I was in Jackson Hole, when we spent so much time together, it gave me a glimpse of what life might have been like if we'd been able to marry when you got pregnant."

Clay swallowed hard. "It would have been so easy to forgive and forget, to reach for happiness together, even at that late date. But, as you may have noticed, Blackthornes aren't too big on forgiving. I chose to get mad all over again. I walked away from you and right into Jocelyn's waiting arms."

"I'm supposed to believe you're suddenly not mad anymore?" Libby asked.

"Having you shove me out the door, figuratively, was a big wake-up call," Clay said. "I realized the last place I wanted to be was on one side of any door with you on the other side."

"How do I know your anger won't come back to haunt us?" Libby asked.

Clay considered for a moment before he answered. "I can't promise it won't. I only want a chance for what your father, and my pride, took from us. The chance to enjoy the good times and survive the bad, just like any other couple. I care enough for you—" He cleared his throat and corrected, "I love you enough to be willing to compromise and work out our troubles together. The question you need to ask is whether you still love me enough to do the same."

"You make it sound so simple," Libby murmured, as she kissed Clay's shoulder, tasting the faint hint of salt.

"Life with you would never be simple," Clay said, kissing her temple in return. "But it would be worth the effort to spend my life with you."

"I don't know, Clay," Libby said. "I've been hurt so much, I'm not sure—"

"Give me a chance, Libby." Clay leaned down and kissed her mouth, urging a response, which Libby gave without thinking about what it might mean to him.

She broke the kiss and looked up into his eyes. "What happens to us if this doesn't work out? What happens if we try to recapture the magic—"

"That's where you're making your mistake," Clay interrupted.

Libby arched an inquiring brow. "My *mistake*?"

"We don't try to recapture the past. We carve out a future for ourselves starting here and now."

Libby stared at Clay, afraid to voice the thought that came to mind. *What are we together without our past?* It was memories of her summer with Clay that had kept her enthralled. Now Clay wanted her to forget the past? "I don't think it's possible to forget the past," she said, as she shifted so she was sitting on his lap, her legs hanging over the arm of the chair, her arms around his neck. "Moreover, I don't think I want to. I have a great many lovely memories, along with the not so lovely ones."

"How about forgetting the bad and remembering the good?" Clay asked with a smile meant to charm.

Libby was charmed, but she shook her head and said, "It's all jumbled up together. I'm not saying we can't go on from here. But what happened between us in the past is part of why I love you. And fear you."

Libby watched Clay's brow furrow with concern and hurried to explain, "If I allow myself to care, you have the power to hurt me again."

"If we're being honest, I think some pain is inevitable," Clay said. When Libby opened her mouth to protest, Clay quickly kissed her. "Think about it. I may say something in all innocence that you take in a hurtful way. The question is whether we'll be able to discuss the things that disturb and worry us about each other and change and compromise."

He made it seem so easy. "Why didn't we talk like this twenty years ago?" she asked.

"You were scared and hurt. I was angry and hurt. We're older and wiser now, and the wounds we inflicted on each other have had time to scab over."

Libby noticed he hadn't said the wounds had healed. Would they ever? Could they ever? "What would it take to heal those wounds?" she asked.

"Living happily ever after," Clay said.

Libby listened for cynicism in his voice, but didn't hear any. "I didn't think you believed in fairy-tale endings."

"I want to believe," Clay said.

"That isn't quite the same thing, is it?" Libby said.

Clay shrugged. "Close enough." He slid his arms

beneath her, scooted forward and stood up, heading for the bed.

"I'm not tired," Libby said archly, as Clay set her down on the bed.

He grinned and said, "I'm glad to hear it."

Libby laughed. "You're incorrigible."

"Does that mean I don't have to play by the rules?" Clay asked as he unbuttoned Libby's jeans, slid the zipper down and began tugging them off.

Libby lifted her bottom when Clay got that far and he slid the jeans down off her legs, leaving her in a pair of peach-colored bikini underwear that would have matched her bra, if she'd still been wearing it. He laid his hand on her flat belly and said, "I wanted to touch you here when you were carrying our child."

Libby felt tears spring to her eyes. "Oh, Clay. I'm so sorry."

"It's a dream I can still realize, Libby. I'm going to hold you to those kids."

"Your turn," she said, scrubbing at the tears with the backs of her hands. "Take off those jeans."

"You aren't going to take them off for me?" Clay asked.

"No," she said with a saucy smile. "I want to watch you strip."

Libby sat up in bed with her legs crossed and watched as Clay reached for the snap on his jeans, flicked it open, then slowly pulled the zipper down. He skinned off his jeans to reveal black, thigh-length jockey shorts, which cupped him very lovingly and left very little to the imagination.

"Come here," Libby said, patting the bed beside her.

"I'd rather be here," Clay said, pulling Libby's legs straight, shoving her back onto the bed, and pulling himself prone on top of her, supporting his upper body on his elbows. "I'm not too heavy?"

"No." Libby welcomed Clay's weight. She put her arms around his shoulders and ran her hands up into his hair. "Do you realize we've never made love in a bed?"

"I remember having my bare butt in the grass more than once," Clay said with a grin.

"You could have stayed on the blanket," Libby said.

"It would have cramped my style."

Libby laughed. "Maybe we should grab a blanket and head outdoors."

"I've grown to like my creature comforts," Clay said as he settled his hips more firmly in the cradle of her thighs. His hands played with her hair as he leaned down to kiss her deeply. He raised his head and kissed first one breast, and then the other. "You're so beautiful, Libby. So perfectly formed."

Libby blushed. If he thought her breasts were perfect, she wasn't going to argue with him. Or point out the silver stretch marks on her belly from her pregnancy. She gave herself up to the moment, breathing in the scent of him, feeling the weight of him, tasting the uniqueness of this particular man, with whom she'd fallen in love once upon a time.

Clay lifted his head from the breasts that had stolen his attention and looked down at her with stormy gray eyes. "I want to make love to you, Libby. I want to put myself deep inside you and—"

Libby kissed Clay to cut him off. What he said sounded wonderful. It was a fantasy she'd imagined for many years coming to sudden life. All she had to do was say yes, and her dreams would become reality.

"Let me love you," Clay murmured against her lips.

"We agreed—"

"We made the rules," Clay said. "We can change them. Say yes."

"Yes," Libby whispered. She wanted the dream to come true. Whatever the future held, she would handle it.

Clay's sudden smile lightened her heart. "I don't know where to start," he said, his smile becoming a grin of delight.

Libby laughed. "Kissing is always nice. Touching is way up there with my favorite things—"

Clay took possession of her mouth as his hands moved upward along her rib cage toward her breasts.

Libby's body arched toward him, as she reached to caress his shoulders and back.

"We don't need these anymore," Clay said, making short shrift of her bikini underwear.

"Or these," Libby said, returning the favor as she shoved Clay's briefs down over his buttocks far enough for him to kick them down and off.

"Are you protected?" Clay said.

"Does it matter?" Libby asked.

"Not to me," Clay said. "So long as you don't mind getting married sooner, rather than later."

"I don't remember hearing a proposal," Libby said. "Did I miss it?"

He stopped and looked deep into her eyes. "I love you, Libby. Will you do me the honor of becoming the next Mrs. Blackthorne?"

"That was hard to miss," Libby said.

"You haven't answered me."

"Ah," Libby said, responding to Clay's touch in a particularly sensitive spot.

"Was that a yes?" Clay asked.

"Ah," Libby said, as she reached between Clay's legs to return the favor.

There was no more discussion as Libby concentrated on touching Clay's body and enjoying his caresses in return. She'd forgotten what it felt like to be adored, to have her body treated as something precious, to have a man touch and taste as though she were the most special person in the world.

And she'd forgotten how it felt to find such pleasure in touching a man, feeling the play of muscle and sinew beneath firm male flesh, and the wonderful coarseness of Clay's beard as he rubbed his face against her breasts. And then there was the aphrodisiac she found most arousing of all—Clay's so evident desire for her.

Libby was almost embarrassed by how wet she was when Clay slid a finger inside her. His grunt of satisfaction made her smile to herself. It was plain that she wanted him, that there was no reason to wait any longer to join their bodies.

Clay met her gaze as he lifted her with both hands for his thrust. Libby rose to meet him, crying out as he sank to the hilt within her. His mouth caught her cry, and Libby arched toward him, wanting to give, wanting to receive.

Could it possibly have felt this good when she was sixteen? How could she have forgotten this enormous pleasure? Clay was doing things with his hands, with his tongue, with his body, that aroused her beyond bearing. She couldn't catch her breath. She couldn't catch up.

"Clay!" she cried.

"Come with me, sweetheart. Come on, love."

Love words in the midst of lovemaking. Clay hadn't used them when they were young. Maybe he hadn't known how. Maybe they'd seemed silly then. Libby relished them now. They raised her higher. They made her feel cherished.

He took his time coming to climax. Which gave her longer to find her own pleasure. Libby felt Clay's muscles tighten beneath her hands, felt her own body begin to spasm and followed his urging to leap into the abyss.

She heard him cry out at the ultimate moment, and exulted in the pleasure she'd brought him, and the joy she'd found herself. Their chests heaved in unison, gasping enough air to keep them alive. Clay sank onto the bed beside her and pulled her into his embrace, shoving her hair back from her forehead to plant a tender kiss in its place.

Libby smiled to herself as she brushed a dark curl back from Clay's sweaty forehead, too exhausted even to lift herself up to kiss him in return.

"How about sharing whatever it is you find so amusing," Clay said.

"That's joy you see, not amusement," Libby said. "I'm happy."

"Good," Clay said. "I'm happy, too. Especially when I consider the fact that we have an entire weekend ahead of us." He waggled his eyebrows, and Libby laughed aloud.

Clay leaned close and kissed her mouth ever so softly.

"What was that for?" Libby asked.

"Just because," Clay said. He turned her so her rear end was spooned into his midsection and settled his hands beneath her breasts.

A moment later, Clay realized she was asleep. And that she'd never responded to his proposal.

As Libby yawned and stretched in bed, her hand brushed against naked male flesh. Her eyes popped open, and she looked beside her. Clay was lying face-down, dead to the world. Libby smiled to herself. The two of them hadn't gotten out of bed at all Saturday except to nourish themselves, before returning to the activity that had left them so famished.

It was no surprise that she'd slept past noon today. They were both exhausted from trying to make up for twenty years in twenty-four hours. She didn't want this interlude to end. She'd been living in a cocoon of happiness since Friday. She didn't want to break out and rejoin the world.

Libby took a strand of her hair and used it to tickle Clay's nose. He brushed at it, grunted, and turned over. Libby grinned. The poor man was exhausted.

"Wake up, sleepyhead," she whispered as she kissed his shoulder. When he ignored her, she said, "Clay, we have to get up."

"I wouldn't be so sleepy if a certain sex maniac hadn't kept me up all night."

Libby laughed. "Open your eyes, Clay. It's morning." She glanced at the clock and said, "Actually, it's past noon."

Clay turned over to face her and pressed his mouth softly to hers. "And that's important because?"

"I'm hungry," she admitted.

Clay laughed. "I'm not surprised."

"And it's time to go back to the real world."

"Which reminds me. You never answered my question."

"What question?"

"Don't be coy," Clay said quietly, looking into her eyes. "Will you marry me, Libby?"

Libby opened her mouth to reply, but nothing came out. The worst thing was, she had no idea why she was hesitating. Clay seemed ready to commit himself to her. Their lovemaking over the weekend had exceeded even her happiest memories. Why couldn't she just say yes and move on to the next stage of her life?

"I'd like some time, Clay."

He laid her flat, then leaned over her, his brow deeply furrowed, his eyes full of concern. "I thought we'd already talked all this out, Libby. I thought you were willing to forgive and forget and move on."

"I thought I was, too," Libby said. "You must admit

this has all been very sudden, Clay. We've waited this long, a few more days shouldn't matter."

"How few?" Clay asked.

Libby eased away and sat up. Then, suddenly embarrassed, she pulled the sheet up to cover her nakedness. "As many as it takes."

"How many is that?" Clay persisted.

"Don't push me, Clay."

"I'm not pushing. I'm asking."

"And I'm telling you I want some more time to think."

Clay turned his back on her and reached for his briefs.

"What are you doing?" Libby asked.

"I'm giving you time to think."

"You're leaving?" Libby asked incredulously. "Right now?"

"I don't want to get my hopes up that you're going to marry me if you're not."

"I just asked for—"

"I know, you just need time," Clay interrupted. "So I'm giving it to you. I'll leave the car for you. You're welcome to stay here as long as you like. I'm flying back to Austin."

"What if I want to fly back with you?" Libby said.

"I'd rather you didn't," Clay said as he pulled on his jeans and sat down to put on his socks.

"Why not?"

"Because I'm afraid if we're alone together on that flight I'll say something I'll regret," Clay said, reaching for his shirt and slipping it on.

"You're angry because you're not getting what you want, when you want it," Libby said flatly.

"We Blackthornes are like that," Clay said as he tucked his shirt in, then zipped and snapped his jeans and buckled his belt.

Libby stared at Clay, who looked completely put together, while she was still sitting naked under a sheet. "I can't believe you're running away. Again."

"I'm not running away," Clay said. "I'm giving you the space you asked for. Believe me, if you come running in my direction, my arms will be opened wide to catch you."

Libby wanted to leap into his arms right then, but his abrupt, dismissive behavior seemed to preclude that sort of spontaneity. "I'm afraid if you leave, this interlude will be over."

"This interlude is over," Clay said. "But you still have the rest of your life. All you need to do is make up your mind to spend it with me."

As Libby stared, openmouthed, Clay strode across the sunlit room and out the door.

16

Kate paced the air-conditioned eight-by-eight-foot concrete space, then pounded on the thick metal door again. She thought she must be in one of the thousands of storage units around Austin that UT students used to store their stuff. This must be one of the better-built, more expensive ones, because no sound was getting past the heavy door. The air-conditioning vent was too small and too high to be an escape route. She'd been left here with plenty of water but no food. Even so, she was more frightened than hungry.

Kate wondered where she was, wondered what day it was. Surely the weekend was past. Surely her parents or Jack or someone would come looking for her and discover she was gone.

Why, oh why, hadn't she paid attention to Jack's warnings? She wondered if Donnie was one of Jack's suspects. She hoped Jack came looking for her and caught the little bastard coming here to retrieve her.

She would have settled for rescue from anyone, but she especially wanted to see Jack.

She wondered if he was thinking of her. She wondered if he'd tried to get in touch with her over the weekend after all, and had realized that she'd disappeared. That was wishful thinking. Even if Jack hadn't been able to reach her, he would have assumed she was with her family. Who assumed she was with Jack.

Kate realized she was totally responsible for the dire situation in which she found herself. She'd arranged it so she would be alone for the entire weekend. No one would be looking for her. Which had given Donnie the opportunity to kidnap her and not be discovered.

She wondered what he planned to do with her. She guessed maybe Donnie might want to exchange her for his own father. Based on what she saw on television, that demand wasn't going to be met. The police didn't negotiate with terrorists.

Her parents must be frantic.

At least they would be together.

Kate slumped down to the floor. She needed a plan for escape when Donnie finally showed up. The room was entirely empty except for a plastic jug of water. He'd taken away her shoes and belt, so she didn't have anything with which to fashion a weapon. The only idea she could come up with was to stand behind the door when he opened it and slam it back into his face.

Kate had no idea how much time had passed, because Donnie had also taken her calendar watch. Which had been a gift from her dad.

Kate sniffled.

She swiped at her nose with her sleeve. She couldn't afford to fall apart. She couldn't count on anyone else to help her. She had to help herself.

The sound of a key in the lock brought her scrambling to her feet. She raced for the door, but it opened before she could get behind it. She considered throwing herself at Donnie to knock him off balance, until she saw the very large gun pointed at her stomach, which did a quick somersault.

"Glad to see you decided to come back," she said, hands on hips. "I don't know what you think you're doing, Donnie, but—"

"Shut up and turn around."

"Why should I do anything you say?" Kate retorted. "You haven't treated me very well, considering—"

"I don't want to put a bullet in you, Kate, but I will. You have a chance to survive if you cooperate."

Kate didn't really believe he intended to let her live. But getting shot right now didn't sound like the way to go. She turned her back to Donnie, expecting him to tie her hands and lead her out to the car.

"Where are you taking me?" she asked.

"I need you to cooperate, Kate. This will all be over soon."

She turned her head to look at him over her shoulder, confused by his answer, and smelled the sickening scent of whatever it was he'd used the first time to put her out.

Kate exploded into action, whirling with fists extended to shove Donnie aside and break for the door. She took only one step into the blinding sunlight before the hand not holding the gun arced around her face, and he covered her entire face, eyes, nose, and mouth, with a soaked pad.

"Help!" Kate cried. Her plea was muffled behind his hand. Kate heard a gunshot, close enough that she could smell gunpowder. She waited to feel pain, but there was none. Before she lost consciousness, Kate thought she heard a familiar voice.

"Mom?" she croaked. Then everything went black.

Libby woke early on Monday morning. Alone in her bed at the Four Seasons in Austin. She groaned and turned over. Why did she always have to make everything so difficult? Why couldn't she just do things the easy way? She couldn't believe she'd let Clay walk out the door and leave her at his family's hunting cabin after he'd proposed marriage.

She'd had a lot of time to think yesterday on the long drive back to Austin. She hadn't wanted to talk to anyone Sunday night. Not Clay. Not Kate. Not North. She'd simply retreated to her room to lick her wounds. And catch up on all the sleep she'd missed over the weekend.

Libby stretched. She wasn't going to sit around this hotel room moping. She would know the right decision to make about her future when she knew it. Until then, she would work on separating Kate and Jack. Libby would have a heart-to-heart with her daughter and point out the difficulties of marrying someone she hardly knew. It ought to be easy to make her argument for waiting to marry when she pointed out the pitfalls that she and Clay had run into, even though they'd known each other for years.

Libby hunted down her cell phone and called her daughter, hoping she'd be able to reach Kate and make arrangements to get together today. She wasn't exactly surprised when Kate didn't answer. Apparently, Kate and Jack had opted for a weekend alone somewhere. Perhaps they hadn't allowed their idyll to end yet. Libby hoped her daughter was doing better negotiating romantic waters than she'd done herself. She left a message asking Kate to call her back.

Then she called Clay, even though she hadn't yet made up her mind what to tell him. Luckily, he didn't answer his phone, either.

"Hello, Clay," she said when his voice message ended. "You can contact valet parking at the Four Seasons to pick up your car."

Libby made a final call to her brother North. Even

though she expected him to be out working on the ranch, she called the house, because she knew he didn't carry a cell phone with him. To her surprise, he answered.

"I didn't expect to reach you," Libby said.

"Then why did you call?"

"I wanted to talk to you, I just didn't— Never mind," she said. "I wondered how you and Jocelyn are getting along."

"Fine. Are you all right, Libby?"

Libby cleared her throat and said, "Clay asked me to be his wife."

North hesitated for so long, Libby asked, "Are you still there?"

At last he said, "Are congratulations in order?"

"I told him I needed more time to think," Libby said.

"I'd think twenty years would be plenty of time to think," North retorted. "Do you want him, or not, Libby? That shouldn't be such a difficult question."

"It's a big decision. I don't want to make a mistake."

"Clay doesn't strike me as a patient man. When were you planning to give him an answer?"

"When I figure out what answer I want to give," Libby said with asperity.

"Why did you call me?" North asked.

Libby sighed. She knew better than to ask, but she asked anyway. "What do you think I should do?"

"It's your life, Libby."

She'd known he would say as much. North had always been there for her, but he'd never tried to push her in one direction or another.

"Call me if you need me, Libby."

Which was North's way of saying the conversation was over. Libby said, "Good-bye, North," and disconnected the call.

Libby stood a long time in the shower. And remembered the shower she and Clay had taken together at the cabin. By the time she turned off the water, her body was fully aroused. She quickly toweled herself off and got out of the steamy room.

Libby had just finished dressing when someone knocked on the door to her hotel room. It was too early to be the maid. And she hadn't ordered room service. She hurried to answer the knock, thinking it might be Clay, telling her he'd made a terrible mistake walking out on her yesterday. Then she realized she still had no answer for him. Libby took a deep breath to calm herself, then opened the door.

But it wasn't Clay.

Libby recognized the boy holding the gun close by his side. He was Bomber Brown's son. The one Kate had befriended.

Donnie Brown gestured with the gun for Libby to step back into the room. He followed her inside and let the door close quietly behind him, then turned to flip the security lock.

Libby stared at the silver gun barrel pointed right at her heart. "What do you want, Donnie?" she asked, stunned.

"I want you to walk downstairs with me without making a scene or drawing any attention to yourself, ma'am."

Libby noted the inconsistency between the boy's courtesy and his menacing voice. He wasn't tall, and she noticed the large gun seemed heavy in his hand. If she could distract him, she thought she might be able to overpower him and take it away.

"I can see what you're thinking," Donnie said. "And that would be a mistake. If you don't cooperate, your daughter is going to suffer for it."

Libby's heart leaped to her throat. "Where is Kate? Is she all right?"

"I have her tucked away safe and sound," Donnie said. "Just come quietly, and I'll take you to her."

Libby started to move toward the door and Donnie said, "Don't forget your purse."

Libby picked it up, hoping she'd get a chance to use the cell phone inside.

Then Donnie said, "Leave your cell phone here."

Libby took it out of her purse and dropped it on the bed. She looked at Donnie and said, "I'll do whatever you say. Just don't hurt my daughter."

"Be quiet, and do exactly as I say. This'll all be over soon."

*   *   *

When Kate woke up she was somewhere else, a smaller, darker place. She was tied hand and foot and gagged. She could see a light under the door and she could tell the floor was made of something light and shiny like the marble on the courthouse floors. She was lying on something that was cutting into her back and could feel something heavy on top of her, crushing her stomach. She scooched an inch or so closer to the light under the door, which was all she could manage, and looked down to see what was causing the problem.

Kate's breath caught in her throat.

She was wearing some sort of vest, and it was covered with blocks of something with wires attached that she was pretty sure were explosives. She carefully lay back down and examined the vest closely, looking to see how she might get it off.

It snapped closed down the front.

Kate tried pulling her legs up to see if she could get her tied hands under her butt and around to the front of her. She quickly realized her legs were tied to something at one side of what she thought might be a janitor's closet, while a rope had been run through her manacled arms and tied off on the opposite side to keep her centered in the room. Which meant she wasn't going to be able to attract attention by kicking the door. The gag meant yelling wasn't an option.

There had to be something she could do. She

looked around the dim light in the room. But Donnie had apparently moved everything she could kick over or knock into out of her reach. She looked down to see if there was any kind of clock running down on the vest, telling her how much time she had before she was blown to smithereens. But there was nothing. Which meant Donnie must have some kind of detonator he could use to blow her up at his leisure.

Kate felt herself hyperventilating and held her breath until she could get control of her breathing. She forced herself to put a lid on her imagination, which was working overtime. She could make a pretty good guess where she was. The shiny floors were the tip-off. Where else would Bomber Boy take the daughter of the judge presiding over his father's trial except to her father's courthouse?

Donnie probably intended to call in a bomb scare, which would mean evacuating the courthouse. Which might give him a chance to rescue his father.

Kate wondered whether Donnie actually intended to detonate the bomb she was wearing. He only needed the threat to free his father. But Donnie actually might want to reinforce the point his father had made in Houston. The Browns really didn't like courts, lawyers, or the federal government.

Kate struggled harder, but that only tightened her bonds. She sent a silent plea to Jack McKinley. *I'm at the courthouse. I'm in trouble. Come find me. Please.*

She wondered how long it would be before her mother and father realized she'd been kidnapped. She wondered how their weekend had turned out. Had they managed to settle their differences? She hoped so. She so much wanted them to be happy. Even if she wasn't going to be there to see it.

Thinking of her mother reminded her of that odd sensation she'd had as she'd been blacking out. Had she really heard her mother's voice? Or was that her imagination? Did that mean Donnie had taken her mother prisoner, as well?

"Donnie better not hurt her," Kate growled beneath the gag. "If he does, he'll have to deal with Daddy. And North. And King." She thought of all her family's powerful resources focused on Donnie Brown. Once that happened, the kid was toast.

Which would be great, assuming she wasn't fried first.

"You shouldn't have interfered," Donnie said angrily. "Then this wouldn't have happened. Now you've ruined everything."

Libby felt faint with pain and loss of blood. She pressed her hand against the gunshot wound in her side, feeling the blood oozing between her fingers. "I need a doctor," she said.

"Don't you think I know that?" Donnie said. "I had everything planned. But this might work out just as well. When the judge gets a call that you're in the hospital, he'll call a recess and leave the courthouse. Once that happens, I can call in the bomb threat."

Libby felt her heart skip a beat. A bomb at the courthouse? Where Clay was sure to be? And where Donnie might have taken Kate? She glanced sideways at the young man who'd acted so friendly in the courtroom, wondering how he planned to silence her, now that she knew about the bomb he'd planted at the courthouse. Another bullet, this time somewhere more damaging?

"Where's my daughter now?" she demanded. "What have you done with her? Is Kate anywhere near the courthouse?"

"She's perfectly safe. For the moment."

Donnie's threat against Kate had kept Libby docile as they'd exited the Four Seasons. She'd sat quietly in the car, while he'd driven to an isolated location with hundreds of storage units. But when Donnie had opened the door to one of them, and she'd seen Kate huddled on the floor, she'd gone berserk.

Libby had only gotten a glimpse of Kate, erupting from the floor and running at Donnie with her fists raised, before she'd charged Donnie herself. Libby had grabbed at Donnie's gun, and it had gone off. The shock and pain of being shot had caused her to lose consciousness. She'd been awake and aware just long enough to hear Kate cry, "Mom!"

When Libby had regained consciousness, she'd found herself belted into the passenger seat of Clay's SUV, with Donnie at the wheel. Kate had been nowhere to be seen. Libby's heart clenched as she realized that while she'd been away with Clay, her daughter had apparently been a prisoner of this youthful psychopath.

She glanced at Donnie, whose brow and upper lip were dotted with perspiration, despite the fact the air conditioner in the car was running full blast. His hazel eyes looked haunted. His sandy hair stood up in spikes where he'd run his sweaty hands through it. The young man was clearly under a great deal of stress.

"You don't have to do whatever it is you're planning to do," Libby said.

"I have to get my father free. Otherwise, the government is going to execute him."

"Killing more people is only going to make the government more determined to hunt you and your father down," Libby said. "You'll never have peace. You'll never be free."

It was plain her words were having an effect, but not the one she wanted. Donnie only seemed more agitated.

"Just shut up," Donnie said. "Or I'll shut you up."

Libby saw they were approaching Brackenridge Hospital, which was not more than a mile from the courthouse. She glanced sideways at Donnie, wondering how he planned to keep her from telling what she knew of his plans. She was terrified that he would shoot her again—and this time kill her. She reached down and surreptitiously released the seat belt, thinking she could leap from the car. Suddenly, an annoying chime resounded throughout the car.

"Buckle up," Donnie said, swinging the gun in her direction. "You never know when I might have to stop fast."

Libby rebuckled her seat belt, feeling her heart sink as Donnie stopped at the beginning of a driveway that led to the Brackenridge Hospital emergency entrance. "You don't have to shoot me," she said. "I promise I won't say anything."

"I know you won't," Donnie said.

"Please," Libby said. She was ashamed to feel so scared, to be pleading with a kid who obviously had no conscience. But she didn't want to die. Not like this. Not with so much of her life unlived. She was surprised how clear her choices became at a moment like this. She wanted a chance to love and be loved by Clay. She wanted marriage and children. She wanted a future with Clay that would include everything they'd dreamed of in the past—and more.

Of course, she was lying to Donnie. She had no intention of keeping his plans to herself. If she had the chance, she would yell them to the high heavens.

Libby understood why Donnie wanted to silence her. She just wasn't ready to be silenced in the only way she could imagine him doing it.

"Please, I—"

"This'll only put you out for a little while," he said, putting the SUV in park, so he had both hands free. He set the gun in his lap and took a capped syringe out of his breast pocket. "But it should be long enough for us to be long gone."

Libby wondered why Donnie wasn't worried about leaving a witness behind who could testify against him. Against *them* she suddenly realized. Donnie had said, "Long enough for *us* to be long gone."

She stared at the syringe Donnie had in his hand, watching as he removed the cap to reveal a wicked looking needle. Maybe whatever drug it contained was intended to kill her, and he just wanted to keep her calm until he could inject it.

But if he'd wanted her dead, he could have killed her and left her in the storage room where he'd been keeping Kate. He'd mentioned he needed her as a lure to get Clay away from the courtroom. Maybe that meant Clay would be safe from whatever devastation Donnie was planning at the federal courthouse. Libby stared at the needle Donnie held upright.

If she fought him, he might shoot her again. The gun was sitting right there in his lap. The needle seemed the lesser of two evils. She held tight to the wound in her side as she felt the prick of a needle in her arm.

"You have about thirty seconds," he said. "Take your purse when you get out. I want them to know who you are."

"Clay and I aren't related. He won't be the one the hospital notifies," Libby said.

"I've left a note for the judge at the courthouse," Donnie said. "He'll come."

Donnie drove up to the emergency room door and said, "Get out."

Libby fumbled with the seat belt with fingers that didn't seem to be working. Donnie leaned across her and unbuckled the belt, then opened the door and repeated, "Get out. Now."

Libby stepped down from the SUV and felt her knees buckle under her. The last thing she saw as she crumpled to the pavement was Donnie Brown driving away in Clay's SUV.

17

"How the hell did this happen?" North demanded, as he stood in the hallway outside his sister's hospital room, his hands fisted on his hips. "For a Texas Ranger working this case undercover, you don't seem to know a helluva lot."

Jack McKinley shoved a frustrated hand through his hair. "Donnie gave me the slip. I thought he was down for the night, but he snuck out of his house before dawn. I had no idea he even knew where to find your sister, much less had the balls to kidnap her. The gunshot wound isn't serious," Jack continued. "The bullet hit Libby in the side, missed all the vital stuff, and went right through."

"That's comforting," North said sarcastically.

"The doctor stitched her up, and she'll be fine," Jack said, uncowed. "Donnie apparently gave her chloral hydrate to put her out. When the drug wears off, we'll be able to talk to her."

"Where is Kate?" North asked.

"I don't know. The last time I saw her was Thursday afternoon, when I told her I couldn't go with her to Bitter Creek."

"She told Clay she was spending the weekend with you."

Jack flushed. "She lied."

"You promised me you'd look out for her."

"I thought the best way to protect her was to keep an eye on Donnie."

"You were wrong."

"I underestimated the kid," Jack said. "He's smarter than he looks. I searched for Kate as soon as I realized I'd lost track of Donnie, but I couldn't find her. Now Donnie's disappeared."

"Do we know for sure that he has Kate?" North asked. "That she isn't with a girlfriend somewhere?"

"None of Kate's friends have seen her since she was late to class on Thursday," Jack said.

"Damn," North muttered. "I was afraid something like this might happen. Who have you got looking for her?"

"Every law enforcement agency in the state has been alerted. We've also got the FBI involved, because it appears Donnie's kidnapped her."

North didn't like the worry he saw in Jack's dark eyes. Jack was good at what he did, and if Bomber Brown's kid had managed to slip away, he was damned clever. Which didn't bode well for Kate. "Find her, Jack."

"I will," Jack said.

North knew Jack would find Kate. The only question was whether he would find her in time—and alive. North stood where he was until Jack disappeared onto the elevator. He glanced back into the room where his sister lay on sterile white sheets and felt his insides clench at the thought of how close he'd come to losing her.

He and Libby were closer than anyone suspected. Their whole lives it had been the two of them against the world. Libby had done most of the caretaking for their siblings, while North had stood between Libby and the younger kids and his father's drunken rages. He'd taken more than one blow to deflect King's anger from the others.

North rubbed at the scar on his shoulder. He and Libby would have left home a lot sooner if they hadn't been worried about what would happen to Taylor and Gray and Tory.

He hadn't been surprised when Libby got pregnant. That was one way young girls managed to force the issue and get out. He'd felt sorry for Libby when King punished her for falling in love with a Blackthorne by threatening to ruin Clay if she didn't stay at Kingdom Come.

He'd seen how unhappy Libby was for the two years before she turned eighteen. And how she was never again quite as happy as she'd been during the summer she'd spent with Clay.

"You and me against the world," he murmured, as he leaned against the portal and listened to the steady beep of Libby's life signs on the monitors. He knew he didn't have the patience to sit beside her bed and wait for her to wake. Besides, he'd left Jocelyn in a family waiting room downstairs. He would have the hospital page him the moment Libby woke up.

North was halfway down the hall when he ran into Jocelyn. "I asked you to wait for me downstairs."

"How is Libby?"

"It looks like she'll be okay. It's just a flesh wound."

"I wanted to leave these flowers for her." Jocelyn held out a bouquet of white daisies in a tall glass vase decorated with a bright yellow bow, which she'd apparently picked up in the gift shop downstairs.

"She'll appreciate that," North said. He stepped back and let Jocelyn pass, then followed her back down the hall to Libby's room.

He hadn't invited Jocelyn to come. But somehow she was here. The woman had insinuated herself into his life so deeply he wasn't sure what he was going to do when September came, and she wanted out.

There was no chance she was going to stay, because she'd made it clear she wanted more than a marriage of convenience. He'd argued that respect and liking were far more lasting than love. She'd replied that respect and liking were absolutely necessary. But so was love.

Love meant being able to forgive, she'd said. Love meant putting the other person first. Love meant tolerance and caring and adoring and— She'd come up with a laundry list of all the things love was.

He'd considered explaining to her why he would never let himself fall in love. How losing the only women he claimed he could ever love had made his father a bitter, angry, unhappy man. How North had vowed he would never let a woman get close enough to hurt him like that. But it would have felt like scraping off a layer of skin, leaving blood and bone exposed, to reveal so much. So he never had.

He'd tried to show her he cared without using the word *love*. He'd spent every night in her bed, so she'd know he wasn't with another woman. He'd brought Breed into the house for meals and spent time with the boy during the day. He'd eaten every bite of the food she prepared for him and asked for seconds. And he'd kept his mouth shut when she changed his home out of all recognition, adding feminine peach and aqua pillows and curtains to his spartan earth tones.

The woman was crazy about flowers. She'd planted black-eyed susans and morning glories and zinnias and marigolds around his back porch. Which would

remind him even when she was gone—after he'd removed the feminine pillows and curtains—that she'd
been there.

"This is a nice room," Jocelyn said, as she set the
daisies on a table beside Libby's bed.

"If you say so," North replied. He'd hated hospitals
ever since the fourth time his mother had taken pills
to end her life—and succeeded. He didn't like the antiseptic smell. He didn't like the shiny floors or the inevitable monochromatic walls. He didn't like the
mechanical sound of the monitors hooked up to sick
and dying bodies. Most of all, he didn't like the effi-
cient and distant doctors and nurses, who'd seen death
often enough to be able to mouth platitudes to families without weeping themselves.

North watched as Jocelyn plumped up Libby's pillow and brushed her blond hair away from her brow,
as though the two of them were friends, which he
knew to be far from the truth.

But that was Jocelyn. Giving. Caring. He didn't
allow himself to think what he'd be feeling right now
if she was the one lying in that bed. His heart
squeezed until it hurt, and he took a deep breath and
let it out.

She came to him, recognizing his distress, and put
her arms around him to comfort him. He gripped her
hard enough to make her squeak and heard her gentle
laugh as he loosened his hold.

She leaned back to look up into his eyes and put her hand against his cheek, because she liked the dark, bristly beard that grew overnight. "Libby's fine, North. She's going to be fine."

He squeezed her again, because she didn't understand it was the fear of losing her that had frightened him. Then he let her go and took a step back. Aware that he had to cure himself of needing her so much. Aware that he was very close to the fine line where he could no longer lie to himself. When he would finally have to admit that he loved her.

"Shouldn't she be waking up soon?" Jocelyn asked, crossing back to Libby's bedside.

"I don't know," North replied, purposely staying where he was.

"I guess she was lucky," Jocelyn said.

North lifted a brow. "Lucky?"

"That he didn't kill her." Jocelyn frowned, then looked at North. "Which makes me wonder why he didn't kill her. I mean, that would have made more sense than leaving her alive, where she could be a witness against him. Why do you suppose he wanted her alive?"

"I never looked at it that way," North admitted. "You're right, though. If Brown had wanted her dead, he would have killed her. Which means Libby serves some purpose by being alive."

North tried to imagine what sort of plan Bomber

Brown's son might have hatched that would work better with Libby alive.

While he was thinking, a harried-looking Clay showed up in the doorway. He shot an anxious look at North and asked, "Is she all right?"

Clay didn't stop, just crossed all the way to Libby's side and took her hand in his. "She feels cold."

"I think that's the air-conditioning in here," Jocelyn said in a soothing voice. "North says she just has a flesh wound. That she'll be fine."

North realized Jocelyn had stepped in as a mediator to make it possible for the two men to communicate without actually having to speak to each other. Which was ridiculous, under the circumstances. If things worked out as North thought they would, Clay Blackthorne was going to become his brother-in-law. Libby would be sure to invite North to family events. And he would attend. Because however much he hated Blackthornes, he loved his sister more.

For Libby's sake, he extended an olive branch. "Jocelyn pointed out something to me. Maybe you'd have a better insight into the situation than I do, since you're more familiar with Brown and his son."

"What is it?" Clay asked.

"Why would Donnie Brown take special pains to keep Libby alive?" North said. "He could have killed her and dumped her somewhere, but instead, he dropped her off at a hospital."

Clay looked aside for a moment. It took North a moment to realize that Clay wasn't ignoring him, he was thinking. Then Clay's chin jerked up, and he focused his gray eyes on North. "I got a note delivered to me in the courtroom, telling me that Libby had been shot, and that she was here at Brackenridge. I didn't question who sent it. Did you?"

"As a matter of fact, I didn't," North said. "I would have called, but I knew you were in court, and Libby's condition is stable. But it's obvious someone wanted you out of the courtroom. Why?"

"I can make a guess," Clay said, meeting North's gaze. "Since I only called a short recess, Brown wouldn't be taken back to the jail. He'd be kept at the courthouse."

"But Brown's son knew you'd be gone long enough for him to arrange a rescue, some sort of incident to distract everybody and give him the chance to free his father," North said.

"It isn't going to be easy getting Brown out of the courthouse," Clay said. "There's a lot of security around him, a bunch of deputies keeping an eye—"

"What if Donnie had a hostage?" North said. "And he was willing to trade his hostage for his father?"

"What hostage?" Clay asked.

"Kate."

North heard Clay take a quick, harsh breath. "He's got Kate? Why wasn't I told?"

"There hasn't been time. Jack just figured all this out in the past half hour. We didn't realize the truth until this morning. Jack didn't check on Kate until after Donnie had escaped his surveillance."

"Kate told me she was staying in Austin to study, but I figured she'd be with Jack. What happened?"

North sighed. "I should have told you this sooner, I suppose."

"Told me what?" Clay asked sharply when North hesitated.

"Jack and Kate aren't really engaged. They aren't even dating. It was all part of a ploy by Kate to get you and Libby together."

"I don't know whether to be relieved or infuriated," Clay said, shaking his head in disbelief. "How did Kate talk someone like Jack McKinley into such a harebrained scheme?"

"I'm to blame for that," North said. "I asked Jack to keep an eye on Kate."

"That sounds like asking the fox to guard the hen-house," Clay said with asperity.

"Jack's a Texas Ranger."

Clay looked stunned. "I've talked to Owen nearly every day at the couthouse, and he never said a word to me about Jack being a Texas Ranger."

"Jack works undercover. Owen might not have known. Or he might have had orders to keep his mouth shut," North said.

Clay's eyes narrowed. "Does Jack have anything to do with Kate going missing?"

"Jack specifically told Kate to stay away from Donnie Brown," North said. "Advice she apparently ignored."

"If I know Kate, and I do, she did the opposite of what Jack told her to do," Clay said.

"It sure as hell looks that way," North agreed.

"I guess we have the answer to why Libby was kept alive," Jocelyn said.

Both men looked at her in surprise.

She looked at Clay and said, "To get you to recess court, so his father would be at the courthouse, but out of the courtroom."

"We need to call security at the courthouse," Clay said. "We need to warn them—"

"I have a feeling it's already too late for that," North said.

"Clay?" a weak voice said.

"You're awake!" Clay said, turning back to Libby. He crossed and sat beside her on the bed, but apparently that wasn't close enough, because he leaned down and tenderly kissed her on the forehead. "I'm glad to see you're awake. How do you feel?"

"Like I've been shot," she said wryly.

North saw the smile on Clay's face before he reached out to brush his knuckle against her cheek. North knew what Clay was doing. Reassuring himself that she was alive. That she was fine. That he hadn't lost her.

"You're going to be fine, Libby," Clay said. "I wish I could stay, but there's an emergency, and I have to get back to the courthouse."

Libby grabbed his arm as he started to rise and said, "Donnie Brown has Kate."

Clay sat back down and said, "How do you know that?"

"He told me so. He's going to make a bomb, Clay," she said, her voice high-pitched and frightened. "He said he's going to call in a bomb scare, but he isn't just threatening to blow the place up. There'll be a real bomb at the courthouse."

"Now that we know—"

"He hates the government and lawyers and judges," Libby interrupted "He's going to hurt Kate to hurt you."

"Kate?" Clay said.

"He's got our daughter, Clay. And he's making a bomb. It isn't too big a leap—" Libby's sob cut her off.

North watched as Clay gently tucked a blond curl behind Libby's ear, love written large on his face. "Don't worry, darling," Clay said. "I'm going back to the courthouse now. I'll find Kate and make sure she's safe."

North was already on the phone to Jack. He listened and then said to Clay and Libby, "Jack says there's no bomb scare. There's nothing at all to indicate there's any problem at all at the courthouse."

"But he said he had a bomb," Libby said. She tried to sit up and cried out in pain and grabbed her side.

Clay eased her back down onto the pillow and said, "Please, stay still, darling. You're hurt."

"Oh, my God," Libby said, tears shimmering in her eyes as she struggled against Clay's light hold to sit up. "Donnie's going to attach Kate to a bomb. I've seen that in the movies. I know—"

Clay eased her back down on the bed. "Easy, baby," he said. "North and I are going to the courthouse, and Jack—he's a Texas Ranger, North says— will be there, too. Between the three of us, we'll find Kate."

"Jack's a Texas Ranger?"

"That's another story," North said. "And we have to go. There'll be a deputy marshal here in a few minutes to guard the door."

"Please don't let anything happen to Kate," Libby said, clutching Clay's arm. "Promise me."

"I'll keep her safe," Clay said.

Libby wouldn't let him go. "Promise me!"

"I promise," Clay said. "I have to go, darling," he said. But he made no move to free himself.

"I'll stay here with you, Libby," Jocelyn said.

Reluctantly, Libby released Clay, her heart in her eyes, the promise she'd demanded still echoing in the room.

It was a promise Clay shouldn't have made, North thought. Because there was no sure way he could keep it.

Kate was surprised when the door to the storage room opened and the light came on. When she saw Donnie, she tried not to look afraid, but her body started shivering, and she couldn't get it to stop.

"Hi, there, sweet thing," Donnie said with a grin. "This'll all be over soon."

Kate wished he'd stop saying that. She shuddered as he ran his hands over her body under the guise of untying the ropes that kept her prone in the closet, touching what she never would have allowed him to touch. She made a disgusted sound deep in her throat and Donnie snickered.

"Might as well let me enjoy it now," he said. "Pretty soon there isn't going to be a big enough piece of you left for anybody else to enjoy."

He didn't take the tape from her mouth, but she called him names that she was sure he understood, because he only grinned more broadly.

She struggled as he hefted her over his shoulder, and when he almost dropped her, he smacked her hard on her bottom. "Stop that," he said. "Or I'll have to put you out."

Kate immediately stopped wriggling. At least if she

were conscious, she'd have a chance to save herself. Unconscious, she was . . . hamburger.

The thought made her giggle hysterically. Which made tears brim in her eyes. She wanted her mom and dad. She wanted Jack. She wanted to live, which seemed the most impossible wish of all.

She wondered where they were that Donnie could move her without fear of discovery. She'd thought they were at the courthouse, but that seemed not to be true. But if they weren't in the courthouse, why all the shiny floors and—

She glanced into one of the rooms as Donnie carried her down the hall and realized they were in a hospital. With shiny floors and an antiseptic smell. Where were the patients? The rooms seemed to be empty.

"They're renovating this floor of the hospital," Donnie said. "So they've got it blocked off to the general population. I've been doing some painting for the contractor—off the books, of course. Nobody's working today because the contractor's mother got killed. Hit-and-run. So sad. We've got the whole place to ourselves."

It didn't take a great stretch of the imagination to figure out that Donnie had been willing to kill an innocent old lady to forward his plan. Kate felt her stomach knot. This freckle-faced boy was a ruthless killer.

He laid her down on a bed, then rolled her on her side and untied her hands. Kate thought this might be her only chance to win freedom, and she made a valiant effort to hit out with her hands. But there was no blood in her limbs, and they were like dead things, useless to fight him.

Donnie used straps on the hospital bed to attach her hands to the bed rails, then tied her feet to the corners of the bed with rope. "You'll be fine here until I need you."

Kate shifted in the bed, trying to find a comfortable position while wearing the vest of explosives.

"I wouldn't move around too much, if I were you," Donnie warned. "You just never know when you might cause a spark and then—*POW!*"

Kate looked at Donnie with narrowed eyes. He must be jerking her chain. Surely, he wouldn't be so nonchalant about carrying her around, if the explosives she was wearing were that volatile.

She looked at the peculiar light in Donnie's eyes, the sweat on his upper lip and brow, and thought maybe he was that crazy. She shivered. She had to get out of here. She had to get free. She looked around the room for some means of escape, or some method of contacting the outside world. She spotted a phone and glanced back at Donnie, who'd apparently followed her darting eyes.

He shook a finger at her, like he would a naughty

THE NEXT MRS. BLACKTHORNE   373

child, and said, "Uh-uh. No phone calls. That would spoil everything." He carefully disconnected the phone jack from the wall and took the phone with him as he headed out of the room. "I may need you to speak to your father to prove you're still alive. But I wouldn't want you calling him before the time is right. See you soon, sweet thing."

Donnie stopped at the door and turned back to her. He reached inside a light denim jacket he was wearing and pulled out a small device. "Just so you know, this is a remote detonator. All I have to do is push this button—"

Kate gasped.

Donnie laughed. "—when I'm at a safe distance. I have no intention of blowing myself up along with you, sweet thing."

I'm not a thing. I'm a person. A human being, you cretin!

"I think it's time I paid a visit to your mom," Donnie said. "She's staying here in the hospital."

Kate's eyes went wide and her heart skipped a beat.

"Oh, yeah. She got shot. Accidentally. Although, I have to say, things are working out well. Your dad's already been here to visit her, along with your uncle and that cheating football hero you like so much. He's a Texas Ranger. Did you know? That sonofabitch had me fooled. But not my mom. Or my brother. Neither of them liked the way he hung around the courthouse so much. I think Jack-the-Texas-Ranger might be worried about you. Much good it's going to do him!"

Donnie laughed as he left the room.

Kate could hear his footfalls echo as he headed down the empty hall. He couldn't know how relieved she was to know Jack was a Texas Ranger. She knew he cared for her. And that he would find her, or die trying.

She struggled to sit as high as she could in the bed, but her hands were secured too far away for her to bend forward and reach them with her taped-up mouth. But she had more mobility now than she had had in the closet, and she went to work trying to rub the tape off her mouth by rubbing her cheek against her shoulder.

That didn't work, so she tried forcing her mouth wide, sticking her tongue through her teeth until her jaws ached. The tape moved. A little. But she was far from free.

Kate was terrified of what Donnie was going to do with her mother. She already had evidence of his ruthlessness. She became frantic when she thought of Donnie simply murdering her mother in her hospital bed and then calling her father to come—which he would, on the run—and capturing him as well.

She closed her eyes and thought of her father and sent him a mental message, hoping it would find its way to him.

Watch out for Donnie Brown, Daddy. He's got me tied up here in the hospital and now he's after Mom. Be careful! We need you to come save us.

And then she realized that however powerful her father might be, he wasn't a lawman. Jack was. So maybe she ought to send a message out into the ether for Jack, as well.

I need you, Jack. Come find me. I'm here at the same hospital as my mom, on a floor that's under construction. I think Donnie is going after my mom, so please protect her.

I forgive you for not telling me you were a Texas Ranger. And for keeping an eye on me as a favor to North. I have to admit that even I find it hard to say no to Uncle North.

I want a chance for a future. With you, I hope. If that last bit scares you, don't worry. I'll make it all right once you've rescued me and this is all over.

The end. Amen.

Kate hadn't realized her message into the ether had become a prayer, but apparently it had. She knew God worked in mysterious ways. He also helped those who helped themselves.

She began to work again on the tape that covered her mouth.

18

❦

"I thought she'd be somewhere in the courthouse," Jack said. "But we've cleared the building, searched high and low, and we haven't found her."

"Not even with those bomb-sniffing dogs?" Clay asked.

Jack shook his head. "Nothing. They didn't find a whiff of explosives. We're baffled."

"Where's Bomber Brown?" North asked.

"On his way back to jail," Jack said.

Clay looked around the courtroom where he'd presided over the surprisingly fast-moving trial. "Donnie didn't show here?"

Jack shook his head. "I don't get it. What was the point of taking Kate if he wasn't going to make a ransom demand or a demand to exchange her for his father?"

Clay's cell phone rang, and he hurriedly reached for it, hoping against hope that it might be Kate. He didn't recognize the number on his caller ID. "Who is this?" he said curtly.

"I think you know who this is," a voice said.

"Where's my daughter? Where's Kate?"

"She's right here," the voice said. "With her mom and her mom's friend."

Clay gestured at North and Jack to come to him. "How do I know you're telling the truth?" Clay held the phone so the two men could hear the other end of the conversation.

"Well, first off, that deputy marshal you sent to guard your woman is history."

Clay swore under his breath and exchanged a bleak look with the other two men. "Just listen to this," the voice said.

In the background Clay could hear women's voices, and then Libby's voice came on the phone. "Clay?"

"Libby? Are you all right?"

"Jocelyn and I are fine, but North would hate it here. We're—"

"Tell him what I told you to say," the voice in the background interrupted.

"Kate is wearing a vest of explosives, Clay. And Donnie has a remote detonator, which he says he'll use if you don't do exactly as he asks. I think—"

Clay heard Donnie cut her off. Then the boy said, "We've left the hospital and gone somewhere else, so don't waste your time looking for us. You'll never find us in time. You have exactly one hour to release my father and get him on a jet headed for South America.

When I hear that he's out of U.S. airspace, I'll tell you where the women are."

"What guarantee do I have that you'll let the women go if I do what you want?" Clay asked.

"None," Donnie said, his voice nasty. "What I can guarantee is that if you don't do exactly as I say, there's not going to be a big enough piece of any of these women left to bury in a Baggie."

Then the phone went dead.

Clay snapped his phone closed and looked into the faces of the other two men, where he saw his own agony and anger and helplessness reflected. "Anybody here think we should let Bomber Brown go free?"

Neither man even moved a hair, the answer was so obvious. They all knew the government didn't negotiate with terrorists. And that the most likely result of acceding to Donnie Brown's demands would be the deaths of the three women. Clay was certain Donnie intended to detonate his bomb no matter what, and in a place where there would be other innocent victims.

"I never should have left Libby and Joss alone at the hospital," North said as he headed for the door to Clay's chambers, where they'd congregated. "I should have been more careful."

"It's that damned kid," Jack said, catching up to him. "He doesn't know what the hell he's doing. Why would he drop Libby off at the hospital if he was going to use her as a hostage later?"

"To keep her alive?" North said sardonically.

"Yeah, but he had to know we'd put a police guard on her," Jack said.

"It sure as hell didn't slow him down any," North said. "You want to ride back to the hospital with me, Jack? Clay, if you take your car we'll have extra wheels. We can stay in touch on the phone."

"I don't take orders from Grayhawks," Clay said, bristling.

"You want to fight with me, or save my sister and your daughter?" North said in a hard voice.

Clay realized North was right. This was no time for egos or old enmities. Whether they liked it or not, he and North would have to work together to save the women they both loved.

"Just tell me how we're going to find this sick son-ofabitch," Clay said, as the three of them left the courthouse headed for their cars. "And get that detonator away from him."

"We start with the videotapes from the hospital garage," Jack said. "That'll tell us when he came in and when he left."

"We don't have that kind of time," North said.

"Then what do you suggest?" Jack shot back.

"I suppose we can have someone in hospital security do that while we're on our way," North said.

Clay had done his share of investigating, first as a district attorney, and later as attorney general. Nothing happened as fast in real life as it did on a one-hour crime show, where high-tech lab work neatly and certainly revealed the criminal. It was daunting to think of finding Donnie Brown in under an hour. Especially when they didn't have a clue where he'd taken the women.

Clay glanced at the other two men over the roof of his car and said, "Maybe Libby left a clue for us in what she said on the phone."

"She didn't say much," Jack pointed out.

"What did she say?" North asked. "I'm trying to remember exactly."

Clay remembered every word. "She said, 'Jocelyn and I are fine, but North would hate it here.'" He turned to North and said, "Does that mean anything to you?"

North laughed harshly. "I hate small, dark places. Does that help?"

"No. Where else do you hate to be?" Clay asked.

"Shopping malls."

"Too public," Jack said. "Where else?"

North's head jerked up. "Libby knows I hate hospitals. Do you suppose they could still be at the hospital, that they never left?"

"It's worth a look," Clay said. He turned to Jack and said, "Should we get the police to cordon off—"

"I'll have them set up a perimeter, but let's give Donnie plenty of room. If he is at the hospital, we don't want him spooked. I can also have the bomb squad standing by, just in case."

It only took ten minutes to get back to the hospital, and they each took a car, which Jack had suggested, in case the hospital turned out to be a wild-goose chase, and they needed to go in different directions later.

"Now what?" Clay said, when they were all gathered in the hospital lobby. "How do we do this search?"

"I talked to the hospital administrator on the way here," Jack said. "They're doing renovations on the sixth floor. The entire floor's empty."

"That's a floor above where Libby was staying," Clay said.

"This feels too easy," North said uneasily. "Could Donnie really be holding Kate and Libby and Joss there?"

"We'll soon find out," Clay said.

"Wait a minute," Jack said, putting out an arm to stop him. "How about letting SWAT do the heavy lifting?"

"As far as we know, Donnie is working by himself," Clay said.

"With a detonator and a lot of explosives," North muttered.

"We also know he's got a gun," Jack said.

"If he starts waving it around, I'll distract him and

you can shoot him," Clay said, eyeing the Colt .45 on Jack's hip.

"Sounds good to me," North said.

"We need a plan," Jack persisted, as they took the elevator to the fifth floor. "Donnie isn't going to give up without a fight."

"He's just one boy," Clay said.

"A damned clever boy," Jack reminded him

"Don't forget the women," Clay said. "If I know Libby and Kate, they haven't been sitting on their hands. They'll have been making plans for what to do when we show up—since they must know we're coming after them."

"You're right," North said. "Joss will be telling him all the reasons he'd be better off to give himself up."

They discussed whether or not it made sense to evacuate the hospital, but they weren't sure Donnie was even there, and so much activity beforehand would alert Donnie, if he was there.

"What if we do find Donnie, and he's sitting on a big bomb?" Jack said. "What then?"

"Then it's too late to evacuate," Clay said. "And we figure out a way to get Donnie and the bomb out of the hospital before he detonates it."

"You seem to think you're going to be able to reason with this kid," Jack said.

"And you don't?" North said.

Jack shook his head. "There wasn't enough warning given before Brown blew up the federal courthouse in Houston for everyone to get out. I think he and his father gave called in a bomb threat just so they could watch the ants scurry, so to speak. They wanted to see the fear, the confusion, and the terror they'd created."

"You think Donnie was involved in that bombing?" Clay said.

"I always have," Jack replied. "But I could never prove it. We'd better split up," he said. "No sense letting Donnie know how many of us there are."

"I think I should be the one to reveal myself to him," Clay said. "I'm the one he most wants dead."

"He's liable to shoot you and not think twice," Jack said.

"I don't think so," Clay said. "I think he's going to want to savor the moment. Which should give you two plenty of time to sneak up on him and get the detonator away."

None of them mentioned the fact that they might have guessed wrong. That Donnie might not be at the hospital. That they would then have to live with the loss of loved ones for which they would forever blame themselves. They were all men of action. They didn't know any other way to be.

"He's going to be suspicious," Jack warned Clay. "He's going to think you've got a gun—or a SWAT team—hidden behind the door. You have to make him believe you're alone and unarmed."

"I can do that," Clay said.

They'd reviewed the floor plan before they'd come upstairs and decided that North and Jack would take the stairs up from five and hide themselves on the sixth floor while Clay made a direct approach, simply taking the elevator to six and walking down the hospital corridor, calling loudly for Donnie to show himself.

"Ready?" Jack said, looking each of the other two men in the eye.

Clay nodded and saw North do the same. "I'll give you three minutes to get set," Clay said. "Then I'm on my way."

He watched as the other two men made their way onto the floor and into the places where they'd decided to wait. He eyed his watch, waiting for a second hand that seemed to be standing still. At last, the three minutes had passed, and he stepped out into the corridor and started walking.

The first two rooms Clay passed were empty. He called out, "Donnie, I know you're here. I just want to talk to you. Come on out."

He was met by silence. Not a scraping chair. Not a squeaking bedspring. Not a woman's whimper.

Clay's heart was pounding in his chest. He'd never been so terrified, more afraid that Donnie wouldn't show than that he would. "Come on out," he called again. "I'm alone. I'm unarmed. I just want to talk."

He took three more steps, which took him past two

more empty rooms. He felt his heart sinking. The kid wasn't here. They'd badly miscalculated. Donnie Brown was somewhere else. And there was nothing they could do now to stop him.

"Put your hands up!" a voice called out.

Clay stopped in his tracks and slowly put his hands up to show they were empty. The voice had come from behind him, which was disconcerting, because he'd looked into every room he'd passed and they'd all appeared empty. So where were the women?

He started to turn around and Donnie said, "Don't move!"

Clay heard him coming down the linoleum hallway and said, "Where's my daughter, Donnie?"

"You're too late, Judge Blackthorne."

Clay's heart was in his throat when he asked, "The hour isn't up, Donnie. How can I be too late?"

"You should have been more careful about what you allowed into evidence, Your Honor. If my dad weren't looking so guilty to the jury, I wouldn't have been forced into doing what I've done."

"What have you done, Donnie?" Clay asked.

"What was necessary to prove my point," Donnie said.

"What point is that?"

"That the government can't be trusted. That judges are puppets of the government. That lawyers are snakes."

Clay turned, despite Donnie's warning, and was face-to-face with the boy, who was only a couple of feet away. The kid had a gun in one hand, pointed at Clay's chest, and what appeared to be some electronic device—the detonator?—in the other.

"Where's Kate, Donnie?" Clay asked again.

The kid grinned. "Down the hall, Your Honor." The way Donnie said it, *Your Honor* was an insult.

"Which means you can't detonate that vest bomb without blowing yourself up, too."

"Sacrifices have to be made," Donnie said.

The words sent a chill down Clay's spine. If the kid didn't care whether he lived or died, he was considerably more dangerous. "Do you think that's what your father would want? For you to sacrifice yourself for him? Usually it's the other way around."

Donnie grinned again. "Like, you sacrifice yourself to save your daughter?"

Clay nodded. "I'd be happy to offer myself as a hostage in Kate's place."

"But I have you both here now," Donnie said. "Why should I let either one of you go?"

"You haven't heard from your father yet, have you?"

Donnie frowned. "No, I haven't. But I've been watching TV in one of the rooms. I've seen the jet they've got ready for him at the airport."

"That's all for show, Donnie. Your dad isn't going to be freed until you release your hostages."

Donnie shook his head. "I don't trust you, Your Honor. By the way, how did you know I was here?"

"Garage videotapes," Clay said. "Showed you coming in, but not going out."

Donnie's eyes narrowed. "Really? I don't believe you."

"Why would I lie?"

"You never looked at garage videotapes," Donnie said.

"How do you know?" Clay said.

"Because I disabled the cameras in the garage," Donnie said smugly. His eyes narrowed. "So how did you know I was here?"

"I didn't know for sure," Clay said. "But you weren't in the courthouse, and I couldn't imagine how you'd get three women out of here without some sort of ruckus, so I figured you must have stayed on the premises. Which turned out to be the case."

Donnie eyed him sideways, but seemed to accept his story. His gaze drifted to a TV that was on in a nearby room without the sound. "There's that jet on TV again." He gestured with the gun for Clay to move into the room, and he followed him there, holding the gun on him, while he reached over to turn up the volume on the TV.

The newscaster said they were still waiting for Bomber Brown to appear, and that his son was holding hostages and demanding his father's immediate release.

"He's not going to be released until you let the women go," Clay said.

"I guess I'll have to show everyone I mean business," Donnie said, shaking the detonator in Clay's face.

"Don't!" Clay said. "Wait!"

"Why should I wait?" Donnie said, his voice hysterical. "It's clear nobody thinks I'll do anything. I'm going to prove—"

"Wait," Clay said again, holding out both hands in supplication. "They'll believe you if you appear on TV with a federal judge as your hostage."

Donnie paused for a half second to consider, then said, "Too much chance for someone to bushwhack me. A bomb will speak a lot more loudly than I can."

Clay wondered where North and Jack were, and whether they'd located the three women. "I want to speak to my daughter."

"No can do."

"Why not? She's here, isn't she? Somewhere on this floor?"

"You'd think so, wouldn't you," Donnie said. "But actually, no."

"No? Where is she?"

"That's for me to know and you to find out," Donnie said with a giggle.

"What about the other two women? Are they here?"

"Might be."

Clay took that as a yes. Which made him worry all the more for Kate, who was by herself somewhere, probably scared half to death. He regretted all the years they hadn't spent together more than he could say.

He hadn't let himself consider Libby's fate. If she was on this floor, why hadn't she made some noise, done something to indicate she was here? She must have heard him call out to Donnie. Either she wasn't here, and Donnie was lying again, or Donnie had tied Libby hand and foot and gagged her or drugged her— or already killed her.

"Where are the guys you came with?" Donnie asked conversationally.

Clay pretended confusion. "What?"

"You didn't come alone. Where are the other guys?"

"I didn't come with—"

Donnie held the detonator at arm's length and said, "You tell me the truth right now, or I'm going to punch this button. Don't worry, it isn't going to kill us. The bomb's far enough away that we'll survive. But your daughter won't."

"I came with Kate's uncle, North," Clay said.

"Tell him to show himself."

"North!" Clay shouted. "Donnie wants you to show yourself. He's threatening to detonate a bomb and kill Kate if you don't come out."

Donnie gestured with the detonator for Clay to

step back into the hall, and he followed him out, putting his back to the wall as he looked first one direction, then the other, for North to appear.

"Where is he?" Donnie demanded agitatedly.

"I don't know," Clay said. "North!" he shouted. "Get your ass out here!"

But North didn't show.

"What kind of game are you playing?" Donnie said. "Did Kate's uncle come with you? Or not? Maybe you just didn't want me to know you're alone. Which is it?"

"I thought you had all the answers," Clay said curtly.

"Start walking," Donnie said. "That way." He gestured toward the opposite end of the hallway. "Keep your hands where I can see them. Don't get any brilliant ideas about trying to pull a gun or anything."

Why the hell hadn't North shown himself? And where was Jack? All he could hope was that they'd found the two women. And that the women knew where Kate was being held.

Clay looked at each room as they passed by it, but all of them were empty. His heartbeat was erratic, and he was finding it hard to catch his breath, he was so scared. Not for himself. For Libby. And for Kate. And for Jocelyn, of course. Although his feelings for her were never so plain as they were now, when his first concern was for another woman.

Clay kept expecting North and Jack to turn up at

any moment. He became more and more worried when they didn't. What had happened to them? Had Donnie set some sort of trap in which they'd been caught? He searched left and right in front of him, but saw no sign of either man.

Jack listened to Donnie bragging to Clay that he'd disabled the garage cameras, and then heard him say that Kate wasn't on the sixth floor and had a sudden flash of insight. Donnie had said all three women were with him. But Libby had said, "Jocelyn and I are fine." Which meant Kate wasn't with the others.

And suddenly Jack knew where she was.

Jack slipped through the stairwell door and raced down the stairs two at a time until he reached the bridge to the parking garage next door to the hospital. He'd wondered why Donnie had an Escalade, and now he knew. The heavy-duty automobile, which weighed over six thousand pounds, could carry a massive payload of explosives.

He doubted Donnie was going to waste his explosives on a hospital. He was going to drive the Escalade right up to the front steps of the courthouse and explode it there. With Kate inside.

Jack told himself he'd made the correct professional decision, abandoning Clay and North to come hunt for Kate. Once Kate was free, Donnie would lose a powerful bargaining tool.

Jack knew Donnie's license plate number because he'd followed the car. He tried to imagine on which floor Donnie would leave the Caddy parked. Not the first floor—too easy to spot. Not the top floor—too hard to make his escape. So somewhere in between. He jogged the perimeter of the garage starting at the top and following the ramps down, looking for the Escalade. And found it on the third floor.

He could tell there was no one in the front seat, but the luxurious Caddy had darkly tinted windows and it was parked in a dark corner. Jack knew the Escalade had a decent antitheft system, but he doubted Donnie would want any kind of noisy alarm that would attract attention. He peered inside the rear of the vehicle, but could see nothing.

Jack stooped down and took a look at the car's undercarriage, searching for a booby trap that might detonate the car if he tried to get inside. He saw nothing.

That didn't mean something wasn't there, only that Jack wasn't knowledgeable enough to find it. He debated whether to call in the bomb squad, but then thought of Donnie glancing out the window and seeing a bomb van arriving and detonating the whole enchilada. Besides, time was of the essence. The sooner he could free Kate, the sooner Clay and North could confront Donnie.

He wondered how soundproof the car was. He

stood at the window and shouted, "Kate, are you in there?"

He got a thump in return. She must be gagged.

"Good girl," he said, hoping she could hear him. "I'm going to get you out of there."

Two enthusiastic thumps in reply.

Jack debated the best way to get inside the car and decided to break a window. He needed something substantial to break the safety glass, and decided to use the butt of his gun. The next problem was which window to break. He didn't want to take a chance of hurting Kate. And he wasn't sure what kind of explosives Donnie was using, so the less trauma, the better.

He decided on the passenger's side window. He knew Kate wasn't nearby, and he couldn't see any explosives on the seat.

"Here goes," he said.

It took two tries before the glass splintered, and another strong punch to clear the glass from the window. Then he stuck his head inside to see what he could see.

Jack took a deep breath and let it out.

The second and third seats had been removed to make an incredibly long bed. Kate was tied hand and foot and gagged, lying as though in a coffin created by two lines of fertilizer bags stacked to the ceiling on either side of her. He could see she was indeed wearing a vest with pockets containing what looked like Simtex. What he didn't know was whether any of those squares of Simtex were attached to any of the bags of fertilizer on either side of her.

"You're in a pickle, all right, young lady," he said. He meant it to be funny, but it came out sounding grim.

Jack carefully opened the passenger's side door, looking for trip wires, then did another search under the seat, for anything that might be triggered by his weight. He found nothing.

Maybe Donnie had been overconfident. Maybe he'd believed the car would never be found, so he hadn't wired any booby traps. Jack was afraid to hope. It was too dangerous to underestimate Donnie. He wiped the sweat from his forehead with his sleeve and slid a knee onto the passenger's seat, then the other knee, so he was facing the backseat.

He could see Kate's frightened eyes. He felt his insides twist. Oh, God. He cared way too much. His heart kicked into high gear, and his breathing harshened. He forced himself to breathe slowly. He forced himself to move slowly. He needed to stay calm. He needed to stay objective. Kate's life depended on it.

"Okay, kid. Just stay cool and I'll have you out of there in short order."

Jack slid his body into the space above Kate, holding himself up on his hands, which he placed in the narrow area between her waist and the fertilizer, aware of her quickened breathing, aware of her quivering body, aware of the rancid smell of fear that filled the car.

He held himself up on one hand, while he slid the other carefully along the length of her body, from her feet upward, feeling her flinch each time he touched, calming her with his voice, telling her he was checking to make sure it was safe to untie her and remove her from the car.

"Easy. Not too much longer. I've got you."

He eased himself back onto his knees on the passenger's seat and checked the area around Kate's head one more time, to make sure there was nothing connected to anything explosive. He could see the tears slide down the sides of her face, but she didn't make a sound.

At last, he removed the gag.

He heard her cough, and then her croaking voice saying, "I knew you'd come."

"I'm a regular knight in shining armor."

"Don't joke," she said in a plaintive voice. "I prayed. And you came."

"All right, kid. Let's see if I can get you out of here." He carefully untied all the plastic cords that held her in place, watching for a booby trap he might have missed, wanting to be a hero for her, even though there was no future for the two of them.

At last he had her free. He slid his hands under her armpits and tugged her up and over the front seat and into his lap, where it would be easier to remove the vest of Simtex. "You're okay now, kid."

She gripped his arms and pressed her face against his chest and started to sob.

He felt his throat tighten with emotion and held her close, wanting to comfort. "It's okay. I've got you."

She was sobbing something that he couldn't make out. He lifted her chin and kissed her lips and said, "Shh. Shh. I can't understand you."

She swallowed the next sob. And the next. She looked up at him with shimmery eyes and said, very clearly and distinctly, "The vest. There's no way to get it off."

19

"Step into the last room on the left," Donnie said.

When Clay stepped into the room, he found Libby lying on a hospital bed, dressed in street clothes, apparently unconscious.

He made an animal sound in his throat and hurried to her bedside, checking the pulse at her throat to make sure she was alive. When he did, she opened one eye, winked, and closed it again.

Clay was so surprised, he took a step back, which made him collide with Donnie, who'd come running after him. He reached for the hand holding the detonator, but Donnie snatched it away and struck Clay in the temple with the gun.

Clay reeled, stunned. He would have fallen except he grabbed the metal handrail of the bed. He saw Libby's eyes flash open and quickly close again when she realized he was still on his feet.

"Keep your distance!" Donnie said.

"I was checking to make sure she's alive," Clay said breathlessly.

"Of course she's alive!" Donnie said. "It was just a flesh wound." His eyes were frantically searching the room. "Where's the other one?" he demanded. "I left her gagged and tied up in a chair beside the bed."

"How should I know?" Clay said. He felt sure North must have rescued Jocelyn, but he couldn't understand why Libby had been left behind—although the wink suggested there was some plan in motion.

Donnie crossed to Libby, and, before Clay realized what he intended, backhanded her in the face. "Wake up!"

Libby's eyes flew open as she cried out in pain.

Clay reacted instinctively, striking out at Donnie with a powerful fist propelled by rage. Donnie's reflexes were fast, but not fast enough, and Clay caught enough of the boy's chin to snap his head back and cause him to stumble backward.

Clay ripped the detonator from Donnie's hand and hung on tight, not knowing whether it was rigged to go off with additional pressure, or when the pressure was released. He wasn't quick enough to get to the gun before Donnie recovered and trained it on him.

Donnie held out his empty hand and said, "Give me that back."

Clay shook his head, certain that he held his daughter's fate in his hand.

Donnie pointed the gun at Libby's heart and said in a vicious voice, "Give me the detonator."

Clay met Libby's eyes, which were liquid with feeling. Donnie was asking him to choose between his daughter and the woman he loved. It was a choice he couldn't—wouldn't—make.

They were at a standoff.

Then, to his astonishment, he saw Jocelyn coming out of the bathroom behind Donnie, her face taut with concentration, an aluminum bedpan held high.

Donnie must have seen movement from the corner of his eye, because he turned at the last second and put an arm up to stave off the bedpan, knocking Jocelyn backward against the wall. He had his finger on the trigger and was bringing his gun to bear on Jocelyn, when Clay leaped at him.

They went down in a pile, and Clay struggled one-handed to reach Donnie's gun. He was at a disadvantage because he didn't dare let go of the detonator. Jocelyn struggled to her feet, but she was still several steps away when Donnie managed to get his gun pointed at Clay's chest.

"Give me the detonator, or you'll kill us all," Donnie said through his teeth.

"You're done giving orders, Donnie," a voice said from the doorway.

Donnie jerked around, but he before he could get his gun turned, the butt of a shotgun hit the back of his head, and he was knocked out cold.

Clay accepted the hand North held out to him and got back on his feet. Jocelyn leaned down to pick up the gun Donnie had dropped when he fell.

"Just in the nick of time," Clay said. "What held you up?"

"Believe it or not, Donnie had an accomplice," North said. "That gray-haired newspaperman at the courthouse who kept asking Kate such personal questions. I relieved him of this shotgun on my way here. Where's Kate?"

"I don't know," Clay said. He held out the detonator to North. "How does this thing work?"

Jocelyn joined Clay and North, who stepped over to Libby's bedside, so the four of them could look at the detonator Clay held gripped in his hand.

"This looks like a safety catch," Jocelyn said, pointing to a catch on the side.

"What if it's not?" Libby said. "We can't take that chance."

Clay's cell phone buzzed in his pocket. "Can you get that, Jocelyn?" he said, turning his pocket in her direction.

Jocelyn answered the phone and held it out so they could all hear Jack.

"I've got Kate," he said. "We're away from Donnie's

car, but it's full of explosives. I'm waiting to hear from you that Libby and Jocelyn are clear before I call in the bomb squad."

"Donnie's no longer a threat," Clay said. "I'm standing here holding the detonator, but I don't know if it's safe to release it."

"Hang on to it," Jack said. "Better let the bomb guys decide what to do with it."

"How's Kate?" Clay asked.

"She's fine," Jack said. He took a breath and said, "She's still wearing the vest."

"Couldn't you get it off?" Clay said.

"The bomb guys need to do it. I'll call them now."

Clay exchanged a look with Libby, who'd apparently been untied the whole time, as she slid her feet off the edge of the bed. "Where do you think you're going?" he said.

"To be with my daughter."

"That's the one place you can't go," Clay said.

"My baby is in trouble. I'm going to be with her," Libby said determinedly.

Clay looked at North and said, "Who do we know to make all this happen faster?"

"I'm not sure you want someone working fast on a bomb," North said. "But I'd say you Blackthornes know more high-powered Texas folks than we Grayhawks do."

"I can't believe the two of you are colluding to put

pressure on public employees," Libby said. And then, fervently, "But I'm so glad you are."

Clay made a call on his cell phone, and when he hung up, said, "We're supposed to make our way to the ground floor and wait for the bomb detail." He slid his free arm around Libby to help support her.

"I'll stay here with Donnie until the police get here," North said, as Clay and Libby headed for the door.

"I'll stay with North," Jocelyn said.

"You should go with Libby and Clay," North said. "It might be a while before the police get here."

"I want to stay," Jocelyn said to Clay and Libby, who'd paused to wait for her. "You two go ahead," she said.

And they did.

"Let me tie this creep up," North said when they were gone. "I don't want to take a chance of him causing any more trouble."

He handed Jocelyn the shotgun and said, "Do you know how to use this?"

"I shoot skeet," Jocelyn said.

"I should have known," North said as he pulled Donnie's hands behind him and secured them with the plastic rope that had tied Jocelyn to the chair. "This is strong rope. How did you get yourself free?"

"Donnie presumed Libby was more incapacitated than she was. He tied her to the bed and me to the chair, but he didn't tie the chair down. I moved the chair to where Libby could reach the knots, and she untied me."

"If you were free, why didn't you escape?" North asked.

"Unlike you, we knew about Donnie's associate. Donnie told him to shoot us if he saw us on the stairs. And Donnie was blocking our escape by way of the elevator. Anyway, we knew you and Clay were coming, so we figured we'd hang around and help you when you got here."

"*You* decided to help *us*?" North said, his mouth curved in a smile. "Didn't you think we could manage on our own?"

Jocelyn smiled back. "We did help. And of course you managed fine."

North reached for Jocelyn's hand and tugged her out of the room, closing the door behind them. Once they were in the hall, he leaned back against the wall and pulled Jocelyn between his widespread legs, hugging her tight.

She slid her arms around his neck and leaned her cheek against his chest. "I was afraid you wouldn't come in time," she whispered.

"I was afraid, too," he said gruffly. "That I wouldn't have a chance to tell you . . . that I love you."

Jocelyn raised her head and looked into North's warm and welcoming blue eyes. "I've known for a long time how you feel about me, North. I'm glad to finally hear you say the words."

North frowned. "I never— I didn't— I wouldn't say that—"

Jocelyn laughed softly and reached up on tiptoes to kiss him, cutting off his protestations. "Just so you know, I love you, too. I think I have since the first time I laid eyes on you. When you tried to scare me off by—"

This time North cut her off, kissing her long and thoroughly, holding her close. When he released her, he looked down into her eyes and said, "Will you marry me, Joss?"

She grinned. "Yes. Soon, please. Otherwise, your firstborn is going to arrive—"

"You're pregnant?" North said incredulously.

Jocelyn laughed. "I can't believe you're surprised. As often as we—"

He cut her off with another kiss, his hand pressed against her belly, which was barely rounded. "We'll marry today," he said.

Jocelyn laughed again. "I'd like time to buy a gown. And to arrange a church ceremony. That's going to take a day or two."

"A day. Or two. No longer," North said. He set Jocelyn away from him as several policemen stepped off the elevator. "I need to get you out of here, somewhere safe."

"You're not still worried about Donnie's bomb, are you?" Jocelyn said.

"I'm sure the bomb detail is freeing Kate even as we speak," North said. "But I'm not taking any chances that something might happen to you. Or the baby," he added after a hesitation.

North directed the policemen to the room where he'd left Donnie, then headed down the empty hospital corridor with Jocelyn. He felt terrified. What he was feeling must have shown on his face, because as soon as the elevator door closed with the two of them inside, Jocelyn put her arms around his waist and said, "Relax. Everything's going to be fine."

He looked down into her face, unable to keep the worry from his own. "I've wanted a son—or daughter— for a long time. But when I think what the cost might be— Are you sure you'll be all right? Have you seen a doctor? Does he say you'll be able to deliver without any complications?"

Joss's laughter, a sound of joy, filled the elevator. "I'm fine, North. Our baby will be fine. These generous hips of mine are perfect for delivering babies. Don't be afraid, sweetheart."

North felt a heightened terror that now that he'd admitted he loved Joss, she'd somehow be snatched from him. He knew his fear wasn't rational, but that didn't seem to help. He held her close and said, "I'm afraid, Joss."

"I'm here, North," she whispered in his ear. "And I'm not going anywhere."

"Mom! Dad! What are you doing here?" Kate said. "You should get as far away from here—"

"What's the story on that vest?" Clay asked the bomb technician who was standing with Kate behind a shield.

"Where's the detonator, Daddy?"

"The bomb detail has it, Kitten. They took it from me. It had a safety catch, and they attached that, and it's harmless. What about that vest?" Clay asked the technician working behind the shield.

"Clever device," the man called back. "Good thing this young lady didn't try to take it off on her own."

Kate glanced toward a group of police and Texas Rangers off to one side which Jack had joined. He had his back to her. She couldn't believe he was ignoring her, after being so persistent about having the vest removed here, instead of somewhere else.

Kate glanced through the glass opening in the metal shield and saw her father had his arm around her mother. "Have you two worked out your differences?" she said. "I'd like to know. You can see what kind of trouble I've gotten into trying to get you two together. I'd like to know I was successful before . . . well, before . . ." Kate's voice trailed off.

She watched her parents exchange anxious glances.

"Actually, we—" her father began.

"Decided to get married," her mother interrupted.

"That's wonderful!" Kate said. She would have jumped up, but the technician had a grip on her.

"Whoa, lady. Let me snip one more wire—"

Kate watched with bated breath as the wire was cut. She stood perfectly still as the man eased the vest off her shoulders and put it in a special container. She took one step forward, turned her head in his direction and said, "Can I go now?"

"You're clear," he said with a smile.

Kate raced around the edge of the metal shield and threw herself into her parents' arms. "Oh," she said, tears coming to her eyes. "A hug sandwich." It was a name she'd made up when she was six for a hug that included both her parents, with her in the middle. She felt her mother's tears against her cheek, which made her throat swell with emotion.

"I'm so glad you're going to be together," Kate said in a choked voice. "That's the most wonderful news I've ever heard. When are you getting married?" she asked.

"Soon," her father said. "Now that your mother's said yes, I'm not going to let her get away."

"But Mom needs a special dress. She and I have to go shopping," Kate said. "And you'll want to be married in church. That'll take some time to arrange."

"I'll go along with whatever your mom wants," her

father said. "But as far as I'm concerned, the sooner the ceremony, the better."

"It'll be soon," Kate promised. "I'm just so happy for both of you."

Kate saw uncertainty in her mother's eyes, wariness in her father's. "You two are sure about this, aren't you? I mean, I haven't coerced you into doing something you really don't want to do, have I?"

Her father took her mother's hands in his, looked into her eyes, and said, "I want this very much. I love you, Libby."

Kate turned to her mother, whose tentative smile became broader as she said, "I've realized it's what I want, too."

"Then why don't you two kiss?" Kate said. "That's what usually happens when a proposal is accepted."

"How would you know?" her father said suspiciously, shooting a glance from Kate to Jack and back again.

"I've seen it in the movies," Kate quipped. "Go ahead, Daddy. Give Mom a kiss."

"This is a noteworthy moment," her father said. "So I'd better make this good."

Kate watched with delight as her father scooped her mother into his arms, pulled her up on her tiptoes and planted a kiss on her that sizzled. She looked away when the moment became too intimate to be shared. She threaded her hands together and pressed them against her heart, grateful that her lifelong wish had finally come true.

And then she met Jack's glance. He quickly turned away, but he'd been looking, all right. She crossed to him purposefully, unwilling to be ignored any longer. When she reached the group of men, she had to call Jack's name to get his attention.

"Jack? May I speak with you?"

"I'm kind of busy, Kate."

Kate's face flamed. How could he? She'd heard all the times he'd called her "kid" while he'd been rescuing her from Donnie's car. Then it had sounded like a term of endearment, she'd thought. But apparently not. Kate felt terribly hurt. It would have been easiest just to walk away. But Grayhawks never ran. They stayed and fought.

So Kate called Jack's name again. "Jack? I just need a moment of your time."

"Go ahead, Jack," one of the other policemen said. "See what the girl wants."

Kate flushed at the diminutive *girl*. Was that how Jack had referred to her in the other men's hearing? She wasn't a girl any longer. She hadn't been for quite some time. She was a woman. Maybe a young woman, but fully grown, for certain.

Once Jack joined her, Kate walked a few paces away, so they wouldn't be overheard either by the policemen or her parents. "I wanted to thank you again for saving my life."

"It was all part of the job," Jack replied.

Kate turned to face him. "I think it was more than that." That was as far as she was willing to go without some encouragement from him.

She didn't get any.

"It was nice knowing you, Kate."

"Is that it?" she said, disbelieving. "You're writing me off? What about everything that happened between us?"

"I don't know what you're talking about," Jack said.

Kate was furious at his denial of any feeling between them. And humiliated. "I thought there was some attraction between us," she said through tight jaws. "But obviously I was wrong."

"There was some attraction," Jack conceded.

Maybe he'd noticed her tears. She swiped at them because she didn't want his pity. "But?" she said, urging him to continue.

"You're still a kid."

"I'm nineteen!"

"I'm thirty-two. That's a lifetime."

"That's ridiculous!" Kate accused.

"You want better reasons. I'll give them to you," Jack said. "You're headstrong. And spoiled. And aimless. You've spent your whole life feeling sorry for yourself because you didn't have two parents at home. Wake up and smell the roses, kid. Everyone ends up alone."

"Even you?" she challenged.

"I like being alone."

"You like being with me!" Kate retorted. She threw herself at him in what would have been an embarrassing way, except his arms closed around her as their lips met. Kate would have sworn the electricity was life-threatening.

But a moment later Jack pulled her arms from around his neck and said, "No more games, Kate. This was a job. No more, no less. And I'm done with it. And with you."

Kate was too angry to reply. Too hurt to reply. And too stubborn to give up. "The day will come, Jack McKinley, when I'll make you eat those words."

"Kate?" her mother called. "Are you ready to go?"

She felt embarrassed that her mother and father had witnessed the scene with Jack. They were going to want details. They were going to want to know what had happened. They were going to want to know that their little lamb was safe from the big bad wolf.

Kate lifted her chin and said, "Good-bye, Jack. Thanks for the education."

"Kate, I—"

She feared he was going to apologize. If he did, she wouldn't be able to keep from bursting into tears. Kate didn't care what Grayhawks did or did not do. She turned her back on Jack McKinley and ran into her mother's waiting arms.

20

❧

The double wedding was Kate's idea. She'd pointed out to her mother and her uncle, "You both want to get married in a hurry. You'd both want to attend each other's weddings. And you'd both want nearly the same people to be there. So why not?"

She'd glossed over the fact that her father and her uncle had been mortal enemies most of their lives. That Grayhawks and Blackthornes didn't break bread together, let alone attend each other's weddings. It was time for mending fences.

As she looked around the quaint, tiny church that was almost as old as Bitter Creek itself, Kate was pleased by what she saw. Beautiful sprays of white roses and baby's breath decorated the altar and each of the pews. On one side of the altar stood Uncle North and his bride, and on the other stood her father and mother. Both brides wore white.

Kate's mother had protested at first about wearing white, but Kate had insisted that if the dream really was to come true, then her mother should be dressed as the bride she should have been twenty years ago.

There had been one scare today, when Kate had thought the double wedding might end up in a shambles. She'd been talking to Grandpa King at the door, complimenting him on how nice he looked in his morning coat, when Grandpa Blackjack had showed up. Kate had seen a barnyard dogfight coming and tried to steer Grandpa King to his seat in the front pew on the left. But he'd also seen Grandpa Blackjack, and he couldn't be budged.

Unfortunately, Ren wasn't on hand to keep Grandpa Blackjack in line, because she was helping Jocelyn with her veil.

"I see you made it to your daughter's wedding. At last," Grandpa Blackjack said.

"I see your son finally decided to make an honest woman out of her," Grandpa King retorted. "And it's my son I'm here to see wed. I haven't forgiven my daughter for the dirty trick she played on me—consorting with the enemy and giving me a half-Blackthorne grandchild."

"Grandpa King," Kate admonished. "Be nice!"

Her grandfather patted her on the cheek and said, "I admit you turned out to be a blessing in disguise, little girl."

Kate huffed in exasperation. Hadn't anyone figured out yet she was a *grown-up*? "Can I escort you to your

seat, Grandpa King?" she asked, trying again to separate the two men.

But they were too intent on exchanging verbal
blows.

"Seems the trick was on my son," Blackjack said.
"He's the one who got robbed of his child."

"I'm right here, Grandpa Blackjack," Kate said
"Nobody stole away with me in the night."

"At least Bitter Creek is back safe in Blackthorne
hands," Grandpa Blackjack said.

"No thanks to that scapegrace son of mine,"
Grandpa King retorted. "I don't know what possessed
the boy to sell all that stock back to you." Grandpa
King snorted. "Did it as a wedding gift to his sister, he
said. Seems to me you Blackthornes are the one who
got the gift."

"Mom is going to be a Blackthorne in a few minutes," Kate reminded her grandfather.

At that moment, Kate saw North and her father
step out of doors on separate sides at the front of the
church and move toward the altar at the center, to
wait for their brides to come down the aisle.

"Oh, Lord," she muttered. "What if they start talking? It won't take them long to find something to fight
about. With their fists."

In desperation, Kate grabbed Grandpa King's left
hand, and Grandpa Blackjack's right hand and tugged
them behind her down the aisle. When she glanced

over her shoulder, she saw the two men were smiling—
at her. She grinned back. When she got to the front of
the church, she let go of their hands and turned to
face them, lecturing them like a stern schoolteacher.

"I don't care how much you two hate each other, I
love you both very much. I'm trusting both of you to
behave yourselves today. If you can't say anything nice,
don't say anything at all." Kate had a feeling the reception at the Castle was going to be a very quiet affair.

The two men turned their backs on each other and
took their seats in their respective pews. Kate blew out
a breath of air. One disaster averted. *Just call me
Supergirl.*

She hurried back to the room where her mother
was dressing and stopped dead at the vision she found.
"Mom. You're so beautiful."

"You don't think this dress is too much?" her
mother said, tugging here and there at the elegant
white gown and holding out the five-foot train Kate
had insisted upon.

"You'll be the prettiest bride ever to walk down that
aisle." Kate felt the tears brimming in her eyes and
smiled through them as she said, "I can't believe this
is happening. I can't believe you and Daddy are finally going to be married."

"Neither can I," said her mother. "Don't make me
cry, Kate," she said with a half-sob, half-laugh. "You'll
ruin my makeup."

They both laughed then, and Kate hugged her mother and said, "I can hear the organ music that means it's time for me to march down the aisle."

"Is King here?" her mother asked.

Kate realized suddenly that her mother hadn't been at all sure that her father would attend. Which was another reason Kate was glad she'd suggested a double wedding. He wouldn't have missed North's nuptials. "Grandpa King's here. He and Grandpa Blackjack already had a run-in, but I sat them down and told them to be good."

"I'll bet you did!"

Kate grabbed up her bouquet, gave her mother one last hug and hurried out the door to the nave, where she was to start her march. She'd watched for Jack, knowing that North had invited him. But he wasn't there. She felt a pang of loss, but ignored it.

Blackthornes and Grayhawks had ended up aligned on either side of the aisle, which had become a no-man's-land traversed at last by Kate, as her mother's maid of honor, and then the two brides, Jocelyn first, and then Kate's mother.

"Kate?" her mother said.

Kate realized she'd allowed herself to daydream, and stepped up to the altar to take her mother's bouquet of baby-pink roses. She kissed her mother's cheek and then stepped to the side where she could see her parents' faces.

Her mother glowed. Her father looked happy.

She turned her gaze to Uncle North and realized he was actually smiling. Which made her smile. Breed was his best man and he was smiling, too. Kate followed Uncle North's glance to Jocelyn, who was one of the most beautiful brides Kate had ever seen. Of course, Kate thought loyally, her mother was the most beautiful bride in the room.

Kate felt her throat constrict when her father took her mother's hand in his to say his vows. She glanced at Uncle North to see if he would do the same, and was surprised to see he was holding both of soon-to-be Aunt Jocelyn's hands.

Both men spoke in firm voices. Both women answered in soft tones. Kate listened to the words, hearing the promises being made, overwhelmed with so many emotions that she was having a hard time processing them all.

She had a great deal to be joyful about. Her parents had finally acknowledged their love for each other. And Uncle North, whom she'd thought would never love any woman, had found Aunt Jocelyn.

Kate focused her gaze back on her parents as she listened to the minister intone the familiar vows.

". . . for richer or for poorer, in sickness and in health, as long as you both shall live?"

"I will," her father and Uncle North both said.

". . . and do you . . ."

"I will," her mother and Aunt Jocelyn both said.

Kate watched as her father put a simple gold band on her mother's finger. And while her mother did the same to her father. Belatedly, she noticed that Uncle North and Aunt Jocelyn had also exchanged rings, but Jocelyn's was a small platinum band to match the sapphire and diamond engagement ring Uncle North had given her.

Suddenly the minister was telling the two couples they were married, and that the grooms could kiss their brides.

Kate felt a hot tear slide onto her cheek. When her mother turned to her, Kate handed her back the bouquet of delicate pink rosebuds and said, "May I be the first to wish you well, Mrs. Blackthorne?"

"You may!" her mother said with a joyful laugh.

She hugged her parents fiercely. "I love you both so much!"

She watched the two couples as they turned for the enthusiastic applause of the congregation, and then her parents were gone, majestic organ music sweeping them down the aisle.

Kate watched them go, knowing that she desperately wanted what they'd finally found. True love. Lasting love. Family and a future. They were what life was all about.

She was very much afraid that happily-ever-after might elude her.

Before her aunt and uncle escaped, Kate kissed and hugged them, too. Then they were flying down the aisle, laughing and happy and looking forward to their future together.

Breed had slipped out a side door, and Kate realized she was alone at the front of the church. And that her work was done. Aside from a little refereeing at the reception, of course.

Kate waited until the church was almost empty before she headed down the aisle herself. She finally had the one thing she'd wished for all her life—a family of her own. Yet she'd never felt so bereft.

She laughed at herself for being maudlin. She focused on being happy for her parents. And for Uncle North and Aunt Jocelyn. Even though she was going to miss them all while they were gone on their honeymoons.

She felt a tap on her shoulder and turned around. It was Breed.

"What can I do for you?" she asked.

"I need a ride to the reception."

"Sure," Kate said.

As the two of them walked to Kate's car, Breed said, "Mom got married again. The guy's not too keen on me."

"I'm sure North will give you a place to stay," Kate said.

"Yeah. When he gets back, I'm sure he will."

Kate realized her problems were pretty small. So what if she'd had an unfortunate romance. Life moved on. She'd find someone else to love. Meanwhile, someone needed her.

"Tell you what, Breed," Kate said. "I've got a pretty comfortable couch. You're welcome to use it until North gets home."

"Thanks, Kate," Breed said. "I think I will."

Kate put a hand on the boy's shoulder. "It's good to have family, isn't it?"

"Yeah," Breed said. "It is."

Kate realized that Breed's father, her grandfather King, had come to the church—and left—without acknowledging Breed. *Well,* she thought. *Here's another crusade.* She was good at getting people together. Look how well she'd done with her mother and father.

She glanced at Breed and thought, *One of these days I'm going to help you reconcile with your father.*

Meanwhile, Breed's problems gave her something to focus on instead of Jack McKinley. Whom she absolutely, positively never wanted to see again.

"Tell me, Breed," she said, giving him her full attention. "What would you like to do to pass the time until North comes home?"

LETTER TO READERS

Dear Faithful Readers,

I'm already at work on the next book in the Bitter Creek series, which continues the saga of Kate Grayhawk and King's might-be-bastard son Breed. I hope you'll come along for the ride!

Meanwhile, if you enjoy my ranch novels, watch for my hardcover novel, *Texas Brides*, part of my popular Hawk's Way series, available everywhere on September 27.

I always love hearing from you. You can reach me through my web site at www.joanjohnston.com. Be sure to sign up on my mailing list to receive notice of upcoming books.

Take care and happy reading!

Joan Johnston